Mistaken Identity

1⁵⁰/₁

Mistaken Identity

JOSH MCDOWELL
ED STEWART

GREEN KEY BOOKS

Holiday, Florida

This is a work of fiction. Names, characters, locations, and incidents are either the creation of the author's imagination or are used fictitiously, and any resemblances to events, locales, or persons, living or dead, are entirely coincidental.

MISTAKEN IDENTITY

©2005 by Josh McDowell and Ed Stewart.

ISBN: 1932587632

Cover photography: Alan Powdrill / TAXI

Cover graphics: Faith Michaels

Published by Green Key Books
2514 Aloha Place
Holiday, Florida 34691

Cataloging-in-Publication Data on file at the Library of Congress.

Printed in the United States of America

05 06 07 6 5 4 3 2

Prologue

THE RIDER SAW THE SILHOUETTES of two small buildings in the darkness ahead, so he cut the engine and lights on the big Harley and coasted the rest of the way. No need to announce his arrival, as if anyone on this lonely country road even knew he was coming. That was the beauty of it. Nobody out here knew anything about him. And he planned to keep it that way for a few days until he did what he came to do. Then he would be gone forever.

There were no lights anywhere, not even street lights. The faint glow of a quarter moon through wispy clouds was barely enough to illuminate the pavement ahead. The rider rolled past a driveway leading to the larger of the two buildings. It was an old wood-frame church, all right, with a little house behind it, probably the preacher's house. And immediately ahead was a dark stand of trees and brush beside the road, just as the old wino in town had said.

The rider scuffed his boots softly on the asphalt, bringing the bike to a stop without brake lights. With the trees and brush between him and the dark church buildings, he used a penlight to find the dirt path through the brush. It took him a couple of minutes to walk the Harley down the narrow path to an open patch of grass the wino had called a "holler." He found the rustic picnic table he had been told about. There was even a chemical toilet parked under one of the large trees. He clearly wasn't the first transient to crash here in this place, but tonight he was the only one. And that would do just fine.

The darkened church buildings were visible from the hollow. Flicking off the penlight, the rider leaned the Harley on its stand. Then he pulled off his helmet, sat down at the picnic table, and lit a cigarette. It was well past midnight, and he was ready to sleep, but he allowed himself a few minutes to enjoy the silence of a warm spring night in the country.

Gazing at the buildings across a couple of acres of open land, he drew deeply on the cigarette. It had been a very long journey through parts of the country had never seen before. Up until a couple weeks ago, he never imagined he would ever see the state of Washington in his lifetime. He had neither reason nor interest for traveling almost three thousand miles to this little country town. But things change, whether you want them to or not. So here he was.

Stubbing out his smoke, the rider unloaded the Harley and pitched a two-man tent in the dark as he had done so often on this trip. The front end of the tent, next to the zippered entrance, was for his sleeping bag; the back end was for the leather saddlebag containing the limited possessions he had brought on the trip. Stretched out on the bag ready for one more smoke, he reached into his saddlebag for a heavy canvas pouch. Unzipping the pouch, he pulled out his Ruger Mark II semi-automatic pistol and laid it on his chest.

After lighting up, he studied the blued finish on the barrel in the light of the cigarette's flaring embers. Reaching into the canvas pouch again, he retrieved a ten-shot magazine and snapped it into place. He always loaded the gun at night and kept it close. What's the point of having a gun for protection if it isn't loaded? Assured that the thumb-operated safety was on, he laid the piece next to the small duffel he used as a pillow, on the side away from the tent flaps.

Snuffing out his smoke in the moist grass, the rider glanced once more across the field toward the church. He might have to endure some nosy, gawking church people while he was here. The wino had assured him that they were harmless and mostly kept their distance. He wouldn't make trouble in the hollow for the few days he was here. And he hoped they would take the same approach.

Zipping the tent netting closed, the rider roller over, touched the butt of his pistol with his fingers, and fell asleep.

EZRA STUDIED THE CHECKERBOARD FOR A MOMENT. Then, from his side of the desk, he cautiously pushed a red checker one space forward. He was slouched in an old oak swiveling and rocking office chair that neither swiveled nor rocked without a good deal of creaking. "Your move, Thomas," he announced.

Thomas Rasby sat ramrod straight in a wooden chair on the opposite side of the desk. He snatched up a black checker and hopped it vigorously over two red checkers Ezra had left unprotected—*thack, thack.*

"You don't have to make so much noise with your checkers, Thomas," Ezra said in a monotone that lacked any force. He ran his fingers absently through the few shocks of wispy white hair left on his head. Thomas' full head of wavy hair was almost as white, though the church caretaker was twelve years the minister's junior.

"Sorry, Reverend Sturdevant," Thomas said meekly.

The noontime game of checkers in the small office of the old church had been played the same way for more years than Ezra could recall. Ezra always had to remind Thomas not to slap his checkers so noisily on the board. The sound really bugged him, but Thomas had been slapping his checkers for decades, and the minister's harping was only effective for a game or two at best.

"You rascal, Thomas. Look what you're doing to me," Ezra ribbed the caretaker good-naturedly. "I'm ruined. You're beating me once again."

Thomas Rasby was a crackerjack checkers player because the caretaker didn't have much else in his brain to distract him while they played. Ezra often amused himself with this thought.

"But it won't count because you slapped your checkers," Ezra razzed. "Now put my checkers back on the board, and I will make another move."

"Oh no," Thomas chuckled, sounding a little like Goofy in the Disney cartoons. "You can't take your move back, Reverend Sturdevant. It ain't in the rules."

Thomas had lived his entire fifty-seven years by the rules, Ezra knew. As a concrete thinker, life was black and white for him. It sometimes took him a while to understand the choices before him. But the rules deeply etched into that cement block of a brain usually steered him to make the right one. It was a childlike trait long absent among the more intelligent. Ezra admired Thomas' simplicity, even envied it at times.

Conversation was limited to between games because Thomas couldn't talk and play at the same time. "Big thunderstorm coming in tonight," Ezra said, moving checkers into place for another game. "Heavy wind and a lot of rain predicted."

Thomas chewed and swallowed a bite of egg salad sandwich and wiped his mouth with a napkin before answering. Don't talk with your mouth full. That was a rule. "We get a couple of them big storms every spring, don't we, Reverend?"

"You'll close the shutters all around the church, won't you?" Ezra said.

"Oh yes, Reverend," the caretaker assured. "I'll close them shutters, all right. And I'll clean out them rain gutters too. I'll put all my tools in the shed before the storm comes. And I'll make sure—"

"Thank you, Thomas," Ezra cut in, knowing that if he didn't stop him, the caretaker would proceed through the entire litany of his weekly tasks. The daily routine was as important to the caretaker as the rules. Thomas Rasby was predictable to the point of boredom. But he was also dependable and utterly trustworthy, like an aging, finely crafted grandfather clock.

After the next game—which the minister lost in another flurry of slapping checkers—Ezra ate several spoonfuls of leftover casserole from a Tupperware bowl as Thomas set up the board. "Tomorrow I will get them

Sunday school rooms in the basement ship-shape," Thomas recited as he deftly moved the pieces into place.

"But we don't have Sunday school anymore, Thomas," Ezra said between bites, launching into the well-worn explanation that never seemed to penetrate the concrete, "because there are no children in our church. They have all grown up and moved away."

"Maybe some children'll come this Sunday," Thomas said with characteristic optimism. "With God all things are possible."

Thomas' uncluttered view of what was and what could be always seemed to catch Ezra up short. "You're right, of course," he sighed. "With God all things are possible."

Chapel of the Valley had been a "mature" church long before Ezra was called as minister twenty-two years ago. The children of the members had grown up and left the farming community for urban universities and careers and for suburban homes and churches. There were fewer than a 130 names on the membership roll at the old chapel. Ezra could count on one hand those who were younger than sixty, and Thomas was one of them.

During the next break, Ezra said, "What do you think of our most recent guest in the hollow?"

Thomas finished chewing and swallowing a cookie before answering. "You mean Joe?"

"Is that his name—Joe? The young fellow on the motorcycle?"

"That's right, Reverend Sturdevant. He said his name is Joe."

Ezra went on, mainly to himself. "It's only May. The migrant workers aren't due in the valley for a couple weeks yet. So what's a homeless man doing with an expensive Harley? Or is he really homeless?"

It took a moment for the caretaker to sort through the minister's three-part question. "I reckon he's homeless, or he wouldn't be sleeping in a bedroll out there in the hollow. That's where the homeless people sleep sometimes, Reverend, when the pickers aren't there."

The hollow was a seven-acre, pie-shaped parcel of undeveloped church property across a small creek from the church cemetery. It was a peaceful area of wild grass and weeds secluded from the road by a thick belt of trees and bushes. Long before Ezra came to the Chapel of the Valley, transients and migrant workers picking seasonal fruit in this central Washington valley used the hollow for a temporary camping spot, mostly during the warm summer months.

Ezra knew well that such people were technically guilty of trespassing on church property. But as long as these occasional visitors weren't drunk, strung out on drugs, or destructive, nobody at the church made an issue of them camping out in the hollow for a night or two. Nobody except for Jethro Haig, vice-chairman of the church board. Jethro saw more liabilities than assets in just about everything. The milk of human kindness, Ezra mused to himself frequently, had turned sour in Jethro many years ago.

Thomas, who lived in a small cabin overlooking the hollow at the rear of the church cemetery, was the self-appointed dorm parent for all who camped there. The caretaker made a point to meet each person, welcome him or her, and even provide canned goods from his own pantry on occasion. Ezra tried to get down to the hollow to visit the travelers. And Dorrie Sturdevant, before she passed, often sent with him a hot, covered casserole in a disposable tin-foil pan.

"So you've talked to him…this Joe out there?" Ezra said.

"Uh-huh. I went to where he was making his campfire last night. I said I was Thomas and did he need anything. He said he didn't need nothing."

"So what's he look like?" the minister pressed.

Thomas scratched his head, thought a moment, then scratched his ear. "He's got black hair tied up in back with a rubber band."

"A ponytail," Ezra suggested.

"Yeah, a ponytail with his black hair. And he's got a big cut on his face." Thomas traced an invisible jagged line down the left side of his own face from the cheekbone to the jaw line with his index finger.

"You mean a scar?"

Thomas nodded. "And he's got a big bird on his arm too," he added, moving his tracing finger to his upper arm.

Ezra nodded. "A tattoo."

"Yes, Reverend, a big bird tattoo on his arm. And there's something else, Reverend. Joe had—"

Ezra cut in, "Did you tell him he could camp out there as long as he needs to?"

"I sure did, just like I done with all the others. But wait until you see——"

"And if he comes back this evening from wherever he's gone on that motorcycle, I'll go out and say hello."

Finally Thomas blurted out what he had been trying to say. "When you go see him, Reverend, maybe he will show you his gun!"

Ezra dropped the checker he had picked up to move. "Gun?" he said with mild alarm. "Are you saying that this Joe out there in our hollow has a gun?"

Thomas nodded even more vigorously. Then he held up his hand and squeezed an imaginary trigger with his forefinger, careful not to point his invisible weapon at the minister.

"A pistol?"

"That's right, a big black pistol. I seen it on Joe's bedroll. He covered it right quick when I come up."

Ezra grimaced and scratched the back of his head. "I suppose a fellow needs to protect himself from coyotes and stray dogs if he's camping out in strange places," he thought aloud. But he didn't like what he was hearing: ponytail biker with a scar, tattoo, and now a gun. *Jethro is going to have a cow over this one if he finds out,* he thought.

"I think Joe's a nice man, Reverend Sturdevant," Thomas said. "He wouldn't hurt nobody with his gun."

Always looking on the bright side, aren't you, Thomas? Ezra mused. *The cup is always half full, not half empty. Except with you, the cup is always full.*

"I'm sure you're right," he said, retrieving his checker and making his move. He hoped he sounded sure.

Two

"GUN? WHAT GUN?"

The large-boned woman standing in the doorway asked the question matter-of-factly, the same way she might ask, "What tree?" or "What flower?"

"Good afternoon, Velma," Ezra said without looking up from the board.

"Good afternoon, Mrs. Walls," Thomas added, rising from his chair as he had been taught. Then he spat out the details about Joe, sensationalizing as a child would the parts about the scar and gun.

The woman glanced at Ezra, who confirmed Thomas' story with a nod but downplayed the caretaker's excitement by adding an easy shrug. He didn't want his long-time volunteer church secretary to be unduly alarmed.

Velma Walls was dressed in a lightweight blue skirt and white blouse. Her auburn hair—colored that way since the gray strands began to appear thirty years ago—was cut short. In contrast to her two co-workers, the church secretary looked like a corporate executive. During the week, the minister preferred jeans, polo shirt, and sneakers—except when he had to dress up for hospital visitations. Thomas had only one uniform for Monday through Saturday: overalls, long-sleeved cotton twill shirt, and work boots.

"All right, you two," Velma said, moving into the room and setting her large handbag on the desk. "Time to clear out so I can get some work done in here." Thomas and Ezra had started collecting the checkers before she finished her order.

Velma turned back to the caretaker. "Your groceries are in the trunk of my car, Thomas. I bought extra boxes of macaroni and cheese for you this week. They were on sale. And I bought franks and beans for you."

"Yes ma'am, Mrs. Walls, I love franks and beans," Thomas replied with his goofy chuckle as he gathered up his lunch wrappers.

Ezra vacated the office chair and slid the keyboard of the church's old computer back into place atop the wooden desk. Wednesday was report day, and Velma dutifully typed and printed the weekly activities of the church membership: illnesses, deaths, grandchildren born to members, and other information she thought appropriate. Her newsy reports were distributed on Sunday morning with the bulletin, although by then most church members had already heard the news via the rural grapevine.

"Speaking of reports, Velma, I think it's time you told Thomas the big news, don't you?" Ezra said it dramatically to spark Thomas' curiosity, which it did.

"Big news, Mrs. Walls?" Thomas chirped excitedly, turning to the secretary. "Like franks on sale?"

The minister flashed his secretary a knowing look. Thomas was just a young boy trapped inside a lanky, six-foot one-inch, fifty-seven-year-old body. Ezra and Velma had withheld "the big news" from Thomas until practically the last minute so he wouldn't become too distracted by the excitement.

"This is even bigger news than franks on sale, Thomas," Velma said with a little laugh. "Your niece Chessy Carpenter is arriving in Orchard Valley today. She's going to spend a few months visiting you and the rest of your family here. Isn't that wonderful?"

Thomas' eyes flicked wide open and sparkled. "Little Chessy is coming? You mean my sissy's little girl Chessy Carpenter?"

"That's right, Thomas," Velma said. "It's a surprise."

The part of the news Ezra and the secretary would leave out, the part that would only muddle Thomas' brain, was the other reason Chessy was coming. Lydia, Thomas' younger sister, had stayed in touch with Velma by telephone out of concern for her aging, mentally deficient brother. Her daughter, Chessy, who worked with mentally challenged adults as a volunteer, had finished college earlier in the month. Before she settled into a job, she was coming to Orchard Valley to assess if it was time to make plans for Thomas' "retirement."

Ezra didn't think Thomas was ready for pasture yet, and he would certainly miss the caretaker's daily companionship on the grounds of the rural church where they both lived. But the minister had to admit that Thomas had aged noticeably in the last couple of years. And he commended Lydia and her husband Bertram for allowing Chessy to check in on her uncle and bring him a little joy.

Processing the news, the caretaker laughed his Goofy laugh. "I only seen little Chessy once since Lydia and Bertram moved away down to Fresno. She's cute as a button."

"Now listen, Thomas, your niece is not a little girl anymore," Ezra informed. "Your sister left the valley…what…twenty years ago? Chessy has grown up."

Thomas seemed lost in reverie. "Lydia let me hold her sometimes and take her for walks. She was just two years old." Then the grin faded. "Lydia and Bertram had to move to California so Bertram could work in raisins. And little Chessy had to go with them."

"Thomas, your niece Chessy is about twenty-two years old now," Ezra explained.

"Twenty-two years old?" Thomas whispered incredulously. "That's a lady!"

Velma and Ezra exchanged secret smiles at the caretaker's deduction.

"And she'll be driving in sometime today, Thomas," Velma said. "She's going to stay with me in town, in the spare bedroom. She's so happy about spending time with you and the rest of the Rasby family in Orchard Valley."

"Today! My little Chessy's coming here today!" Thomas' eyes glistened with tears of joy. "I'll fix dinner for her one night. I hope she likes franks and beans."

After Thomas left the office to tend to his groceries and return to work, Ezra studied the church secretary as she sat down at the keyboard to work. Velma had become a trusted friend over the years. She was a good woman, a true saint. She had cared for Thomas more than any of his kinfolk had. It wasn't her duty as church secretary to shop for his groceries or do his laundry, but she did it faithfully month after month, year after year. Thomas would always need someone to mother him, and Velma had filled that role ably and lovingly.

"Now about this young man in the hollow," Ezra said, gazing out the office window past the church cemetery to the hollow beyond the creek. He knew the traveler was gone at the moment. He had heard the motorcycle start up and leave at about 9:30. But he was coming back, that was for sure. He had left a small tent behind. Far beyond the church property, wheat fields rolled gently across the valley to the foothills where orchard after orchard of fruit trees stood in close formation like battalions of green uniformed soldiers.

"Another wayfaring stranger?" Velma inquired, tapping away at the keyboard, her reading glasses perched low on her nose.

"Yes, apparently a biker type who told Thomas his name is Joe."

"Which may or may not be his real name, of course," Velma replied. "And he may have a gun, you say."

"A big, black pistol, according to Thomas. Maybe he saw a real gun, maybe he didn't. He said there was a gun lying on the bedroll when he went into the hollow to say hello and that the young man covered it up as he approached. But can we really believe Thomas' claim?"

"It *could* be a gun, and this Joe could be someone more dangerous than the usual transients who come by." There was a touch of alarm in Velma's tone. "He could be running from the law. There seem to be a few gas station robberies in the county every week."

Ezra was still gazing out the window. "I know, Velma. I just don't want our concern about what Joe *might* do to deter us from what we can do for him."

The secretary clacked another sentence before she spoke again. "So what are you going to do about this fellow, Ezra?"

The minister turned back to her. "I'll go down to the hollow when he comes back and have a friendly chat."

"About the gun?"

"Not necessarily, at least not at first. I just want to get an idea what he's like, what he's up to, how long he plans to stay."

"And be sure he has enough to eat," Velma added, smiling.

Ezra shrugged. "Thomas is usually on top of that with all our visitors. But I may take something when I go down to meet him. In the meantime, you should take the usual precautions when you're here in the building alone. Let Thomas know where you are, lock yourself in…you know."

"Yes, I know, Ezra. I'll be careful. Thank you for the reminder."

"Well, I'd better get dressed up," Ezra said, collecting his empty lunch bowl and stepping toward the door. "Jethro and Bradford will be here in about twenty minutes, then I need to go into town and see Buck at the nursing home."

"Jethro and Bradford?" Velma said without looking up from the monitor. "Why are the two church board mucky-mucks coming out here on a Wednesday?"

"I want them to take a gander at what Louise Wilkerson has done for us."

Velma's eyes snapped up at him. "Ezra, don't tell me it's still here—in the office," she said, scolding him like a big sister with every word.

"Now Velma, don't worry, it's safe," Ezra explained sheepishly. "It's locked up tight in a metal box, and the box is locked up in the bottom drawer. Nobody even knows about it except you and me. I'll take it into the city the next time I go."

"You should have put it in a much safer place yesterday," Velma continued to scold, "as soon as the box was delivered."

"And I will, Velma, I will. But remember, Louise had it under her mattress for more than forty years, and she never locked her front door. It's safer here than there."

Velma glowered at him in silence.

"I'm going into Yarborough tomorrow morning," Ezra conceded. "I'll take it then."

"Promise?"

"Yes, I promise."

After a few more seconds of glowering, Velma let him off the hook by turning back to her monitor. "Now shoo so I can get something done."

Ezra crossed the short distance between the side door of the church building and the back door to the parsonage. Thomas waved to him from across the cemetery as if they had not seen each other in days. He was pulling on work gloves for an afternoon of gardening. Ezra waved back.

The minister stopped outside his door to listen. The inviting, pleasant sounds of the spring afternoon were being swallowed up by another noise, the familiar roar of a Harley-Davidson approaching on the country road in front of the church. Ezra could hear the motorcycle decelerate abruptly near the driveway to the property, then he finally saw it: a black and chrome beauty of a machine moving slowly between the trees, nosing into the hollow in the distance.

Astride the bike and gunning the engine was a muscular young man wearing a tight-fitting black T-shirt, black jeans, and black boots. *The man in black*, Ezra mused, *apparently right down to a "big, black pistol."*

The young man guided his bike to the small tent he had pitched in the hollow. He cut the engine, dismounted, and set the kickstand.

Ezra watched him pull out a cigarette, light it, and sit down cross-legged on the hollow's grassy carpet. The minister could not deny a sense of apprehension. But it was time to find out what this man called Joe was all about. He stepped into his kitchen long enough to retrieve from the refrigerator two cold bottles of lemon-flavored iced tea, his favorite drink. Then, breathing a prayer, he headed out toward the hollow.

Three

CHAPEL OF THE VALLEY OWNED EIGHTEEN ACRES of property alongside the country road between rural Orchard Valley and Yarborough, the county seat, eighteen miles to the north. The land was deeded to the church at its founding in 1923 by charter member Merwyn Rasby, the caretaker's grandfather. The elder Rasby was a God-fearing farmer who wanted his family to attend a local, country church instead of driving into the city every Sunday. So he and a few like-minded families in the valley chartered the church and hired its first minister. Rasby sold a chunk of his property to the newly formed Chapel of the Valley for the sum of one dollar.

Two and a half of the eighteen acres were developed for the original wood-frame church building (which was still standing), a parking lot (first dirt and then oil and gravel), and a modest parsonage at the back. The main floor of the church served as the sanctuary with a small anteroom / office just off the chancel. The full-sized basement provided a few classrooms and a fellowship hall.

Another two and a half acres of property became Chapel of the Valley Cemetery, the final resting place for many deceased church members. A caretaker's cabin and equipment shed were later built in the southwest corner of the cemetery, parallel to the parsonage but separated from it by an expanse of cemetery lawn. Stately evergreens and sprawling maples shaded the church grounds and cemetery.

Six acres on the south side of the original property were left in crops, leased to the farmer across the road for barely enough money to pay the taxes. The remaining seven acres, a depressed, roughly triangular piece of land wedged between the cemetery and the church's farmland, was left undeveloped. Secluded from the road by a stand of trees and carpeted with wild grass and weeds, it was known simply as the hollow.

For years, the hollow had served as an unofficial campground for transients and migrant farm workers. Several years back, Thomas had carved out a fire pit in the hollow and ringed it with bread-loaf-sized stones. He also built a large wooden picnic table so visitors wouldn't have to eat on the ground. Each summer, one of the farmers in the church had a chemical toilet delivered to the hollow and maintained it for workers during the picking season.

Ezra crossed the lush, green cemetery lawn—dappled with sunlight and shadow—toward the hollow. Thomas kept the cemetery and church grounds verdant, clean, and weed-free, and his flowerbeds and borders were the envy of every gardener in the valley.

As Ezra started down the slope from the cemetery to the hollow, the young man in black was hunched over the motorcycle tinkering with the engine. The man paid no attention to the approaching visitor, but Ezra was sure the biker had seen him coming.

"Hi there," Ezra called out as he came near, trying to sound friendly. He stopped next to the picnic table, a few steps from the motorcycle.

The young man kept tinkering with his bike as if he hadn't heard anything.

"I'm Ezra Sturdevant, the minister at the church here," Ezra continued, standing in the brilliant sun. Beads of sweat were already forming on his face and on the bottles of tea.

Flicking a glance at Ezra, the biker offered a barely cordial, "Yeah, hi." Then he was back at his work.

Undeterred, Ezra said, "I thought you might like a cold drink. Must be ninety degrees out here already." He waited a moment. "So I brought you an iced tea." Another pause. "It's real cold...or at least it was when I pulled it out of the fridge."

Seconds ticked by and Ezra just watched. He had put up with less friendly visitors in the hollow—even rather hostile ones. He could wait out this one too.

Finally the young man laid his screwdriver and shop rag on the grass and stood. "My name's Joe."

He was an inch or so short of six feet, Ezra assessed. But muscular arms, thick chest and neck, and sturdy legs made him look big, like a linebacker. He appeared to be in his mid-twenties.

Ezra put the bottles on the table and stepped forward. "Nice to meet you, Joe," he said, offering his hand. The kid lifted both of his hands, which were conveniently soiled with grease, meaning no handshake.

Ezra nodded and quickly dropped his hand. "How about a cold drink?" he said, retreating to the table.

Joe stayed put. "I have everything I need, Reverend. But thanks."

"It's nice and cold," Ezra lifted one of the glistening bottles toward the biker.

Joe shook his head once.

Sitting down at the table, Ezra unscrewed the bottle cap and took a long swallow. "Mind if I sit and visit for minute?" he said.

Joe shrugged. "Suit yourself. I'm not much of a talker, but it's your property." Then he returned to a crouch next to the bike, picked up the screwdriver, and tinkered some more.

Ezra studied the young man. His dark hair was pulled back into a ponytail that fell to the top of his spine. He was at least two days removed from his last shave, but the scar on the left side of the man's face stood out through the stubble. He sported a well-worn silver band on his left index finger. The tattoo high on his arm pictured a fierce-looking eagle diving for a kill.

Joe's clothes were not tattered or badly soiled, and his boots looked to be almost new. The designer sunglasses now perched on top of his head were not cheap, Ezra knew. The Harley-Davidson wasn't new, but it had been nicely maintained. This wasn't a panhandling biker just trying to make it to his next meal. Ezra guessed that the young man could afford to stay at a hotel if he wanted to.

"What brings you to our valley?" Ezra said after another swallow. As he waited for an answer, he casually glanced toward the door of Joe's small tent. The flaps were tied open, but Ezra could see no gun.

Still focused on the engine, Joe said, "Just…traveling. Seeing the sights."

Ezra sipped his drink, waiting for more information. Joe offered none. The minister asked a few more small-talk questions, trying to draw out the young man, but he got nowhere. He commented on the nice-looking Harley and asked questions about it to show his interest. Joe provided only basic information in short answers.

"Where do you call home, Joe?"

"At the moment, I guess I call this little rest stop home."

Ezra sipped his drink, waiting. Finally, Joe added, "I'm from out east."

"Eastern Washington? Spokane? Pullman?"

Joe shook his head, still intent on his work. "Way east… Pennsylvania."

It was a small victory, Ezra thought. Joe had supplied some real information. Buoyed with confidence, he pressed on. "And where are you headed, Joe?"

Joe wiped his screwdriver clean with the shop rag and dropped it next to other tools spread on a shop rag. Then he stood and took a couple of steps toward the table. "Do you interrogate everybody who spends the night here?" he said, glaring at the minister.

A cold flash of fear shot down Ezra's back. If this young man became hostile he could do some serious physical damage. Ezra brushed away the momentary shock and locked eyes with the intense young man. "I 'interrogate' simply because I'm interested in the people who stop here. Maybe I'm old-fashioned, but I don't think you are here by accident. And if there is some divine purpose behind your visit, I'm just curious to know what it is. If I come across as nosey, I apologize."

The hard edge left Joe's gaze and he glanced away. "Okay, Reverend," he said. Then, "I'll be around the area a few days—if that's all right—then I'll be heading home."

"You're welcome to stay here as long as you want to, Joe," Ezra said, standing. "And if you need anything—"

"I don't need anything, Reverend," Joe inserted pointedly. "Just a place for my tent and bedroll."

"Of course. But if something comes up, just tell Thomas."

"Your gardener?" Joe said.

"Thomas is the church caretaker. You've met him, haven't you?"

Joe nodded. "He seems a little…" He finished the sentence by tapping his forehead with his index finger.

"Thomas suffered brain damage at birth," Ezra explained. "But he's loyal, dependable, and he has a big heart."

Ezra cautiously pressed on to the issue he wanted to broach with Joe. "Speaking of Thomas, he mentioned something about seeing a gun down here. Do you have a gun, Joe?"

Joe scowled briefly at Ezra. Then he looked away as if crafting an answer. "It's a pellet gun," he said at last, "to scare away animals."

Was he telling the truth? Ezra had no way of knowing. Joe made no move to get the gun and show it to him, and Ezra wasn't about to press the issue.

"That's good enough for me," the minister said. "We get a few pesky coyotes around here, so you're smart to have something to ward them off."

The muscles in Joe's forearm relaxed a little.

"One more thing," Ezra said, picking up the iced tea bottles. "The weather service is predicting a big thunderstorm in the valley tonight. It could get very noisy and wet out here. You're welcome to move into the church basement for the night if you like."

"Like I said, Reverend, I don't need anything," Joe said. "I have a good tent. I'm ready for the weather. But thanks just the same."

"You're welcome, Joe."

Joe nodded. Then he retrieved a wallet from the hip pocket of his jeans and pulled out a twenty-dollar bill. Holding out to Ezra, he said, "Here's a little something for the hospitality. You can put it in the collection or whatever."

"Not necessary, Joe," Ezra said with a wry smile. "God doesn't need anything either. But thanks just the same." He turned and began walking back toward the church, leaving Joe standing with the twenty dollars dangling from his hand.

Ezra angled across the cemetery to where Thomas was working. He told the gardener that Joe's gun was "just a harmless pellet gun for plunking coyotes." He hoped he was right. Thomas wanted to chatter about when his niece might arrive. Ezra said, "Chessy will get here when she gets here," which left Thomas with plenty to think about.

On the way back to the parsonage, Ezra stopped beside a modest granite headstone colored dusty rose and admired the inscription: DORIS M. STURDEVANT—SERVANT OF GOD, BELOVED WIFE. Stooping down to brush off a few pine needles that had collected on the stone, he said, "This one would be a challenge for you, Dorrie. He acts tough, and he's as self-sufficient as they come. You would probably bake him a batch of your peanut butter cookies and melt the sharp edges right off him."

Ezra glanced out to the hollow once more. Joe had started up the Harley and was revving the engine noisily. It sounded well-tuned after Joe's tinkering.

At that moment a late-model silver Cadillac sedan turned sharply into the church parking lot, kicking up gravel and dust. Ezra glanced at his watch. Jethro Haig, vice chairman of the church board, was three minutes early, chauffeured as always by his stepson Rusty. Jethro loved being seen in nice cars, but he hated driving them. Ferrying Jethro around in the Caddie, watching the auto races on TV, and sponging off his late mother's husband were about all Rusty had proven to be good at in forty-five years of living, Ezra assessed.

Board chairman Bradford McDermot would arrive soon in his red three-quarter-ton farm truck. Bradford's 200-acre farm started to the south where the church property left off, but the farmhouse was on the far side of the spread. So even though they were the church's nearest neighbors, Bradford and Esther still had to drive whenever they came to church.

"Wait until they see what Louise Wilkerson has done, Dorrie," Ezra said over his shoulder as he hurried to the parsonage to change clothes. "It will really give Jethro something to harp about."

As he stepped inside, Ezra heard the Harley roar through the gears as it raced down the country road.

Four

JETHRO HAIG STARTED IN ON THE MINISTER the moment they were both in the church office. "Have you seen what we've got out there on our church property, Ezra?" he snapped, laying his hat on the filing cabinet. "A motorcycle gang member! A no-good transient! Another panhandler desecrating our land!"

Ezra stole a quick look at Velma over Jethro's shoulder. Her eyes launched into a familiar here-we-go-again roll. Rusty, in dress jeans, western shirt, cowboy boots, and a NASCAR cap, leaned in a corner absorbed in a car racing magazine.

Jethro Haig was a small, wiry, tinny-voiced seventy-two year old with a sparse comb-over that stood straight up when a breeze caught him from the side. The board vice-chairman was a farmer who fancied himself a high-rolling businessman. In both arenas, his shrewd dealings had netted him success and wealth. Preferring gabardine to denim jeans and flannel shirts, today Jethro sported a lightweight brown business suit, silk tie, and panama hat. But the scuffed and dusty steel-toed work boots he always wore belied the image he sought.

"The kid isn't panhandling, Jethro," Ezra explained. "He has his own gear, his own food. He hasn't asked the church for anything."

"What if he gets drunk and breaks his leg on the church's property?" Jethro steamed. "We'd be liable, you know. A lawsuit like that would wipe us out."

"Well, I suppose there is a little bit of risk," admitted Ezra. "But when people are in need, we can't always put safety first."

Jethro bored in. "I'm not just talking about safety, Ezra; I'm talking about survival. In case you hadn't noticed, the church treasury is barely above water, and it's not getting any better. Every time one of our old pensioners transfers membership from the sanctuary to the cemetery, the church loses another small income stream. And there are no replacements in sight. Our kids have all moved away, and we can't attract new members with no-account trash polluting our property."

Bradford McDermot walked into the small office as Jethro spoke. Thomas Rasby tagged after him like a puppy. "Hello Mister Haig. Hello Rusty," he said as if greeting family. "My niece Chessy Carpenter is coming today." Neither man acknowledged the greeting.

The interruption didn't slow Jethro for a moment. "This building is a wreck held together with rusty nails and wishful thinking. It needs paint inside and out. The roof leaks, the pews are falling apart, and the wood floors need refinishing. The furnace won't make it through next winter. And even if we could get these things fixed, something else is bound to break down or fall apart. I just wonder how long we'll be able to keep the church doors open. It's obvious we need to revisit the topic of selling off some property."

Bradford and Ezra exchanged knowing glances. They had been down this road with Jethro many times before.

"And you're still in the market for that thirteen acres out there, I gather?" Bradford said, unfazed by Jethro's bluster.

Jethro wheeled toward the farmer, who was taller, huskier, and two years younger than himself. "You know good and well I want that thirteen acres, Bradford. It's a standing offer. I'll pay a fair price, enough to fund all the needed repairs and still leave something in the bank."

"Jethro, you know the church's position on that property," Ezra said. "We've gone over it for years in the board meetings. That land has been dedicated for future ministry. This valley needs a facility to house and care for migrant workers and their families. We can have a significant impact on hundreds of people every summer."

"Yes, I am well acquainted with your vision," Jethro said. "But you need to get your head out of the clouds and face the facts. This church can't support the facility it already has, let alone build and maintain another. It's just not good stewardship to hold onto property that could be turned into desperately needed operating capital."

Jethro allowed a few moments of silence before speaking again. "Of course, that thirteen acre parcel is too small to do me much good if you won't sell me your place next door, Bradford. You haven't received any offers lately, have you?"

Bradford McDermot was one of the hardest working farmers in Orchard Valley, and his crops were renowned for quality year after year. But at seventy, Bradford and Esther were eyeing retirement. Their three children had pursued other careers away from Orchard Valley. So it meant selling their large, successful farm. Ezra knew the McDermot spread had been on the market for nearly a year.

Bradford smiled and shook his head. "Not a single one, Jethro. It seems that you're the only person around interested in taking on 200 acres of wheat and cherries—though I'm sure the land won't be in crops long once you get your hands on it."

"Now Bradford," Jethro said, softening his tone, "it's no secret that I might turn that land over for a profit if the right deal came along. I'm a businessman trying to prepare for retirement, same as you. But whatever I might do with your land shouldn't have anything to do with you selling it to me."

"Well, if you offered me a decent price for it, I might think about it for longer than half a second. But I can't let my farm go for fifteen percent below market value."

Jethro cocked his head and smirked. "If you were receiving other offers, I'd say you might have a decent bargaining position, my friend. In the meantime, my offer is still on the table. I'll take the farm off your hands so you and Esther can start taking those cruises you've been talking about."

"I just want a fair price," Bradford replied, "and I'm sure someone will offer it eventually. Until then, we're doing just fine."

"Bah!" Jethro spat, "You'll never get what you want out of that land, Bradford." Then, wheeling toward Ezra he grumbled in the same tone,

"Now what's this 'emergency meeting' all about, Reverend? The day is wasting way."

Ezra nodded. "This is a semi-official church meeting, so Rusty, if you wouldn't mind…" He left the familiar unfinished request dangling in the air. Rusty was not a church member and did not attend the services on Sunday with Jethro, preferring to sit in the Caddie outside and listen to the auto races on the radio.

Jethro's cowboy stepson was lost in his magazine and had missed the hint. "Rusty, wait outside," Jethro barked.

Rusty looked up casually. "All right, Boss," he drawled, then he scuffed out of the office.

Saying nothing, Ezra unlocked the bottom desk drawer, removed the metal box, and set it on the desk. "I want to show you something that has a direct bearing on the issue of our church's financial status. Being leaders of the board, you should know about it, but nobody needs to know right now, so keep it under your hat."

Bradford and Jethro shuffled a few inches closer to the desk. Thomas peered around Bradford's shoulder for a better look. Ezra hadn't invited him to the meeting, but when the caretaker trailed Bradford into the office, Ezra didn't have the heart to send him back out in the heat. Velma sat quietly in front of the keyboard.

Ezra unlocked the box and lifted the lid. He retrieved four bundles from the metal box and casually laid them on the desktop side by side. Each bundle was about the size of a brick. Then he waited, letting the two board members take in the sight.

"What did you do, Reverend, rob a bank?" Jethro huffed, staring at the bundles.

"You're looking at $22,455, mostly in hundreds and fifties," Ezra announced. "It was bequeathed to the church by a former member, Louise Wilkerson. I buried her in the cemetery last week."

"Wilkerson," Jethro repeated, the hard edge suddenly gone from his tone. "Her husband did fair to middling in sugar beets, as I recall."

"At ninety-six she outlived both him and their daughter, who died an old maid. Louise's last will and testament specified that her entire estate, which was the cash she kept under her mattress in her apartment, be delivered to the church just as you see it here. Louise's lawyer brought the box out to me yesterday."

Ezra watched Jethro's eyes riffle through the bills as if suspecting that the minister had sneaked out a twenty when nobody was looking.

Bradford pushed his John Deere cap back on his head with his thumb and whistled his amazement. "That dear, dear old lady," he said, shaking his head in wonder. "She was a McDermot, you know. My father's cousin. Her husband Mort was board chairman maybe fifty years ago, long before I got here. What a legacy she leaves for the Chapel."

The sneer returned to Jethro's face. "That woman had no business giving away that kind of money. She lived as poor as a church mouse ever since Mort died. We can't accept it."

"It will be a little difficult giving it back to her, Jethro," Ezra said, unable to hold back a wry grin. "And according to her lawyer, Louise has no living heirs, and nobody has contested the will. So I'm afraid we're stuck with her money."

"I think it's a wonderful gesture, a real God-send," Velma put in.

"I been praying for a miracle so I can fix up some things," Thomas put in. "I think Sister Louise's money is a miracle." Then he began a lengthy litany of repairs which were needed.

"I can't believe you people!" Jethro snorted when Thomas took a breath. "Your 'miracle' has been here all along. I've been offering the church enough money to fix up everything with plenty left over. You keep turning me down flat, and now you're crowing over a widow's mite. You've got things turned upside down. It just doesn't make sense."

"Louise's gift can't do everything," Bradford replied, "but it will help us do some things and allow us to keep the church's vision for our unused thirteen acres intact."

"Vision!" Jethro huffed. "Twenty-two thousand dollars will barely get the church started fixing the problems we've got. Face the facts, people. This church will never be able to afford a camp for migrant workers out there. Can't you see that the Chapel of the Valley is dying right under your noses? And if you don't sell that land, it will die even sooner."

Jethro snatched up his hat and stepped toward the door. "As for you, Bradford, if you have any sense at all you will take my offer for your spread before I invest the money somewhere else and you're stuck with your precious farm." Then he thrust the panama onto his head and stalked out the door. "Where are you, Rusty? Let's get out of here," he barked just before slamming the door.

The four left in the church office were so used to Jethro being Jethro that his carping passed without further comment.

"That's a wonderful, timely gift," Bradford said, nodding to the bundles as Ezra returned them to the metal box. "And I'm sure we can make it go a long way toward repairs. The good Lord is watching out for us, that's for sure."

"All things are possible with God, Mister McDermot," Thomas intoned reverently. The others hummed agreement, and Velma resumed her typing after the long interruption.

"I've got to get back to work," Bradford said, tugging his cap down into place. "You'll be taking that money into the bank in Yarborough directly, won't you Ezra?"

"Yes, directly." The minister winced inside at the intentional vagueness of his reply. He was sure "directly" to Bradford meant today, but to Ezra it meant tomorrow.

JOE OPENED UP THE ACCELERATOR until the Harley reached seventy miles per hour on the country road. Mainly he was listening for the steady, high-pitched growl of the engine, assuring him that his carburetor adjustment had been adequate. He also thrilled at the opportunity to open it up and feel the warm wind buffeting him. And traversing the quiet, scenic farm roads of Orchard Valley gave him plenty of time to think. Joe had a lot to think about.

Over and over he had second-guessed his decision to come west. Chances were high that his journey was in vain. He was not merely searching for a needle in a haystack, he still had to find the right haystack. And maybe there was no needle at all. He kept telling himself it was no big deal if he didn't find her. But if it was no big deal, why had he uprooted his life and come three thousand miles on a motorcycle to a country town he couldn't even find on an atlas? Why would he spend so much of his meager savings on fuel and food when he could live more cheaply at home—and sleep in his own bed instead of a sleeping bag?

But he was here now. If nothing else, coming west to "find his roots"— that's what Joe had told a few of his friends back home—was a convenient way to leave his sadness behind, at least for a while. And his trip would serve as a clean break with the excesses of his younger days, the trouble he had been in and the hurt he had caused. Whether he found what he was looking for in Washington or not, he would return home in a few days to start a new, productive life.

Joe slowed the bike as he approached a four-way stop at the intersection of two farm roads. He yielded right of way to a water truck apparently making its way from the hydrant to the field. Then he turned left and gunned the bike through the gears until he was up to fifty.

Up to speed again, Joe tugged at the uncomfortable chin strap of his helmet. He hated helmets, which were required for minors in his home state but not for adults, and he had planned his trip from Pennsylvania to Washington through northern states that had similar laws. But Washington required helmets for all cyclists, drivers and riders, so he wore one which barely met the state's safety requirements for headgear. And it would go back on his sissy bar the moment he left the state on his way home.

It had taken him all the way from western Pennsylvania to Montana to admit it to himself, but Joe was indeed homesick. Not so much for Pittsburgh or for the old house perched high on the hillside overlooking the Ohio River; he was homesick for the one who had made that house his home for twenty-four years. Joe had hoped that the long journey west might help him cope with his recent loss. But being away only fueled the fantasy that his Mom would be waiting for him on the porch when he returned, just as she had been so many times when he had wandered far from home. Joe would return home again some day, and it saddened him to think that she would not be there.

About twenty minutes later, Joe decelerated on the main road as he approached the country church and the hollow where he had pitched his small tent. He guided the bike down the gentle, grassy incline through the trees to his campsite and parked. He had left his tools spread out on a shop rag in the grass. He could almost hear his mother chastising him about leaving his things lying around where they could get lost. Satisfied that his machine was running well, he hurriedly returned his tools to the vinyl pouch and stowed it in his saddle bag.

He had just sat down at the picnic table and lit a cigarette when the caretaker ambled into view. Joe cursed under his breath. If this half-wit was going to pester him several times a day, he may have to abandon the ideal campsite and find another.

"Hello, Joe," the caretaker called out as he approached. "Did you get your bike fixed good?"

Joe took another drag on his cigarette. "Yeah, it's fixed," he said.

"Mighty glad to hear it," Thomas said, grinning and nodding like a bobble-head doll. "I come out here to tell you there's a big storm coming in. There'll be—"

"Heard all about it," Joe cut in. "The preacher already told me. I'll be just fine."

"I got my cabin over yonder," Thomas persisted. "Got a couch you can sleep on."

"Thanks, but I like to be by myself. And my tent's waterproof."

"That tent will be your miracle tonight, Joe," Thomas said. "We already got two miracles today already. My little niece Chessy Carpenter coming all the way from Fresno to visit me. That's a miracle."

Joe didn't have a clue what he was talking about and didn't care. "Yeah, great," he said, exhaling.

"And Sister Louise gave the church a box of money," Thomas jerked a thumb over his shoulder toward the church office.

Joe looked up. "What are you talking about?"

"It's a big, *big* miracle, Joe," Thomas said excitedly, his weathered face crinkled into a big smile. "Sister Louise gave the church twenty-two thousand dollars when she died last week. I never seen so much money before. Did you, Joe? Reverend Sturdevant has it locked up in his desk."

"Are you talking about cash, man?"

The caretaker nodded. "It's all in dollars of green cash. I seen it on the desk. Reverend Sturdevant will take it to the bank in Yarborough tomorrow. Then we can get a new roof for the church. But it's a secret, Joe. Don't tell nobody." Thomas lifted a finger to his lips in a shushing motion.

Joe surmised that the man's story was the product of his childish, retarded imagination. Nobody keeps $22,000 in cash in a desk drawer.

Thomas excused himself to make preparations for the storm. Watching the caretaker ascend the slope to the cemetery, Joe thought of the irony. Here was a little church in the middle of nowhere, allegedly the beneficiary of some widow's savings—over $20,000. Could it be true? If so, why couldn't this woman have been related to him? He could use some cash like that.

A LITTLE AFTER 4:00 P.M., Velma heard a car drive into the parking lot through the open side window. She walked through the sanctuary to the front door of the church to see a red Jeep Liberty with a trail bicycle mounted to a rack on the back. The occupants were strangers to her, but she was expecting guests, so she hurried out to meet the visitors and locked the door behind her.

A pretty young woman stepped out of the passenger's door, pulled off her sunglasses, and smiled as Velma approached. "Are you Mrs. Walls?"

"Yes, and you must be Chessy," Velma answered, extending her hand, "our dear Thomas' niece."

"Yes, that's me," the girl replied with a light laugh, warmly shaking the woman's hand.

The driver had come around from his side. He was in his mid forties, Velma guessed, trim, graying at the temples, and California tanned.

"I'm pleased to meet you, Mrs. Walls. And I would like you to meet Doctor Richard Denny, one of my college professors."

"Doctor Denny, it's a pleasure to meet you, too," she said cordially as they shook hands.

"My students call me Doctor Rich," he returned, "but to everyone else I'm just Rich."

"All right, Rich," Velma said.

Chessy continued, "Doctor Rich is on his way to Seattle. He volunteered to give me a ride to Orchard Valley on his way."

Chessy's eyes drifted behind Velma, and the girl's face suddenly glowed. "Oh, is this my Uncle Thomas?" she squealed.

Thomas was lumbering toward the SUV from across the cemetery. Velma had never seen his face stretched into such a broad grin. Chessy ran to embrace him. They were certainly a mismatched pair, Velma thought. Thomas was wiry, weathered, stork-like. Chessy was petite, fair, and the picture of fashion. Yet it was obvious that after twenty years, she was still Thomas' "little Chessy."

Turning to the professor, Velma said, "Are you traveling on to Seattle tonight?"

He nodded. "That's the plan."

"There's a storm front coming in from the west that could turn your drive through the pass into a nightmare," Velma said.

Rich glanced at the dark clouds boiling on the far western horizon. "I was afraid of that."

"We have a spare room in the parsonage," Velma said. "It's for visiting missionaries and guests, which are few and far between for us. You're welcome to stay here tonight. And our minister always enjoys the company."

Rich objected. "I'm sure the minister wasn't planning on a guest for the night."

"It's no trouble at all," she assured. "Chessy will be staying at my home; it's all been arranged. And the parsonage guest room is always ready."

Rich touched the small of his back with his right hand. "Well, parking the Jeep for the night sounds very appealing. But are you sure your minister wants to take in a boarder sight unseen?"

Velma laughed. "I've known Ezra for twenty-two years, so I think I can speak for him. You're as welcome as the flowers in spring. He is used to coming home to find a guest in his spare room."

The two of them began walking toward Thomas and his niece, who were standing under a huge elm at the edge of the cemetery, hands clasped, chattering and laughing in happy animation.

"They seem to have bonded already," Rich said in amazement. "Hard to believe they haven't seen each other in twenty years."

"I love it," Velma exclaimed. Then she lowered her voice. "Did Chessy tell you anything about Thomas, I mean, his...limitations?"

"She told me as we traveled," Rich said discreetly.

"He may be disadvantaged mentally, but his big heart more than makes up for it. He's a teddy bear, a people person—and he's like this with everyone he meets. Every Sunday morning he stands near the front door just to greet people arriving for church. It's not his job; he's just happy to see people, and he lets them know it."

"Maybe congeniality runs in the family," Rich replied. "I've only known Chessy for a year, but no one is a stranger to her. She was very popular at the college with both her fellow students and the faculty. She's always a delight to have around."

Velma called out to uncle and niece. "Hey, you two, let's get out of this heat. Ezra has some iced tea in his fridge. We can talk inside." Turning back to Rich, she explained, "Ezra always leaves his door unlocked. He thinks of the parsonage as an extension of the church."

The four of them sipped cold tea in Ezra's living room. Thomas babbled to Chessy about everything he thought she needed to know about Orchard Valley and the Chapel of the Valley. Velma announced that Rich had accepted an invitation to spend the night in the parsonage before leaving for Seattle in the morning.

In response to Velma's questions, Rich, a lifetime bachelor, explained that he was beginning a six-month sabbatical with a month of vacation. "I'll be visiting my sister and her husband on Vashon Island in Puget Sound. I'm looking forward to a little fishing, exploring Mount Rainier on my trail bike, and catching up on my reading until July. Then I plan to spend the rest of the year in theological studies and guest lectures around the northwest until after Christmas."

After twenty-five minutes of chit chat, Velma stood to leave, needing to finish a few things in the office before heading to her home in town. They agreed to meet at the Country Skillet at 7:00 P.M. for supper. "The best and only supper restaurant in our little town of Orchard Valley," Velma boasted. She gave Rich directions to the restaurant, which was in the little town of Orchard Valley three miles west of the church. She would arrange for Ezra to meet them there.

Thomas dutifully declined the invitation to supper because he was behind on his storm preparation chores. But he did agree to give Chessy a quick tour of the church property while Rich hauled his luggage into the parsonage and took a power nap before supper.

Thomas walked Chessy through the church building, leading her by the hand as if she was still a little girl. He showed her the sanctuary, the office, and the classrooms and fellowship hall in the basement. With each new room, he proudly explained what he dusted and mopped each week and where he had patched and painted.

Outdoors, Thomas marched Chessy around his flowerbeds and neatly trimmed lawn. As the afternoon shadows grew long, they strolled through the cemetery. Thomas had a sentence or two for a few headstones, usually a tribute to the dear saint planted beneath it.

Finally he led his niece to the side-by-side graves of his mother and father, Chessy's maternal grandparents, who had died while Chessy was a child. He spoke of them in loving, respectful terms, and Chessy was touched. "I wish I had known them," she said.

Thomas showed Chessy his own cabin in the back corner of the cemetery. The four small rooms—living room, kitchen, bedroom, and bathroom—were plain but tidy. Thomas delighted in telling the joke someone had once made—and then explained to him—about his tiny living quarters: "It's so small you have to step outside to change your mind."

As the two of them crossed the cemetery toward the church, Chessy noticed the hollow for the first time. She saw a man hovered over a motorcycle, polishing chrome to a brilliant luster. "Who is that, Uncle Thomas?" she said, stopping to watch.

"That's Joe," Thomas said. "He's on a trip, so he's camping out in the hollow." He filled Chessy in on Joe in three short sentences highlighting his scar, tattoo, and pellet gun. Then he explained that many people camped in the hollow during the summer—migrant workers, travelers, and people with no homes at all. "Reverend Sturdevant and me, we make sure them people in the hollow got plenty to eat," he added. "Like Reverend Sturdevant says, you never know when one of them might be an angel."

Chessy watched the biker work for several seconds. "Well, I don't see any wings on that one, Uncle Thomas."

Thomas got the joke and laughed. "No, Chessy, Joe ain't got no wings."

At that moment, the young man looked up. Seeing Chessy, his eyes lingered a moment. Chessy smiled and waved as if adding her welcome to that of the minister and the caretaker. Joe turned back to his work without responding.

Seven

CHESSY RELAXED IN THOMAS' CABIN while her uncle hauled a ladder from window to window around the sanctuary closing shutters. Ominous charcoal clouds were steadily rolling in from the west, dimming the normally bright evening sky of late spring. Twice during the process a gust of wind nearly toppled the ladder with Thomas on it.

Thomas waved goodbye to Chessy and Dr. Rich as they left for supper in town a few minutes before seven. Taking the ladder to a back corner of the church, Thomas climbed up on the roof and began scooping needles out of the gutter and dropping them to the lawn below. The caretaker was on the church roof several times a year for one reason or another, so he knew to be careful climbing around on the fairly steep pitch. He had fallen off when he was much younger and less cautious, breaking a bone in his foot. He never forgot how painful it was.

Gusts of wind pushed at him, but he stayed low, scooping out needles by hand. One strong gust made him grip the roof edge with both hands. It passed, but as it did he heard a loud clatter from the back of the church. Something had fallen in the wind. He crawled carefully back to the place where he had climbed onto the roof and looked down. There was the rickety old ladder, collapsed on the ground.

Thomas studied the ladder for several moments. He hadn't considered the possibility of it blowing over. Such a thing had never happened before. But now he was stuck on the roof with no way of getting down. He worried about it for only a minute before realizing that he didn't need to get down yet. He still had more gutters to clean. So he crawled back to where he had left off and continued his job.

When he finished and returned to the back corner of the building, the ladder was still lying right where it had fallen. The seriousness of the situation began to dawn on him. It was getting darker, and the wind was picking up. Soon the rain would start, followed by lightning and thunder. And he would be stuck on the roof in the midst of it all. He couldn't jump down. It was too far. He might break his foot again—or a leg or an arm.

Furthermore, the church was empty and dark. Rev. Sturdevant, Chessy, Mrs. Walls, and Dr. Rich were in town at the restaurant. Rev. Sturdevant and Dr. Rich would return to the parsonage in a couple hours—no, it would be even longer. Thomas remembered that they had to unload Chessy's luggage at Mrs. Walls' home. By then Thomas would be soaked to the skin. He didn't like thunder, and he didn't like being outside when the lightning flashed. He knew about farmers who had been struck by lightning, and one of them died from it.

He stared out toward the hollow. In the diminishing light, he could see Joe's tent and motorcycle, now covered with a plastic tarp. But he couldn't see Joe, and there was no campfire or light anywhere in his camp. He called out Joe's name twice, as loudly as he could, but the words seemed to die in the noisy wind. Joe must have walked somewhere, he thought.

Thomas did not know what else he could do, so he just sat down on the edge of the roof and prayed as worry buffeted him like the wind.

• • •

Velma sipped her cup of decaf and looked happily at her companions around the restaurant table. The meal had been excellent, and discussion around the table had been warm and spirited. She could see immediately that Chessy would fit in just fine. Ezra and Rich had hit it off right away, and Velma was sure they would be compatible dorm mates in the parsonage for one night.

They talked about Thomas in light of his sister's claim that he may need closer supervision and care as he moved into his sixties. Velma and Ezra sympathized with Lydia's concern, but they assured Chessy that Thomas was still doing well, especially with the two of them close enough to watch over him. However, Ezra emphasized, his long season as minister at Chapel of the Valley was in its twilight. When Ezra was done, Velma would also retire from her volunteer position. Until then, they were most happy to be Thomas' loving guardians.

A low rumble of distant thunder caught everyone's attention. "We'd better not stay out too late, Rich," Ezra said. "I don't want us driving home in a downpour."

"We can't leave yet," Velma objected with a mock scowl. "Ezra and I don't know anything about you, Rich, like how you became a Bible college professor. Did God call you into the ministry as a boy or young man?"

"I only wish I had started on my current path at a young age," Rich said ruefully. "But I didn't come to Christ until I was in my mid-twenties. I grew up in a non-Christian home and was quite a trouble-maker as a teenager—drugs, alcohol, fast motorcycles."

"You, a wild-living biker?" Velma's eyebrows arched in disbelief.

Rich glanced at Chessy, who had already heard his story, then back at Velma. "Yes, I'm sorry to say. Many wasted years roaming the country, poisoning my body, living for myself."

"Reminds me of Joe," Ezra put in, looking at Velma.

"Joe?" Rich said.

"There's a young fellow—mid-twenties, I'd guess—camped in the hollow behind the church," Ezra explained. "He's riding a big motorcycle. Harley-Davidson. Nice one. Rode it here from Pennsylvania, he says. Joe appears to have sown a few wild oats."

"I saw him this afternoon from across the cemetery when I was walking with Uncle Thomas," Chessy said.

"I'd be cautious if I were you," Ezra advised. "I went out to meet him shortly after he arrived. The young man has a hard edge to him, and I don't know what he's up to."

"Uncle Thomas said he has a gun," Chessy added.

"Joe told me it was only a pellet gun, but he didn't show it to me," Ezra replied. "He may be just a harmless traveler, but you never know. We need to show him the love of Christ, just as we do for everybody else. But it's wise to be a little careful."

"That's what brought me to Christ," Rich said. "Some wonderful Christians at a shelter in San Francisco welcomed me, fed me, and didn't try to cram religion down my throat. It was their love and acceptance that drew me in."

Another loud clap of thunder rattled the dishes on the table. Ezra was on his feet in a hurry. "I hate to break up the party folks, but we need to get on the road. Let's get Chessy's luggage over to Velma's, Rich, and point our cars toward the barn."

"I hope you stay around tomorrow long enough for us to hear the rest of your story, Rich," Velma said.

"I'm in no big hurry to get to Seattle," Rich said. "In fact, I wouldn't mind nosing around your beautiful valley tomorrow and perhaps head for the city on Friday—if Ezra doesn't mind having a roommate for another night."

"Not at all, Rich, I'd enjoy the company," Ezra assured. "But right now, we need to get back to the church. I don't like leaving Thomas alone in bad weather. Like a lot of kids, he's afraid of thunder and lightning."

•　　•　　•

Thomas had lost all track of time. He sat huddled and shivering on the roof. There was barely enough light leaking through the clouds to help him make out his cabin, the headstones in the cemetery, and other landmarks around the church grounds. But he could see no people. Whenever a car passed by on the road, which was infrequently, he waved his arms and shouted for help. But nobody heard him or saw him.

The first big flash of lightning illuminated the landscape like daylight for an instant, startling the caretaker. He wrapped his arms tightly around his knees and counted to himself, *One one-thousand, two one-thousand, three one-thousand,* waiting for the thunder clap. Whatever number he was counting when the thunder hit was how many miles away the lightning struck. Someone had told him that once.

He got to fourteen-one-thousand before the thunder boomed like a cannon blast to the west. But he only got to eleven between the next flash of light and peal of thunder. Then a few flashes later, it was down to seven.

By now the rain was pelting Thomas sideways in the strong wind. As the water quickly drenched his clothing, he strained a look toward the road leading to Velma's house in town. No cars were in sight. He was beginning to tremble, as much from fright as from the wind blowing through his wet clothes. The roof was slippery, so Thomas anchored the heels of his boots in the rain gutter. Each gust of wind caused him to tighten his grip. And the blinding flashes of lightning were getting closer. He didn't want to jump off the roof, but he feared that if he didn't jump soon, he would be blown off.

"O Jesus, Jesus, Jesus," he whimpered, trying to shield his eyes from the driving rain.

He opened them again and, looking out over the church lawn, he thought he saw the shadow of someone or something moving furtively through the darkness near the front of the church building. He could not tell if it was man or beast, but he cried out in terror. "Help, please! Help, please!" The shadow stopped for a moment, then quickly disappeared under the eaves of the building. With wide eyes and limbs trembling, Thomas watched the shadows where he had seen the movement, but it did not appear again.

The noises of the storm engulfed Thomas, and his terror mounted. The wind howled through the eaves of the church, and the old building creaked and popped. All around he could hear dead branches falling from trees. Suddenly a blinding flash and a reverberating crack split the air, followed immediately by a heavy thud that shook the building. He looked up to see the great elm standing near him split down the middle as if a giant ax had swept down on it from above. Half of it fell hard onto the roof just in front of him, collapsing a section of the roof over the office. Thomas also heard the sound of shattered glass. He shuddered violently and shrieked in terror but managed to keep his life-saving grip on the gutter.

Thomas began to edge toward the tree, thinking he might somehow find a way to climb down on it. But suddenly he had something more to worry about. He thought he smelled something and sniffed the air to check it out. Smoke! His eyes widened and his heart jumped into his throat. Smoke was wafting from the hole in the roof. He bent over the edge of the roof to see better. Smoke billowed from the office window as well, and through the panes he could see a flickering orange glow.

The church was on fire.

Eight

JOE PRESSED THE LIGHT BUTTON on his digital watch. The green numerals told him it was 9:56. He had been holed up in his tent against the elements since about 7:30, reading by his penlight. But now the batteries were dead, and there was nothing to do but wait out the storm. The wind and rain buffeting his tent, along with the cannonade of thunder overhead, made it sound like he was camped in the middle of a battlefield. And despite his best attempts to keep his stuff dry, Joe's sleeping bag felt clammy.

A lightning flash and thunder clap hit at almost the same time, causing him to flinch. *The core of the storm must be right overhead,* he thought. It might be another hour before it was quiet enough for him to sleep, so he fumbled for the pack of cigarettes he had stowed in his boot. Lighting up, he unzipped the tent six inches for ventilation. It mattered little that it let in a few more raindrops because the floor of the tent was already damp. He dropped back on his sleeping bag, took a long drag, and exhaled into the darkness.

With the next flash of light came a noise unlike any Joe yet had heard during the storm. The crack of thunder was followed immediately by a reverberating snap and a thudding crash. He could not be sure above the noise of the wind and rain, but he thought he also heard the crash of broken glass.

The cacophony brought Joe up on his elbow. He waited and listened in the darkness, hearing only the low howl of wind and the spatter of rain pelting his tent. Not satisfied, he unzipped the tent door until it was fully open, tossed his cigarette outside, then stuck his head into the rain for a look around.

At first he saw nothing but large trees and the dark church building against the churning black clouds. Then something caught his eye—a small flicker of light. Joe squinted against the rain hitting his face, staring into the darkness in the direction of the old church. There it was again, fingers of orange and yellow light. *Flames!*

Joe reacted instinctively. Quickly pulling on his jeans and boots, he burst from the tent and sprinted across the soggy hollow toward the church. His pants and T-shirt were soaked within seconds. With each of his splashing steps, the flames seemed to glow brighter. The fire was coming from a window near the back of the church not far from the minister's house. "Hey! Fire! Fire!" he yelled as he ran.

As he raced up the slope and started across the cemetery, another strobe-like flash illuminated the landscape long enough to tell the story. The huge elm near the back corner of the church had been hit by lightning. It had split down the middle, half of it crashing down on the church roof. On the way down, the tree had apparently snapped a power line that ran into the church and ignited something inside.

The little country church was on fire.

Joe had to slow to a jog as he crossed the darkened cemetery, weaving around the headstones and heading toward the minister's house.

"Reverend, wake up!" he yelled, approaching the dark house. "The church is on fire! Call 9-1-1!" Mounting the back steps, Joe banged his fists on the door, repeating his urgent cry. He tried the doorknob, and it opened. Flipping on the wall switch by the door, Joe found himself in the kitchen. He grabbed the phone on the wall, dialed emergency, and in clipped phrases, reported a fire at the Chapel of the Valley.

A quick check of the bedrooms revealed the house to be unoccupied. But when he raced out the back door, he suddenly stopped. He thought he heard a cry.

"Help me! Oh God, help me, please!" it came again, seemingly from the top of the church building.

Joe looked up to see a dark figure huddled at the edge of the church roof.

"Somebody help me, please!" came the call again.

The caretaker! Joe leapt down the steps and ran to the spot just beneath where Thomas cowered. "Where's your ladder?" he yelled above the noise of the storm.

"It fell down. It's 'round the back of the church. Hurry please, Joe!"

Joe found the fallen ladder and dragged it back to Thomas' precarious perch. In seconds he had the ladder in place and climbed up two rungs. "Come on down, man. I'll steady the ladder." Thomas wasted no time getting on the ladder and down to the ground.

"Oh, Joe, I'm so glad you came. The Lord must have sent you—"

"No time to talk now," interrupted Joe. "Got to get that fire out. Where's a water hose?"

The quaking caretaker pointed to the corner of the building nearest the parsonage. Joe followed his finger and found a long, green garden hose coiled neatly around a caddy attached to the building. Spinning the faucet handle fully open, he pulled the hose free of the caddy before the water reached the nozzle. In seconds he was directing a full stream through a broken window.

Joe looked back at the caretaker, who seemed frozen in terror at the scene before him. "Move the ladder over here! Do it now!" he ordered.

The firm words seemed to bump the man into gear. He carted the ladder from the corner of the building to the window where Joe stood.

Hose in hand, Joe clambered several rungs up the ladder. Heat and smoke billowing from the window prevented him from getting too close. From his improved position, he aimed a stream at the center of the small inferno. The water might slow down the flames for awhile, Joe thought, but the stream was too small for the fire. The whole building could go up in smoke without professional firefighting equipment.

"Oh, look! Someone's coming," cried Thomas.

Joe turned and saw two pairs of headlights bouncing up the driveway into the parking lot. A red Jeep Liberty slammed to a stop, and behind it, a small sedan. A man jumped out of each vehicle and ran toward where

Joe stood on the ladder. He recognized the reverend but not the younger man.

"Fire department is on the way!" Joe yelled down to them, keeping the garden hose trained on the blaze in the office.

"I've got to get into that office," the minister shouted up to him, obviously distraught. "There are some...valuables in there."

Joe remembered what the caretaker had said about a "miracle" of $20,000 cash, and he knew if the money was simply stashed in a desk drawer, it would be gone soon.

"No way, Reverend," Joe called out, "nobody can get in and out of there alive right now." The minister's face was drawn with grief.

Soon they heard the sirens in the distance. The county fire department rolled in quickly and doused the fire in less than ten minutes. Remarkably, fire damage had been confined to the small church office, though the damage was extensive. The fire captain commended Joe for acting quickly, saying the building would likely have burned to the ground had he not started pouring water into the office when he did.

"I knew there was reason for you being here, Joe," the minister said as the fire fighters put away their gear. "If you hadn't seen the fire start, the church and perhaps the parsonage would likely be just a pile of smoldering embers by now."

The other man, whom the minister had called Rich, stepped forward. "I want to add my appreciation, too," he said. "Thank you for doing what you did. I thank God for your quick response." He grabbed Joe's hand and pumped it vigorously.

Joe just wanted to return to his tent. He didn't like all these people making over him. God didn't bring him here to save anything; he came on his own with his own agenda. He was no angel of mercy; he just happened to be in the right place at the right time to do what he did. It was no big deal.

When the fire captain called the minister aside, Joe saw his chance to slip away. The storm was moving on to the east and a few stars were now visible through the trailing clouds. It was only then that Joe realized he was soaked to the skin with his arms and face smudged with soot.

He felt something odd under his heel inside his boot. He pulled it off and fished out a flattened, soggy wad—his last package of cigarettes. He cursed under his breath.

"Do you want to take a bath, Joe?" Thomas the caretaker was standing next to him, looking as disheveled as he felt.

"Bath? Me? No, I'm fine."

Thomas paid no attention to his response. "You're all dirty, Joe, and your clothes is all wet. You can't go back to your tent like that. You can take a bath in my cabin. And you can put your clothes on the radiator. They'll dry out right quick."

Joe hesitated. He would rather take care of himself; that was his style. But he hadn't counted on getting soaked and dirty. A hot bath and dry clothes sounded tempting.

"I don't want to put you out, man," he objected weakly. The adrenaline rush that had sustained him during the crisis had abated, and he suddenly felt exhausted.

"You can take a bath," the caretaker said, oblivious to his objection, "and I'll make you some tea or hot cocoa."

Joe shrugged and then nodded. "I have to get my saddlebag. So I'll meet you over there, all right?"

The caretaker hustled off toward his cabin to prepare for his guest.

Conditions in the tent were worse than Joe expected. There was a half inch of water on the floor. The sleeping bag was wet throughout. He had no place to sleep tonight. Fortunately, the saddlebag was waterproof. He retrieved it, zipped the tent flaps closed and started across the hollow toward the caretaker's cabin.

Joe watched the two fire trucks drive away. There would be a lot of work in the morning just to clean up the place. Then the office had to be gutted and repaired, and the fallen tree had broken a hole in the roof, which would probably require major reconstruction. It might have been better had the church burned to the ground. At least they could start on a brand new building instead of trying to patch together this old place.

The caretaker's cabin was a cracker box, reminding Joe of a few tree houses he had built as a kid. Thomas pointed him to the tiny bathroom which was dominated by an oversized claw-foot tub. Joe took his bag in with him. He would have soaked in the hot water for an hour had he not been a guest, but after ten minutes of luxurious warmth and comfort, he washed and got out.

When he emerged into the living room wearing dry jeans and T-shirt, Thomas greeted him with a mug of steaming hot cocoa. Then the caretaker left to take his bath. Joe sat down on the couch—really a threadbare old loveseat—which occupied half the floor space in the living room. The few furnishings were decades out of style, but the place was clean. He allowed himself to sink into the old cushions while he sipped the warm cocoa.

What a strange old duck, Joe thought of the caretaker as he savored the warm, sweet drink. *The man is several bricks short of a full load, but what a trusting soul, sharing his living quarters with a stranger as if welcoming an honored guest.*

Placing the empty mug on the table beside the sofa, fatigue overtook Joe like a powerful sedative. His head dropped back to the cushion, and he was asleep.

Nine

EZRA KNEW HE WOULD NOT SLEEP until he was sure. He was bone tired after a long day of work and a harrowing night of fire. As he made small talk with Rich at the kitchen table over cups of coffee after the fire crew had left, he was silently tormented by three dark realities: *Louise Wilkerson's bequest was in the desk in the office. The office suffered substantial fire damage. Louise's gift—over $22,000 in cash, which he should have taken to the bank yesterday—was consumed in the blaze.*

But the third reality had not been confirmed because the firemen had warned Ezra not to sort through the office debris in the dark even though he had not mentioned precisely why he wanted to get in there. With the fire extinguished, the fire captain urged them to wait until morning to assess the damage.

Ezra feared the worst. Money is only paper, and paper burns in intense heat. He would be awake all night wondering if indeed the bundles of cash were lost, so he decided to find out. Bradford McDermot and Jethro Haig had not called the parsonage after the fire, so apparently neither of them had heard about it. Ezra was not about to call them until he had something concrete to say about the money. Morning would be soon enough, but that meant finding out what happened to the cash tonight.

Turning to his roommate, he said, "Rich, there's something especially troubling to me about this fire. Can I tell you about it?"

Rich was attentive and empathetic, which was an immediate comfort to Ezra. But Rich's next words were even more encouraging: "Let's get a couple of flashlights and find out what happened in there."

The two men stood in the doorway of the church office, sweeping the fire damage with flashlights. The sight made the minister heartsick. The walls were badly charred and the water-soaked carpet was littered with fallen, burned ceiling tile fragments. The furniture and equipment, including the computer and printer, were ruined, destined for the scrap heap. Most of it belonged to the church, but the old oak desk had been his and Dorrie's for many years. Now it was charred beyond repair.

"Where was the box?" Rich asked as their flashlight beams criss-crossed the room.

"In the bottom desk drawer," Ezra answered. "I keep it locked." He pulled out his key ring and searched through the keys for the right one.

Rich stepped around the desk to the drawer side. Aiming his beam at the bottom drawer, Rich was silent for a moment. Then, "I hate to tell you, Ezra, but it's not locked anymore."

Ezra looked up from the key ring. "What? The bottom drawer is unlocked?"

"That's right, none of the drawers are closed all the way, and the bottom drawer is wide open."

Rich kept his beam trained on the bottom drawer as Ezra stepped around the desk to look.

"Good gracious!" Ezra gasped. "The drawer is empty. The money box is gone!"

"You're sure that's where you put it?"

"Positive. I returned the box to the drawer this afternoon, then locked the drawer."

Rich hunched down with the flashlight for a closer inspection.

"Maybe one of the firemen opened the drawer," Ezra reasoned. "I can't believe one of them stole the box."

"Mm, not likely," Rich said. "It looks like the box was gone before the fire started. See, the bottom of the drawer is evenly scorched. If the box had been here during the fire, I think there would be some outline of it, but there is none."

"Then the box must have disappeared sometime before—"

"And look at this," Rich persisted. He was fingering the brass keyhole on the front of the drawer. "The lock has been jimmied with something sharp, like a knife or an ice pick or a screwdriver. You can see how it's been chewed up. Somebody purposely pried open the drawer to get to its contents."

"Good gracious, we've been burglarized," Ezra uttered in disbelief. "It must have happened this evening while we were at supper before the fire broke out. Perhaps the thief set the fire himself to cover up the burglary."

After a few seconds of silence, Rich stood, shaking his head. "The captain said a power line was cut by the falling elm. He thinks sparks started the blaze. I doubt that a burglar was resourceful enough to schedule a thunderstorm."

Ezra sighed deeply. "I've been praying that the money wouldn't burn up with the building. How was I to know that someone had already made off with it? It was very foolish of me to leave that much cash in the drawer. The board members will be disappointed in me…and at least one of them will be furious."

"Don't be so hard on yourself, Ezra," Rich encouraged. "Thank God no one was hurt or killed. Money can be replaced."

"Tell that to Jethro Haig," Ezra muttered more to himself.

"Who could have done this?" Rich pressed. "Certainly not Thomas Rasby?"

The minister shook his head vigorously. "Unthinkable. Thomas has neither the heart nor the imagination to steal the church's money."

"Who knew the money was here?"

"Thomas and I. Velma Walls, our secretary. Bradford McDermot and Jethro Haig from our board. None of them would do such a thing—even our cantankerous Jethro."

"What about the kid with the motorcycle," Rich said, "the one who was pouring water on the fire when we pulled up? Did he know about the money?"

"No. At least I don't think so."

Ezra had entertained the dark thought that standoffish, self-sufficient, mysterious Joe was capable of burglary and perhaps worse crimes.

Thinking aloud, he argued, "If Joe stole the money, why would he stay around Orchard Valley instead of hightailing it out of here? Why would he risk his life to put out the fire? And why would he accept Thomas' offer of a dry bed right under our noses? It doesn't make sense." Ezra decided not to mention the mystery of the alleged pellet gun.

"Maybe that's just what he wants you to think. Maybe he's a pro, a real con man." Before Ezra could respond, Rich added, "It doesn't make sense to me either, but it's a possibility that should be considered."

Ezra sighed again. "I'm a minister, Rich, not a detective. I'll call the local police first thing in the morning after I break the news to our board leaders. Chief Jurgen will sort it all out."

"Then we'd better get out of the room before we taint any evidence," Rich said. So the two of them cautiously retraced their steps out of the office, locking the door behind them.

IT SEEMED TOO GOOD TO BE TRUE. Mom was fixing him bacon and eggs, and it wasn't even Saturday. She never fixed him a big breakfast during the week; she had to be at work before he got up. But Saturdays were special. Mom delighted at laying out a delicious spread for him— crispy bacon, eggs over easy and biscuits with homemade jam.

Joe woke up, eyes still closed, and welcomed the sizzle and the smell of bacon coming from the griddle in the kitchen. Then it hit him. He wasn't at home, and his mother wasn't cooking breakfast. She was gone now. It had been a cruel dream. But he could still hear bacon frying very near, except it didn't smell exactly like bacon.

He lifted his head to look around. Seeing the mug on the small table brought everything back to him. He was lying on a small sofa where the caretaker must have covered him with a blanket. Daylight streamed into the room through the small windows on the east.

"Good morning, Joe." The caretaker stood over him with a spatula in his hand. "It's almost eight o'clock. I'm fixing up some breakfast for you, if you'd like some."

Joe sat up slowly and pushed the blanket aside. He rubbed his face with his hands, willing himself fully awake. Thomas was still standing beside the sofa waiting for some kind of response. Joe wasn't in the mood for socializing, but a hot breakfast was too good to pass up.

"Breakfast? Yeah, sure," he said, rising slowly.

The spread on the table wasn't anything like the one in Joe's dream. The caretaker hadn't fried up bacon; he had taken two wieners, sliced them lengthwise, and fried them. The eggs were scrambled hard and generously flecked with black. Instead of his mother's homemade biscuits and jam, a stack of dark toast sat in the middle of the table next to a half-full jar of grape jelly. Still, the big mug of coffee looked hot and black, and this breakfast still beat anything Joe had in his tent.

They sat down at the table and Joe was about to pick up his fork when the caretaker closed his eyes and pronounced a prayer of simple, rhyming words, something a little kid might say before a meal. Joe waited but didn't close his eyes.

"The church is a real mess, Joe,"Thomas said as the men dug into their breakfast. "The big elm split in two and fell on the roof and made a big hole. The church office is all burned. Bradford says it's gonna take a lot of money and work to fix it."

"Who's Bradford?" Joe said between mouthfuls of eggs. The fried franks actually tasted pretty good. And a healthy layer of jelly did a fair job of covering the burnt toast.

"Bradford is the chairman of the church board. His farm is right yonder."Thomas pointed his fork toward the south. "Reverend Sturdevant called him early this morning. He come over about seven, and we been looking at the damage ever since. I just come in to fix your breakfast."

"You didn't need to do this," Joe said.

Thomas didn't seem to hear him. "Your tent got all wet inside, so I opened it up and put your bedroll out in the sunshine to dry."

Joe put his fork down. "That's *my* stuff out there, man," he said, a little indignantly. "I can take care of my own stuff."

Thomas gazed at him across the table. He didn't seem offended at Joe's mild rebuke. Instead he smiled broadly, "I wanted to help you, Joe."

Joe held his tongue. He knew the man meant well and wondered if he ever got upset at anything. Maybe he was on medication that kept that silly smile on his face.

Joe ate quickly, eager to get on with his day, but the caretaker tried to keep a conversation going. "My niece Chessy Carpenter just come here from California."

Joe put it together. "You mean that blonde who was walking around the church with you yesterday?"

"Yep, that's Chessy. I'm her Uncle Thomas," he stated proudly. "She's a real nice lady. Maybe you can meet her today if she comes out to the church."

Joe hummed noncommittally. From a distance the girl seemed nice looking. And she was also young, dispelling Joe's theory that there was no one connected with this church under sixty years old. Still, from what he knew about the caretaker, Joe had no inclination to meet his niece. Stupid genes might run in the family. Besides, he would not be here long, maybe not even until the weekend.

"What's your real name, Joe?"

Joe pulled the coffee mug away from his lips at the surprising question. "What do you mean? My real name is Joe."

"No, I mean your *real* name. My real name is Thomas Merwyn Rasby, but people call me Thomas. What is your real name?"

Joe took a gulp of coffee while he considered the liability of giving Thomas more information about himself. He could think of none. "Joe Caruso, that's my real name."

The inquisitive caretaker kept up the grilling. "Why did you come to Orchard Valley?"

"Just to see the country."

"Didn't you come to see somebody? That's why Chessy came to Washington."

"No, but I'm kind of looking for someone." Joe wished he hadn't said so much.

"Who are you looking for, Joe?"

"Just someone. They probably don't even live here anymore."

After another moment, Thomas asked matter-of-factly, "How did you get a scar on your face?"

Joe snapped his head up at the question. Most people probably *thought* the question when they saw him, but not many people *asked* it, especially strangers. But then this man was not like most other people mentally. He had a kid's brain, and kids often blurt out their thoughts.

Joe took a bite of toast. He could feel the caretaker's curious gaze, a sensation he did not like.

"I cut myself on broken glass when I was a kid," he said, hoping it satisfied the man. It didn't.

"You mean like a glass bottle or dishes? Did you fall down on some glass, Joe?"

Joe shoveled in the last forkful of eggs, ready to excuse himself and get outside. "It was a glass window, it shattered, and my face got cut. It happened a long time ago, man. It's no big deal." He stood and opened his mouth to thank Thomas for the meal and the bed, but Thomas spoke first.

"Did it hurt?"

Joe's patience was running thin. "Of course it hurt. It was a bad cut."

"Does it still hurt, Joe?" Thomas was touching the side of his own face as if checking to see if he had a scar too.

The words were ready to pop out of his mouth, *Only when snoopy people like you bug me about it,* but Joe bit them off. "No, it doesn't hurt. Like I said, it happened a long time ago. And I don't talk about it."

"So it's kind of like a secret, right, Joe? The broken glass is a secret, something you don't talk about. We don't talk to nobody about secrets or they ain't secrets no more."

Joe sighed. "Yeah, okay, it's kind of like a secret," he said, trying to appease this simple man who was wandering too close to the truth. Then he picked up his plate and utensils and took them to the sink. When Thomas was in the kitchen, he retrieved his saddlebag.

"Thanks for the breakfast and the couch," he said when Thomas turned back to him. He wanted a cigarette in the worst way, which meant he would have to ride into town to replace the pack that got soaked last night.

"Are you an angel, Joe Caruso?" Thomas asked.

The question struck Joe as comical, and he almost laughed. "An angel? Are you kidding?"

"Reverend Sturdevant says the people we help may be angels. But Chessy said she didn't see no wings on you."

Joe opened the door, ready for a quick escape. "Well, the girl is right. I'm no angel." Then he was out the door before Thomas could ask another stupid question.

Eleven

CHURCH BOARD LEADERS Bradford McDermot and Jethro Haig did not respond to the disappearance of the money as Ezra had expected they would. Telephoning them both at home before 7:00 A.M., he braced for Jethro's wrath. Perhaps the vice chairman was incapable of a full boil at such an early hour because he didn't explode at Ezra over the phone. It was as if Jethro had already heard about the empty drawer, but he insisted that he didn't learn about the fire before retiring at 10:00 P.M.

Jethro was clearly irritated over the misfortune, and he couldn't resist a dig at the minister for foolishly leaving over $20,000 in cash in a desk drawer. But his harshest words were aimed at the "reprobate motorcycle gangster" camped in the hollow. As far as Jethro was concerned, Joe was guilty of stealing the money, period. Even when Ezra explained that Joe's brave intervention kept the church from burning to the ground, Jethro's judgment was undeterred.

Bradford's disappointment coming through the phone was palpable. He seemed almost in tears over the loss of Mrs. Wilkerson's generous bequest. He did not infer that Ezra was at fault, but neither did he offer his minister the words of encouragement Ezra had anticipated. When Ezra had mentioned Joe's heroics in quelling the fire, Bradford perked up. "I can't wait to meet this young man," he said without any inference of suspicion that Joe was the thief.

Ezra made two other early morning calls. He told Velma Walls about the fire and what it did to the church office and equipment. "So you won't need to come out to work today," he added. Velma, near tears, assured him that she and Chessy would be out later in the morning to see the damage.

Then Ezra called the chief of the small local police department to report the burglary. George Jurgen was one of only three full-time and four part-time law officers in Orchard Valley. The chief had been out to the church briefly during the fire, but Ezra didn't say anything about the money, hoping against hope that it had survived the blaze. Hearing the new information, the chief promised to get out to the church before noon.

Bradford arrived at the church within twenty minutes of Ezra's call. Jethro, wearing a dress shirt under his overalls, arrived ten minutes later with Rusty at the wheel of the big Caddie. Ezra and Rich described what they had found in the charred office—and what they had *not* found. Ezra explained that he had put in a call to Chief Jurgen in town, who would be out in a couple of hours to investigate the scene. Ezra asked the board members not to mention anything to anyone else about the burglary. They agreed, Jethro reluctantly.

After the men surveyed the damage to the office, Bradford said, "I suggest we schedule a church workday Saturday to clean the debris out the office and get it ready for remodel."

"Remodel?" Jethro said with a cynical laugh. "The church will have to go into debt to fix that hole in the roof let alone remodeling the church office. Of course, if we could strike a deal on that property out there we—"

Ezra cut short Jethro's familiar diatribe about buying the church farmland and the hollow. "I like Bradford's idea. I'll have Velma call the men in the church to come around eight on Saturday morning. We can get the office cleaned out and do something about patching the roof."

"I'll call a few fellows I know at the Baptist church," Bradford put in. "They'll be glad to help."

"You'd better not wait 'til Saturday to take care of that roof," Jethro huffed. "Chance of rain again tonight."

Ezra sighed. "I don't see any of us getting up on that roof today."

"What about the young fellow who put out the fire?" Bradford said. "Maybe he could get up there and eyeball the damage for us."

"A total stranger? A transient?" Jethro scorned. "What good could he do us?"

"He's already done us a fair piece of good," Bradford answered. "At least the building is still standing."

"That's Joe there," Ezra said, pointing across the cemetery, "the man who used a garden hose to fight the fire until the fire department arrived."

Bradford turned to see a young man leaving Thomas' cabin with a black leather saddle bag tossed over one shoulder and heading across the back of the cemetery toward the hollow. The morning sun was bright and warm, and the sky was clear in marked contrast to the destructive storm of only hours ago.

"We need to thank him personally, Jethro," Bradford said, "and show him a little Christian charity. We can ask him if he will get up on the roof and tell us what it'll take to pull down that elm and cover the hole till Saturday."

"Bah! You can talk to him if you want to, Bradford," Jethro growled, "but you'd better check his tent for that money box first. I'm going off to work." Jethro left Bradford, Ezra, and Rich standing beside the split elm, barking at Rusty to start the Cadillac.

Bradford then strode off in Joe's direction as quickly as his arthritic knees and hips would allow. "Say, Joe," he called out, waving his arm on his way. "Can I talk to you for a minute?"

The young man kept moving toward his camp as if not hearing the call. Bradford called out even louder, "Joe, I just want to thank you!"

The young man eased up and waited, although his body language communicated to Bradford that he regarded the meeting as an interruption.

"Hello, Joe," Bradford said, puffing as he approached. At close range, he could see that the muscular kid was good looking under a veneer of toughness. "My name is Bradford McDermott, and I'm the church board chairman." He stuck out his hand, and the young man shook it but said nothing.

Ezra had told him that conversation with Joe took effort, kind of like trying to untangle a wet, knotted rope. "The minister told me all about what you did last night, getting Thomas off the roof, calling 911, and fighting the fire. I want to thank you sincerely, young man. The building could have burned to the ground. And Thomas...well, he could have been seriously hurt or even killed in the fire."

"It was no big deal," Joe said. "I did what anyone else would have done."

"The fact that you were out here, that you saw the fire start, and that you actually did something about it...I'm just amazed at your helpfulness and courage."

"I'm glad I could help," Joe said, edging toward his camp.

The idea recurred to Bradford to show interest in this tough-looking kid. "I don't want to impose on you," he said, "but I wonder if I could ask one more favor of you."

Joe stopped edging away. "What's that?"

"Well," Bradford said with a little laugh, "as you can see, the minister and the caretaker and I are not as nimble as we once were, and that other fellow isn't exactly a spring chicken. Could I talk you into climbing up on the roof over there to tell us about the damage? It shouldn't take very long."

The young man was quiet for a moment. "Okay, I guess I could do that. Can you give me five minutes?"

"Of course. We'll get the ladder set up."

By the time Joe got to the church, Thomas had erected the old ladder close to the building. "Now, be careful up there, Joe," Ezra warned. "We appreciate all you're doing, but we don't want you falling through the roof."

"I'll be careful," Joe said, starting up the ladder.

"I'd like to go up with you, Joe, at least to the top of the ladder," Rich said. "Maybe I can be of some help."

Joe glanced back at him and shrugged. "Whatever," he said.

The two younger men ascended the ladder while Bradford and Thomas steadied it from below. The kid was both confident and cautious about what he was doing, Bradford observed.

"Hey, Reverend," Joe called down from the roof. He had been crawling over the leafy elm, peering into the hole it had punched in the roof. Rich had also ventured up the incline for a look.

All eyes below looked up. "The hole in the roof is not your only problem. You have dry rot underneath, lots of it. The roof has probably been leaking in a lot of places for a lot of years."

"Joe's right," Rich added. "I pulled up a few shingles here and there, and it looks pretty bad."

"I wouldn't patch up the hole, if I were you," Joe added. "I'd peel off the whole roof, plywood and all, and start over again. You may even need to replace some of the beams."

Ezra turned to Bradford. "Insurance should cover the damage, don't you think?"

Bradford shook his head. "We cut back on our policy a few years ago to save money. Insurance will patch up the hole, but it won't cover long-standing dry rot."

"In the meantime," Joe continued, "you need to get this tree down. I suggest you cut it apart with a chainsaw up here and toss it down piece by piece. Trying to pull it down could cause even more damage."

"And you need to get something to cover the hole in the roof until repairs can be made," Rich advised. "You could get another cloudburst tonight. A big tarp might do it."

"A tarp—good idea," Bradford said.

Joe called down again. "Does anybody have a chainsaw?"

"Thomas has one in the shed, don't you Thomas?" Bradford said. Thomas nodded.

"Get the saw, and I'll start cutting the tree apart," Joe said. "You guys can stack it up or cart it away."

"That's mighty good of you to offer, Joe," Ezra said, "but you don't have to do that."

"No problem, Reverend," Joe said, stripping off his T-shirt in the mid-morning heat. "I'm already up here, and I can get it done in a couple of hours."

Bradford gazed up at Joe in wonder. Then, turning to Thomas, he said, "Get the saw, Thomas."

Ezra said, "I'll call Calvin and Elmer and ask them to come out to help," Ezra said, beaming at their windfall. "This man is ready to go to work."

Twelve

BRADFORD FEARED THAT AT LEAST ONE of the old men on the ground would have a heart attack before it was all over, and he knew he was one of the candidates. Joe tore into the fallen elm with a vengeance, operating the chainsaw skillfully. Rich stayed on the roof with him, tossing cut-up limbs over the side. Bradford, Ezra, Thomas, and two other church men could barely keep up with them.

The men dragged the leafy branches off to a burn pile beyond the cemetery. They loaded the logs, which Joe cut into eighteen-inch lengths, into a wheelbarrow and hauled them to Thomas' cabin to be stacked alongside the equipment shed. While the team worked, the utility company arrived, replaced the severed power line, and restored power to the church building.

Joe and Rich kept working nonstop, but the men on the ground couldn't. Whenever they stopped for a breather and a drink of water, Bradford and Ezra discussed plans for dealing with the damage. The short range plan, they agreed, was to secure a large tarp and tack it down on the roof to cover the gaping hole. The weather report called for scattered thunderstorms. Bradford said he would go into Orchard Valley during the afternoon and round up the needed supplies.

The long range plan was a little more difficult. They estimated that repairs to the roof and the church office, even with volunteer labor, would far exceed Louise Wilkerson's benevolent gift, when and if it was recovered. They were sure that Farmers Bank in town would provide an equity loan to the church, even though another monthly payment would further burden the church's operating budget. But the repairs had to be made, so Bradford would see about the loan when he was in town. Ezra said he would encourage the congregation to contribute toward the building fund above and beyond their regular giving.

Joe finished just before 11:00 A.M. Climbing down the ladder with the chainsaw, his face, arms, and torso glistened with sweat. Patches of sawdust stuck to his skin looked like a pale rash.

Rich came down after him. "That was some workout," the professor said, beaming. "This guy is a tiger with a chainsaw."

Joe used his T-shirt to brush sawdust from his chest and shoulders. "You didn't do too badly yourself," he said to Rich.

"It was mighty nice of you to help us out, Joe," Bradford said. "Where did you learn to work a chainsaw like that?"

"I spent a couple of summers on a work crew back home," Joe said. "Brush clearing, a little construction, stuff like that."

A car turned into the church parking lot. Bradford recognized the old green Toyota belonging to Velma Walls. He continued, "Well, you're a handy man to have around. I could use a fellow like you working for me on the farm."

Joe shook his head, "Thanks, but I won't be around long."

Velma Walls approached the group of men standing by the ladder with Chessy right behind her, carrying a picnic basket. "We heard there was a crew working out here this morning," Velma said, "so we put together some cold cut sandwiches. Anybody hungry?"

The men lifted a chorus of approval, except for Joe, who was backing away from the group as he pulled on his T-shirt. Bradford noticed. "Hey, Joe, you worked harder than anyone here. Come have some lunch with us."

Joe fumbled with an excuse, but the men quickly voted him down. He could not help but notice the beautiful girl walking with the older woman toward a patch of shady grass on the church lawn. Reluctantly, he accompanied the group, and Thomas came over from his work at the equipment shed.

"Joe, I don't think you met our church secretary," Bradford said as Velma passed out individually wrapped sandwiches made of sliced turkey and ham. "This is Velma Walls. Velma this is Joe. He's been a big help to us today. Spent the last two hours on the roof cutting up the elm."

"I'm pleased to meet you, Joe," Velma said, handing him a wrapped sandwich. "And thank you for your help today. That was very nice of you."

"My pleasure, ma'am," Joe mumbled, taking the sandwich. "And thank you for the lunch."

"And that's my niece, Chessy Carpenter, Joe," Thomas put in, beaming with pride. Chessy was pouring lemonade into paper cups and passing them out to the men. "Chessy come up here from California. She goes to the Bible college where Doctor Rich is the teacher."

Chessy finished pouring a cup of lemonade and smiled as she held it out to the young man. "Hi, Joe."

But as he reached out to take the cup, it slipped from the girl's hand, bounced off Joe's knee, and spilled cold lemonade down his jeans and into his boot.

Joe jumped up, sending his uneaten sandwich flying. The girl looked mortified. "Oh, I am so sorry," she said. "I can't believe I did that. I'm... *so sorry*." Velma sprang into action, thrusting a wad of napkins into Joe's hand.

He dabbed at the large wet spot on his pant leg as the girl apologized again. "It's okay," Joe said, looking embarrassed.

Velma pulled another wrapped sandwich out of the picnic basket and passed it to Joe. "We have plenty, Joe," she said. "Don't worry about the other one."

He relaxed a little, deciding that no real harm was done. Besides, he was very hungry. So he sat down again and pulled off the soggy boot.

"I'm going to try this again, Joe," Chessy said with an embarrassed little laugh. She poured a fresh cup of lemonade and held it out to him. "Do you trust me?"

Her musical laugh made him smile. "Sure, I trust you," he said, receiving the cup.

Joe leaned back against a tree trunk and savored the sandwich. He had actually enjoyed dismantling the elm and working up a good sweat.

It had been a few weeks since he had done any satisfying physical labor, and he basked in the satisfaction of a job well done, a job no one else in this circle could have done with the possible exception of the man who climbed up on the roof with him. This professor, who didn't really look like a professor, had busted his tail tossing cut-up limbs over the side. The guy was well into his forties, Joe guessed. But anybody who could keep the pace he set for two hours had to be in pretty good shape. Joe gave the professor a few points for that.

The noisy chainsaw hadn't allowed for much conversation on the roof, which suited Joe just fine. He didn't go up there to socialize. And whenever there had been a lapse in the noise—while gassing up the saw or moving to a new position—Rich didn't have much to say. Joe gave the Bible professor a few more points for not pushing his religion.

But what about this girl with the unusual name—Chessy? Joe assessed her with several furtive glances as he ate. She either knew these people well or she was endowed with an enviable measure of social ease. She engaged them in pleasant conversation, not just the secretary and her uncle the caretaker, but the other men as well. She was either deeply interested in people or she was putting on a very good act. It was obvious that the caretaker's genes did not run through the whole family. He could tell Chessy was a sharp girl.

And she was beautiful. Small but not tiny. Lithe and athletic-looking without sacrificing an ounce of femininity. Her soft, straw-colored hair was pulled back with a scrunchy. Chessy wasn't trying to showcase her looks for anyone, but he couldn't help but watch her when he was sure no one was watching him. When Chessy glanced his way, which she did a few times, he managed to look away before their eyes met.

"What do you think, Joe?"

Joe snapped his eyes from Chessy to the speaker, Bradford McDermot. Had he caught him looking at Chessy? Surely he wasn't asking what he thought of her. "Uh, what do I think about what?"

"We were talking about what we need at Builder's Mart," Bradford said. "I'm thinking two heavy-duty nine-by-twelve tarps tacked down over the damaged areas, top one overlapping the bottom one. Do you think that will take care of the problem until we decide on a more permanent solution?"

Joe had assessed what needed to be done while he was still on the roof. "Yeah, two tarps ought to do it," he said. "But you also need thirty or forty feet of one-by-six. Rough grade will be fine. You'll want to tack down the tarp with a border of one-by-six to keep the wind from ripping it off the roof."

"Good point," Bradford said. The other men nodded.

"And I would tack the edge of the top sheet just over the other side of the ridge, running one-by-six the whole width," Joe went on. "Then make sure the overlap and the edges on this side are all tucked under your boards."

"Sounds like you've done this before," the minister said.

Joe shrugged. "A little of this, a little of that," he said.

His eyes wandered casually back to Chessy, and she was looking directly at him. Their eyes locked for a heartbeat or two, then Chessy looked away. Joe didn't regard himself as an expert on women, especially what they might be thinking—far from it. But he thought he saw something in Chessy's soft blue eyes during that brief flash of time. He thought he saw the same interest he had been struggling not to reveal to her.

But he discounted his hunch immediately. This girl wasn't any different from the others. She was just sneaking a look at his scar while the left side of his face was turned toward her. Or was there really something else in those eyes?

Thirteen

BRADFORD DRAINED THE LAST OF HIS LEMONADE and stood up, signaling to Joe that the lunch break was over. "Anybody want to ride into the Builder's Mart with me?" Bradford offered.

Ezra and Rich declined, saying the police chief was coming out to talk with them about the fire. The volunteers also declined and headed for their pickups. Thomas said he still had storm debris to clean up. Joe overheard Velma explain to Chessy that her uncle didn't like to go to town very much, either Orchard Valley or the "big city" of Yarborough eighteen miles north.

Joe was ready to break away, too. He wanted to get cleaned up and ride into Yarborough. He had put off what he came to do long enough. It was time to get on with it and then head home.

Chessy spoke up before he could make a move. "I'd like to go with you, Mister McDermot." She was on her feet, brushing grass clippings from her shorts.

"I would enjoy the company, young lady," Bradford said, obviously pleased. "In fact, I'll give you a little tour of this end of the valley. You and Thomas have some relatives out here. I'll take you by their farms on the way. Then we have to get back and tack down those tarps."

"I'll be glad to help with getting the tarp in place," Rich put in, "if the preacher will let me stay another night in the parsonage."

Ezra laughed. "My pleasure, Rich. The room is yours as long as you want to stay. And your help is greatly appreciated. Stay for a week if you like."

"I may take you up on that, Ezra," Rich said, standing and gazing out toward the hills rimming the valley. "This place is something special—and so are the people."

Joe picked up his boot, ready to make good his escape. Bradford caught him before he could take a step. "What about you, Joe? Would you like to ride along and see a little of our valley? We'll only be gone an hour or so."

Had the old farmer asked him before Chessy had volunteered to ride along, Joe would have turned him down flat. But Chessy was looking at him again, waiting for his response.

Joe hesitated, not wanting to seem too eager. "Sure, I'll go with you," he said in an I-can-take-it-or-leave-it tone. "I can give you a hand with the one-by-sixes."

He asked for a few minutes to change clothes. Bradford said he and Chessy would wait in his pickup, the red one with the extended cab and bed. He would get the air conditioning cranked up against the early afternoon heat.

After rinsing his face, arms, and boots in the creek, Joe slipped into his small tent and changed into clean blue jeans and a faded navy T-shirt bearing the logo of Penn State University. He locked his saddlebag, which contained his pistol, loaded the bag onto the Harley, and secured the bag to the bike with another lock. Firing up the engine, he rode up the slope to the church and parked the bike in the shade next to the building where Thomas and the others could keep an eye on it.

"So you're a Harley man," Chessy said as Joe slipped behind her to sit in the cab's back seat. Bradford had insisted Chessy ride in front where she could see better.

"Yeah," Joe replied, settling into his seat, disappointed to be looking at the back of her head.

"Sportster 1200?"

"Yes, how did you—"

"Ninety-six?"

"Good guess," Joe said, masking his surprise. "Ninety-seven."

"It was no guess," Chessy explained. "My dad was into Harleys for several years. He's had a couple of Sportsters. Just got rid of his Softail a couple of years ago. Mom wanted a motor home."

Joe smiled to himself. How many girls knew the difference between a Harley and a Honda, let alone a Sportster and a Softail?

Bradford turned south on the side road just north of the church, which led into the community of Orchard Valley, population 5,600. *The old farmer drives with spunk,* Joe thought with admiration. *Not like some of the near-retirees clogging up the highways these days.*

Bradford began pointing out the sights right away. Sprawling farms of wheat, clover, sugar beets, and sweet corn stretched for miles on both sides of the road. One of Chessy's second cousins owned this one, another Rasby relative used to own that one, and Thomas' parents built that one, Bradford explained with the enthusiasm of a tour guide. He could name every Rasby by birth or marriage living on each spread. Some of these people would be in church on Sunday, but many attended the Baptist church in town. Chessy said she had not met, or did not remember meeting, any of them.

Joe noticed a police car heading toward them on the highway. The lights weren't flashing, but the sight still made him flinch, a conditioned response from his past, a life he wanted to leave behind forever. "That's our police chief and one of his officers," Bradford said, flashing a wave as the car sped by. "George Jurgen and Raul Tapia. George used to buck hay for me when he was in high school. Turned out to be a nice fellow."

Joe had never used the words "police" and "nice fellow" in the same sentence.

Bradford proudly pointed to a couple of farms worked by some of his relatives. "Here's how you can tell the difference between a Rasby farm and a McDermot farm," he said. "If the workers are standing around having a good time, it's a Rasby farm. If the workers are working, it's a McDermot farm." He laughed heartily.

"That's not what I heard," Chessy grinned. "I heard that Rasby farmers are poor but happy while McDermot farmers are rich and dull from overwork."

Bradford roared with laughter. "That's what I like, Chessy. A Rasby who can dish it out as well as take it." Then, speaking over his shoulder, he said, "You just have to face it, Joe. The Rasbys march to the beat of a different drummer. Actually, I don't think they even have a drummer. They just seem to bumble about on their own."

Chessy gave him a playful slap on the arm, and they both laughed again.

Joe didn't think the light-hearted barbs were all that funny, but he was amused at how spunky little Chessy stood up to the burly farmer. And he was enjoying the scenery. The professor was right. This valley was something special with its quaint farmhouses surrounded by deeps rows of sweet corn or plush carpets of clover.

•   •   •

Chief George Jurgen had turned forty-six last Saturday. Ezra knew this because George's Aunt Flora was a church member who reveled in keeping the minister current on family news from Sunday to Sunday. So Ezra relayed the news to Professor Rich Denny during the introductions. Rich said he was forty-six on his last birthday nearly a month ago. The proximity in age didn't register as important to the police chief.

George Jurgen was another product of the valley who had left the farm after high school for life in the big city. After two years of community college near Seattle, he joined the King County Sheriff's Department as a deputy, working his way up to sergeant and then lieutenant by the time he was forty. However, the interdepartmental politics soured him on a lifetime career with the county, so when he heard that his hometown was looking for a police chief, he applied for and got the job.

George had Orchard Valley in his blood, but his professionalism at police work set him apart from the "good old boys" he had grown up with in the valley. The chief was casual and countrified in demeanor but hardnosed when it came to the law. Ezra appreciated both qualities.

"List for me the people who knew about the money in the drawer," George bored in after Ezra's explanation of the missing box.

The minister related the short list: the secretary and caretaker, the two board members, Rich and himself. He quickly dismissed them all as possible suspects, but George wrote down every name anyway. Ezra added that he was not going to tell Thomas about the missing money just yet and that those who knew about the burglary were going to keep it quiet. George said he would have to talk to everyone eventually and agreed that Thomas didn't have to know the details.

Ezra pointed to the black Harley parked in the shade of the eaves. "There has been a young man camped out in the hollow for a couple of days, George," he said, "but he hasn't been inside the church, and I'm pretty sure he didn't know we had cash in the office."

"But there were other items in the office a thief might want, is that right?" the police chief said.

"Office supplies, books, a computer and printer, not much of value to a—"

"But a stranger wouldn't know what you have until he got in there and snooped around, Ezra. Maybe he was just hoping for loose change and hit the jackpot."

Ezra detailed Joe's heroics on the previous night. George listened, then asked for the biker's name. "It's Joe—that's all I know," Ezra said. George instructed his subordinate, a thirty-four-year-old Latino named Raul Tapia, to jot down the Harley's license number so they could run the ID back in town.

"You'll tell me what you learn about Joe, won't you George?" Ezra said.

The chief nodded.

George and Raul spent twenty minutes inspecting the church office and sorting through debris. Ezra and Rich watched with interest from the doorway. After moving a few ceiling tile fragments in a corner, Raul held up an item in his latex-gloved hand. "Does this belong to you or the church, Reverend? This could be the way the thief got into the drawer and opened the money box."

It was a medium-sized screwdriver with a clear red handle. "I've seen that kind before, but not around here," the minister said. "We don't keep tools in the office, and Thomas' hand tools in the shed all have a black handle."

"That screwdriver is from a pricey set of tools, Ezra—Pierponts," George said. "The fire would have melted the handle on a cheaper one." Then turning to Raul, "Bag it up as potential evidence."

With Thomas cleaning up debris behind the parsonage, Ezra took the officers to the church's tool shed. A quick check confirmed that there were no red-handled screwdrivers in the church's set of tools. George said, "It's likely that the burglar took the money box with him, but if you or Thomas or anyone doing repairs finds the box on the grounds, be sure and let me know."

Ezra agreed, and George and Raul left to handle other business in town.

Returning to the parsonage to wash up after the morning's work, Ezra pondered the church's double-barreled misfortune: a destructive fire and a stolen bequest. Changing into a clean set of work clothes, he whispered a quick prayer. "You saw the person who broke into the office and stole the money box. Please throw your light on this crime and expose the persons responsible and help the police find them. And please protect Louise's gift until it can be recovered."

He was brushing his wispy gray hair in front of the bathroom mirror when two dots suddenly connected in his brain. The revelation was so startling that he stopped the hairbrush in mid-stroke. He had told George Jurgen that he had seen red-handled screwdrivers before, but the church didn't have any. Just now he remembered the last time he had seen not just one red screwdriver but a set of them. It was in the hollow yesterday when Joe was tinkering with his motorcycle. The screwdriver in his hand and others lying by the Harley all had clear red handles.

•   •   •

The town of Orchard Valley was another eye-opener for Joe. Bradford seemed to know everyone, and everyone knew him. The farmer charged the lumber, tarps, and other supplies at the Builder's Mart without so much as signing his name. "Put this on the church tab for me, will you, Murray?"

"Sure, no problem, Bradford. How's Esther?"

Chessy didn't know anybody in town, but you couldn't tell it from the way she interacted with the people she met. And when Bradford introduced her as Thomas' niece, they practically gave her the key to the town. She would have spent time talking to everyone had Bradford not kept the three of them moving. There was work to be done this afternoon, he said like a true McDermot.

Joe tried to blend into the background like a hired hand, but Bradford introduced him around as if he was a relative and recounted with relish how Joe had saved Thomas from the roof and cut up the fallen elm. The townspeople were courteous and friendly even though Joe noticed a few cautious glances at his long hair, tattoo, and scar.

On the way back to the church, Chessy asked more questions about Joe's motorcycle. She talked some about her father's Harleys, and Joe was impressed at what she knew.

As they turned into the church parking lot, Chessy abruptly swung around in her seat and faced Joe. "Hey, Joe," she said, smiling. "Will you take me for a ride on your Harley sometime?"

NO ONE ASKED HIM TO DO IT, and he could have easily excused himself and gone about his business, but Joe volunteered to help nail the tarps into place. The blazing sun felt good on his back, and he relished the satisfaction of seeing a project completed—and done right. Besides, Chessy was hanging around the church helping her caretaker uncle pick up storm debris. Joe could always go into Yarborough tomorrow and do his business. What was the big hurry?

He and Rich climbed onto the roof to secure the tarps. They worked quickly and efficiently together with Rich following Joe's lead. Bradford kept them supplied with lengths of one-by-six and cheered them on from the ground.

"You're wearing a PSU T-shirt," Rich said as they lined a board up with the vertical edge of the tarp. "Do you attend Penn State?"

Joe had a couple of nails in his mouth. He spiked them into the wood with the hammer before answering. "Yeah, I'm at Penn State," he said.

"What are you studying?"

Joe worked his way down the slope, pounding nails into the board, to where Rich was holding the bottom edge in place. Then he looked up. Joe hated small talk—filling the silence with words just because there was silence—but Rich sounded genuinely interested. Joe was suspicious, however, that the Bible professor was fishing for a way to turn the conversation to sin and salvation.

"I'm working on a graduate degree in engineering," he said.

"What was your undergraduate degree in?"

"History."

"From history to engineering?" Rich said with surprise, moving the next board into position. "I need to hear that story."

Joe pounded a few nails before answering. "No big story. A career in history would have locked me up in a classroom or an office. That's not me. I need more freedom than that—building something, fixing something, making something work right. So I switched over to engineering."

"I can see that in you just from the short time we've worked together," said Rich. "You seem to know how to get things done."

Bradford had been listening as he climbed the ladder and slid one-by-sixes up to them. "I sure can't see you teaching in a classroom, Joe," he said, huffing and puffing from the heat and exertion. "Sounds like you made a good choice."

Funny, Joe thought, that two men who barely knew him would take his side so quickly. Several of Joe's friends had criticized his decision to go into engineering. Even his mother had questioned him long and hard about "throwing away" his history degree before finally coming around to his way of thinking. What did these two strangers see that those who knew him much better had trouble seeing?

They finished off the tarps without much more discussion, which was fine with Joe. It was in the low nineties in the sunshine, and he could tell the heat was taking a toll on the old farmer on the ground. But the man kept working hard, typical of what Joe had heard about McDermot industry. Even Rich, who seemed to be in fine shape for forty-something, was wilting in the heat. When Joe looked around for Chessy, she was in the shade, leaning on a rake, and talking to her uncle.

"Great job, you two!" Bradford shouted as Rich and Joe descended the ladder. "I don't know how we could have done it without you."

"Glad to help out," Rich said. Joe let his partner's answer serve for the both of them.

"We're putting together a workday for Saturday," Bradford continued. "Lot of cleanup and repair to be done, especially that roof. Could sure use some extra muscle if you two are available. Starting at 8:00."

"You can count on me," Rich answered immediately. Then, with a laugh, "Your minister might turn me out if I didn't help." Joe again said nothing. He might be gone by Saturday.

Rich excused himself to wash up in the parsonage. Bradford engaged Joe before he could get away. "How would you like to come out to the farm for supper tomorrow night, Joe? I'd love for you to meet Esther and see our place."

Joe hesitated. "Well…" He hoped it wasn't obvious that he was trying to fabricate an excuse for bowing out. "I have some business to attend to tomorrow, stuff I didn't get to today."

"But you have to eat supper somewhere," Bradford countered with a mischievous smile. "How about seven? We'll eat out on the patio."

If Joe had said a quick "no thanks," Bradford probably would have let him off the hook. But his hesitation just gave the farmer an opportunity to up the ante.

"We have a big package of baby back ribs in the freezer that I have been saving for a special occasion," he said, eyes gleaming. "I make my own sauce—secret recipe. I'll slather those ribs and cook them up on the barbecue. Esther will steam some vegetables fresh out of our garden. What do you say, Joe? It's the least I can do for all your help."

Why is he doing this? Joe wondered. *What is he after?* Does this old man intend to pitch me on religion himself? Is he trying to butter me up to help with the repairs on the church? Or is he just as he appears—good-hearted and grateful, eager to share with a stranger, no strings attached?

"Yeah, all right, tomorrow at seven," Joe heard himself say. The rib dinner did sound tasty.

"Wonderful!" Bradford said. "My place is just south on the highway here. Go to the first mailbox on the right, turn in the driveway, and follow it back to the farmhouse right over yonder." He pointed across the cemetery and to the southwest. "You can't see the house from here on account of the trees. But you can get there in about three minutes."

Bradford clapped him on the shoulder. It was a manly gesture, on a par with a friendly punch on the shoulder. Joe could feel the affection in it. Then Bradford said goodbye, got in his truck, and left.

Joe found the garden hose at the back of the church building. He rinsed off his arms and hands and then, undoing his pony tail, he bent down and let the cool water pour over the back of his head and dark wavy hair. He just let the water flow, soaking his hair and dripping off his face into the flower bed.

Shutting off the water, he threw his head back to shake off the excess water. He heard a small yelp behind him. Turning, he found Chessy standing there wearing a look of surprise. Water was dripping from her nose, chin, and a few strands of hair. Her top was splattered from the sudden spray. She was carrying a rake and a push broom.

"I'd say you got me back for the lemonade," she said, starting to laugh.

Joe felt very stupid. "I'm sorry. I...I didn't know you were back there."

"Yeah, right!" Chessy grinned. "Revenge is sweet, isn't it?"

"No...no...really. I'm sorry."

"Hey, Joe, it's all right. No harm done. In this heat, I'll be completely dry in thirty seconds."

"So what are you going to do now?" He immediately wished he hadn't asked. He didn't want to set himself up for a disappointment.

"Velma's going home in about a half hour. She lives in town, and I'm staying at her house. After I help Uncle Thomas put all the tools away, I'll be going home with her."

Except she didn't keep walking toward the shed. She stayed there, the sun shimmering on her golden hair and sparkling in her sky-blue eyes. "What are you going to do now?" she asked.

Joe didn't have an answer. He had thought about taking a ride, but he couldn't tell her that. She might think he was offering to take her. He had some dirty clothes to wash, and he had seen a laundromat in Orchard Valley. "I have to do laundry," he said at last.

"I'd still like to take a ride on your Harley," she said.

He mentally kicked himself. She would have gone with him if he had asked. But now he had already told her what he was going to do. "Maybe we can...sometime."

"What about now...before I go home?" Then Chessy wrinkled her nose. "I'm sorry, it wasn't right of me to ask. You have laundry to do. Maybe some other time, if it works out. I'll see you, Joe." She turned and started toward the shed with the tools.

"Besides, I don't have an extra helmet," Joe called after her. "They're a little anal about helmets out here in the west."

Chessy turned back to him. "Rich has a helmet in the Jeep. He's a trail rider. I'm sure he'd let me borrow it."

It was all the encouragement Joe needed. "Then we could take a ride now, out in the country. And I'll drop you off in town and do my laundry."

"That sounds great," Chessy said eagerly. "I'll tell Uncle Thomas and Velma, then get the helmet." She headed for the shed.

Joe jogged down to the hollow. The warm day had thoroughly dried out his sleeping bag and tent. He slipped inside long enough to change his perspiration stained T-shirt and soiled jeans. Then he ran a comb through his hair and secured it into a ponytail again. After stuffing his dirty laundry into a small duffel, he headed back toward the church.

Chessy was waiting for him with sunglasses on, a small backpack slung over her shoulder, and a blue helmet strapped on. Joe pulled on his own helmet and shades, straddled the Harley, and turned the starter.

"We can head out to the south," he said above the throaty rumble as Chessy climbed on behind him. "I heard there's a good road through those hills. Then we can double back and head for town. How does that sound?"

"Great. I'm ready. Let's go."

Joe drove slowly across the parking lot to the road. He gunned the cycle into the southbound lane and raced through the gears. Chessy slipped her hands around his waist and held on tightly.

Fifteen

JOE DIDN'T CARE WHICH WAY THEY WENT. The farmland stretched for miles in all directions around the church, some of it flat, some of it hilly. And it was all beautiful, freshly washed from the storm, brilliant with color on a late spring afternoon. So he sped south to the first farm road and headed for the hills that bordered the valley.

He could tell that Chessy was an experienced rider. She leaned into the turns just as he did, and she didn't dig her nails into his flesh in fright every time he goosed the accelerator. Though she didn't cling to him like a girlfriend might, a person couldn't ride on the back seat and not be in constant contact with the driver. The warm breeze and Chessy's closeness brought a sense of peace to Joe that he hadn't felt in years.

Had he been on the bike alone, he might have gone faster. But he wanted this to last. And it was fine with him that the noise of the engine overpowered all efforts at conversation. It was enough to ride in silence with this unusually fine and friendly woman. He still could hardly believe she showed such interest in him. Maybe she had a religious agenda. If being a "prospect" was the price he had to pay for a pleasant, peaceful ride in the country, so be it. He could hold his own in such a debate.

After nearly a half hour on the road, they came to a four-way stop. To the left was a roadside produce stand next to a large orchard of Red Delicious apples. A couple of kids, likely the children of the grower, worked the stand. Chessy waved him toward it. He took the clue, pulled over, and shut off the bike.

Chessy lifted off her helmet, and her hair was matted with perspiration. "I need to ask about a rest room," she said. "Then I'll treat you to a glass of

cold cider." She pointed to the handmade sign: FRESH COLD CIDER—
50¢.

"Sounds good," Joe said, removing his helmet and shoving his sunglasses
to the top of his head.

Joe stayed by the Harley until she came back. She paid for two glasses
of cider and chatted with the two kids—a brother and sister team, she
found out—while they served her.

"So tell me about yourself, Joe," Chessy said as they sat on a bench in
the shade sipping the cider.

"Ladies first," Joe said.

"Okay, but you're not off the hook," she replied. "I was born in
Yarborough, but my folks lived out here in Orchard Valley. When I was
about four, Mom's brother in California asked Dad to join him to work a
raisin farm near Fresno. Dad is a maintainer, so he could have stayed here
his whole life, but Mom was ready for an adventure. I guess she talked him
into the move.

"So I grew up in the farming country around Kingsburg, California.
Dad and Uncle Claude grew raisin grapes, and Mom worked in the local
school district with special ed kids. After high school, I attended Fresno
State for a year. Then I decided to switch to a small Christian college in the
area just to learn more about the Bible and my faith. That's where I met
Doctor Rich." She took a long sip of cider. "That's my story in a nutshell,"
she concluded.

"What was your degree in?" Joe probed.

"Pastoral ministry," Chessy said.

"You? A woman pastor?" Joe said with disbelief.

Chessy shrugged it off with a laugh. "I'm not planning to be a pastor
in a church like Reverend Sturdevant. And I don't plan to teach theology
or church ministry like Doctor Rich. It was just the major that got me the
education I wanted."

"So what do you plan to do with your degree?"

Chessy laughed lightly. "That's a good question. I'm not sure yet."

Joe narrowed his eyes. "Didn't you have a career goal in mind when
you started the program?"

"Not really. I went to college to learn. I just don't know where or how I'm going to apply what I've learned."

Joe scratched his head and grinned slightly. "Is that what Bradford was saying—that the Rasbys just kind of wander through life without a plan?"

Chessy bumped his shoulder with her own. "Wait a minute; I had a plan. I planned to finish college and get a degree. The rest will fall into place at the right time."

"What are you going to do until you find your niche?"

Chessy thought for a moment, then replied, "During summers, I volunteered at a center for the mentally challenged, people kind of like my uncle Thomas. I felt I was really making a difference in their lives. Now that I've graduated, I've been offered a part-time job at the center. I'll probably take it and continue taking classes."

Then Chessy turned the conversation to Joe. "Your turn, Joe. What's your story?" She locked onto his eyes without letting go. Joe hated it...and he loved it.

"Okay, I grew up in Pittsburgh. Parents divorced when I was eleven. Lived with my mother through high school. Four years at Penn State, history degree. Grad studies toward an engineering degree. That's about it."

"Did you stay in touch with your father after the divorce?"

Joe involuntarily broke away from her penetrating gaze. "No. He moved to West Virginia...remarried."

"In other words, he didn't stay in touch with you."

"Right."

"Do you see him...ever? Birthdays? Holidays? Did he attend your graduations?"

Joe shook his head. "It was pretty much a clean break. It was better for everybody."

Chessy continued searching gently with her eyes and words. "Are you and your mother close?"

"Yes...I mean...we were close. My mother passed away two months ago."

"Oh, Joe. I'm so sorry."

Joe felt a swell of emotion in his throat at her genuine words of sympathy. He chased it down with a swallow of cider.

"So, you're alone. Your mother is gone, and your father is out of the picture."

Joe nodded. "I guess that's about it."

"Any brothers or sisters?" Chessy said.

"None that I know about." Joe wished he hadn't said it that way. Maybe Chessy wouldn't pick up on it.

"What do you mean?" she said.

Joe wavered before deciding to answer. "I mean I was adopted as a newborn, a closed adoption. My adoptive parents had no other children. I don't know about my birth parents. I don't know who they are."

Chessy's eyes were probing his for more information, but Joe glanced away.

"Does that bother you?" she continued, speaking in a private tone. "I mean, does it bother you not knowing who your birth parents are?"

"My adoptive parents were my parents," Joe asserted. "Mom and I were as close as any two family members can get."

Chessy seemed to be drinking in his words. Revealing his mother's death had gained her sympathy, and his slip about being adopted only seemed to deepen her personal interest.

She asked the things he expected a woman to ask: what his mother was like, the details of her illness, their last days together, and the funeral. Joe provided the basic information without embellishment. Chessy repeated her feelings of sympathy several times.

Then she asked, "Why did you ride all the way out to Washington?"

"I haven't taken a vacation since I started college."

"It probably feels good just to get away for a while after all you have been through with your mother."

He nodded.

"But why did you come to Washington? And why Orchard Valley of all places?"

Joe winced inside at perpetuating the lie. "Never been here before. Heard it was beautiful, so I decided to see for myself." The answer seemed to satisfy her, but he wasn't sure she bought it. "Shall we get going?" He started to get up.

"Can I ask you another question first?"

Joe knew what was coming. He was surprised she had waited so long to ask it. "Sure."

"Will you tell me about your scar? If you don't want to talk about it, it's okay."

Joe had found that if he didn't make a big deal about it, other people didn't either. "I fell into a plate glass window when I was nine."

Chessy grimaced. "Were your parents at home? Did they have to call an ambulance?"

"My father was home, but Mom was at work. Dad figured he could drive me to the hospital before the ambulance could get there, so I held a compress to my face while he raced me to the hospital."

He noticed that Chessy was focused on his eyes, not on the side of his face.

"Are you ready to go?" he said, standing and collecting her empty cup.

Chessy stood also. "Sure. Thanks for sharing your story with me."

"Yeah," Joe said, "and thanks for the cider."

Joe was relieved to be back on the motorcycle with the conversation over. But feeling Chessy close behind him again, he didn't want this ride to end. She seemed to be holding on a little tighter as they roared past fields of hops and corn.

He had not told the whole truth, but no harm was done. He might tell her about the real reason that brought him to Orchard Valley some day, and he might even tell her the real story behind his scar.

"Are you going to be around the church later tonight?" Chessy asked as she climbed off the bike in front of Velma's house.

"Yeah, I guess," Joe answered. "Why?"

"Uncle Thomas wants to build a campfire out in the hollow and toast marshmallows. Apparently, it's one of his favorite things to do on a nice evening. He's invited me and Doctor Rich and the minister, and he said he'd like you to come, too. It'll be later—maybe around nine. Will you join us at the campfire?"

Joe hoped his delight at the prospect of seeing Chessy again didn't seem too obvious in his smile. "It just so happens that all my appointments tonight were cancelled," he said. "And since the campfire is in my front yard, sure, I can make it. Do you need a ride out to the church?"

"Thank you, but I'll have Velma's car tonight. She plans to stay in."

"See you tonight, then."

"Great, and thanks again for the wonderful ride."

•   •   •

Ezra answered the phone in the parsonage at just after 8:00 P.M. He and Rich had been enjoying a theological discussion over a bowl of soup for supper.

"Sorry to call so late, Ezra. This is George."

"It's not too late for me, George," Ezra said. "But I thought you were off duty at 6:00."

"Just thought you'd like to know what I learned about your latest guest in the hollow."

"Yes, I would."

"The Harley is registered to a Joseph Martino Caruso, residence in Pittsburgh, Pennsylvania."

"Joe Caruso," Ezra said. "So that's his name."

"Right, age twenty-four, height five-eleven, weight 175, eyes brown, hair black."

"Sounds like him all right."

George continued, "Driving record isn't close to perfect, but no outstanding tickets or warrants."

"That's a plus."

"As for his criminal record…" The chief paused. Ezra could hear pages rustling. "Mister Caruso had some trouble during his college years. Drunk and disorderly. Destruction of property. College boy things, I reckon. No robbery. No burglary. No jail time."

Ezra hummed. "So we're not likely to see him on one of the crime-stopper programs."

"Don't think so. Just be careful. Like we were taught at the academy: any person is capable of any crime at any time."

"We'll keep our eyes open, George, just like always."

"Is there anything about him waving a red flag for you, Ezra?"

Ezra thought it ironic that the chief would phrase it that way. As positively as he wanted to think about Joe Caruso, the red screwdrivers in the kid's tool kit had raised a red flag in Ezra's mind. It could easily be a coincidence that the tool Raul uncovered in the office looked like the tools Joe carried in his kit. But what if it wasn't? He hadn't told Rich about it or anyone else. Should he tell George? He decided not to.

"Like I said, George, we'll keep our eyes open," he said.

"I still want to interview your people out there, including this kid," George said. "Maybe I'll talk to him first, sometime tomorrow perhaps."

"That'll be fine, George, if he's still here."

"Wherever he is, we can find him if we want to."

"I'm sure you can, George. See you tomorrow then."

Sixteen

"WOULD YOU LIKE ANOTHER MARSHMALLOW, JOE?" Thomas said, holding out the bag. "Your first one was perfect—golden brown."

Joe reached in and pulled out a spongy white cylinder. "Thanks."

Not wanting to seem eager, Joe had let the others enjoy the fire for twenty minutes before casually sauntering over from his campsite. He didn't even like marshmallows, but he had to toast a couple of them and force them down or it might seem obvious that he came to the campfire for a different reason.

Actually, there were several reasons. Joe couldn't deny a strong attraction to Chessy Carpenter. She was a most welcome and unexpected surprise on his trip to the west. He wasn't really looking for a girlfriend; he had other important things to do and a life to get back to. And he disdained long-distance romances, so there was no point in getting romantically involved so far from home. But that was all before he met Chessy.

Chessy was the main attraction, Joe knew, but she was not the only pleasant surprise for him in Orchard Valley. He hadn't intended to get acquainted with anyone on this trip. The thunderstorm and the fire had thrust him into a community of church people he would have never chosen to enter. An old, semi-retired minister who wasn't intimidated by Joe in the least. A scarecrow of a caretaker with straw for brains and the heart of a saint. A college professor who was intelligent without flaunting either his knowledge or his credentials. And a gaggle of old farmers who were genuine salt-of-the-earth types—clean living, hard working, neighbor loving.

And this interesting cast of characters even had room for a non-religious stranger on a motorcycle. Joe found himself liking these people in spite of himself because they seemed to like him when they knew practically nothing about him.

This reality caused him a twinge of discomfort. Would these people be as neighborly and accepting if they *did* know about him, specifically, if they knew about his less than saintly life in years past? The dark cloud always looming on the eastern horizon caused Joe to doubt that Chessy's apparent interest in him would survive what he balked at telling her. But he still could not keep away from her.

Conversation around the fire was easy. Joe asked questions about the valley because he was intrigued by what he had seen. Ezra and Thomas eagerly told him more than he wanted to know, but he was fascinated by this quaint, sprawling vegetable garden called Orchard Valley. All the while he kept a furtive eye on Chessy, who likewise seemed to be drinking in the information.

Thomas put away the marshmallows and toasting sticks, then he stoked the embers and added two more logs. The fire grew bright against the dark sky.

Someone mentioned Bradford McDermot. Rich said, "It must be great to have a godly man like Bradford as the spiritual foundation of your church."

"Yes, Bradford is a wonderful Christian man, Rich, and he's one of my dearest friends," Ezra said. "But he hasn't always been the saint he is today. He traveled a hard road before finding his peace with God."

"Really?" Chessy said with surprise. "He's such a kind and wonderful man. I can't imagine him as anything else."

Joe turned up the collar of his sweatshirt against the chill at his back. Then he leaned in, ready to hear more.

"Bradford was an alcoholic and quite a rounder in these parts as a young man," Ezra began.

Rich shook his head. "I never would have guessed it."

Ezra continued. "His lifestyle nearly cost him his farm and his family. If there is a real saint in this story, it's Bradford's wife Esther. All her friends told her to take their three kids and leave that drunken sot. But she wouldn't do it. She was a member of this church before I came here, and she kept praying for him. One day her prayers were answered."

Chessy asked the question that Joe wanted to ask. "What happened?"

"There was big family crisis, and Bradford got roaring drunk. And when he was drunk, he was ornery. He drove over here in the middle of the night, kicked in the door of the church, stormed inside, and started yelling at God, cussing him out. My wife Doris and I had only been at the church a few months. We were awakened by this awful ruckus coming from the sanctuary. It sounded like a gang of vandals wrecking the place."

Joe was enthralled by the story, and the others around the fire were also.

"I got up and called the police," Ezra went on. "Then I locked Dorrie in the house and crept over to peek in the front door. Here was Bradford, this hulk of a man, yelling obscenities, kicking over pews. He was unsteady on his legs, and while I watched, he took a swing at a pew with his foot and missed. He fell, banging his head on the corner of a pew on the way down.

"Well, that calmed Bradford down in a big hurry. I approached him cautiously and saw blood running down the side of his neck. He was dazed, didn't even know what hit him, didn't even know he was bleeding. I went and got a cold compress and tended to the cut on the side of his head. Thank God, he let me do it. He didn't have any fight left in him."

"But the police were on the way, right?" Chessy said.

Ezra nodded. "Two Yarborough County Sheriff's deputies arrived a few minutes later. I told them I had everything under control."

"You sent them away?" Rich said, amazed.

"Yes, I didn't think a trip to jail was what Bradford needed. I helped him back to the parsonage, and Dorrie made coffee. I pumped him full of caffeine while Dorrie bandaged his head."

"Did you lead Bradford to Christ that night?" Rich probed.

"No, we just listened to him," Ezra said. "He babbled on and on, talking about his troubles, his hard life, his rebellious kids. Dorrie went back to bed, but I kept the coffee flowing and let him talk. About 6:00

A.M., he was sober and subdued. I told him to come back anytime just to visit. I was interested in him. Then I sent him home in his truck."

"But something happened in Bradford's life that night," Chessy advanced.

"Apparently so," Ezra said, "because he came by the church every week or so. Not to the services. He just came to visit. We would talk about fishing and farming and current events around the valley. But one day he wanted to talk about God. He was ready, and I prayed the sinner's prayer with him."

Joe tugged at the sleeve of his sweatshirt. He felt uncomfortable with the simplicity of the "sawdust trail" ending. Religion and God are fine for the people who need it. But alcoholism is a disease, and alcoholics need therapy, not a "sinner's prayer." He wasn't about to argue the point at the risk of alienating himself from Chessy. So he changed the subject "Reverend, you mentioned your wife. Is she still…with you?"

Ezra gazed into the fire for a moment, then he looked up. "No, Joe, my wife passed on nineteen years ago."

Chessy was first to respond. "I'm so sorry." Rich added a word of sympathy. Joe didn't know what to say, so he kept silent.

"Missus Sturdevant has her final resting place in our cemetery, Joe," Thomas put in, trying to be helpful. "You can visit her if you like."

The image of his mother's face filled Joe's mind. He had some idea how the minister must have felt back then, the deep sense of loss, the hopelessness of a loved one gone forever. Joe thought about his mom and missed her almost every day.

Covering his momentary reverie, he mumbled, "That's too bad."

Rich turned to Joe. "Chessy told us that you lost your mother recently."

Flicking a quick glance in Chessy's direction, Joe said, "Yeah, that's right." He wondered what else Chessy had revealed about him before he came to the campfire.

The professor expressed his sympathy appropriately, as did the minister. Rich asked a few more leading but respectful questions about

Joe's mother and her illness. Joe answered them factually but without elaboration. Rich took the clue and let the topic rest.

Thomas seemed to be waiting for the chance to ask the next question. "Did you find the somebody you're looking for, Joe? Chessy said you were on vacation, but I told her that you were kind of looking for somebody, like you said."

Joe felt a twinge of guilt in his gut. He berated himself for letting those careless words slip out in front of the caretaker this morning. She was looking at him now. He could feel it. *Stay cool,* he told himself. *You'll be fine.*

"I heard that there are a lot of Harley owners in the Northwest," he said casually. "I was hoping I might run into some of them on the road, but I haven't so far."

It wasn't the truth, at least not as the others around the campfire might define truth, Joe mused. But it was true enough for the time being. The answer seemed to satisfy the simple caretaker, but Joe couldn't read Chessy's silent response.

After a few moments, Chessy stood. "Thank you, Uncle Thomas, for the nice supper and the cozy campfire. I need to get back to Velma's and do a little reading."

The other men stood like real gentlemen, so Joe stood too.

"Doctor Rich has me working on an on-line study project," Chessy explained, "and I'm a little behind."

"Why am I not surprised?" Rich laughed good-naturedly.

"You know me too well, Doctor Rich," Chessy said with a cute little giggle. "But I'll get it done on time. Good night, gentlemen."

Rich and Ezra bid her goodnight, then Thomas took her hand to escort her to Velma's car. After a few steps from the campfire, Chessy turned. "Will I see you again, Joe?"

The question caught him by surprise. It sounded like she was saying, "If you're leaving soon, have a nice trip," as if she didn't care if he rode off tomorrow. But his gut told him she was more interested, that she cared about seeing him again. At least he hoped that sentiment was behind her question. He decided to chance it.

"I'll be around for a while," he said. "I thought I might help with the work project on Saturday, if it's all right with the minister."

Ezra brightened up immediately. "That would be wonderful, Joe," he said with excitement. "We could sure use your help."

Chessy's smile nearly buckled Joe's knees. The firelight sparkled in her eyes. "Then I'll probably see you tomorrow," she said. With another warm smile, she turned and walked into the darkness at her uncle's side.

"I'm going to turn in, too," Ezra said. "Last one to leave, kick some dirt on the embers. Goodnight." Then the minister headed up the slope toward the cemetery on a line with the parsonage.

Rich made no move to go with him. Instead he sat down on the bench and tossed another log on the fire as if he planned to stay awhile. Joe stood there for a moment. It was only ten o'clock, and he wasn't ready to crawl into his sleeping bag yet. Rich was an interesting guy. It could be fun talking to him. But did the professor want to talk to *him*?

"I've never been to Pennsylvania, Joe," Rich said, stoking the fire until it sprayed sparks. "Sit down and tell me about it."

Seventeen

JOE SAT DOWN AGAIN, welcoming the opportunity to talk about home with someone who seemed interested. He regaled the professor with descriptions of the Allegheny Mountains, Penn State University, quaint Amish communities in and around his home state, the rich history of Gettysburg and other historical sites, and the excitement of watching his favorite football team, the Pittsburgh Steelers. Rich seemed to drink it all in, which made Joe want to tell him even more.

After about twenty minutes of sounding like the Pennsylvania Chamber of Commerce, Joe turned the conversation to Rich. Tossing a few wood chips into the fire, he asked, "What caused you to get into your line of work?"

Rich gazed into the fire for several seconds. Then he said, "You remember the story Ezra told us about the drunk named Bradford whose life was completely turned around when he gave his life to God?"

Joe flicked another chip at the fire. "Yeah, I remember."

"Well, when I was about your age, the same thing happened to me. I won't bore you with the details, but by the time I was twenty-five I had royally fouled up my life—partying, drugs, stuff like that."

Joe tried to mask his surprise. It had never occurred to him that the Bible professor could have such a wild past—a past like his own. Joe was sure the details wouldn't bore him, and he wanted to hear them, but he kept still as Rich continued.

"Then I met some Christian people in San Francisco who accepted me as I was and introduced me to Jesus, just like Ezra did for Bradford. In their words and actions, I saw for the first time who Christ really is, so

I committed my whole life to Him. From that point on, I have wanted to share with the whole world why Christ came to earth. Teaching in a Bible college seems to fit that goal, so that's how I got where I am."

Joe knew his question had thrown the door wide open for Rich to preach at him, but he couldn't resist taking it a step further. "So you're out to save the whole world," Joe stated more than asked with a slight smile.

"No, not really," Rich responded matter-of-factly. "I quit trying to save people a long time ago. I just introduce them to Jesus Christ and let God take it from there. I've learned that when people understand who Jesus really is and why he came, it makes all the difference in the world to their lives. In many respects, Christianity has gotten a bad rap for trying to 'save people,' and I feel badly about it. But when we present Christ as he is, people see authentic Christianity and welcome a loving relationship with God."

Rich poked at the embers with a long stick. Joe waited, expecting Rich to go on, but he didn't. The two men sat in silence gazing into the fire for several moments.

Finally Joe spoke. "You don't seem like the typical Christian, Rich."

"What do you mean?"

"Most of the Christians I've met are pretty pushy about their religion. It's kind of refreshing to know one that isn't trying to convert everyone to their brand of beliefs and religion."

Rich nodded, then spoke. "Christianity is not about pushing beliefs or getting people to join a religion. It's about a man—Jesus Christ—who came to earth and claimed to be God in the flesh. Jesus stated that we are alienated from God the Father and that our sin has brought us eternal death. He also said that he came to earth to destroy sin and give us eternal life by sacrificially dying in our place. Jesus cared enough to do this for us because he wants an eternal relationship with us. It's really that simple; Christianity is a relationship, not a religion. And that's what I want to share with people wherever I go."

Joe thought about the words as the fire snapped and hissed. "I've never heard Christianity explained that way—you know, simple," he said, shifting his gaze from the fire to Rich. "And I appreciate that you're not pushy about it."

Rich hummed understandingly. Then he said, "When I was a kid, my parents took me to a church where religion was crammed down my throat. It was all about following rules and getting punished when you didn't. I hated it, and I wasn't interested in knowing a God who was so mean and demanding. As soon as I was old enough, I got as far away from church as I could."

Joe thought of his own childhood experience with church, which was remarkably similar to what Rich described. The difference was that Joe walked away from religion as a fifteen-year-old and never looked back while Rich had obviously found a convincing reason to become a Christian.

The question fell out of Joe's mouth. "So what brought you back?"

Rich poked at the fire, and Joe watched a smile grow on the professor's face. "I came back to God, Joe, when my friends in San Francisco helped me see that what Jesus Christ did for me is infinitely more important than anything I could ever do for him. I finally realized how much God gave in order to turn the human race back to himself. I realized that if I had been the only person alive, Christ would have died on the cross to deal with my sin so I could enjoy a loving relationship with the God who made me."

Joe had just been preached to, and he knew it. The professor could have just as easily put Joe's name into his last sentence, insisting that Jesus died for his sins, too. Joe remembered that much about sin and salvation from his religious training, but it never sounded as attractive as Rich had just put it.

If Rich had wanted to move in for the "kill," now was the time. Joe waited for the professor to open fire on him, reminding him how sinful he was, harassing him to kneel down in the dirt and repent, but he didn't. Silent moments slipped by in the flickering firelight.

When Rich finally stood and spoke it was to say, "I'd better call it a night, Joe. I'm really beat. Enjoyed our chat, though. See you tomorrow?"

"Have to go into Yarborough, but otherwise I'll be around."

"Great. Want me to help you smother the fire?"

Joe shook his head. "I think I'll stay for a while."

"Good night then, Joe."

"Good night."

The professor disappeared into the darkness in the direction of the minister's house. Joe moved closer to the fire to enjoy its warmth and think about Rich's winsome words.

Eighteen

WHEN JOE CRAWLED OUT OF HIS SLEEPING BAG on Friday morning, water beads dotted the outside of his tent and gleamed like jewels in the bright morning sun. Apparently, it had been a light rain because he had slept like a hibernating bear, hearing nothing.

After splashing himself awake with water from the creek and shaving for the first time in four days, he slipped on a pair of cotton slacks and a polo shirt instead of his usual jeans and T-shirt. Afterward, he ate a nutrition bar, smoked a cigarette, and brushed his teeth. Just before eight o'clock, he pulled the plastic tarp off his Harley, fired up the bike, worked his way out of the hollow to the road, and roared away north toward Yarborough.

Joe kept assuring himself that what he was about to do was no big deal, that it was probably a fruitless exercise. But he had come all this way to do it, and he was determined to follow it through. There would be no more displacement activities—that was what Mom used to call them. When you keep finding all kinds of other stuff to do—even good stuff— to put off doing what you need to do, that's displacement. The church fire hadn't been his doing, of course. But getting involved with the repair work yesterday had conveniently delayed his trip into Yarborough a full day.

Displacement might have been the word Mrs. Caruso used to describe why Joe arranged another large part of his day yesterday to be with Chessy Carpenter, but Joe would have disagreed with his mom over that one. Connecting with the caretaker's niece had suddenly become as important to him as the reason that brought him to Washington. He wanted to spend more time with Chessy. He hoped to see her today, but for now it was time to get down to business.

After fifteen miles on the country highway, Joe passed a sign stating *Welcome to Yarborough—Population 83,620.* This was the big city in this region, sporting malls, multiplex theaters, a number of high-rise building, a modern convention center, traffic, and a cluster of county administration buildings. Most people in the country avoided coming into the city if they could. But for Joe, who loved rural Orchard Valley but had been raised in the city, there was something familiar and comforting about the corridors of concrete buildings, street lights, and office workers moving at a quicker pace than their neighbors in the farmland.

He stopped first at a coffee shop a few blocks from the county buildings and ordered a large breakfast of eggs, sausage, pancakes, and coffee. He looked over the local paper while he ate alone in a booth. His mother might have said it was another hour of displacement, but he needed something decent to eat, and he wanted to make sure the office would be open when he arrived.

A few blocks away, Joe drove into a parking garage adjacent to a county building. After locking up his bike and saddlebag, it took him several minutes to find the office with gold block letters on the door: AUDITOR—RECORDS. The large room was spread with a number of workstations but no cubicles dividing them. Office worker bees were buzzing at half the desks in the office, and the other stations looked like they were expecting occupants at any minute. A long wooden counter just inside the door separated the work area from incoming visitors. The two clerks working the counter were busy with other people. Joe stood quietly and waited.

A matronly, fifty-something woman two desks from the counter saw him and stood. "May I help you, sir?" she said, stepping to the counter.

"Uh, good morning," he said.

"Good morning," she returned, waiting for his request.

Joe was surprised at how nervous he felt. He began with the words he had rehearsed several times over the last weeks during his travels. "I was born in this county, but I was raised out of state by adoptive parents. And I want—"

"You want to locate your birth parents," the woman finished the sentence for him as she reached under the counter and produced a form. "Am I right?" she added, still smiling.

"Well...um...yes. How did you...?"

"Since the state relaxed the regulations on closed adoptions, we've had a lot of requests for information about reuniting birth parents and children. Just fill out this form completely and return it to me. It will take a few days to process your request, but we will contact you."

"A few days?" Joe said. He had hoped they had a database on the computer. They could punch in a few items of information and he would know right away if his parents could be found or not. He hadn't counted on waiting around a few days.

"I have their names," he explained, "and I have my birth certificate." He pulled a folded sheet of paper from his back pocket.

"Most people who come to us have names or a certificate of live birth," the woman said, pushing the form a little closer to him on the counter. "If they don't, an inquiry takes much longer. Just fill out the form, and we'll do our best."

"Do you have a pen I can borrow, please?"

"Sure." The woman pulled a cheap ballpoint from under the counter and handed it to him. "You can keep it if you like."

"Thanks."

"By the way," she added in a more private tone, "I don't want to discourage you, but many of these inquiries turn up nothing. Parents of adult children leave the state; mothers marry and change their names. Good luck, but don't get your hopes too high."

Joe appreciated the personal aside. "My hopes weren't too high to begin with," he said. Then he held up the form. "Maybe just going through the process will satisfy me." It was a highly personal thing to say, but somehow it was easier to a total stranger.

"Closure, you mean."

"Yeah, closure."

"Did you just find out about your adoption?" she inquired, seeming genuinely interested.

"No, my parents told me as a child that I was adopted. They were very open about it."

"What brings you here from…?"

"Pennsylvania."

"Pennsylvania," the clerk said with surprise. "You've come a long way to find your roots. So why did you decide to go on this search now?"

"My adoptive mother passed away recently."

"I'm so sorry," the woman said with the empathy of someone who knew what it was like to lose a mother. "You didn't want to begin your search until she was gone, then. Afraid it would hurt her."

Joe bowed his head. What was he doing telling his story to a stranger? Except she wasn't really a stranger. This person understood closed adoptions and adult children who sought to reunite with their birth parents. She dealt with it every day. Though she seemed businesslike and matter-of-fact in many ways, a streak of compassion showed in her questions. Perhaps she had been on a similar quest.

Joe looked up. "Just before she died, my adoptive mother gave me a letter written to me by my birth mother. I never knew about it. Mom said she kept it secret because she was afraid I might choose to return to my birth mother."

"A normal, realistic fear," the clerk said.

"Yes, and I understand," Joe replied, "even though I never would have left her."

"What was in the letter—if you don't mind me asking?"

"Nothing special, just a mother's simple wish that the child she would never see again would have a healthy and prosperous life. The letter also mentioned that she had separated from my father before I was born and that he had joined the army and disappeared from her life."

"A lot of people are searching for their mothers knowing that their fathers are unknown or out of the picture."

"So now that Mom is gone," Joe concluded, "I thought I would at least make an effort to connect with my birth parents. If it doesn't happen, it's okay. I had a great mother anyway."

The clerk smiled pleasantly. "Thanks for telling me your story—and good luck."

Joe turned away to find a quiet corner where he could do his paperwork.

The form was three sheets of legal-sized paper, each packed with blank lines and large empty boxes. He had hoped for a few blank spaces or a multiple-choice format so he could check a few boxes and be on his way. This seemed more like a graduate level midterm exam.

The only short answers requested were his personal data and the names of his birth parents, if known. Joe carefully copied the names from his birth certificate to the appropriate lines: Wallace Ray Barnes and Becky Ruth Barnes. Familiar questions flooded back to him. Were these two people still alive? If so, how many thousands of miles could they be from this place? Did they ever think about the child they produced twenty-four years ago?

The "essay questions" related to his adoptive family and what he knew about his birth family—which was limited to the two documents he had brought with him: the birth certificate and the letter from his birth mother. Joe told his story as concisely as he could. Several times he fought off the temptation to wad up the form and pitch it in the waste bin. What good would it do? But he urged himself on. He would never learn anything if he didn't try.

The pleasant clerk Joe had talked with was not in the office when he returned to submit the completed form. Another woman received the papers and deposited them in an inbox that was already stacked above its sideboards. Joe left the office feeling he had wasted his time. He considered packing up his gear and leaving for Pennsylvania before he had to say anything to anybody.

He quickly dismissed the idea for three reasons. The first reason was Chessy Carpenter. He couldn't walk away from her, not yet anyway. Second, he had committed to eat supper with Bradford McDermot and his wife tonight, and he was halfway looking forward to it. Third, he had said he would stay around to help with the big church workday tomorrow, and another day of labor would help keep his mind occupied.

Leaving the county building, he lit up a cigarette while walking to the parking garage. There was nothing to keep him in the city any longer. He was eager to get on the road back to Orchard Valley and the hollow. Of all the places he had been over the last six weeks, that little country town was beginning to feel like home.

•   •   •

Later that afternoon, Brenda Long sat at her desk in the back corner of the records office routinely sorting through forms. Even after a long, busy day on the job, the forty-two-year-old widow continued to be energized by her task of seeking to reunite adult children with birth parents they had never known. Her colleagues knew well that she respected the position of birth parents who, for a variety of reasons, did not wish to be found. But they also knew that Brenda Long was never more fulfilled than when she persuaded a birth parent to reconnect with the child he or she gave up in a closed adoption. Her greatest joy was to schedule and witness those tearful reunions.

She picked up the next form from the thick sheaf of papers on her desk. She looked first, as she always did, at the names of the birth parents. Her memory was not photographic, but a name from these forms would often take her to another form in her file where an adult child was seeking someone by that name. She studied the two names: Wallace Ray Barnes and Becky Ruth Barnes. Then she noted the name of the adult child seeking information: Joseph Martino Caruso, age twenty-four.

Brenda read through the form carefully. Her heart warmed at the story of a young man whose dying adoptive mother presented to him a letter from his birth mother which she had kept secret all his life. After the woman's death, the young man had driven across the country to seek a reunion with birth parents he knew he might never find.

The supervisor studied young Caruso's description of his adoptive family, which was split by divorce before he reached his teens. The story affected Brenda deeply, bringing tears to her eyes.

"Kathryn, do you remember the person who submitted this inquiry?" Brenda asked her coworker, who was straightening her desk, getting ready to leave for the weekend. "It has your initials in the corner."

Kathryn stopped and took the papers to study them. Brenda waited. "Oh, yes, the young fellow from Pennsylvania," she said at last. "He came in sometime this morning. He told me a little about his story, the letter and all. Why?"

"It's a very interesting story," Brenda replied, "especially with his adoptive mother keeping the letter a secret. What did he look like?"

"He was a strong, good-looking kid, around six feet—not an ounce of flab on him, kind of like a football player. Thick, dark hair in a ponytail. The only thing that would keep him from being fashion model was a rather prominent scar." She touched the side of her face as she said it.

"A scar? On his face?"

Kathryn nodded. "Looked like a pretty bad cut."

Brenda pointed to the form. "He gives his temporary residence as a church out in Orchard Valley," she said. "That's strange. Was he wearing a minister's collar? Did he look like a homeless person?"

"No, he seemed like a pretty clean kid. No collar. Just dressed like men his age dress—nice slacks and a knit shirt, as I remember."

Brenda thanked Kathryn for her help and wished her a happy weekend.

On her way back to her desk, Brenda stopped at the copy machine and duplicated the young man's inquiry. She returned the original to the stack and slipped the copy in her briefcase.

As a supervisor, Brenda Long could not get personally involved in many records cases that came across her desk. But the story of Joseph Caruso moved immediately to the top of her list. This one would not go through the regular channels; Brenda would handle it personally. And that meant a drive out to the country tomorrow for a visit with young Mr. Joseph Martino Caruso.

Nineteen

LIKE EVERYTHING ELSE JOE HAD DISCOVERED about Orchard Valley, Friday evening's supper with Bradford and Esther McDermot was more enjoyable than he expected. The meal of barbecued ribs and fresh vegetables concluded with deep-dish berry pie topped with a mountain of ice cream. His mother had been a good cook, but Joe had to admit that Esther's supper was one of the best home-cooked meals he had ever eaten.

Joe had feared that an evening with a pair of seventy-year-olds might bore him to sleep. However, the big farmer and his small, white-haired wife kept the conversation alive with questions about his home, his mother, his education, and his dreams for the future. Joe shared what he thought they needed to know—general information he would feel free telling anyone. Esther interrupted him frequently—"More ribs, Joe? More iced tea? Another slice of pie?"—interruptions Joe didn't mind at all.

At times, his thoughts strayed back to the county auditor's office and the written inquiry he had submitted this morning. His hosts would probably be interested in his quest to locate his birth parents, but he wasn't ready to expose that facet of his history.

After supper, Bradford and Joe moved from the picnic table to comfortable lawn chairs near Esther's garden and an outdoor fountain, which bubbled melodically. Joe had offered to help Esther clear the table, but she wouldn't hear of it. She said mealtime cleanup was a woman's work while the "men folk" talked. This couple was definitely from another generation. Joe smiled to himself.

"We have a good crew of men coming to help with the church workday tomorrow," Bradford said, waving away a pesky moth. "Most of them will be our own church members, of course. But two or three fellows are coming from the Baptist church. We helped them when they put a new roof on their building a couple of years back. And there may be a few men from town coming out who don't attend church anywhere."

"It's kind of like a barn-raising, then," Joe said. "When one group in the community needs help, others pitch in to get the job done."

"That's the way it works out here. Farmers help each other bring in the crops. You never know when you're going to need a helping hand, so it's smart to be helpful toward those whose help you may need some day. The golden rule, you know."

"What do you hope to get done tomorrow?"

"Hope is the right word, my friend," Bradford replied, chuckling. "As you noted yesterday, the damaged roof needs to be torn apart and replaced. Jethro Haig ordered all the materials. The truck should arrive at about eight in the morning. That's when I asked everyone else to show up."

"I'll be there, too," Joe assured him.

"That's great, Joe! I appreciate your willingness to help us. I would also like to clear out the church office tomorrow and get all the debris hauled away to the landfill. Thomas can work on replacing the damaged flooring and wallboard over the next few weeks. We'll furnish the office as funds become available. In the meantime, Ezra and Velma will have to work out of their homes, I suppose."

"Won't your insurance cover all the damages?"

Bradford grimaced. "Unfortunately, no. The board decided to cut back our insurance coverage in hopes that what we save in premiums would allow us to fatten up the building fund. But there have been so many repairs lately that the fund is depleted."

"So how will the church pay for what is being done tomorrow?"

"Another benefit of a small, friendly community," Bradford said. "The local bank vice-president is a member of the Methodist church in town.

We have a men's fellowship breakfast there once a month. He set up an equity line of credit for the church for such emergencies."

"What if you max out your credit line?" Joe posed. "Repairing the storm damage seems like just the beginning. A building that old can nickel and dime you to death."

Bradford didn't have a ready answer. The farmer's expression told him that he was wrestling with that question, too. Finally he said, "We have an opportunity to sell off thirteen acres of undeveloped church property, the wedge of land that includes the hollow and the parcel just south of it that we lease out for farming. The proceeds of that sale would get the church out of the red and provide a nice little nest egg of cash for future needs."

Joe was still reading the man's face. "And you think that's a good idea?"

Bradford shifted in his chair. "Yes, I'm beginning to think I do. I haven't always thought that, but lately I've been coming around. You need to know something about our church to understand why." He explained the minister's long-standing hope that the unused land eventually be developed into a care facility for the many hundreds of migrant workers who, with their families, populated the valley during late spring, summer, and early fall. A good number of church members shared this dream, but it had never become a reality because the existing facilities required more upkeep than the small congregation could afford. The damage from the storm under-scored the point.

"Many people, including my dear friend Ezra, still think the dream could come true," Bradford went on. "But in the meantime, what we do have is falling apart. So I am beginning to think that selling the land to Jethro is the only thing to do."

"It makes sense to me," Joe said. "How can the church think about expanding when it can't meet its everyday expenses?"

Bradford cocked his head at him. "Exactly. I'm happy to know somebody else sees it like I do."

"Great minds think alike, sir," Joe quipped.

Bradford roared with laughter. "Great minds. Yep, that's us, all right."

It wasn't that funny, but Joe found himself laughing, too. Then he said, "Who is Jethro?"

"Jethro Haig, another church board member. You probably saw him early yesterday morning. Man about my age but smaller, kind of stoop-shouldered. Drove off in a silver Cadillac about the time I talking to you."

"There was another guy driving the Caddie," Joe inserted. "Wearing blue jeans and a ball cap. Looked to be kind of middle aged."

Bradford paused to think. "Ah, yes. Rusty. Jethro's stepson. Moved in shortly after Jethro's wife died a few years back. Just drives him around, runs errands. Laziest man I've ever known. A little slow upstairs, too, if you ask me. Jethro puts up with him out of respect for his wife, I guess."

Joe hummed. "So Jethro wants to buy that land?"

Bradford nodded. "Jethro has been very successful at farming, so he has quite a stash of money. He's a big man in town, too. Was mayor for a couple of terms and still has a lot of influence in the area. He's been after the church property and my place, too."

"What does he want with more land?"

Bradford's forehead creased into a frown. "Jethro is a wheeler-dealer. He thinks he can interest a land developer in the property—you know, a company that will plop a shopping mall or housing development out here in the middle of the farmland. He hopes to turn it over for a huge profit—one more shrewd deal before he retires. And packaging the church property in with mine gives him the advantage of additional highway frontage."

"Are you wanting to sell?"

"Well, yes and no." Bradford paused to scratch his chin. "I'm seventy years old, and it's time for me to retire. My dear wife wants to take a cruise or two, and I promised her we would. Then she wants to get a smaller place, perhaps a home in town, something we can take care of in our twilight years. I owe her that after all I've put her through."

Joe remembered Ezra's story about Bradford from last night. He found it difficult imagining that this good-hearted farmer would have ever caused his sweet wife any grief.

Bradford went on, gazing out at the wheat fields as he spoke. "But I really wish I didn't have to give up this old place. The good Lord has been gracious to me. He has blessed my work even though I didn't deserve it. My blood, sweat, and tears have watered the land, and the crops have been better than average. And to tell you the truth, I've resisted selling to Jethro not only because of the money but because none of the people out here want to see a shopping mall go up on this land."

Bradford paused, and Joe wondered if the man would get emotional on him, but he pulled himself together quickly. "Our kids are grown and gone, and they don't want the place. So I need to sell out. Problem is, nobody's looking. My realtor says he hasn't even received an inquiry yet. So Jethro's offer, unfair as it is, gets more attractive every day."

"Why don't your children want the farm?"

Bradford dismissed the question with a wave. "They have their own lives, and I can't blame them. Our son and his family live in Boise. He's an engineer, and a good one. As for our two daughters, farming apparently wasn't what they had in mind. Perhaps if things had been different when the kids were younger..." His voice trailed off and his eyes got misty.

Joe realized that it was a veiled reference to Bradford's early alcoholism, but he played dumb and let the statement pass.

Again, Bradford recovered quickly. "Say, Joe, how would you like to jump in the pickup with me and see our place? I'd love to show it to you. Have you ever toured a working farm before?"

Touring a working farm sounded pretty dull to Joe, but he liked the old farmer and decided to humor him. "Sure, I'd like to see your place."

The next hour and a half changed Joe's mind. As the golden spring evening settled over the valley, he fell in love with the spread where Bradford McDermot had made his living for the past forty-seven years. He knew that farming was more than throwing out seed and water and waiting for harvest. He just didn't realize how much more.

Bradford's farm was mostly in wheat, but he also had several acres in sweet corn and a good-sized cherry orchard. Each crop required special care. Bradford walked Joe through the orchard explaining the year-long cycle of pruning, spraying, thinning, more spraying, weed control, and harvesting. At every step, the crop was in jeopardy if the correct measures were applied either early or late or ignored altogether. The farmer talked about the variables of weather, such as freezes and thunderstorms, that could wipe out an entire year's crop. This week's storm, Bradford noted, would have been devastating had it occurred in the summer, just before wheat harvest.

Bradford took him through the barn, and Joe marveled at the amount of high tech equipment needed to maintain this operation. Not one tractor but four, plus their various attachments, and other vehicles. He tried to calculate the value of what he saw, and the numbers were staggering. This was a costly operation, and he could readily see how a farmer might lose it all through carelessness, poor planning, or lack of industry.

They returned to the house after sunset. Joe thanked his hosts for the wonderful evening and made his exit after declining another slice of berry pie. He promised Bradford that he would be ready to go to work on the church roof at eight in the morning.

On the short ride back to the hollow, it occurred to Joe that Bradford and Esther had not asked him about the scar on his face. It was as if they were so interested in his story that they hadn't noticed his old injury. He had relaxed in their presence without even realizing it. He hadn't thought once about turning his face away. He had let his guard down and had a wonderful time with the old couple.

What kind of place is this? he pondered as he rode down the slope to his tent. *The preachers don't cram their religion down your throat, and old folks are so accepting and hospitable that even I can feel a peace.*

"What are these people doing to me?" he said aloud shaking his head.

Twenty

AS JOE STRODE ACROSS THE CEMETERY toward the church building at two minutes to eight, two things surprised him. First was the number of volunteers who had already arrived ready to work. There were nearly twenty men standing around on the grass in clusters of two or three, many of them sipping coffee they had brought with them. And every couple of minutes another pickup truck pulled into the parking lot with yet another worker or two. Joe was impressed that so many men would give up a beautiful Saturday to work at the church.

Even more surprising was the age of the volunteers. Joe didn't see anyone—except for Rich—who looked younger than fifty. Most of the men wore faded caps bearing the logos of farm implement companies or feed stores. Many had tool belts strapped around their waists. The over-the-hill-gang was ready to work. Except for Rusty Ewing, Jethro's chauffeur, who was closer to Rich in age. The man was leaning on the fender of the Caddie listening to country music through the car's open window.

A couple of the men greeted Joe as he approached, but most gave him little more than a glance. Ezra made a special point to greet Joe and thank him for coming. As he clapped the young man on the back, Jethro Haig walked over, and Ezra introduced him to Joe.

Jethro mumbled a curt greeting without offering to shake his hand. Then he quickly turned back to the minister. "Has Chief Jurgen been here yet?" he asked rather gruffly.

Ezra's expression and furtive glance his way hinted to Joe that Jethro's question was inappropriate in his hearing. Joe got the hint and sidled casually away. Yet he overheard Ezra's hushed response: "George came out on Thursday, and he said he'd be back to talk to some of us. But remember, Jethro, we're keeping this to ourselves for right now."

Jethro mumbled a response Joe couldn't understand, then tromped away.

Ezra walked over to Joe immediately and spoke in the same serious, secretive tone. "I want to ask you something, Joe. It may not make any sense to you. But I have a good reason for asking, and I hope you'll trust me on that."

Joe had a bad feeling about this. But over the last two days he had come to believe that the preacher was an okay guy. Not knowing where Ezra was going with this conversation, he said, "Sure, what do you want to know."

"The afternoon I came out to meet you, you were working on your motorcycle. Do you remember?"

"Yeah, carburetor adjustment."

"I noticed you had some nice tools, especially that set of red-handled screwdrivers."

"Pierponts, one of the best made. Mom gave the set to me for Christmas a couple years ago. Why?"

"How many screwdrivers are in your set of Pierponts?"

"I don't understand, Reverend," Joe said, unable to hide his perplexity over the minister's line of questioning. "What do my tools have to do with anything?"

Ezra locked onto Joe's questioning gaze. "Can you trust me on this, Joe?"

No way could Joe deny the minister's sincerity. After a moment's pause, he said, "I have four of them, two flatheads and two Phillips'."

Ezra dropped his gaze for two seconds as if phrasing the next question. Looking up, "Have you lost any of them, Joe—one of the flatheads, for example?"

Joe could feel his perplexity escalate to annoyance. "No, Reverend, they're in my tool kit. I don't know what you're after, but I take good care of my stuff."

Ezra studied Joe's eyes for several moments, and Joe obliged him with a glare. "Thank you, Joe," he said at last. "I just needed to hear it from you." Then he gave Joe a fatherly pat on the bicep and walked away.

Bradford McDermot was the recognized foreman of the crew, and he wasted no time sorting the men into work groups and making assignments. He put Joe in the group assigned to tear off and rebuild the roof. He directed another group to gather roof debris and haul it away. A third group was to unload supplies from the trucks and feed them to the crew on the roof.

By 11:30, the old shingles, tar paper, and plywood were torn off, and some of the rotted beams had been removed. Bradford estimated that they would have all the beams replaced and the new plywood tacked down before evening. The new paper and shingles would have to wait for another day. Local weather reports promised that the next few days would be clear and warm.

As he worked, Joe listened to the ongoing, good-natured ribbing between members of the two largest families in the church. The McDermots poked fun at the Rasbys for taking too many breaks and for standing around gabbing when they should have been working. The Rasbys countered with comments like, "It's all right to fellowship while you work, Ted" and "Lighten up a little, Phil." Joe figured the friendly verbal sparring had been going on for years, maybe generations.

He was amazed at how the McDermots and Rasbys tended to play out their roles. The Rasby men did take more breaks and seemed more chatty while the McDermots, from Bradford on down, kept up a furious, no-nonsense work pace. It wasn't that the Rasbys didn't work, because they did. And the McDermot clan was far from anti-social. Still, the general traits seemed to hold true.

Thomas Rasby was the exception to the rule, Joe observed. The cheerful caretaker worked at a pace that would make a McDermot proud, yet he kept a stream of chatter running to the men around him. Working on the ground with the supply crew, Thomas seemed to anticipate what the roof crew needed. As the man in the middle, he caught barbs from both families, but he obviously enjoyed the banter and fun. The man was as dense as a sack of concrete, Joe thought, but he had never seen a harder worker with such an amiable disposition.

Perched on the peak of the roof just before noon, Joe noticed a police car approaching on the highway. It slowed and turned into the parking lot crowded with pickups. Two officers stepped out. The one with gold stars on the epaulets of his dark brown uniform had a manila envelope in his hand.

As Joe watched and worked, the cops sought out the minister, who was scooping up debris from the lawn with a shovel. They talked, but Joe couldn't hear anything above the racket and chatter on the roof. For all he knew, they were volunteering for the work detail, but he couldn't help but wonder if Ezra's crazy questions about his tools had something to do with it. Yet none of them once looked his way.

Joe's attention was diverted by the arrival of a green Toyota. Chessy and Velma Walls were among a number of ladies coming to serve an outdoor picnic dinner to the workers. Four long tables had been set up in the shade next to the cemetery. One of them was filling up with homemade salads, side dishes, watermelon, bread, and fried chicken. Some of the men were ringing the other three tables with folding chairs brought up from classrooms in the basement.

After placing a covered dish on the food table, Chessy looked up, smiled, and waved at Joe. With his hands busy, Joe returned her smile. Then Chessy turned back to a conversation with two other women. When Joe looked around for the cops, he saw them standing several paces away from the workers on the ground. The senior officer was talking to Thomas Rasby and showing him whatever he had in the manila envelope.

Joe was one of the last men off the roof in response to Velma's "dinner bell" —a metal pot lid she banged with a serving spoon. He stood in line to wash his hands and face at the outdoor faucet. Then he pulled a T-shirt over his sweaty torso.

When he turned toward the tables, Ezra and the two cops were standing in his path. "Joe, this is George Jurgen, our police chief, and officer Raul Tapia."

Joe immediately made the connection. Bradford had pointed out the police cruiser on the road into Orchard Valley and mentioned George and Raul by name.

"George, this is Joe Caruso, our guest in the hollow."

Joe couldn't mask his surprise. He hadn't told Ezra his last name. He hadn't even told Chessy. Then it dawned on him. Addressing the chief, "You ran my plate, and you gave my name to the reverend." The chief nodded.

The cops knew more about him than his name, Joe realized. His life was now an open book in Orchard Valley, Washington, even the stuff he wished he could forget.

"Joe, the chief would like to talk to you for a minute," Ezra said in a discreet tone. The four of them were standing alone near the faucet while the other men started through the buffet line. "The congregation doesn't know about it yet, but something of value was taken from the church office Wednesday before the fire. The chief is interviewing those of us who were on the property Wednesday, and that happens to include you."

The picture was suddenly crystal clear to Joe. Whatever happened, he was probably the prime suspect because he was the stranger in town, and the cops had discovered that this stranger had an arrest record. He decided to be proactive. "Did this 'something of value' happen to be cash? Like around *twenty thousand* in cash?"

The surprise on the minister's face confirmed Joe's guess, so he answered the obvious question before Ezra could ask it. "Your caretaker let it slip that afternoon. I didn't know whether to believe him or not."

The chief turned to Ezra. "When we talked to Thomas just now, he said he had shared the 'secret' with Mister Caruso."

Ezra sighed. "I shouldn't have let Thomas see the money. But then if I had taken the money to the bank as I should have, this wouldn't have happened anyway."

Turning back to Joe, the chief said, "I want to ask you a few questions, Mister Caruso. Ezra, will you excuse us?" The minister nodded then left to join the work crew at the tables.

Joe's answers to the chief's opening questions established that he lived in Pittsburgh and arrived in Orchard Valley in the early morning hours of May twenty-second. Joe subsequently related during questioning that he was born in Yarborough, had been taken east by adoptive parents, and had come west on this trip to look into the whereabouts of his birth parents, who were unknown to him. He added that he had submitted an inquiry form at county records office in Yarborough.

"Why did you decide to stay out here?" Chief Jurgen continued, motioning toward Joe's tent in the hollow.

"I like camping instead of moteling," Joe answered. "And it's much cheaper."

"But why camp here instead of a campground? We do have campgrounds in this county, you know."

"It was late when I arrived in town. I asked a guy on the street for a recommendation. He directed me out here. It's quiet and free, so I stayed."

"Where were you on Wednesday afternoon?"

Joe thumbed toward the hollow. "Out there. When the storm started rolling in, I zipped myself in for the night…at least I thought I was in for the night."

"So you were on the property all afternoon? You didn't leave at any time?"

Joe thought back. "I left a couple of times. My carburetor was acting up, so I worked on it out there and then took off for a test ride."

"A couple of times?"

"Two times, yes."

"How long were you gone on those test rides?"

"Ten minutes, maybe twenty minutes each, something like that."

Joe ventured a glance at the picnic lunch in full swing. It was festive and noisy, and Joe wished he was there eating with the rest of the crew. He couldn't see Chessy anywhere. No one else seemed to be looking his way.

The chief reached into the manila envelope. Joe had an inkling what was coming next, having pondered all morning the minister's enigmatic question about his tools.

"Do you recognize this?" the chief said. He displayed a medium-sized Pierpont flathead screwdriver sealed in a plastic freezer bag.

Joe smiled to himself. *Ezra knew what was coming today and gave me a head's up,* he thought. "Yes, I carry a set of Pierponts in my tool kit," he answered. "Same red, see-through handles. I'm pretty sure I have one that size."

"And your screwdrivers are in the tool kit right now? Out there with your bike?"

"To the best of my knowledge, yes."

The chief bored into Joe's eyes. "Mister Caruso, the screwdriver in this bag was discovered in the church office after the fire. We also determined that the desk drawer containing the money box was jimmied with a sharp instrument, possibly this same screwdriver. Do you understand what I'm saying?"

The point of the chief's questions had been crystal clear since he produced the bag containing the Pierpont screwdriver. "Yes sir, I understand. I'll be happy to show you my tool kit."

Joe and the cops strode down into the hollow in silence. Under the chief's watchful eye, he retrieved his tool kit from his saddlebag. The "kit" was simply a black, soft vinyl bag with a Velcro flap into which he dumped his travel tools.

"On the picnic table," the chief directed. "Just dump out the bag."

Of the small assortment of tools which tumbled onto the table, only three had clear red handles. Two Phillips' head screwdrivers and one flathead screwdriver. Joe's other Pierpont screwdriver was missing, the one matching the screwdriver in the chief's plastic bag.

Twenty-one

"YOU SAY YOUR MISSING SCREWDRIVER WAS IN THE TOOL KIT on Wednesday afternoon?" the chief said after Joe performed a cursory but fruitless search for his missing tool in his saddlebag and in and around his tent.

"Yes, I used the smaller flathead for the carb adjustment," Joe explained, "and I took it with me during my test ride."

"You took your tool kit with you when you rode that afternoon?" the other officer asked.

"No, just the small flathead, stuck in the back pocket of my jeans in case I needed to make another tweak or two. I left the rest of the tools in my pouch."

"Where did you leave the pouch while you were riding?" the Latino officer continued.

"On the grass where I was working."

"And was the other flathead in your pouch when you returned?" the chief asked.

"I don't know. I didn't look," Joe said. "The job was done, so I dropped in the small flathead and put the pouch away in my saddlebag."

Joe was sure that he and the two cops agreed on one thing: The chances that his missing Pierpont screwdriver was *not* the one in the evidence bag were too astronomical to warrant serious consideration. But Joe doubted that they were convinced of what he knew to be true—that he did not break into the church office, jimmy the drawer with his screwdriver, and make off with the money box.

"Do you mind if we look through your things, sir?" the chief said.

"Help yourselves, officers," he answered.

They didn't find his screwdriver, but they did find his pistol as Joe knew they would. "It's a target pistol, sir," he said to the chief. "You know, for coyotes and stuff."

"But it's not a pellet gun, is it?" the chief pressed. "It's a twenty-two caliber firearm."

Joe knew where that comment came from. "I didn't want to scare the minister, sir. So I told him I had a pellet gun."

"Do you have a permit for this firearm, Mister Caruso?" the chief asked, handling the pistol. Joe was relieved that the cops kept themselves between the gun and the church instead of waving it around.

"Yes sir, there's a pocket inside the case."

The chief found the laminated card bearing Joe's picture.

"When's the last time you fired this gun, Mister Caruso?" the chief asked as he studied the permit.

"Indoor practice range back home about six or seven months ago."

The cop returned the permit and the gun to the case, zipped it up, and returned it to the saddlebag. Joe released a silent sigh.

"How long are you planning to camp out here?" asked the chief as he slipped the bagged screwdriver back into the manila envelope.

"I don't have any set plans, officer," Joe said. "A few more days, at least until I get some kind of response on my inquiry at county records."

Chief Jurgen pursed his lips and tapped his boot on the grass for several moments. Finally he said, "Do you have any idea how your screwdriver got into that church office?"

"No sir, I don't."

"You won't be able to get it back for a while, you know. It's evidence in a crime, and we need to hold onto it."

"I understand."

"And if you go running off without telling anyone, it'll look mighty suspicious. You know that, too, don't you?"

"When I settle my business in the city I'll check in with you. If you need me to stay longer, I can probably do that."

The chief's next question caught Joe off guard, which he assumed was the purpose of it.

"Have you told us the complete truth today? Because if you took the church's money, we *will* find out."

It was a stark departure from the gentlemanly albeit cool "sir" and "Mister Caruso." And there was an intentional fierceness in the chief's glare, leaving no doubt that Joe was a suspect.

In the past, Joe had reacted harshly to not-so-subtle insinuations against his character. He had roughed up guys and broken up stuff when someone dared to call him out this way. Joe felt the fire just now—hot words ready to explode from his mouth, an urge to plant a fist in the cop's face, but he wasn't about to give the chief a reason to bust him with a nightstick and carry him off in handcuffs.

"No sir, I did not take the church's money," he said coolly. "I swear on my mother's grave."

Joe knew that his oath meant nothing to the cops, but if they knew what it meant to him they would immediately clear him of all suspicion.

"How can we get in touch you, Mister Caruso?" Officer Tapia asked, returning to the phony politeness as the chief started edging toward the patrol car. "Do you have a cell phone?"

"No phone. I'll be here or in town or in Yarborough. I'm not going anywhere, at least not today."

"We appreciate your cooperation, sir."

• • •

Joe had taken only a couple of bites from his plate before Bradford stood up at the next table and addressed the work crew as they ate. "I don't know if you all had a chance to meet Joe Caruso," he said, glancing Joe's way. "Joe is from Pennsylvania, and he's visiting in our valley for a few days. You might have heard that he was a hero the other night, helping put out the fire. Well, you heard right. The good Lord brought him along just when we needed him. And he volunteered to work with us today before heading back east. Joe, thanks for your help today."

Joe was surprised to hear a ripple of applause from the group. He could have done without the attention, but he felt genuine appreciation in the applause. He acknowledged the recognition with a quick wave then dove back into his dinner.

Two minutes later, a slender feminine arm reached out from behind Joe to pick up his cup. "It sounds like you're leaving soon. Is that true?"

Joe turned to see Chessy filling his cup with lemonade. The words just tumbled out. "Why do you want to know?"

Chessy seemed stunned by Joe's directness. She stopped pouring and looked at him. The sunlight filtering through the giant elms danced in her eyes. "Well, I…I was hoping for another motorcycle ride," she said, seeming a little self-conscious.

The men sitting on either side of Joe were jawing with others at the table, paying no attention to the couple's conversation. Still, Joe kept his voice low. "I don't know when I'm leaving. I have some things to finish here. It could take a few days."

Chessy broke eye contact long enough to finish filling the cup. Handing it to him, she said, "So you're not leaving tomorrow?"

Her eyes gripped his. Several seconds elapsed before Joe realized she was waiting for a response. "Uh, no. Not tomorrow."

It was a Mona Lisa smile, Joe thought. Slight, secretive, mysterious. Chessy added a slow nod. "Good," she said, then walked away to fill more cups.

Turning back to his plate, Joe realized that conversation at his table had subsided. The men sitting next to him were craning their necks toward another table where the conversation was animated and intense.

"It's a simple matter of stewardship," he heard someone say emphatically. "It's foolish to think of expansion when we can't even take care of what we have."

"So you think caring for the less fortunate is foolish, do you?" came the stern reply. "You'd better be careful what you're calling foolish."

Taking a closer look, Joe saw that old Jethro Haig was one of the men involved in the discussion, but his usually pasty white face glowed with ardor. "Chester, it is foolish for the church to hold onto that worthless parcel and go into debt"—Jethro dropped his fist firmly on the table when he said *foolish* and *worthless*—"when the proceeds could pay for all these repairs and much more."

Jethro's words were directed at a man sitting near the other end of his table—Chester. Joe had heard others call him Chet, and Joe thought he was a Rasby. Everyone was now listening to the suddenly sharp exchange. Even the women had stopped serving to pay attention.

"I'll tell you what's foolish," Chet snapped, pointing his plastic fork down the table at Jethro. "Giving up land that is dedicated for ministry and turning it into a strip mall."

Jethro had opened his mouth to reply, but Ezra, who was also sitting at that table, spoke first. "All right, you men," he said in a calming tone, "I know you both feel strongly about this, but let's not blow a gasket."

Joe looked first at Jethro and then at Chet, waiting to see who would erupt next. Neither of them did, but the displeasure on their faces revealed that the argument was far from resolved.

After several tense seconds, a few men began eating again and other conversations resumed. Then a man at Joe's table spoke up. "Reverend, since the subject has come up, maybe we need to talk about it a little more." There were murmurs of agreement at each table. Chet and Jethro kept silent.

"Sure, we can talk about it, Larry," Ezra said, "as long as we do it in a civil manner."

Larry, whom Joe remembered was in the McDermot clan, continued. "I know the board has voted a number of times not to sell our surplus land. But seeing all this damage, I'm thinking it's time to talk about it again."

"This isn't even the half of it," another man put in. "Our old church is in need of many more repairs. The wiring is old and not up to code. I think we're in danger of another fire."

"There's rust in all the pipes," someone else put in.

"And the parsonage needs a new roof."

The litany of needed repairs brought up by the men snowballed until Ezra stepped in again. "Yes, these things are all on the list. We just have to take them one at a time as the funds become available."

Bradford stood to address the rapt group. "Jethro's suggestion is worthy of consideration. It's been awhile since the board discussed the issue of selling off those thirteen acres. Perhaps we need to put it on the agenda again."

"And you'll keep putting it on the agenda until it passes." Chet Rasby, who was still steaming, said it as an aside, but Joe heard him, and he was sure most everyone else did.

"Easy there, Chet," Ezra said, more charitably than Joe thought he deserved, "It's also a chance for the board to reaffirm its decision to save that land for a future ministry site for migrants and their families."

"The board has already spoken on that point," said a man at Joe's table who sounded irritated. "So why bring it up for another vote?" The man had been talking with some of the Rasbys earlier, so Joe thought he must be in the family. Was this issue the root of a long-standing family feud?

"Things change, Fred," someone answered him. "We have a crisis on our hands here with this building, and we have to consider every option."

From there the heated words flew between the tables.

"But selling the property is not an option."

"It's practically our only option."

"We have to keep that land. The transients use it as a temporary shelter."

Ezra held up his hands in a silent plea for restraint. His effort went unheeded.

"The homeless shouldn't be allowed to use the land. They trash the hollow."

"If we sell out now, we won't ever be able to build a ministry center."

"Nobody said we were selling out. We're only going to revisit the question."

"We can always buy more land when—or if—this building is restored and the church is on a firmer financial footing."

"But we can't lose our ministry of serving the migrant workers."

Jethro Haig jumped to his feet, livid. "Wake up, you fools!" he shouted in a gravelly voice. His eyes bored into Chet Rasby. "Get your heads out of the clouds. If you don't turn that land into cash, this church is finished. It will fall down around you."

Chet was on his feet, glaring at Jethro. "You are pushing this through to line your own pockets, Jethro Haig."

"This is not about me, Chester. This is about what is best for my church."

"*Your* church! You're selling out *your* own church for thirty pieces of silver."

"Chester, you are a fool!"

"Jethro, you are a Judas!"

Those final two cannon blasts silenced the group. Only then could they hear an equally urgent yet more subdued sound. Joe turned in its direction. Leaning against the trunk of a large maple, Thomas Rasby held his hand to his heart as if in severe pain. He was sobbing uncontrollably.

Twenty-two

CHESSY SAW IT THE MOMENT JOE DID. "Uncle Thomas!" she cried out. She was at his side before anyone else. She knelt beside him as Joe looked on. "What's wrong? Are you in pain? Is it your heart?"

The heated discussion was forgotten for the moment, and a few more people came to Thomas' aid, including Ezra and Joe. Someone urged him to sit down on the grass, so he did, with Chessy's help. Whispers around the tables speculated on the problem—heat stroke, respiration problems, heart attack.

It took a moment for Thomas to regain his composure and answer Chessy's question. "It hurts my heart," he said, whimpering.

"What makes your heart hurt, Thomas?" Ezra said, also on his knees beside the man.

"The words, Reverend Sturdevant," he said, sniffing. "The words make my heart hurt."

"You mean what we have been talking about at the tables?" Ezra pressed.

Thomas nodded slowly. "My heart hurts real bad when you talk like that." His eyes swept across the group of onlookers.

Joe's breath caught in his throat. He suddenly understood. He painfully remembered his own anxiety growing so intense in his chest that he felt his ribs closing in on him, making it hard to breathe, making his heart literally ache. It happened when his parents fought, when they screamed at each other, when they threatened each other. That's what Thomas was feeling right now, Joe knew. This was the caretaker's family, people he loved dearly. To hear them argue scared him so badly that it hurt.

"I'm sorry the words hurt you, Thomas," Ezra said in a comforting tone. "It's going to be all right now. Our discussion just got a little carried away. Everybody's fine. Don't you worry."

Chessy wiped the tears off her uncle's face with a paper napkin. "Are you okay now, Uncle Thomas?" she said, patting his shoulder.

He took a few deep breaths, and he was no long pressing his hand against the center of his chest. "Thank you, Chessy," he said with a weak smile. "I'm okay now."

The people around Joe seemed to release a collective breath.

As the men wandered back to their jobs and the women to the cleanup, Joe saw Chessy attempting to help Thomas to his feet. He moved in quickly to lend a hand on the other side. "Thank you, Joe," he said, back on his feet. "My heart feels better now."

Yes, the slashing, visceral pain subsided quickly, Joe remembered, but the anxiety churning in his stomach would last for days. He hoped Thomas got over it sooner than he had.

Chessy's eyes, which were still shadowed by concern, met Joe's. "Yes, thank you for helping," she said.

"Sure," he said, hoping she read the interest in his gaze. "Are you all right?"

"Yes, and thanks for asking."

"If you need any other help…" Joe left the offer hanging open. Chessy nodded.

Thomas excused himself to use the bathroom in his cabin before getting back to work. Joe motioned to the table where the heated exchange had taken place. "What did you think of all that?"

Chessy frowned. "I think I know a little how Uncle Thomas felt. It's so sad to see church people fighting."

"Especially when the issue is so clear cut," Joe added.

Chessy cocked her head questioningly. "What do you mean?"

"That church property out there," Joe said, waving his hand to the south, "is an albatross, worthless. It's money just sitting there waiting to be used. That old guy Jethro may lack diplomacy in his argument, but he's right. The church needs to sell that land and put the money to good use around here. It's ridiculous to borrow money when the cash is within easy reach."

"What about the people who use that property?" Chessy said. "What happens to them?"

"You mean people like me?"

"Yes, but I'm also referring to the transients and homeless who stay there, people who don't have nice motorcycles or homes in Pittsburgh, the people my uncle and the minister help throughout the year."

"Are you saying that you don't agree with Jethro's argument?"

Chessy answered without hesitation. "Think about it, Joe. Those thirteen acres have been set aside to help people—eventually migrant workers and their families. If that land is sold off, that opportunity is lost."

"But what about this place?" Joe countered, gesturing toward the church building. "The upkeep? The repairs?"

Chessy glanced around at the men getting back to work. "Looks to me like it's getting done," she said as if Joe had missed the totally obvious.

The comment about Chessy being a Rasby crossed Joe's mind again, but he didn't dare speak it. Instead, he said, "Then you side with those who are not willing to sell the land even if the existing plan falls apart."

"It won't fall apart, Joe," Chessy said.

Her air of confidence hit him the wrong way. "How do you know?" he said, feeling his face flush warm.

Chessy gazed at him with that irksome Mona Lisa, I-know-something-you-don't-know smile on her face. "I just know," she said.

A rush of words flooded Joe's mind, all argumentative, all sharpened to puncture or cut. Chessy was as dense as all the other Rasbys. She couldn't see the obvious, and he wanted to put her in her place for it.

It must have shown on his face because Chessy said, "You don't agree with me, do you?" Had she said it argumentatively, Joe might have let her have it. But she didn't. It came out almost playfully, as if the point of their argument—*the* argument—didn't really matter to her all that much.

Joe envied Chessy's ability to let things go. He found himself smiling. "I guess it doesn't matter anyway, does it? Because they're not going to let us vote."

"But if they did," Chessy added with a little laugh that made Joe's heart skip, "it sounds like our votes would cancel each other out."

Joe laughed and agreed. He felt the sudden urge to collect Chessy into his arms, put her behind him on the motorcycle, and ride away with her—far away, forever. And the light in her eyes caused him to think she would go with him despite their obviously differing opinions about things.

There wasn't much camaraderie among the men through the afternoon, no more of the good-natured ribbing from the morning's work session, nor did the argument between Jethro Haig and Chet Rasby resurface. Joe watched from the roof as he worked, and the two men avoided each other. The heat and Thomas' episode had apparently drained the fight out of everybody. Thomas was back up to speed, but the clash even seemed to turn him more inward and quiet during the long afternoon.

As a result, the men poured their energy and attention into the tasks at hand. On the roof, Joe and his coworkers finished their job earlier than expected. They had replaced all the rotted support beams and tacked on new plywood in preparation for tar paper and shingles. To Joe, it was a monumental achievement for one day. And he had enjoyed every minute of the hard work.

After cleaning up the dinner mess, most of the women went home, including Velma and Chessy. If the pretty California blonde waved goodbye to him, Joe was too busy to notice it. The hot sun and steady, demanding task had dulled his earlier fantasy about riding off with Chessy. She was very different from him, as their brief clash after lunch had revealed.

Chessy thought like a Rasby; he most definitely did not. And yet there was something about that relaxed, relational view of life that attracted him. Furthermore, Chessy had this Christian religious thing going. Joe had dismissed Christianity for himself because of its intolerant view of other religions. His talks with Rich were showing him an entirely new side of what Christians believe, how they think, what they do—and why. But Joe wasn't ready for a radical religious experience.

There may be little hope of a lasting relationship with Chessy Carpenter, Joe had concluded as the afternoon wore on. Yet there was no reason to walk away from what hope there may be.

Just after 4:00 P.M., another unexpected occurrence caused Joe to think that the old saying, "Bad things happen in threes," might be true. Ezra, who was collecting and carrying discarded lumber to the burn pile, took a fall. Joe heard the cry of pain and turned to see the minister crumple to the grass. He learned later that Ezra had stepped on a board and rolled his foot off the side under his full weight. He landed heavily on the wood he had been carrying, scraping his hands and driving a rusty nail into his forearm.

According to the men who gathered around to help him, Ezra had suffered either a very bad ankle sprain, a broken bone, or both. Joe watched from the roof as two men helped him into the passenger seat of a pickup truck. Before leaving for the emergency care facility in town, Ezra asked Rich if he would be willing to preach the morning service tomorrow since he might be off his feet for a few days. Rich agreed. Then one of the older men drove off with the injured minister.

As the men gathered their tools and prepared to head home, Bradford thanked each one personally for his contribution. The big farmer had put in a full day himself keeping the ground crew organized and productive. By the time the last sheet of plywood was in place on the roof, every piece of scrap lumber had been disposed of. The men on the ground had also policed the entire church yard picking up any debris left over from the storm.

"I can't thank you enough for your help today," Bradford said, meeting Joe as he descended the ladder. He gripped Joe by the arm and gave him a manly squeeze. "We wouldn't have finished nearly this soon without you."

The farmer's face was red from exertion and much of his shirt was wet or stained from perspiration.

"Glad to help, sir," Joe said, really meaning it. "I think the day went well."

"Except for poor Ezra," Bradford lamented. "He really took a fall. Guys our age don't bounce as well as you young fellows."

"Yeah, I feel bad for him."

"Joe, I need to apologize about what happened at noon today," Bradford said, brow furrowed. "You know, the friction over the property."

"No problem," Joe said. He could tell the clash was still bothering Bradford.

"I'm really embarrassed that you had to see that. The church is supposed to be about faith, hope, and charity, but sometimes our own passions and priorities get in the way. We're not perfect, and sometimes it's a little too obvious."

"Don't worry about it," Joe said. "Eventually they'll realize that the smart thing to do is to sell the property."

"As you know, Joe, that's my position. But it's not the right decision if we alienate half our congregation."

"It sounds like you're going to alienate half of them either way."

Bradford gazed at the horizon for a moment, then turned back to Joe. "That's what we need to avoid," he said. "We need God to help us work this out. And I know he will."

Joe thought he saw the same brash confidence in Bradford's eyes that he had seen earlier in Chessy's. Had Joe asked him, "How do you know?" he thought the old farmer would answer as she did: "I just know."

Before Joe could respond, Bradford said, "We have a big house, Joe, and we kind of rattle around in there all by ourselves. If you would like to sleep in one of our spare bedrooms for the rest of your stay, you're welcome to it. There's a separate shower. You could eat with us if you like."

The offer was very tempting, and not only for the comfort of a bed and a shower. This old man and his kind wife made him feel comfortable, at home, and at ease. No airs, no expectations, no judgments. It was more than Joe had anticipated during this brief visit, and he knew he would miss these people when he left for home.

"I appreciate the offer, sir," he said, "but I'm fine right here."

"All right, but it's a standing offer," Bradford said, smiling. "Will we see in you church tomorrow?"

Joe shrugged and wagged his head, "Maybe."

Bradford laughed. "Good! We'll look for you then, son." Then he said goodbye and headed for his pickup in the parking lot.

As Joe walked back to his campsite to clean up, the dark cloud of his earlier encounter with the police returned. He was clearly suspected of a serious crime in which one of his tools had been used. Throughout the afternoon while his hands were busy pounding nails, he had pondered his situation. It bothered him that he had been a good guy since he arrived in the hollow and now he was turning out to look like a bad guy. What kind of God would reward his heroics and helpfulness by making him look like a criminal?

Two tumblers suddenly clicked in his brain as he walked, as though his subconscious had been working on the problem and finally spit out some data. First, since he had not taken the church's money, obviously somebody else had. While the cops had been pestering and threatening him today, the real perpetrator was likely out there in the world somewhere spending the cash. Second, that somebody had apparently used his expensive Pierpont screwdriver in the burglary. How did the tool get from his tool kit into the thief's hands? Joe remembered returning the screwdriver to his kit. Or had he just imagined it? Had he instead lost the red-handled screwdriver on the road or on the church grounds?

The only persons to venture all the way out to his campsite had been the minister and the caretaker. Had one of them found the screwdriver and innocently taken it to the church office where it was discovered after the fire and linked to the burglary? There had to be a logical explanation, but unless Joe discovered it he would have the cops breathing down his neck.

Grabbing a towel from the tent, he went down to the creek for a marine shower. He hoped his subconscious would continue to work on the problem.

Twenty-three

BRENDA LONG HAD DRIVEN PAST THE CHURCH at about 3:00 P.M. There was a project going on with perhaps ten men working on the roof and twice that many on the ground. It did not seem like a good time to stop in, so she turned west and spent an hour and a half strolling around the quaint little country town of Orchard Valley. It had been more than twenty years since she visited some of these shops. She recognized a few of the proprietors, but no one recognized her. Brenda had changed.

By the time she got to the church, it was almost 5:00 P.M. The last pickup was just pulling out of the parking lot and turning south as she slowly approached the driveway from the north. She pulled into the empty lot and parked. At first glance, the place looked deserted. Then she noticed a white-haired man astride a small riding mower near the back of the church cemetery.

Brenda stepped out of her champagne-tinted Honda Accord and locked it. Even though it was Saturday, her visit to the church was technically official business. She was dressed in office attire—a beige suit and white blouse—though she would have preferred shorts and a sleeveless cotton top. She also carried her leather briefcase.

The main doors to the church were locked. Even the parsonage looked deserted. Seeing no one, she started across the church's back lawn toward the cemetery and waited for the caretaker to notice her.

"May I help you, ma'am?" He had stopped ten yards away, shut down the engine, and stepped off the mower. "Reverend Sturdevant is at the hospital, and Missus Walls went home. My name is Thomas."

Brenda recognized the man, though she knew he would not recognize her. It had been a very long time.

"I'm looking for a young man by the name of Joseph Caruso. Is he here?"

The old caretaker's face broke into a big smile. "You mean Joe," he said proudly. "That's Joe's place out there." He aimed a finger past the cemetery toward a small tent nestled into the trees close to the main highway. "That's his motorcycle, and there's Joe down by the creek."

Brenda saw a young man in jeans, bare from the waist up, squatting at the edge of the creek. He was facing away from her, patting his neck and chest dry with a towel.

Before Brenda could object, Thomas took a step toward the hollow and yelled out Joe's name until he stood up and turned around. Then Thomas made an exaggerated pointing motion toward the guest and waved for him to come up to the church.

The young man stood and stared for a moment. Then he signaled that he would come up. Brenda thanked Thomas, who was already getting back on the mower to continue his work.

Five minutes later, the young man walked up the rise from the hollow toward Brenda, who waited in the shade near the front corner of the church building. He had pulled on a navy T-shirt that clung to his muscular torso. His long dark hair, pulled back into a ponytail, still glistened with moisture, and the scar on his face was as unsettling as her coworker had described it.

"Joseph Caruso?" she said as he approached.

He looked at her suspiciously. "Yes. Are you with the police?"

The question caught Brenda off guard. "The police? No. Why do you ask?"

The young man waved it off. "Never mind. What do you want?"

"I'm Brenda Long, supervisor of records in the county auditor's office." She thrust out her hand as she continued, "I'd like to talk to you about the inquiry you submitted to our office yesterday."

The young man shook her hand in businesslike fashion. It was quick and impersonal. "You people work on Saturdays?" he said.

"Not usually, but your situation seemed rather…unique."

"What do you mean?"

"Since you are visiting from out of state and your temporary residence is, well, a church, I thought it might be helpful to put your inquiry on the fast track."

The young man studied her for a moment. "I didn't expect such fast service. The lady at the counter said it might take several days to process my form."

"Yes, the paperwork is tedious at times," Brenda said, "but I read your file yesterday, and I was touched by your story. So I decided to look you up today. Besides, I enjoy a pleasant drive out in the country once in a while."

Joe smiled. "Well, I'm impressed. But I guess I shouldn't be surprised. This valley has been full of pleasant surprises since I arrived here."

"May we sit down and talk for a few minutes?" Brenda said. "Is now a good time for you?"

Joe shrugged. "Sure, I can talk now."

One long table and several folding chairs remained outside from the picnic. Joe suggested that they sit there since it was in the shade. She quickly agreed.

Brenda pulled a file folder out of her briefcase and laid it on the table, unopened. "Why don't you begin by telling me your story, Joe," she said.

"I wrote out my story yesterday," Joe replied. "You said you read it. Isn't it in your file?"

"Yes, I have your form in here," she said, laying her hand on the folder. "But I would like to hear you relate the story. It will help me get a better feel for your relationship with your adoptive parents and your search for your birth parents."

She could tell from his expression that Joe didn't think it was necessary to go through his story again, but after a moment's delay, he began the story. Brenda had read through Joe's inquiry form several times last night, and what he told her now was just as she remembered it—except for the added detail she had hoped to hear. Occasionally, she interrupted to ask more about his home in Pittsburgh, his adoptive parents, his schooling, his friends, and his parents' divorce.

Brenda bored in on the topic of Joe's relationship with his adoptive father. "We were never very close," he said, head down and searching the tabletop. "Maybe he was doing the best he could with what he had. Mom told me when I turned thirteen that my father had been against the adoption in the beginning. She had talked him into it, and she apologized for not giving me a good father."

Brenda fought hard to keep her sadness from showing on her face. "How did you feel when your mother told you that?" she said. Joe had written nothing about this on his form.

"In a way, I was relieved," he said. "It wasn't that my father was against me personally as much as he was against having a kid at all. It kind of explained his distance. At the same time, I think it brought Mom and me closer. She wanted me all along, and she still wanted me."

Joe grew more solemn as he related the events leading up to his adoptive mother's death. Brenda could sense his deep admiration for the woman. She also noted that the pall of grief was still upon him, and she choked back tears of her own.

Finding her courage, she asked, "Do you mind telling me about your scar?"

Joe looked at her, a mixture of puzzlement and irritation clouding his face. "What does that have to do with locating my birth parents?"

"Nothing really, and I'm sorry if I offended you," she said. "You don't have to tell me about it. It was a personal question, not an official one."

The young man relaxed a little at her apology. "It happened when I was a little kid. I was rough-housing in the living room and fell into a plate glass window." He explained how his father raced him to the hospital as blood seeped through the towel Joe held against his slashed face.

The mental picture brought a wave of grief that turned Brenda's stomach, but she held herself together. "Thank you for sharing that with me," she said.

Then she quickly changed the subject. "Will you tell me about the letter your mother gave you near the end, the one from your birth mother?"

"I didn't write about that on my form," Joe said.

"I know, but Kathryn—my coworker—mentioned that you told her about a letter your adoptive mother gave you just before she died."

"I call her my mother, not my *adoptive* mother," Joe said.

"I'm sorry," she said. "Yes, she was your mother." Brenda sensed that the young man's tolerance for questions was wearing thin, so she added, "This is my last question for today. Whatever you can tell me will be helpful."

"And how soon will I know something about my birth parents?"

Brenda tried to convey her assurance through a smile. "Like I said, I'm putting your case on the fast track."

Joe told his story. He related his surprise and shock when his dying mother gave him the letter his birth mother had sent along with him as the adoption was finalized. "Mom admitted that she kept the letter hidden because she didn't want me to leave her in search of my birth mother," Joe explained. "I told her I never would have done that. She was my mother, and that's all I needed to know. That letter actually brought us even closer for those last few weeks. I think she finally realized that I loved her, that I was proud to be her son."

"What did the letter say?" she probed, realizing she was asking another question.

Joe didn't seem to mind. "It was very short, just a few lines. Maybe she dashed it off at the last minute, just in time to tuck into my diaper bag. She said three things: "Please forgive me for giving you away; I will always love you; I pray we will meet again someday."

Brenda stood up abruptly. "I need to get something out of my car. I'll be right back." Leaving her briefcase and Joe's file folder behind, she grabbed her small beige purse and hurried toward the parking lot.

She walked to the back of the Honda and popped the trunk open. Shielded from the young man's sight by the trunk lid, Brenda burst into a storm of tears, stifling the sound of her sobs with a wad of tissues pressed to her mouth.

Twenty-four

JOE PONDERED HIS CONVERSATION with Ms. Brenda Long as he awaited her return from the car. The county worker had looked him up on her day off, apparently putting his request for birth parent information on the "fast track." Weird. The woman had peppered him with questions about his background and adoptive family as if she didn't believe a word of what he wrote in his inquiry. Weird. And she was so into her work that she was emotionally touched by his story—to the point of tears. Very weird.

The woman appeared to be in her forties. She was well-dressed and well-groomed, plain but not unattractive. She seemed intelligent and articulate, a knowledgeable and capable civil servant. This same person in the governmental system in Pittsburgh would likely be a cool, businesslike, by-the-book kind of worker. He could not imagine a county employee back home giving up personal time to grease the slow-moving wheels of bureaucracy. Joe chalked it up to the cultural differences between urban and rural life, or perhaps between the east and the west.

Still, he was ready to be done with Brenda Long for today. She had more than enough information about him. He was tired of revisiting the details of his mother's life and death which had picked at the scab of his slowly healing grief. Now if Brenda Long would be just as diligent at digging up information about Wallace Ray and Becky Ruth Barnes.

The woman returned from the car after three or four minutes. She was carrying a sturdy paper sack with handles. As she sat down, Joe noticed that her eyes were rimmed with red. She had been crying again.

"Is there anything wrong, ma'am?" he said. He flashed back to Thomas Rasby's breakdown earlier in the day and wished there was someone else around in case the woman fell apart on him for some reason.

She ignored his question. "I have something very important to say to you. Then I want to leave you some things and let you think about it."

Joe just waited, saying nothing. The thought crossed his mind that this woman was not really a county worker at all, but that she was some kind of emotional wacko who stole his papers and got a morbid thrill out of invading people's lives.

Her words came out slowly and carefully, as if she was afraid they might spill and cause a big mess. "If everything you have told me today is true, then I think your birth mother has been located." She barely finished before clouding up again. Tears spilled down both cheeks before she could catch them with a tissue.

Joe studied her for several moments. "Yes, what I told you, what I wrote on the form, it's all true," he said emphatically. "What do you mean that my birth mother has been located? You haven't even looked for her yet."

The woman held together and pressed on. "Twenty-four years ago, I unofficially changed my given name because I didn't like it. I got over it eventually and started calling myself Brenda again. But during my late teens and early twenties I preferred to be called Becky...Becky Ruth."

Joe just stared at her. *She is wacko*, he thought. *She's trying to pass herself off as my birth mother.*

"I was a wild, rebellious girl back then. I got myself pregnant at age eighteen, and I talked my boyfriend into marrying me. But it didn't last. He ran away when I was six months pregnant, and I have never seen him since. His name was Wallace Ray Barnes, and I was known as Becky Ruth Barnes. I named my baby Daniel Lee Barnes."

"Just a minute, lady," Joe said, standing. "I don't know what your game is, but I've had enough of it. Maybe you work in the county auditor's office and maybe you don't. Somehow—I don't know how—my papers fell into your hands. It's all in there—my birth parents' names, my birth name, the dates. You have some angle, some scheme, and you're playing on my emotions to make it work. But you haven't told me anything yet to prove to me that you are anything but a con artist or a psycho."

The woman remained remarkably calm. "I don't blame you for not believing me," she said, her tears well in check now. "I didn't believe it myself when I first saw your inquiry form yesterday. That's why I came out here today, why I grilled you about your background. I had to be sure. I was afraid someone may have been playing a cruel joke on me."

"What do you mean?" Joe said, hands on his hips.

"If you will give me a few more minutes, I'll try to explain."

A soft, warm breeze wafted through the trees above, creating a moving kaleidoscope of light and shadow on the table and lawn around them. The droning of Thomas' mower continued as he methodically worked his way across the cemetery lawn. Joe had the urge to get away, to climb on the Harley and ride. But the woman was right. From her perspective, he was the con artist or the psycho, playing on her emotions for some hidden or hurtful purpose. He had to hear her out, so he sat down again.

"Shortly after I gave my baby up for adoption, I had the marriage annulled and moved to Seattle. I took a job with King County and worked up to a supervisory position in the auditor's office there. I didn't plan to get into records; that's just where I ended up. Along the way, I married a coworker, Dennis Long, and I started calling myself by my legal name again. We were unable to have children, and Dennis did not want to adopt, so we remained childless."

Joe stole a glance at Brenda's ring finger to confirm what he had noticed earlier. She was not wearing a ring.

"The years went by, and before we knew it, Dennis and I celebrated our twentieth anniversary. Two days later he ran a red light downtown and was broad-sided by a bus. He died instantly. That was five months ago."

The woman paused to quell a fresh outpouring of tears.

"I'm...I'm sorry," Joe said. Then he silently remonstrated himself for saying anything. The woman who called herself Brenda Long hadn't proven anything yet.

She continued. "I never stopped thinking about my baby, wondering where he was, hoping he was healthy and happy. It occurred to me that he might want to reconnect with his birth parents some day. I was determined never to intrude into his life, but if he decided to look for me, I would welcome such a reunion. Knowing that you—I mean, *he*—would probably start looking here in the valley, I decided to move back…just in case. So I was able to get a job in Yarborough County."

Joe squirmed on his chair. She didn't sound like a wacko now, and if she was conning him, she was a top-rate liar.

"I never really believed anything could come of it," Brenda went on, "until yesterday when your inquiry came across my desk. But I was skeptical, just like you are. So I had to check you out. And now, I am sure that you are the child I gave up for adoption twenty-four years ago."

"How can you be sure?"

"The letter," Brenda answered. "You knew the contents of the letter I scratched out and slipped into your diaper bag before handing you to the adoption agent."

"Maybe the other lady at the office yesterday just told *you* about the letter," Joe posed. "After all, I revealed what it said; you didn't tell me."

"Yes, you have grounds for skepticism too," she answered. "But let me tell you one more part of my story."

Joe listened eagerly.

"When Wallace left me, I was eighteen years old, six months pregnant, and very alone. The only one I had in the world was my baby, who was still in the womb, so I began keeping a journal of sorts, writing letters to my baby. Through the remainder of my pregnancy, I wrote a page every two or three days—nothing very important, just my thoughts and feelings, things I would tell a close friend. I also wrote down my hopes and dreams for my child and his future.

"After delivery, I decided that the best thing for my baby was adoption. Once I made the decision, it all happened very quickly. The agency called one morning, informing me that a suitable couple had been found. I didn't know anything about them—their names, where they lived. The lady from the agency arrived before noon to take you away. You were only two weeks old."

Brenda dropped her head into her hand and fought back tears. Joe noticed that she did not correct herself. She said, "take *you* away," not "take *my* baby away." He decided to overlook it.

"I had just a few minutes left with you, so I took my journal and scribbled off a quick note to you. Like you said earlier, it's wasn't very profound…just a mother's last wishes. I tore the note out of my journal, tucked it into the diaper bag, and said goodbye."

Brenda reached into the large bag which was sitting at her feet. She placed on the table in front of her a stack of four dog-eared books, each of them no more than an inch thick. "I never stopped writing to…my Danny," she said, touching the journals. "I had no reason to believe that you would ever read them, but I wrote anyway, telling you about my life, wondering about yours."

She paused to dab her nose with a tissue. Joe could not take his eyes off the books sitting in front of her.

She picked up the top book, found a small slip of paper serving as a book mark, and opened to that page. Looking up at Joe, she said, "Do you still have it?" she asked.

Joe knew what she meant. He reached for the billfold in his back pocket and extracted a folded sheet of paper and unfolded it. It was old and discolored. As he spread it out, Brenda slid the journal across the table, opened to the stubby remains of a sheet which had been hastily torn out.

Joe carefully placed the letter into the book, sliding its jagged edge next to the stub between the pages. The edges matched perfectly. The letter had been torn from this very book. Joe stifled an expletive of amazement. Brenda simply smiled contentedly. She knew the page would fit.

"I want you to have these journals," she said, sliding the other three volumes across the table. "Read them if you like—they're all addressed to Danny, which is what I have called you all these years. Then, if you want to meet again, feel free to call me. My number is inside the back cover of the last book."

She stood, picked up her purse, and pulled out her keys. "I have no intention of barging into your life. Nor do I expect you to change your life in order to fit me in. I just thank God that he allowed me to see you again, to realize that you are all right and that you have turned into a fine young man. I would love to talk to you again, but it's completely up to you."

Joe stood. "I...I don't know what to say." He glanced down at the books, then up at her again. "This is...incredible. I... I..." He couldn't find words.

Brenda smiled, almost laughed. "I've had twenty-four hours to get used to the idea that you might be my son. It sounds like you need some time to let this sink in. Take all the time you need."

She stepped away from the table. "Thank you for telling me your story. Thank you for coming to Washington to look for me. Thank you for...today."

She began walking to her car. Joe caught up with her. "I will call you," he said.

"That would be wonderful. Goodbye...Joe."

Joe let her go on. Should he have shaken her hand? Should he have hugged her and kissed her as family members do? No, not yet. Brenda was still a stranger to him. He needed to find out more about her. He needed to start reading the journals.

The Honda left the parking lot and turned north toward Yarborough. Joe watched it go until it disappeared behind a roadside crop of eye-high sweet corn.

Twenty-five

THE BOSS LET HIM OFF WORK at 5:30 today, and Jud couldn't be happier. Sometimes he had to work until after 9:00 on Saturday nights. Jud didn't much care for his boss, who barely paid him a living wage. But he smiled and said, "Thank you, have a nice night. See you in the morning."

When he got to his tiny, musty apartment, Jud didn't feel like eating a TV dinner and hunkering down in front of the TV with a six-pack for the night. It was Saturday night—party night in town, although that usually didn't mean much to him this late in the month. Jud got paid on the first, and after about three weeks he was usually down to his last sawbuck. But May was different—*way* different. This month he had plenty of money to party, and it would be like this for many months to come.

It was as if God just handed it to him and said, "Judson, have yourself a high old time on me." It couldn't have been easier. He had heard about a box of greenbacks stashed in a drawer out at the old country church. A big, noisy storm brews up to cover him while he makes the snatch, and a transient biker is right there to take the blame. Jud laughed out loud at his good fortune.

Jud rolled a cigarette, lit it, and took a long, bitter drag. After propping his smoke in an ashtray he had swiped from a hotel he and his boss had stayed at once, he retrieved the money box from under his bed and set it on the soiled chenille bedspread. The lock was busted, so he lifted the lid, pulled out the four bundles, and commenced to count them once again. When he had a pile totaling $5,000, he took another, long satisfying puff on the cigarette.

He had never been very good with numbers, especially big ones, so he had to start over twice and roll another smoke. *Twenty-one thousand three hundred and forty-five dollars. Or was it twenty-two thousand?* Then he laughed again and cursed. *What's the difference? I'm one rich cowboy and it's time to start enjoying the fruits of my labor!*

Leaving the money spread out on the bed, Jud changed into clean jeans and a western cut shirt, pulled on his best boots, slicked back his hair, and splashed on plenty of aftershave. Returning to the bed, he snapped up a small wad of hundreds and peeled off five of them. He'd never spent half a grand partying in his life, and he probably wouldn't tonight, but it felt good having it rolled up in his jeans pocket.

Jud gathered the rest of the bills into bundles, secured them with rubber bands, stashed the bundles in the metal box, and shoved the box under his bed. Turning out the lights, he grabbed his favorite cap from the rack mounted by the front door. Then he stopped. This was his work hat, but it was party time, not work time. So he returned the cap to the rack and selected his straw cowboy hat. Tugging it on, he checked the mirror. Satisfied, he gave himself a quick salute, stepped outside, and locked the door behind him.

•   •   •

Joe took the highway into Yarborough to a Mexican restaurant he had seen yesterday. He took Brenda's journals with him and began reading the first one as he waited in the noisy cantina for a table in the crowded dining room. Finally settled at a table for two with a tamale combination plate and beer, he continued to read.

The earliest entries in the journal told about Brenda's shock, confusion, and then excitement at being pregnant. She talked about Wallace Barnes a lot, obviously smitten with him. They had met at a party in Yarborough, started dating, and ended up in bed. There was a devil-may-care tone to her entries. Her mother—just "Mom" in the journal—was deeply hurt that she had gotten pregnant out of wedlock, and "Dad" was incensed.

Brenda was sorry she had hurt her mother, but she seemed to be glad that she had touched off her father. She was a wild one, all right.

After supper, Joe withdrew some cash from an ATM and bought supplies and cigarettes at the local market. He thought about stopping at Velma's to see if Chessy was there. He was still a little numb from his visit with Brenda Long. Part of him wanted to tell someone about it, and he wanted to see Chessy again, but he decided he wasn't quite ready to talk to anyone about the sudden appearance of his birth mother.

Returning to the church, he was flagged down by Thomas. The caretaker said he would not be building a campfire tonight since not many could come. The minister had returned from the emergency room with a severely sprained ankle and a few cuts and bruises, Rich was preparing a sermon for tomorrow morning, and Chessy was staying in town with Velma tonight. Joe was glad for the change of plans. He had some serious reading to do.

Joe sat down at the picnic table in the hollow to read Brenda's journals in the warm twilight. He didn't miss the stifling humidity of the east which kept his clothes sticky with perspiration. Had Brenda not given him up for adoption, he likely would have grown up here in Washington, perhaps even in this valley. It was a pleasant thought.

Most of the early pages of Brenda's journal were filled with sentimentality and angst, a teenage girl's emotions exploding into words. Joe halfway expected to see dried teardrops dotting the pages, but the words were more sober during the second half of the pregnancy. The honeymoon was over. Wallace and Brenda—Becky at that time—were not getting along. Wallace lost his job, got another one, and then lost that job. Becky was working part-time as a restaurant hostess in Yarborough.

The more Joe read about his birth father, the more he disliked him. The guy was a loser, a girl chaser. Joe suspected that Wallace had no intention of sticking around to take care of a wife and raise a kid. Marrying the girl he had impregnated was only an act. When Wallace got what he wanted out of Brenda, he would leave her high and dry, and great with child. Joe cursed his luck. He had been saddled with two fathers in his lifetime, both of them losers.

After Wallace finally left Becky, the journal pages focused more on "Danny," the name Becky had already selected for the little boy, Daniel— or if a girl, Danielle—she would soon bear. *We're going to do this and that, Danny. You and I are going to be so close, Danny.* Clearly, Becky's hopes were mounting that a child would fill her loneliness and provide purpose for her life.

There was a significant gap in journal entries before April 23rd— Joe's birthday. A month earlier, Becky gave up her job at the restaurant and the apartment she and Wallace had rented. She moved into a home for unwed mothers where Daniel Lee Barnes was born. Joe couldn't imagine growing up as Daniel Barnes or Danny Barnes or Dan Barnes. He had to keep reminding himself that the Danny he was reading about was him.

Darkness closed in on the valley, so Joe moved into his tent for the night. He switched on the battery-powered lantern he had bought in town to read a little while longer.

In one of her first entries after the baby's birth, Becky broached the subject of adoption. *I love you, Danny, more than I have loved anyone or anything,* she wrote, *but I don't know if I can give you the best home. You may never have a father to play ball with. What kind of a life is that for a little boy?*

A few pages later, Becky announced to Danny her decision to give up him up for adoption. She apologized profusely—*I'm so sorry. I love you so much. I can't believe I'm doing this. It breaks my heart.* The next time Becky wrote in her journal, little Daniel Lee Barnes of Yarborough, Washington was gone. Unknown to his mother, he had become Joseph Martino Caruso of Pittsburgh, Pennsylvania.

Joe snapped the book shut and dropped it beside his sleeping bag. He lit a cigarette and switched off the lantern to smoke in the dark. It was nearly midnight. The tent flaps were tied open so he could see the stars in between puffs of cigarette smoke.

He was angry at Becky Barnes, and he was angry at the person she had become—Brenda Long. Joe ran his hand slowly across the side of his face, feeling the familiar lines of an old scar. *Had Becky Barnes realized what kind of father her son would grow up with,* he thought, *she would never have signed those papers.* He wished Mom was still alive. He wanted to thank her again for not giving up on him when Dominic Caruso was finally out of their lives.

After a final puff, Joe ground out the butt and flicked it outside. He didn't fall asleep until after 1:00 A.M.

•   •   •

It took all evening, but Jud succeeded in blowing two of the Franklins he had brought with him to Paco's Restaurant and Cantina in Yarborough. The "grande combo" of chile rellano, beef enchilada, rice, and beans—washed down with three margaritas—had only set him back $60. But he stayed in the cantina boot scooting' until almost midnight and treated several unattached females on the floor to drinks.

Climbing into the old red Ford pickup his boss let him drive as his own, Jud assessed that the evening would have been perfect except for one thing: seeing the biker from the church sitting at a table when he walked in. The guy, whose name was Joe, had his face buried in a book while eating supper, so Jud had asked for a spot on the other side of the restaurant. The kid never saw him. Of that, Jud was sure. But Jud saw him, and it made him mad.

Why wasn't the kid in jail by now? He knew the cops had found the screwdriver he had purposely left in the office, and he knew they had traced the tool back to the biker in the hollow. Why hadn't they locked him up for burglary? They had him dead to rights, but there he was in Paco's, feeding his face and reading a book like he didn't have a care in the world.

Jud figured that if the cops weren't sure Joe was guilty they might be looking for someone else. That made Jud very uncomfortable. He didn't want the cops to *wonder* if Joe stole the money; he wanted them to be *sure*. He wanted Joe in jail so he could spend his windfall right under the cops' noses.

Jud turned over the engine and ground into gear. Apparently, the cops needed more proof. So, he decided right there in Paco's parking lot to give it to them. By 3:00 A.M., he had planted another item of evidence against the biker in the hollow.

Twenty-six

JOE HAD PLANNED TO SPEND SUNDAY MORNING reading the journals. As much as he disliked his birth mother's decision to give him up, he had decided to give her the benefit of the doubt. Right or wrong, good or bad, she did what she did, and there was nothing either of them could do about it. Joe felt he owed it to his birth mother to read her story.

The chiming of the church bell at 9:30 A.M. reminded him that the Sunday service would begin in half an hour. Church attendance had never been a big part of Joe's life. His parents were lapsed Catholics before adopting him. Joe had attended a Baptist Sunday school with a friend when he was ten, but the kids there were just as cruel to him about his blemished appearance as any of the kids in public school, so Joe never went back.

Here, the melodic chimes pealing over the valley called to him. For one thing, Chessy would surely be there, as well as other people Joe had grown to like, such as Bradford and Esther McDermot, Thomas Rasby, and Ezra the minister—if he was able to hobble from the parsonage to the sanctuary. Dr. Rich was supposed to deliver the sermon. Joe had enjoyed their fireside chat, and he was intrigued to hear what the professor would say.

Furthermore, Joe was curious to see what impact yesterday's verbal skirmish over the property might have on the congregation. Would there be another shouting match between Chet Rasby and Jethro Haig and others who lined up on opposite sides of the issue? Joe wanted to find out. It could be entertaining if nothing else.

Joe decided to attend the service. He cleaned up and put on the pants and shirt he had worn to the county auditor's office. Not very "churchy," but they would have to do. He walked up the slope and across the cemetery to the church, joining a small throng of worshipers entering the building. Thomas Rasby was waiting at the door to greet people. His face lit up as Joe came up the cement stairs.

"Joe, you came to church!" he exclaimed, pumping Joe's hand furiously. He looked none the worse for wear from yesterday's emotional trauma. "You'll like the service, Joe. Missus Walls will play the organ, and Doctor Rich will bring the sermon. Chessy and me, we'll be down front. You can sit with us." Joe forced a smile and kept walking. No way was he sitting near the front of the church, even if Chessy was there. He slipped into a rear pew to the left and stepped past two old ladies in order to sit near the wall.

People entered in ones, twos, and threes to find their favorite pews. They were all old—no teenagers, no young couples, no children. He saw many men he remembered from the work party.

Jethro Haig entered alone. He was a widower, Joe had learned, with just his middle-aged, stand-offish stepson Rusty for company. Jethro greeted a number of people on the right side of the church. He paid little attention to the left side, and the reason became obvious when Joe noticed Chet Rasby and his wife sitting five rows ahead of him on left side. The left side was the Rasby side, and the right side was the McDermot side. Was the separation of the clans a coincidence or the manifestation of a house divided?

Just then Velma Walls and Chessy Carpenter walked in, heading down the center aisle for a seat in the front. She was beautiful in a white, sleeveless dress accented in navy blue. Joe did not want to seem eager, but he could not look away from her. He hoped she would look up and scan the congregation, searching for him. A moment later, as if triggered by his wish, she did. Seeing him, she smiled. Then she motioned subtly for him to come up front and join her. He declined with one small shake of the head. Chessy smiled again and sat down next to Velma. They were sitting on the McDermot side. So much for a house divided—at least totally divided.

The last to enter from the rear were Bradford and Esther McDermot, who strode quickly down the aisle and sat down in the third row, McDermot side. A side door opened, and Ezra Sturdevant came in on crutches. He moved directly to the empty front pew where he could elevate his ankle. He was followed by Dr. Rich. The professor's slacks, sport jacket, shirt, and tie were stylish. He took his place next to the minister.

During the first part of the service, Joe paid more attention to Chessy than to the hymn book one of the old ladies thrust into his hands. He made no pretense of singing hymns he had never heard before, although he enjoyed watching Chessy sing and Velma play the old Hammond organ.

Standing with the aid of crutches, Ezra explained to the congregation the receipt of the late Louise Wilkerson's surprise gift to the church and the burglary that took it away just as quickly. He tearfully confessed his fault in leaving the cash in the office on the night of the big storm and explained that the police were working to solve the crime and recover the money.

As the minister sat down, Bradford McDermot stood and addressed him, speaking for the small congregation, absolving him of responsibility and affirming their love and support for their pastor. Church members underscored the board chairman's statement with nods and applause. Thankfully, no one looked back toward him, suggesting that the police chief's visit with Joe in the hollow yesterday apparently had not triggered suspicion among the congregants.

Rich's sermon kept Joe's attention. It seemed to be an extension of their fireside conversation. The professor shared that all people were God's creation but were alienated and alone because of sin. He went on to say that Christ's death was meaningless unless Jesus was truly who he claimed to be. "If Christ was not the true Son of God," Rich stated emphatically, "then what he has to offer you and me is not real at all." Rich went on to offer convincing evidence that Christ was the Son of God and, therefore, a transformed relationship, including forgiveness of sin, was a reality.

When the service was concluded, Joe remained standing in his row as the parishioners exited. "How did you like the service?" Chessy asked brightly as she came up the center aisle toward him. She and Velma were among the last to leave the sanctuary. Velma went on as Chessy stopped to talk.

"Fine. Rich is a good speaker."

They stood at the back of the sanctuary and talked for several minutes about nothing much of consequence. Joe felt relaxed in her company. He wanted to spend more time with her.

"What are you going to do now?" Joe said.

"Relatives," she said with a thin smile and a sigh. "My mother's aunt and uncle are taking Uncle Thomas and me out for Sunday dinner."

"You don't sound thrilled."

"It will be fine."

"But not nearly as much fun as going for a ride on the Harley."

"Not nearly." Then she turned pink with embarrassment and looked around to see if anyone else had heard her say it.

"Maybe later then," Joe said. He wanted to tell her about Brenda and the journals. She would listen. She would understand. She would care.

Before she could respond, they heard hurried footsteps in the vestibule. "Chessy! Chessy!" It was Velma's voice, and there was keen urgency in her voice.

The secretary rushed into the sanctuary. Seeing Chessy she said, "Thomas needs you. Jethro and Chet started arguing in the parking lot, and your uncle is in tears."

Twenty-seven

JOE CAME UP BEHIND RICH, who was standing just outside the front doors. He seemed to have a good view of the action. Most of the church members were huddled in small groups, except for Ezra, Velma, and Chessy who were escorting the tearful Thomas to his cabin.

Joe kept his voice low. "What happened?"

"Jethro and Chet got into it again," the professor said at a whisper.

Joe easily spotted the two rivals. Each was at the center of two separate discussions on opposite sides of the walkway leading to the parking lot. Even Jethro's driver Rusty had been drawn away from the radio in the Cadillac to watch the conflict from the fringes of the congregation.

Rich continued. "A preacher always hopes that people want to talk about the sermon after church. But by the time I got out here, most everyone was debating the property issue. And like yesterday, Jethro and Chet and a few others kind of let their emotions get the best of them. For a minute I was afraid it would come to blows."

"What about Thomas?" Joe said.

"When he came outside, the words were flying hot and heavy across the sidewalk. He watched for a minute, then the tears started to flow. It breaks his heart to see these people bickering."

Bradford had been moving from group to group, trying to calm the troops. He stood on the sidewalk now. "Folks, listen to me please." It took a moment, but he finally collected the group's attention. "I know you have strong feelings about this issue, but snipping at each other about it is not the way to settle it. So as board chairman, I'm calling a congregational meeting for tomorrow evening at seven o'clock. I want you to come prayed up and ready to voice your concerns in a calm and logical manner."

"Nobody will ever change my mind," Chet Rasby called out, "I'm never going to vote to let that land go." A number of heads on Chet's side of the walkway nodded vigorously.

Bradford raised his hands in an attempt to quiet the two men, but Chet ignored his stop sign. "I can tell you right now, Jethro. If the church votes to sell that land, a lot of us will be leaving with it." This time, there was a chorus of agreement around him.

"That sounds real logical," Jethro said mockingly. "If you don't get your way, you're going to leave. Do you run away from all your problems?"

"Stop it right now, all of you!" Bradford boomed over the growing din. "I don't want to hear another word." His commanding voice and presence quieted the crowd immediately.

"I am so embarrassed in front of our guests," he went on, glancing back at Rich and Joe. "Now I want you all to go to your homes, eat your Sunday dinner, and think about this...this...travesty. Then you come back tomorrow night ready to discuss this calmly. And don't you dare come without spending some time in prayer."

No one moved. Bradford waited only a few seconds before barking, "Go on, now!" The church members began moving toward their cars and trucks without a word. Six minutes later, the parking lot was empty except for Bradford, Esther, Rich, and Joe.

Joe could see the dejection in Bradford's eyes. The board chairman apologized for the congregation's behavior, and he seemed on the verge of tears. Then he and Esther excused themselves to check on Thomas and the others before going home for dinner. Rich and Joe were left alone on the front steps.

"Looks like we're on our own," Rich said.

Joe nodded. He felt a little shell-shocked from the outburst.

"I need to go into Yarborough to get a few things," Rich said. "Do you want to ride along and grab a burger? I won't be gone too long."

It was a warm and genuine invitation. Joe sensed that Rich enjoyed his company and that he wasn't at all bothered by Joe's religious skepticism.

And Rich was one of the few people who knew about the stolen money, but he had never once intimated a suspicion that Joe was behind it.

Still, he felt torn. He was captivated by Brenda's story. He had planned to spend the afternoon reading, trying to learn more about her and perhaps about himself, but being with Rich for a couple of hours sounded appealing. And he had to get something to eat anyway.

"Sure, a burger sounds great," he said.

With Thomas' permission, Joe locked his Harley in the equipment shed. Then he hopped into Rich's Jeep for the ride into town. On the way, they talked about the church conflict they were witnessing. Rich was less concerned about which side was right than about how the people were allowing the issue to drive a wedge between them. He was especially worried that half the church could leave, depending on how the people voted on the property. Joe sensed that the man cared deeply for the church as a whole, as he had evidenced in his sermon.

Rich said that he would be staying around another week. "Ezra would like me to preach again next Sunday since he's not likely to be on his feet by then," he explained. "And he said he would appreciate the moral support this week in the midst of the upheaval among the members."

Joe was glad to hear that Rich would be staying.

Over burgers, fries, and Cokes, they talked about motorcycles, sports cars, engineering fields, and workout regimens. In response to Rich's questions, Joe extolled the manifold virtues of the Harley-Davidson and explained that he was leaning toward a career in civil engineering. "As long as people use toilets," he quipped, "civil engineers will be in high demand." The comment gave Rich a good laugh.

Joe cautiously introduced the subject of Rich being in his forties and still single. "Yes, I would like to be married someday," he said while dragging a french fry through a small pond of ketchup on his plate. "But only to the right woman. And so far, I just haven't found her."

Rich turned the question back to Joe. "What about you? Do you have a girlfriend back home?"

If he did, Joe thought, it would embarrass him to admit it to Rich. Joe was sure his interest in Chessy had not escaped the professor's notice. "No, not me," he said. "I don't have time for a girlfriend." That sounded pretty stupid, Joe thought. He could always find time for a girl; he just couldn't find a girl who had time for him. He hoped Chessy was the exception he had been waiting for.

"Who was that woman you were talking with late yesterday?" Rich asked. "I came to the sink for a glass of water about 5:30. I saw you out the kitchen window. You were sitting at the table out back talking to someone."

Joe searched his plate, trying to decide how to respond. He picked up a slice of dill pickle he had pulled out of his hamburger. He didn't care for dills. He ate it anyway, thinking.

Finally, he said, "That woman claims she is my birth mother, and I think she might be right."

Rich's eyes widened. "Your birth mother?" he said discreetly, as though trying to keep a secret. "There must be a story behind this."

It wasn't a demand to tell all. It wasn't even a request. But the interest in Rich's expression said, "I'd love to hear about it if you want to talk."

Joe told his story, beginning with his birth and adoption in Yarborough, continuing with his decision to come west in search of his birth parents, and culminating with Brenda Long's visit to the church yesterday and the captivating journals she had left with him. Hearing himself tell the story, it sounded to him like something out of a syrupy novel.

Rich kept shaking his head and saying, "That's amazing." He asked questions which drew out Joe's thoughts and feelings about what was happening as much as the details of the story.

"I am very happy for you, Joe," he said as they left the restaurant. "What are you going to do now?"

"I'm going to read the journals, then I'll probably call her."

Rich kept digging. "Then what?"

Joe had already asked himself that question, but he didn't have an answer. "I don't know," he said. "Maybe we just shake hands and go on with our lives."

Joe had one more thing to say about his story, but it took him several minutes to say it. "I plan to tell Chessy about my birth mother. But until I do, I would appreciate it if you didn't say anything to her."

"No problem, Joe," Rich said. "It's your news to tell. I won't say a word."

Joe spotted the police car in the church parking lot from a quarter mile away. He could see two uniformed officers standing beside it, waiting. "What's this all about?" Rich wondered aloud as he turned into the driveway. Joe's stomach knotted in dread. He feared they were waiting for him. Rich parked four spaces away from the patrol car.

Stepping out of the Jeep, Joe recognized Chief George Jurgen, but the other officer was new to him. He was younger, taller, and burlier than the Latino officer who was with the chief yesterday. Only the short-sleeve brown uniform shirt and badge identified him as a policeman. He was also wearing faded blue jeans and old basketball shoes. Joe assumed he was one of the part-time officers on Chief Jurgen's tiny force.

"Will you step over to the car please, Mister Caruso?" the chief asked, all business-like.

Joe complied while Rich stood by the Jeep to watch.

At the chief's direction, Joe emptied his pockets on the trunk lid and assumed the pat-down search position. The chief quickly inspected Joe's wallet while the husky officer he called Nate patted him down. Without another word from the chief, Nate pulled Joe's hands behind him and snapped on the handcuffs.

"Hey, what's this for, Chief?" Joe argued. He had been handcuffed once before in his life and hated it.

"Suspicion of burglary," the chief said, slipping Joe's wallet and loose change into a plastic bag.

"Just because of a screwdriver? That's ridiculous."

"The screwdriver and this," the chief said as he inserted a key in the trunk lock of the patrol car. He turned the key, and the lid popped open. Joe's black leather saddlebag was inside. And next to it, lying on top of a plastic grocery sack, was a metal box with a busted lock. "We found this right where you buried it in the brush next to your camp. The minister identified it as the box stolen from the church office. We haven't found the money yet, so we're taking you to the station. You can tell us all about it there. Read him his rights, Nate."

As Nate read monotone Miranda rights from a card, Joe fought hard against the urge to lash out—to curse and kick and resist in any way he could. He knew it would only make things worse, but old habits are difficult to tame. When asked if he understood his rights, he hissed acknowledgement.

"Your motorcycle is still in the shed," the chief said, slamming the trunk lid. "You have somebody to watch out for it?"

Joe glanced at Rich who offered a weak smile and a don't-worry-about-it wave. The chief tossed Rich the keys. Then Officer Nate guided Joe into the back seat of the patrol car and shut the door.

As Joe left the church in the custody of the Orchard Valley Police, one menacing thought drummed in his brain: he'd been set up.

Twenty-eight

JOE REGARDED HIS INTERROGATION AS A JOKE. He answered
every question truthfully, and for many of them the truthful answer was,
"I don't know."

"How did your screwdriver end up in the church office after the
burglary?"

"I don't know."

"How did the empty money box end up buried near your campsite?"

"I don't know."

"Where is the money now?"

"I don't know. I never saw the money."

And whenever Joe stated his conviction that someone was setting him
up to take the rap for the crime, they asked him, "Who?"

"I don't know."

"Why is this mystery person setting you up?"

"Probably because I'm an easy target."

After forty-five minutes on this merry-go-round, the chief fingerprinted
Joe and ushered him to a cell, one of only two in the small police facility,
the other one being vacant. Suspects arrested by the Orchard Valley police
were held at the station for processing and interrogation. If inmates were
eligible for bail but it was not posted, they were moved within twenty-
four hours to the county jail in Yarborough.

"A county detective is going to come by in a day or two and dust the
box for prints," the chief told Joe. "You're probably too smart to leave
prints, but we still have enough to hold you. The judge will decide what

to do with you at a hearing, but you'll be lucky to see him in a week's time."

"My rights said I get a lawyer, a public defender."

"Yeah, Seth Uelander will come in sometime today to talk to you," explained the chief reluctantly. "He's a hotshot lawyer who's trying to climb the ladder in the county, so he still makes jail calls on Sunday."

"What about bail?" Joe asked the chief.

"I called the county D.A. at home. Bail is set at five grand. Is there anyone around here who will post your bail?"

Joe dropped his head. "Probably not."

"You get a phone call, you know. Is there anyone you want to call?"

Joe had met a lot of wonderful people during his few days in Washington, some who could easily cover his bail. He wasn't about to impose on any of them. If his mom was alive, he could call her, and she might help him out. Brenda Long apparently was his birth mother, but Joe didn't feel any better about calling on her than on his other recent acquaintances. "No," he answered, shaking his head.

Left alone in the cell, Joe pondered his predicament. The evidence was stacked against him, and perhaps the real thief had fabricated even more evidence intended to sink him. There was no one to post his bail and no one to look for the real culprit. He was stuck and out of ideas. He had plenty of time to kill.

"God, what's happening to me?" He intended "God" as a curse, but then thought about what he had just said aloud in his cell. It hadn't ever bothered him before. Maybe it was because he had been surrounded by decent church people that he felt embarrassed about using God's name that way. So he added in a whisper, "Sorry about that. But if you can help me out here, I'd sure appreciate it."

After pacing the cell for several minutes Joe accepted that he would probably be here or in Yarborough County Jail until he was formally charged in a few days. He called out to Nate, whom the chief had left in the office while he went on another call. The officer stepped to the barred window of the cell door.

"There are some books in my saddlebag—journals," Joe explained. "May I have them please? I'd like to read."

"They're not stolen property, are they?" the officer asked.

"No, they belonged to my mother. It's a long story. I'd just like to read them."

Joe could see Officer Nate pull out the four volumes and inspect them for hidden weapons or drugs. Satisfied that the books were harmless, he passed them through the barred window.

The eight-by-eight cell had a narrow cot with a thin mattress and even thinner foam pillow. There was a stainless steel toilet in the corner. Joe flopped on the cot, doubled the pillow behind his head, and began reading where he had left off.

I suppose you want to know something about your extended family, the next page in the journal began. Becky was alone when she wrote these pages, Joe realized. Her son, Daniel Lee, had already been transported to Pittsburgh and given a new name. How did I get there? Joe wondered. Did my adoptive parents fly out to pick me up? Did they drive out as I did recently on the Harley? Apparently Becky Ruth Barnes knew nothing about where he went or how.

To be honest, your grandfather—my dad—is a drunk and a wife-beater. He slaps Mom around for the lamest reasons: the meatloaf wasn't cooked right, his best shirt wasn't ironed, etc. It made me scream inside. I schemed about putting rat poison in my father's liquor bottle, but I could never actually do it. If he didn't die, he would probably kill me. And if he did die, I would go to prison for life or to the gas chamber.

Page after page described the man's abuse and Brenda's rage over it. Joe felt anger building in him for this evil monster of a husband and father.

I always got along with mom, but Dad and I started butting heads early, and it only got worse as I got older. Truth be told, Dad not only slapped Mom around, but we had our own private war going on. My younger brother and sister (I'll write to you about them someday) always toed the line, and Dad didn't do much to them. But his rules were ridiculous, so I didn't pay much attention to them. And he made sure I paid for it.

When I turned fifteen and began trying out my wings of independence, Dad turned his anger toward me when he was drunk. If I was late for supper or if I slept in too late on Saturday morning or if I talked on the phone too long or if my room was messy, I got a beating with the strap. And if I talked back to him or tried to grab the strap, he just beat me more. He never broke the skin, but I always had at least one welt on my backside or legs from his punishment.

Joe pictured Brenda sitting across the table from him yesterday. He couldn't believe she wrote these lines. Becky Barnes and Brenda Long seemed like completely different persons. Joe could not visualize the nicely-dressed, articulate county records supervisor as a rebellious teenager who was physically abused by her father.

Joe's reading was interrupted by the arrival of Seth Uelander, the lawyer from the county public defender's office. Even premature baldness couldn't hide that the tubby counselor wasn't much older than Joe.

Uelander didn't shake hands, didn't even sit down in the visitor's area. Glancing at the arrest sheet, he scoffed at the "flimsy circumstantial evidence" which got him arrested. He said the judge would throw it out of court in a New York minute at the hearing on Thursday or Friday. Joe hoped he was right. The lawyer said he would be in touch and left.

Joe returned to the journal.

One day, in the middle of one of his drunken beatings, something inside me snapped. I wasn't going to take it any more. I flew at my father like a cornered cat, slapping him, scratching him, trying to hurt him. He is a big man, and I probably didn't hurt him very much. Instead, he just got more violent with me, using his hands instead of a strap. I lost the bout, but I vowed never to let him touch me without striking back, no matter how badly he hurt me. And whenever he started pushing Mom around, I would fly into the middle of him with my fists swinging, only to get knocked down again.

Nate, the jail officer for the day, opened his cell door and handed him a white sack with the logo of a fast food restaurant. It contained two cheap burgers, an order of cold french fries, and a large cup of water. *Dinner compliments of the taxpayers of Orchard Valley,* he thought wryly. He nibbled on one of the burgers as he continued to read.

It occurred to Joe that Becky had not mentioned her father's name in her journal, nor had Brenda Long given her maiden name when they talked yesterday. Joe wanted to know more about the jerk who batted his mother and grandmother around. If "Dad" was still alive—and Joe hoped he was dead—Joe thought he might try to look up the old guy and tell him off.

When I turned seventeen, I'd had enough, so I left home. I hated to leave Mom and my brother and sister in that hell of a home, but I had to get out. I moved in with a girlfriend in Yarborough to finish my senior year there. Dad threatened to come after me and drag me home, but he never did. I had always hated my name— did I tell you that my real name is Brenda, not Becky?—mainly because it was the name Dad picked out for me. Mom had wanted to name me Rebekah after a woman in the Bible, so I changed my name to Becky—not legally, but that's how I filled out my registration forms at school in Yarborough.

Injected into the ongoing commentary about Becky's hatred for her father were entries tracking her weekly activities. She got off to a rough start after the baby was gone. She moved back in with a girlfriend from high school, but she yearned to be out on her own. The pages recorded a string of failed job interviews and Becky's increasing discouragement. *I have good work skills, Danny,* she wrote. *Why won't people give me a chance to demonstrate them? I can't stay with Annie too much longer. I have to get out on my own. I have to get a job. I just have to.*

In one way, I'm glad you don't have to suffer through this with me. I would have to place you in child care or something. Besides, it's best that you are not anywhere near my drunken excuse for a father. I'm afraid he might have hurt you in some way. But you will never have to be afraid of him, sweet baby. He never saw you, he never held you, and he never will. And it gave me great satisfaction to tell him that in a letter. I can never hurt him physically; he is too strong for me. But I can keep him from ever seeing or knowing his first grandchild and hope it hurts him as deeply as he has hurt me. Do you think I'm being too harsh?

Joe thought about the question. No, it wasn't too harsh. Joe supposed it wasn't harsh enough for what she had suffered.

The page concluded, *I'm comforted to know that you are being loved and cared for by a mom and dad who are devoted to you. But I still miss you, my Danny darling. Wherever you are, part of my heart will always be with you.*

Joe read a few more pages until Becky had finally secured a full-time job as a waitress. She said it wasn't the best job in Yarborough, but it allowed her to get a small apartment and start her life at the age of nineteen. *I don't want to be a waitress all my life, Danny. I have too much potential for that. Maybe Yarborough is too confining for me. Maybe I need to break away, get out of this city, and really see what I can do. Maybe I need to move to someplace like Seattle.*

Joe laid the book down and smiled to himself. Becky Ruth Barnes eventually did move to Seattle, she had told him, and she did all right for herself. He suddenly felt very proud of the woman who had given birth to him. She wasn't satisfied with the status quo. She had the drive to make something happen, a drive he shared. And she had pulled it off.

Suddenly Nate's face appeared in the window. "Caruso, you have a visitor."

Joe jumped up and peered past the officer to see a young blonde sitting on the other side of the screen in the small visiting area outside the cell. "Chessy!"

• • •

Jud had to work a few hours Sunday morning as usual. It was tough to rise and dress by 9:00 A.M. after his late night at Paco's and even later activities out in the country. It had been as easy planting the empty metal box near the biker's camp as it was stealing the box when it was full of cash. He had even thought to wipe the box down with rubbing alcohol to remove his fingerprints, just like he saw once on TV. After cleaning it, Jud kept his leather gloves on until the box was buried. It would have been better if he could somehow have gotten Joe's prints on the box, but at least his own were not.

Jud had done a fair bit of shoplifting and burglary in the past with a few misdemeanor arrests. But that was only nickel and dime stuff. This little caper netted him over twenty grand without breaking a sweat, and somebody else was going to take the fall for it. Relishing the thrill of his success and new found wealth, Jud challenged himself to keep his sites set high. It would be difficult going back to TV dinners and cheap beer after the feast and fun he enjoyed last night at Paco's.

On Sundays, the boss usually took him out to lunch, and today had been no exception. When the old man went to the restroom, Jud slipped out to the pay phone in the lobby and placed his call to the Orchard Valley Police. As a "concerned church member who wanted to remain anonymous," he told about seeing the transient in the hollow digging a hole early this morning and burying something. "I'm just doing my part, but I don't want to get involved." Then he hung up.

The police would know from caller ID that the call came from the restaurant, but it was so crowded with church people eating Sunday dinner—several of them from the Chapel of the Valley—that nobody would be able to single out Jud as the caller. Once again, it was too easy.

The boss gave Jud the rest of the day off, so he spent the afternoon in his room sipping beer and dozing in the chair while the TV blared. *Where should I go for supper and drinks tonight?* he wondered. It felt real good just to know he could go anywhere he wanted and buy any meal on the menu. For the second evening in a row, he dressed up, splashed on plenty of after shave, and headed for Yarborough.

Rolling on the highway north, he wondered if the biker was in the slammer by now. It wouldn't be smart to try and find out, but Jud was sure the metal box had done the trick. "His dinner won't be near as good as mine," he said aloud with a laugh.

Twenty-nine

IF CHESSY HARBORED ANY SUSPICION that Joe was really a thief, she didn't show it. Instead, she said she was concerned about him and related that Rich, Ezra, and others at the church were praying for him. Joe reiterated his innocence and advanced his conviction that someone had used him as the scapegoat for the crime, someone who was still at large. Chessy seemed to understand, but she stopped short of clearly saying, "I know you didn't do it." And she never brought up the topic of bail.

Joe asked about Chessy's afternoon of visiting relatives. She gave the highlights, rolling her eyes about how farm people cook such large meals and expect you to eat two or three helpings of everything.

"How is Thomas feeling? Do you think he's all right?" Joe said.

She frowned. "I think he's all right physically," she said softly. "He has no history of heart problems, at least according to Velma and the minister, who have known him for twenty years or more. Velma takes him in for a physical exam every couple of years, and he always checks out fine—'disgustingly healthy,' the doctor says. I also called my mom, and she says the Rasbys have strong hearts.

"But I'm really concerned that he's taking this property conflict so hard. It's breaking his heart—almost literally, it seems." Then she added, as if to herself, "In reality, it is heartbreaking to see Christians at each other's throats."

"What do you mean?"

Chessy explained that Christians are supposed to be known for their love and forgiveness, for the ability to work through disagreements in a positive, edifying manner. "People are imperfect, so there will always be some conflicts," she said, "but Christians should be able to deal with conflicts without attacking one another. It was the verbal attacks and threats of leaving that seemed to be tearing Thomas' heart out."

Joe shifted uncomfortably in his chair. There was only a desk and a wire screen between them instead of the inch-thick bullet-proof glass in more secure facilities, but the screen felt like a wall. He hoped that wall wouldn't be insurmountable after what he was about to say.

"I have to tell you something, Chessy," he began. "Actually, I have to apologize to you." She looked at him questioningly.

Gazing at her, appreciating her beauty, yes, even beginning to feel love for her, Joe thought twice about admitting that he had intentionally deceived her. He didn't want Chessy to think less of him, especially now that he was accused of burglary. He wanted to win her, and how can you win a girl by telling that you lied to her?

But he had to finish what he started. "I led you to believe that I am just out here on a vacation—no other reason to be here. It wasn't the whole truth. Like I mentioned to Thomas, I did come out here to look for somebody—and I don't mean other Harley owners, the lame answer I gave the other night."

"Who did you come to look for?" Chessy said.

"I came to look for my birth mother," he began. Chessy said nothing, didn't even blink, so Joe just kept going. He told the whole story of his adoption, the letter from his birth mother, and the events leading up to his meeting yesterday with Brenda Long. He told her about the journals without going into detail about their contents. He hoped for other opportunities to tell Chessy more of his story.

"I don't know why I couldn't tell you this earlier," he concluded. "Maybe I was embarrassed about being adopted or about searching for my roots. Anyway, I'm sorry I misled you. I want you to know the truth about why I came out here."

Chessy now looked stunned. Joe couldn't tell if she was reacting to what he had shared or to his openness to share it.

"Thank you for telling me, Joe," she said, "and I accept your apology. I'm just…I'm blown away. And I'm so happy for you that you have reconnected with your birth mother. You must feel very fulfilled."

Joe weighed the word for a moment. "I don't know if *fulfilled* is how I would put it," he said. "It's not like I didn't have a mother. I had a great mom. It's more like finding the answer to a question that, until recently, I didn't know I needed to ask."

"I see," Chessy said. "So what does it mean to you to find your birth mother?"

"I'm not sure I know what you're asking."

"How will this affect your life? I mean, are you going to stay in touch with her? Are you going to see her periodically? Will you do anything differently now that you have found her?"

Joe didn't have an answer. "I don't know."

"So you come all this way to look for your birth mother. You find her—miraculously. And now you're just going to turn around and go back home—end of story?"

"Chessy, I told you I don't know what's going to happen next," Joe said, feeling a little defensive.

"Don't you want to build a relationship with this woman?"

"Maybe she doesn't want a long-term relationship." It sounded weak, and Joe didn't think Chessy would let it pass.

She didn't. She bored into him like a caring sister. "Joe! She's been waiting for you to find her. She moved here to the valley in case you came looking for her. You are her only child. It doesn't matter that she gave you up for adoption or that she hasn't seen you for twenty-four years. She's been thinking about you every day since then. The journals prove that. Of course she wants a relationship with you."

Joe backed off. "All right, maybe she does."

"Your mother probably feels badly about relinquishing you to another family. She won't push herself on you. I'll bet she's waiting for you to say you would be interested in staying in touch."

"But I can't move out here."

Chessy laughed. "I don't think she would want you to live with her or change your entire life to accommodate her. I'm talking about initiating a relationship—telling her you want to write to her or email her, talk on the phone, plan to visit her occasionally, invite her to Pittsburgh to show her where you grew up."

Joe felt stupid, though he realized Chessy was not at fault. He understood that she was just being as helpful as she could be. "Yeah, I know," he said, hoping he sounded convincing.

"So you *are* going to call her."

"Yes, I'm definitely going to call her. And I think I would like to meet with her again before I go home. But, as you can see, I have a little problem to solve first."

"People are praying for you, Joe," Chessy said. "I know God will help you."

"Well, I wish I could be that sure," Joe said as if to himself.

Chessy ignored the aside and went on. "So that's why you have been hanging around Orchard Valley? You've been waiting for the county to process your inquiry?"

Joe felt cornered. Having just apologized for a half-truth, was he ready to perpetrate another one? "Yes, that was part of my reason for staying."

"Why else would you want to stay?" she asked coyly.

Two can play at this game, Joe thought. "Well, for one thing I love this valley. The people have been great. And I enjoyed working on the church. I'm having a great vacation."

Chessy gazed at him. "Any other reasons?" she said, clearly baiting him.

Joe couldn't play any longer. Locking onto her gaze, he said, "Chessy, I don't want to lose contact with you either. Being with you has been... special...for me. I didn't expect this. I didn't expect you. And the worst thing about all this"—waving toward his cell—"is not being able to see you."

He gingerly lifted his hand to the screen and held it there, wanting to be as close to her as possible. To his surprise, she put her hand on her side of the screen where it would touch his. The sensation of her hand on his took his breath away.

They held the pose for several moments. Then Chessy withdrew her hand. "I didn't expect this either, Joe," she said with some of the sparkle leaving her eyes. "And I'm not sure what to do about it."

"What do you mean?"

"I have really enjoyed getting to know you, Joe. And I like you. I like you very much, but I don't know that this surprise we have found is realistic."

"You mean, you living in California and me living in Pennsylvania," Joe advanced, "the long-distance relationship thing."

Chessy nodded slowly. "That's a big consideration, of course. But there's much more to it than that. We have different lifestyles, different goals, different values."

Joe saw her slipping away. "Goals can change. Lifestyles can change," he offered helpfully.

"Yes, they can—and should—when two people are in a relationship. It's the values part that cannot be compromised. At least I cannot compromise my values."

Joe glanced away for a second. He knew where she was going. Turning back, he said, "You mean religion."

"Not religion, Joe. Christ. I have committed my life to Jesus Christ. I know I'm not perfect, but I want Jesus at the center of all I am and all my relationships."

Instead of feeling rebuffed by Chessy's line in the sand, Joe was attracted to her even more. She knew where she was, and she knew what was important to her. She reflected the qualities Rich had been describing in a Christian. Seeing people like Chessy, Thomas, and others only made the professor's descriptions more reasonable.

"I understand," Joe said. "You can't compromise your values, and I wouldn't want you to."

"Thanks, Joe." Chessy nodded. "And you know, you may have come here looking for your physical roots, but I think God brought you here to find your spiritual roots, too. That could be why you ended up camping at a church."

Joe said nothing. After several minutes of silence, Chessy said she had to go. She promised to come back tomorrow if he was still here.

"I hope I'm out tomorrow," he said with a weak laugh. "I'd like to be at the church meeting tomorrow night. It's kind of like a soap opera. I'm hooked, and I have to find out what happens next."

Chessy didn't smile. Joe thought about the pain the conflict had caused her uncle. He wished he hadn't said anything.

"In spite of the circumstances, tonight was special for me, Joe," she said as they both stood. "Thank you for sharing with me about your birth mom and for understanding where I am."

"You, too," he said, "and for being up front with me about how you feel."

Alone in the cell, Joe found himself talking to God. *What's this all about, and why are you even interested in me?* There were no answers, but Joe felt as if his words were heard, as if God was somehow in the cell with him.

•   •   •

Brenda Long sat at the desk in her pajamas and robe. She enjoyed reading or watching TV in her comfortable Yarborough condo on Sunday evenings, her last few hours of relaxation before a busy work week. But the television had not been on all day. She had spent the afternoon attending to some personal business and spent the evening poring over a mountain of papers related to her afternoon's activity.

Her concentration wasn't as sharp as usual. Thoughts of Joe Caruso and her visit with him yesterday kept interrupting. Along with the thoughts came, alternately, excitement and apprehension. The prospect of getting better acquainted with her son and perhaps beginning a long-term relationship thrilled her. However, Brenda was acutely aware that Joe may not want such a relationship, may not even want to talk to her again. And she didn't want to consider such a possibility.

In the meantime, there was still business to attend to. Brenda shuffled through the papers again, checking figures as she had several times already this evening. She came to the final page and the line awaiting her signature. She wasn't sure why she felt led to go through with this transaction, but the leading to this point had been definite and clear. It was a step she never dreamed of taking. It could come to nothing at all, or it might change the rest of her life. She knew she had to find out.

She picked up the pen and breathed another prayer. Hovering over the line for a moment, she then touched the tip to the paper, signed her name, and added the date. Switching on the fax machine, she dialed the number on the letterhead. In seconds the deed was done. She removed the originals and filed them, then turned off the machine.

"What in the world do you have up your sleeve, God?" Brenda said aloud. Then she headed for bed.

• • •

The graveyard jailer came on duty at 10:30 p.m. He was a Latino with a deeply lined, leathery face and plenty of salt in his pepper-black hair. The officer brought him a blanket and dimmed the light in the cell, abruptly ending Joe's reading for the night.

Joe wasn't close to feeling sleepy. So he laid back on the bunk and got angry thinking about the person who should be in this cell tonight instead of him—the one who put him here. It had to be somebody local, he thought, instead of a hit-and-run burglar who could have been in Canada in five hours. Otherwise, why would he go to the trouble of framing Joe? He was deflecting attention to someone else because he was still around and was planning to stay around without suspicion.

Joe considered some options. Could it be one of the church members? The thought almost made him laugh. Talk about an over-the-hill-gang. There were some cranky old men in the bunch, and Jethro Haig was the undisputed president of that club. But they were all long-time members. Why would any of them steal money that could help their church? Unless...

It suddenly made sense, but Joe couldn't believe he was thinking it. Jethro Haig stole the money in order to force the church to reconsider his offer to buy the thirteen acres of church property which included the hollow. The shrewd old curmudgeon seemed greedy for land, including Bradford McDermot's 200-acre spread, perhaps because he had a developer in his hip pocket ready to pay megabucks for it. Even a churchman—and Joe didn't see Jethro Haig as a model of Christian charity—might steal a relative pittance from his own church if the greed was strong enough.

"Caruso!"

Joe jumped, startled. He turned to see the Latino jailer peering in his window. The lights came up, and he heard the sound of keys jingling.

"Get your stuff. You're out of here."

Joe gathered up the journals and stepped out of his cell. Waiting to greet him with a warm smile and a bear hug was Bradford McDermot.

Thirty

IT'S BEEN SEVEN MONTHS since you went away, Danny, and I'm finally getting my life together again, the next journal entry began. *I have a job and an apartment. I should be able to put a down payment on a used car pretty soon. But now your grandfather stirs everything up again with a letter.Why can't he leave me alone?*

Joe was still in his sleeping bag, but the early morning light illuminated the tent, allowing him to see the page. Driving him back to the church at almost midnight, Bradford had again offered Joe a room in their farmhouse. Joe was grateful for the big farmer's generosity, promising to pay him back for the money he had advanced for his bail. But he again declined the offer of free room and board. Bradford was a literal Godsend, but Joe had to be on his own. And with all his stuff back with him—except his pistol, which the police kept as a precaution—he was ready for whatever his unseen enemy threw at him. But for now, he felt compelled to continue the fascinating story chronicled by his birth mother.

He read with deep interest as his mother told about a letter she had received from her father, who had written to apologize for the harm he had done to her. He had apologized many times before, she said, usually after he sobered up. But this time her father's letter went farther than the previous apologies. He confessed over several pages the ways he had abused her, the hateful words he had spoken, the hurtful things he had done. It was like an inventory, and Becky said that—to her amazement—it was all there, even some things she had forgotten. Furthermore, he included a list of his cruel behavior toward Becky's mother. He had apparently asked for her forgiveness, and she had granted it.

It seems that your grandfather was really ticked off when he got my letter saying he would never see his grandson, Becky wrote. *He went on quite a bender, he told me in the letter, smashing things in a drunken rage. Then he claims to have had a religious experience that sobered him up and transformed him from foul-mouthed drunk to a church-going square. He closed his letter by asking me to forgive him.*

But he's not getting off this easy. He didn't leave any physical scars, but I'm still bleeding inside from the way he treated me. What does he expect me to do with all the hurt he caused—just forget about it? If he does, he's crazy.

Joe could feel the pain and bitterness coming through the words on the page. He couldn't blame Becky. He agreed that such a man did not deserve her forgiveness.

Becky explained that she would not even dignify her father's request for forgiveness with a reply. Instead, she tore the letter to pieces and flushed it down the toilet. Even if her father's dramatic change was real—and she seriously doubted that it was—it would make no difference in her life. "Good for you, Becky," Joe heard himself say aloud. "The old man is incorrigible; he'll never change. Don't let him ruin your life."

When his watch beeped at 7:00 A.M., Joe laid the book aside to get dressed, clean up at the creek, and eat a power bar and an apple he had stashed in his saddlebag. The morning sun was already bathing the valley in warmth. In an hour or so, Joe would knock on the door of the parsonage to get his Harley keys from Rich.

As he ate, Joe wondered what "evidence" of his guilt would turn up next. If the real thief was still around the valley, he would soon find out that Joe was free on bail. What other tricks did he have up his sleeve designed to keep the focus on Joe? And if Jethro Haig was behind all this, how could he find out? The old man would be at the big church meeting tonight. Would he be surprised to see Joe there? Joe couldn't wait to find out.

Finding a comfortable place in the sunshine next to a tree, Joe resumed reading Brenda's fascinating journal. *Happy birthday, Danny. You're a year old today!* Joe looked at the date on the page: April 23, his birth date.

I cried a lot today, thinking about you, imagining what you look like. You're probably walking by now—or at least trying. And I can almost hear you saying your first words—probably 'Dada' and 'Mama.' I know you love your mother and father, and I'm sure they love you. But today I miss hearing you say that word to me: Mama.

The pages flew by. Becky Ruth Barnes's writing gradually transformed from that of a flighty, emotional teenager to a mature young woman with career aspirations. She described her bold move to Seattle and her elation at landing an entry-level job with King County. That's when she became Brenda again, explaining that it was a more professional-sounding name.

Brenda introduced Danny to Dennis Long, a coworker who had caught her eye. Over a period of several months they dated and had fun, but Brenda kept the relationship from getting serious. She explained that she still felt burned after her brief marriage to Wallace Barnes. But when Dennis finally proposed, Brenda was ready. They were married in a simple civil ceremony with just a few friends from the office in attendance.

Joe skimmed the next two volumes, slowing only to read in detail Brenda's comments on special days in Joe's life: birthdays, holidays, graduations from kindergarten, elementary school, and high school. Most of Brenda's school dates were off a year because Joe's parents had held him back in school, but the sentiments she wrote convinced him that he was still very much a part of her thoughts.

Occasionally, Brenda would make reference to another letter from her father. He remained contrite and hopeful that she would forgive him. He assured her that he had remained sober and that Jesus Christ had become the focus of his life. Even Brenda's mother insisted that her dad had changed. Brenda wrote back to her mother, but said nothing about her father as if he was dead. And she never responded to any of her dad's letters.

At about 8:30, Joe walked over to the parsonage for the keys and retrieved his bike from the shed. Both Rich and the minister, who was still on crutches, seemed glad to see him. They didn't ask about his time in jail, and Joe only said that the public defender thought the charges were ludicrous. His hearing would be later in the week. Until then, he was free. Nor did Joe say anything about his suspicion that Jethro Haig had something to do with his arrest. The truth would speak for itself when Joe found out what it was.

By mid-morning Joe was racing through the final volume of the journals. Brenda's life with Dennis sounded tolerable but lacking in excitement. His mother regretted that she and Dennis were unable to conceive a child and that Dennis was unwilling to adopt. Joe wondered if his mother would have stopped writing letters to him in the journal if another child or two had filled the emptiness in her life.

Two events near the close of the journal caused Joe to read each page more attentively. First came Dennis' death in January of this year. Brenda's expression of shock and grief was sincere. Dennis had been a good husband. She was going to miss him. Brenda's mother, whom she had seen only a few times since she left home, surprised her by attending the funeral. *Your grandfather did not come to the service, Danny,* she wrote. *Mom said he was ill and could not make the trip to Seattle. Perhaps it's just as well that Dad could not come. I'm not in any condition to deal with him. I haven't talked to him since the day I walked out of his house almost twenty-five years ago, and he stopped writing to me ten years ago.*

The second arresting event occurred only a few weeks after Dennis's death. *Danny, I have wonderful news,* she began. *I have just become a Christian.*

Joe rested the book on his knee and gazed out at the farmland in the distance, stunned by what he had just read. Brenda had written about agreeing to attend church with a caring friend from work. The woman had invited her a few times before Dennis's sudden death. Several days after the funeral, she asked again, and Brenda thought a church visit might somehow help soothe her grief and get her friend off her back. But something happened to Brenda at church and in the days following her Sunday visit, culminating in her surprising leap of faith.

In the succeeding pages, Brenda related to Danny the wonderful changes that were happening in her life as a result of her conversion: purpose instead of aimlessness, peace instead of emptiness, enriching dependency upon God instead of the dogged independence which had characterized her life and career. *I'm now praying for you every day, Danny,* she concluded one page. *I pray that you will also find God's love in Christ if you haven't already. I also pray that God will allow me to see you again, not just to know you are alive and well—which is important to me—but to share with you what God has done for me.*

Many of the entries after Brenda's conversion were prayers she wrote for Danny and his adoptive family. She acknowledged to God that if, in his wisdom and plan, she was never able to see her son again, she could accept it. She knew that Danny was in God's hands, and he would do what was best for her son. *But my greatest joy, Lord,* she wrote, *would be to see Danny again. Please bring him to Washington, if it is your will.*

Joe snapped his head up from the page. He suddenly realized that Brenda's prayer of only a few months ago had been answered. How did that happen? He had unwittingly cooperated with Brenda's petition. What caused him to do that? It was his own idea to come west after his mother's death, not God "moving" him. But it was just what Brenda had asked for. The idea of such a coincidence gave him a chill.

Joe had to keep reading. In a few pages, Brenda turned her attention to her father, whose name had yet to be divulged in the journals. Brenda was having a change of heart toward the man who had attempted to restore their relationship for many years.

God has helped me forgive your grandfather, Danny, she wrote, *which is a miracle in itself. I never thought I would say this to anyone, but I want to reconnect with Dad. I finally understand what he was trying to tell me about Jesus Christ changing his life. And all these years I doubted that anything significant had happened to him.*

But Dad has probably given up on me by now. I would have if I were him. I said some horrible things to him. I robbed him of ever seeing his grandson. I flushed his apologies down the toilet. I guess he finally lost hope. Next to seeing you again, Danny, my greatest desire is to somehow return to my father, to make things right between us. But I'm afraid it may be too late. How can I even approach him after what I have done? Reuniting with you and Dad is something only God can do, but my Christian friends tell me that nothing is impossible for God.

The last several pages of the journal summarized her move to Central Washington: a new job, a new home, and a growing anticipation that her prayers would be answered. Then the journal abruptly ended. Joe checked the date. Brenda had stopped making entries just over two months ago, only a few days after moving into her Yarborough condominium. It was as if she didn't need to write anything more, that she was waiting to tell her beloved Danny the rest of the story in person when God answered her prayer.

Joe closed the book and held it reverently. It was uncanny, scary. Ever since arriving in this valley, he had sensed that God was circling him. Thomas Rasby, Bradford McDermot, and the other people of this little church had been preaching to him through their loving, God-fearing ways. Chessy, a beautiful Christian girl who shouldn't have given him a second glance, had looked past his tough exterior to something good within him. Then there was Rich's "evidence" for a gracious God and a sacrificing Savior who offered a real relationship because he was truly who he claimed to be.

Even more astounding, he discovered that the birth mother he came west to find had been waiting for him, praying to God for his return. And somehow this God loved Brenda so much that he prompted Joe's cross-country trip—without Joe even realizing it.

Joe scarcely breathed as these thoughts replayed in his mind. He had to talk to somebody. Maybe this God could do something impossible for him. Maybe this loving, powerful God could help him clear his name in Orchard Valley. But that meant he had to tell someone about the trouble he was in. Who should he tell? Rich? Chessy? Ezra? Bradford? He wasn't sure.

In the meantime, Joe had to fulfill his promise. He had told Brenda he would call her when he finished the journals. He would do better than that. He would drive into town right now and take her to lunch. He would thank her for letting him read the journals. And he would ask her one burning question: Who is my grandfather?

In five minutes, Joe was gunning the Harley north on the road to Yarborough.

Thirty-one

BRADFORD WALKED THROUGH THE ORCHARD surveying the ripening cherries and assessing the harvesting that needed to be done when the migrant workers arrived, but his heart was not in his work. The cell phone clipped to the front pocket of his overalls chimed. Bradford welcomed the distraction.

It was Ezra. "Bradford, we have to talk about this mess before tonight's meeting. I was up half the night stewing and praying about it."

"I was about to call you, my friend," Bradford said. "I didn't sleep very well either. I'm just heartsick over this whole thing."

"Do you have time to come over for a while?" Ezra said. "I want to talk to you and pray with you about tonight's meeting. I'll ask Rich to pray with us if you don't mind. Somehow we've got to rein in Jethro and Chet. Jethro will listen to you, and I may be able to talk some sense into Chet."

"Excellent idea," Bradford affirmed. "Give me ten minutes."

Bradford huddled with his foreman, quickly explaining what had to be accomplished the rest of the day. He was climbing into the truck for the short drive to the church when his cell phone sounded again.

"Yes?" he said, settling in behind the wheel.

"Mister McDermot, this is Alan Snyder at Certified Properties. How are you?"

"Alan," Bradford said, surprised. "I haven't heard from you in quite a while."

Snyder laughed. "Unfortunately, there hasn't been a good reason for me to call, at least until this morning."

Bradford lifted his eyebrows. "What's up?"

"Well, sir, we received an offer on your farm this morning."

"An offer? That's strange. Nobody has even been out to look at it."

"Apparently the prospective buyer knows the area pretty well."

"Is it a commercial outfit—like a land developer?" Bradford quizzed.

"No, it's a private party."

"Then it must be Jethro Haig again. I can't believe he—"

Snyder interrupted. "The buyer's realtor wouldn't give a name."

"Then it's Jethro for sure," Bradford asserted. "He must be embarrassed about trying to lowball me again."

"Mister McDermot, the buyer didn't come in low," Snyder said.

"Really," Bradford said guardedly. "What is the offer?"

"Full asking price, cash deal."

Bradford was momentarily speechless. Then all he could say was, "You're kidding, Alan."

Snyder laughed again. "This is no joke, sir. I have a firm offer in my hands—in writing—and a check for ten thousand dollars."

"Any contingencies?"

"Not a one. This deal is as clean they come."

"Then old Jethro's had quite a change of heart," Bradford said, more to himself.

"The realtor stated that the buyer wishes to remain anonymous until the offer is accepted. Is that a problem for you, Mister McDermot?"

Bradford thought for a moment. The offer was a direct answer to prayer. He and Esther had asked God specifically to send them a buyer who would agree to their asking price and cash them out. Perhaps God had changed Jethro's heart in order to answer their prayer. Or perhaps Jethro was so confident that the congregation would vote to accept his offer at tonight's meeting to purchase the church property that he decided to bite the bullet and pay full price for the McDermot's place. Either way, the McDermot's petition had been granted.

"Sir, do you have any problems with this offer?" Alan Snyder pressed.

"I don't think so, Alan," Bradford said, "but let me talk to Esther first, then I'll call you right back."

Bradford called his wife at the house. Esther was elated at the news. She didn't think Jethro was the prospective buyer. "He never pays full price for anything, Bradford. That's why he has so much money." But Esther agreed that the offer was the answer they had been seeking.

After hanging up, Bradford dialed Alan Snyder at his office in Yarborough and asked him to bring the papers out to the farm later in the afternoon. Snyder said he would be there by 4:30.

Driving out his long gravel road, Bradford thanked God for the answer to prayer. He already felt a burden lifting. They would soon be free of this responsibility. Hopefully the buyer would allow him to come out occasionally and share some of his farming experience. He didn't want to see the farm misused. It had been their home for forty-seven years.

Pulling into the church parking lot, Bradford was aware that another burden remained heavy on his heart. It also involved Jethro Haig. The property issue was tearing at the heart of the Chapel of the Valley. The meeting tonight could split the church down the middle, ruining dozens of long-term, close relationships.

"Dear Lord," Bradford prayed as he parked the truck, "if you can redeem this old sinner and sell my farm for full price, you can surely knit these hearts together again. Please do it. Amen."

• • •

Supervisor Brenda Long was already at lunch when Joe arrived at her office at ten minutes until noon. The clerk he talked to said it was a celebration lunch for a woman in the office who was retiring. Brenda should be back by 1:00 P.M., she explained.

Since he was already in the city, Joe decided to wait. He tooled around town until he found a fast-food chicken place, where he devoured a white-meat combo meal. When Joe got back to the office, Brenda was still out. He sat on a bench outside the auditor's office and waited.

Joe saw her coming down the hall with a group of women. She was engrossed in conversation and didn't see him. Having read the journals, Joe now felt relationally connected to Brenda Long. He had no doubt that she was his birth mother. He would never know this woman as intimately as he knew the mother who had raised him, but he could not ignore the genetic link. Her blood flowed in his veins. He shared a few of her physical traits and probably some of her personality traits. And her family history was also his. Like it or not, he was related to the beast of a man, called her father, who had ruined her childhood and driven her out of his home.

As the group of women approached, Joe stood. It was the kind of respect his adoptive mother had earned. It suddenly seemed right for Brenda Long, too.

"Hello, Joe," she said, finally seeing him. Her face registered surprise. The other women turned into the office, leaving the two of them alone in the hall.

"I'm sorry I didn't call before coming over," he said. "I finished reading your journals this morning, so I decided to come into town and see if you had some time to talk."

Brenda's eyes widened. "You read them all?"

"Yes. They were fascinating."

"I must admit, I wasn't sure you would be interested in reading them."

"You poured a lot of time and effort into those books," Joe said. "Thank you for doing it, and thank you for letting me read them."

Brenda's smile communicated her pleasure at the compliment.

"If you can't talk now, I can come back later," Joe said.

Brenda shook her head. "I've been waiting for this for a long time, and the county owes me plenty of comp time. Give me a minute, then we can find someplace to talk."

While Brenda was in the office, Joe paced the hall nervously. He felt like he was charging recklessly into his past. It was all happening so quickly. You didn't ride fast on a motorcycle in new territory because the unknown or unexpected could hurt you. Joe felt that same way about the sudden exploration of his history with Becky Ruth Barnes, a.k.a. Brenda Long.

When Brenda emerged from the office, she had a briefcase as well as her purse. "I'm taking the rest of the day off," she said brightly, "so we can talk as long as you want. And I know just the place to be on a beautiful day like today."

They walked to Brenda's car in the parking garage adjacent to the county building. She drove two miles to a tree-shaded park situated like an oasis in the middle of a commercial district. "This is Founder's Park," Brenda explained as she parked. "I brought you here the day before you... went away. It was our only real outing together."

"Why did you bring me here?"

"I wanted you to see one of my favorite spots in Yarborough. Even though you weren't even two weeks old, I hoped it would make an imprint on your brain, that this is where your life began."

They walked into the park, found an empty bench in the shade, and sat down. Joe felt awkward. He had met this woman only two days ago, yet he had been linked to her his entire lifetime.

"I'm sure you have some questions after what you have read," Brenda began, appearing relaxed. "I'll be happy to tell you anything you want to know."

"You may also have some things you want to ask about me," Joe countered.

"Yes, there is much I want to know about you," she said, smiling. "But you can be first."

Joe's head was filled with questions. He hadn't itemized or organized them, but two of them always seemed to hover at the top of his consciousness. He asked the one he thought would be the easiest for Brenda to answer: "What was my father like?"

She looked away for a moment and sighed. Then she said, "I can tell you what I know about Wallace Barnes, but I didn't know him well. We were together a total of eight months—from first date to the day he left. We weren't even friends. We didn't think the same at all."

Brenda talked about Wallace's appearance, noting that Joe and his biological father shared similar traits: a mildly cleft chin, wide-set eyes, rather small hands. Joe was surprised that his mother had noticed these things about him. She described Wallace's personality as introverted and sullen. His glaring faults were a foul temper, a foul mouth, and a propensity for stealing.

Joe moved on to his next category of questions. "Your father—my biological grandfather—is he still alive?"

Brenda did not answer immediately. Joe had been right. This was still a delicate issue with his birth mother.

"Yes," she said at last, "he's alive and well from what I understand."

"You still haven't reconnected with him?"

"No."

"But you say you are going to."

"I want to. And I think I need to. It's just that…" Her words trailed off to a grimace.

Joe finished the thought for her. "You don't believe that he will see you."

"Yes, I'm struggling to believe that Dad wants anything to do with me. Remember, I have ignored him for my entire adult life."

Brenda's history with her father was fresh on Joe's mind from the journals. She had a point. Even a good man may not be able to forgive his daughter for nearly three decades of rebellion.

"You never mentioned your father's name in your journals," Joe said.

"I didn't?" Brenda said in surprise.

Joe shook his head. "No first name, no last name. Just 'Dad.'"

"I'm surprised you haven't run in to him out in Orchard Valley."

"Maybe I have and don't know it."

"Your grandfather—my father—is named Bradford McDermot."

Thirty-two

BRADFORD AND EZRA HAD BEEN FRIENDS for over two decades. They had also worked closely together as church leaders at the Chapel of the Valley for most of those years. In the course of their relationship, Bradford had heard Ezra weep before, but never like this. As the minister, the board chairman, and the professor prayed together in the parsonage living room, Ezra's fervent petition gave way to sobs of grief over the conflict between the factions in his congregation.

"Whatever it takes to heal the wound, O God," he said with his voice quavering, "I ask you to do it. Visit us tonight in a special way. Melt our hard hearts and fuse us together as one for your glory."

Bradford's eyes brimmed with tears as his friend's passion touched his own heart. He echoed the prayer, asking God to somehow bring together Jethro Haig and Chet Rasby as well as all those who lined up so tenaciously behind either of them.

Even though he had been around the church only a few days, Rich prayed with a fervor that matched that of the minister and board chairman. In addition to his prayer for church unity and a resolution to the seemingly insurmountable barrier between the Rasbys and the McDermots, Rich also prayed for Joe Caruso, whom he believed had not come to the church by accident.

After the time of prayer, Rich thanked the two men for inviting him to share the burden with them, then he excused himself to drive into Orchard Valley.

"I want you to know where I stand, Ezra," Bradford said when Rich was gone. "You know that I am partial to selling the property. In my mind, it seems like the most reasonable solution to our financial problems. But if that's not what God wants for the church, then I don't want it either. I won't be pushing an agenda tonight, and I will talk to Jethro today and make sure he keeps himself under control."

"Thank you, my friend," Ezra said. "I know your heart is in the right place, and I agree that we need God's solution tonight, not just a majority opinion. While you are talking to Jethro, I will be talking to Chet. If we can keep these two from getting into another shouting match with one another, we should be able to lead a reasonable and productive discussion."

Once they finished planning the meeting, Bradford relaxed a little in his chair. "We got an offer on our place today, Ezra," he said.

The minister's eyebrows rose. "Jethro again?"

"The buyer has asked to remain anonymous, so I don't know for sure. If it is Jethro, he's had a change of heart."

"How so?"

"The offer is for the full asking price, cashing us out," Bradford said.

Ezra whistled. "That's wonderful, Bradford." Then he added, "But you're right. That doesn't sound like Jethro Haig."

"And why would Jethro want to remain anonymous?" Bradford wondered aloud. "For that matter, why would anyone want to remain anonymous?"

"Maybe it's a developer," Ezra said.

"No, the realtor assured me that it's a private party," Bradford said. "I can only hope it's someone who wants to keep the farm going."

"So you're going to accept the offer," Ezra said.

Bradford shrugged. "It's what Esther and I have been praying for all these months. This must be the answer."

Ezra fluffed the pillow under his injured ankle on the sofa. "Then you will have to decide where to move."

Bradford sighed. "Yes, our realtor has been watching the listings for places in town. Now I suppose we will have to look at some of them."

The big farmer rose to leave. "Don't trouble yourself to get up, Ezra."

"One more thing, Bradford," Ezra said from the sofa. "Have you heard anything else since the funeral?"

Ezra was always good to ask about Brenda occasionally. The last time he asked, Bradford told him about the sudden and tragic loss of his daughter's husband Dennis.

"She moved back to Yarborough, I hear," Bradford said, suddenly glum.

"When? Where?" Ezra pressed with interest.

"Two or three months ago I think. I guess she's living in town. We don't know where."

"She hasn't contacted you?"

Bradford pursed his lips and shook his head slowly. "No, she hasn't."

"Brenda is always in my prayers, Bradford," Ezra said.

Bradford nodded. "Esther and I trust that God will bring our daughter back to us in his own time."

"It will be a great day, Bradford," Ezra said.

Bradford felt the encouragement in his tone. The minister always knew how to keep his hopes alive. "I would give up everything to hasten that day, Ezra," he said, tears returning to his eyes.

Ezra stretched out his hand, and Bradford gripped it. Ezra said, "I know you would, my friend. Let's just see what God will do."

●　　●　　●

For a moment, Joe couldn't find the breath to speak. Finally he stammered, "Bradford McDermot? He...he's your father?"

Brenda eyed him closely. "Yes, he's my father. What's the matter, Joe?"

"The Bradford McDermot who owns the big farm next to the church out in the valley?"

"That's right. I grew up on that farm."

Joe spoke the words slowly, as if one wrong syllable would trip an alarm. "You're saying that Bradford McDermot is my flesh-and-blood grandfather."

Suddenly Brenda's eyes widened with insight. "You've seen him, haven't you? You've been staying at the church, and you've seen him around there."

Joe's story tumbled out in a rush of words: the fire at the church, working on the building with the men, the conflict over the property, Thomas' emotional breakdowns, and finally the evening he spent at the farm with Bradford and Esther. He explained that he thought very highly of Bradford. His grandfather seemed to like him, too.

"I can't believe it, Joe," Brenda gasped. "You ate supper with my parents, and you had no idea that they're your grandparents. And they don't know who you are."

"And to top it all off," Joe continued, "it was Bradford who showed up last night at almost midnight and posted——" He caught himself. He was beginning to feel at home with Brenda Long as his mother, so at home that he almost blurted out that he had been in jail.

Brenda's eyes narrowed. "Were you going to say what I think you were going to say?"

Joe rubbed his forehead with the back of his hand. Then at just above a whisper, "Yeah, that's what I was going to say. I was in jail last night. It just felt like you already knew, that I might have told you."

"You can tell me if you want to, Joe."

It was all the invitation he needed. If his other mom were alive, he would have told her about being implicated in the burglary. Brenda seemed just as interested and just as safe. So he told her the story, except for the haunting suspicion that Jethro Haig might somehow be out to frame him.

Brenda offered understanding but no advice. "I'm sure things will work out for the best, Joe. I can't believe God would bring you back to me only to have you end up in jail on a false charge."

Then Joe directed the conversation back to Bradford. "The father you described in your journals, that physically abusive drunk, is not the man I know as Bradford McDermot."

"He wrote to me about his conversion," Brenda said, "but I didn't believe him. He was so terrible to us—to me. Until recently, I don't think I allowed myself to accept that a person can change so drastically."

"What do you mean by 'recently'?"

"When I turned my life over to Christ," Brenda said without hesitation. "I could not accept that a mean drunk could be transformed into a loving husband and good man until I experienced a similar change myself."

Joe recalled some of the most recent entries in Brenda's journals. She described her life as brand new. She claimed a completely different outlook on life as a result of her spiritual conversion. It was the same message he had been getting from Rich, the same message he had seen in so many people over the last five days.

"Then why haven't you gone to Bradford and cleared up your differences?" Joe pressed. "He's not anything like what you knew as a teenager. He's a wonderful man."

Brenda grimaced, and Joe saw that she was near tears. "In my head, Joe, I think I understand that," she said. "And in my heart, I have forgiven him—as best I know how to forgive someone—for what he did to me and my mother. But look what I have done to him. I'm forty-two years old, and I have spent my adult life punishing him for something God forgave him of twenty years ago."Tears filled her eyes. "I feel so…so…unworthy of my dad's love."

"I'll talk to him," Joe said. "I'll explain that I'm your son. I'll tell him how you feel and—"

Brenda cut him off. "No, I don't want you to do that. Please."

"Why not?"

"If he knows who you really are," she explained, "it may influence him too much in my favor. I need to do this, but I have to do it on my own. I want him to respond to me just as I am."

Joe stared at her for several moments. "Are you saying that you don't want him to know that I'm his grandson?"

Brenda flashed an expression of inner pain. "Just for a little while longer, until I can talk to him…please. If you say something, they will know that you have talked to me. I would like to see them first."

Joe felt agitated. "How long is 'a little while'?" he said. "I see Bradford just about every day. And if I'm his grandson, I would like him to know it."

"I know, and I'm sorry, Joe. I promise, I'll make contact with him soon. I'm just waiting for, well, the right time."

"Are we talking a week, two weeks…?"

"No, no, just a day or two. Will you promise not to say anything until I talk to them?"

It was not what Joe wanted, but Brenda had a point. Revealing his identity too soon might make the reunion with her parents doubly difficult.

"All right, I promise," he said.

"Thank you. It will be soon."

Then Brenda said, "I mentioned my commitment to Christ earlier. Did you read those pages in the journal where I described how I came to Christ after Dennis' funeral?"

"Yes, I read them." He considered telling Brenda about his long conversations about Christ and Christianity with Rich Denny. He knew much more about Christianity than she thought he knew, Joe assessed. But he didn't want to get into it, at least not now.

Joe needed to get back to the valley. He wanted to find Jethro's farm while it was still light in case he needed to do a little looking around when it was very dark. Brenda drove him back to the county garage where the Harley was waiting. Brenda reaffirmed her intention to talk to Bradford and Esther very soon. They said goodbye, then Joe headed for the farmland around Orchard Valley.

Thirty-three

JOE KNEW THE GENERAL VICINITY of Jethro Haig's big farm. At supper Saturday night, Bradford had mentioned that the place was out a farm road called Lateral D east of Orchard Valley. Joe found Lateral D and headed east. It was another hot, dry afternoon, so the slipstream flowing around him felt good.

The farms on this side of town were a patchwork quilt made up of multi-acre squares of sweet corn, feed corn, wheat, timothy hay, sugar beets, hops, and peach, prune, and cherry orchards. Four miles out of town, Joe stopped to ask an old guy lumbering slowly along on a tractor where Jethro's place was. "About another two miles, big white farmhouse, garage, and barn about half mile off the road." Joe nodded thanks and sped off.

Joe didn't know what he would do once he got to Jethro's farm. He wasn't ready to ask him point blank if he had stolen the money and planted the false evidence. He needed more to go on than that, but maybe the element of surprise would give him something. He wanted to read the old man's face when he rolled up to his front door on the Harley.

He spotted the cluster of white buildings with dark green trim from half a mile away, encircled by a sea of wheat and sugar beets. Slowing to take in the sight, Joe noticed about a dozen farm hands working the spread, a few near the buildings but most out in the field. Several of them were moving giant irrigation lines into place for tomorrow morning's watering. Joe assessed that Jethro Haig was rich enough to hire out all the help he needed, leaving him plenty of time for bugging the minister and chirping about how the church property was being mishandled. Had he used some of that free time to break into the church office and try to ruin Joe's reputation? Joe intended to find out.

He took the long, gravel driveway back to the complex. The farmhouse was a large, two-story wood-frame structure with a shaded porch that extended the length of the front. The place looked at least fifty years old, but it was well cared for, and the yard was nicely landscaped. Near the house was a two-car garage with what appeared to be a small mother-in-law apartment above it. Parked alongside and to the rear of the garage was a couple of old pickup trucks, one black and one red. *Farm trucks no doubt,* Joe thought. Next to them was a balloon-tire ATV and an electric golf cart. Joe imagined that the smaller vehicles were just for getting around the farm.

A very large barn and even larger equipment shed were about a hundred yards behind the house. There was no one standing near the house, and the garage doors were closed, so Joe idled farther down the drive toward the barn.

He rolled up to a couple of young Latinos dressed in khakis. Still astride the idling Harley, he said, "Where can I find Jethro Haig?"

The two glanced at each other. Then one replied in fractured English, "Señor Haig...no is here."

Joe dusted off a little high school Spanish to ask where he was. "*Donde esta Señor Haig?*"

The worker did his best to murder the words "Orchard Valley," but Joe got it.

"*Con Rusty?*" he added, assuming that Haig's stepson was with him.

After a few seconds of thinking, the kid's eyes brightened. "Oh si, Rusty," he said, smiling broadly with his hands making a driving-the-car motion.

Joe mimicked the motion. "Rusty *con* Señor Haig."

Both men nodded vigorously. "Si, si."

"*Yo es amigo Señor Haig,*" Joe said pointing to himself. The kids kept nodding. He thought about asking when Haig and his lackey would be back but didn't think his Spanish would get him there. So he goosed the engine and said, "*Muchas gracias.*"

None of the workers seemed to care that he was there, so Joe tooled around the buildings just checking things out. When he drove past the house again, a plump Latino woman in a house dress and apron was standing on the porch watching him. *The cook or the housekeeper,* Joe thought. He waved and smiled at her. She waved back but without smiling. Joe was amused at how Jethro might react when she told her boss about his visit. If he was involved, Joe might get a clue when the old man showed up for the showdown at the church tonight.

Having seen enough, Joe picked up speed on the driveway back to the road. Turning toward town on Lateral D, he gave the farmhands an exhibition of the Harley's power and roar.

Soon after Joe parked in the hollow, Thomas came out to meet him. "We have a big meeting in the church tonight, Joe," the caretaker explained. "I have to move a big table from the basement to the platform. Will you please help me carry the table, Joe?"

Joe said he would be glad to help, so they walked together to the basement. The folding table had to be collapsed and carried up the stairs. It was more awkward to handle than heavy, but Thomas knew exactly where and when to turn and lift.

As they carried the table into the sanctuary, Joe asked, "How are you feeling about tonight's meeting?"

Thomas waited until they had the table set up on the platform. "Me and Jesus, we been crying about this meeting, Joe," he said. His face mirrored inner pain. "And I been praying real hard about it all day."

"It hurts you to see people argue with each other, doesn't it?" Joe said.

"It hurts me deep inside, Joe. And Jesus says it hurts him deep inside."

"What is Jesus saying about this meeting?" Joe probed, humoring the man.

Thomas shook his head forlornly. "Mostly he's just crying about it, Joe. And when Jesus starts to crying, I can't help crying, too."

Joe studied the man's lined and weathered face. His eyes were puffy and red. Joe thought Thomas might be imagining the sorrowful Jesus living inside him, but there was no denying that the caretaker himself had been in tears much of the day.

Thomas continued. "Fighting is not what the church is for. It's for loving one another and serving God together. When church people leave off loving and go to fighting, it's like Jesus bled and died for nothing. That's when I hear him crying."

The old man's chin began to quaver. Joe found himself moved by Thomas' sensitivity. Most men he knew, including himself, stifled sentimentality and tears.

They made a second trip to the basement for two folding chairs to place behind the table on the platform for the minister and the board chairman to occupy during the meeting. As long as they weren't talking about the meeting, Thomas seemed like his old self.

"I'm going to fix franks and beans now, Joe," Thomas said when the job was done. "Would you like to come for supper?"

Joe glanced at his watch. It was already 5:30, and the meeting would start at 7:00. He could probably find something more appetizing to eat in town than franks and beans, but if he ate supper in the cabin, perhaps he could help keep Thomas on an even emotional keel before the meeting.

"Franks and beans sounds wonderful, Thomas," Joe exaggerated. "Thank you for the invitation."

Joe told Thomas he would meet him at the cabin in a few minutes. Then he retreated to his tent and changed into the cotton pants he wore to church the day before and a clean pullover shirt.

Thomas' table wasn't fancy. Two large bowls of beans with sliced franks, a half a loaf of sliced white bread still in the cellophane bag, butter, a jar of grape jelly, salt, and pepper. But Joe was glad to be there. Thomas intoned a simple but heartfelt prayer of thanks for the meal. He added a sentence of petition for the meeting at seven o'clock. If God listened to anybody's prayers, Joe thought, he must listen to Thomas'. The man talked to God as if they were best friends.

Buttering a slice of bread, Joe thought again about Bradford McDermot. The reality of being his grandson was still so new to him. He wondered what Thomas would say when he found out. Joe hoped the news would be common knowledge soon.

"You have Jesus in your heart, don't you, Joe?"

Joe's mouth was full of bread when Thomas posed the surprising question, so he had a moment to think about his response. He didn't want to mislead the sweet old man, but neither did he want to get into a theological discussion. He swallowed and replied, "I'm closer to Jesus than I have ever been, Thomas." Considering that he was sitting with one of God's good friends and that everybody at the church seemed to be talking to Joe about Jesus, he knew there was a lot of truth in his answer.

"That's good, Joe," Thomas said. "I pray for everybody who stays out yonder in the hollow. So I been praying for you every day since you come here. Is there something you want me to ask Jesus for?"

The simple, saintly invitation seemed to be issued from Jesus himself, as if the Lord was gazing at him through the caretaker's eyes and welcoming his concerns. Before he could talk himself out of it, Joe began to unload. It seemed perfectly right to tell his troubles to someone who seemed so close to the only one who could help him.

Joe put down his half-eaten slice of bread. "You know about the money that was stolen from the church office, don't you?"

"Missus Wilkerson's money," Thomas said.

"That's right. Well, the police think I stole that money. But I didn't take it, so I need you to ask Jesus to find the real burglars." Joe hoped his bare-bones explanation would be sufficient for Thomas.

"I think I seen the person who took the money, Joe."

Joe's jaw dropped. "What? You saw someone break into the church?"

Thomas nodded while chewing a mouthful of beans and franks. Then, "When I was stuck on the roof and crying out to Jesus, before you come and got me down, I saw somebody by the church door."

Joe's hopes began to rise. "Who was it? Did you recognize him?"

"It was dark, Joe. I just seen a shadow. I thought maybe it was you."

Joe shook his head vigorously. "No, Thomas, it wasn't me. I was in my tent. I didn't come out until I saw the fire. That's when I brought you the ladder."

"Then the shadow wasn't you; it was the burglar," Thomas said.

"Right, and I need to find that person and take them to the police. I need to get the money back for the church."

Joe allowed himself one small spoonful of beans before going on. "When you saw the shadow, do you remember seeing a car in the parking lot, someone driving in or driving out during the storm?"

Thomas shook his head. "I only seen cars and trucks on the road, and they didn't stop to help me."

Joe's hopes quickly deflated. "All right, then that's what I need from Jesus. I need him to tell us who that person was and what he did with the money."

"He can do that, Joe," Thomas said with characteristic optimism, "because he's Jesus. I'll ask Jesus to help you, Joe. I'll ask him when I pray."

"Thank you, Thomas," Joe said with genuine gratitude. "And I would appreciate it if you didn't tell anyone else about my 'problems'—anyone except Jesus, of course."

"I don't have to tell nobody else," Thomas said, smiling. "Telling Jesus is enough."

Joe finished his supper quickly and thanked his host again. Thomas said he would clean up, change clothes, and see Joe at the meeting. Joe left the man to his tasks.

Walking back to the hollow, Thomas' words about Jesus rang in his mind. His expectation that Jesus would help Joe injected him with hope. What if God—the God Thomas and Ezra and Rich believed in, the God who had transformed his birth mother and grandfather—what if this God was available to help him, too? What if this God could do something to clear his name in the burglary? Would this God do it for him, even though he didn't have "Jesus in his heart," as Thomas termed it? What if this God, who apparently had his hand in bringing Joe and his birth mother together, could keep him and Chessy together?

Walking out to the hollow, Joe thought about what Thomas had said about a "shadow" appearing near the church door on the night of the burglary. Thomas had insisted that there was no vehicle in the parking lot.

Whoever did it needed wheels to get out to the church and then escape after the burglary. Where was that vehicle during the burglary? Joe thought about one possible answer and decided to check it out.

Thirty-four

WALKING STRAIGHT PAST HIS CAMP, Joe ascended the footpath through the trees and brush where the police had discovered the buried metal box. It had poured on the night of the theft and the fire. Someone might have parked on the road behind the cover of the trees while breaking into the church. In all the noise of the storm, even Joe, whose tent was only forty or fifty yards away, would not have heard the car come and go, especially if the driver intended not to be heard. But there might be something that would tell him a car had been there. It wasn't much to go on, but he felt compelled to look.

Joe began walking the road between his camp and the church driveway, keeping an eye out for traffic—mostly pickups and other farm vehicles—and of which, fortunately, there was little. It was a stretch over one hundred yards long that could not be seen from the church building, even from Thomas' vantage point on the roof. Joe searched the sun-hardened dirt alongside the pavement all the way to the driveway. He didn't see anything unusual or worth closer inspection.

He backtracked and went the other way from his camp on the same side of the road. He walked over two hundred yards in this direction with the same result. He crossed to study the three hundred yards of shoulder on the far side of the road. About twenty yards past the footpath, he found something: a surprisingly clear tire impression baked in a small patch of yellowish clay-dirt, apparently from the passenger's side of a vehicle. Joe had noticed patches of this yellow clay around his campsite and beside the creek.

A few feet farther ahead he found a second print, not as clear because it was in soil instead of clay. Joe glanced across the road toward the church. The building was blocked from view by a stand of elms and birch near the road. From this point, the thief could jog silently to the door of the church in under a minute, and he would only be visible the last thirty yards. And at the height of the storm, Thomas was lucky even to see a shadow as the culprit entered or exited the church door.

Returning to the print in clay, Joe squatted down off the road to study it. If the guy parked on the correct side of the road, this would be his right rear tire. Joe didn't know much about tires, but this print didn't look like it came from a new one. The tread wasn't deep, and it was thinner on the right side of the print, suggesting uneven wear. As for a pattern, to Joe it just looked like garden variety tire tread.

Joe went back and forth between the front and rear prints several times before he was sure they were from two different kinds of tires. The front tire also had thin tread with uneven wear; in this case, less tread in the center of the print than on the outside. But the tread patterns were slightly different. Joe was sure the two prints were from the same vehicle. He guessed that it was an older car on which front and rear tires had been replaced at different times with different brands. Or a truck, perhaps. The prints could be from a light-duty pickup truck, and it seemed that every farmer in town had one.

Joe made mental notes about what to look for. Car or light truck. Front tire: thin center tread. Back tire: thin outer tread, possibly evidence of yellow clay. Joe knew he didn't have to go searching for tires to inspect, at least not right now. In less than twenty minutes, the church parking lot would be full of vehicles, and their owners would be inside attending the meeting. Joe would check them out one by one, and he would start with the Cadillac that belonged to Jethro Haig.

•   •   •

Jud's boss had given him a couple hours off, but the old man wanted him later in the evening. Jud hated working weeknights, especially now that he had money for being out on the town. If he could pull off a few more profitable jobs around the valley, his stash could last him several months, enough time to disappear from this state and leave his boss to fend for himself.

But at this moment Jud still had loose ends to tie up from the church job. He didn't believe it when he heard that the biker kid—Joe Caruso, by name—was on the loose and flaunting himself all over the valley. Jud had to see for himself. And then, as he was rolling down the main highway past the old church, there he was, squatting by the side of the road, tracing something in the dirt with his fingers. At fifty-five miles an hour, Jud was by him in a hurry. He turned his head away as he passed the kid, just in case he looked up at the pickup. He didn't. Glancing in the rearview mirror, Jud saw him still intently focused on the dirt.

Jud knew what was happening back there, and it made him mad. The kid was smarter than he looked. He had found the spot where Jud had parked the truck that night. He was looking at tread marks in the dirt. Was he smart enough to figure out where they came from? That would ruin everything. The law couldn't keep Joe Caruso off his trail, so Jud would have to do it himself. And in that instant, he knew just what to do.

About a mile and a half down the highway, Jud pulled the rusty red pickup into a driveway and turned around. Staring up the road, he ran through the gears until he was up to sixty. The front end shimmied a little at this speed, but in a fifty-five zone, he was close enough to legal. And after contact at sixty miles per hour, Joe wouldn't be around to argue when Jud explained that the kid had just bolted across the road in front of him without looking.

Jud could see the form still crouched by the road. He tugged the bill of his cap low on his forehead and sighted in on his prey. But when Jud was still a quarter mile away, the kid stood up and looked both ways on the highway, then he jogged across and into the brush toward the hollow. As Jud raced past, he again glanced away in case the kid was looking. Slowing at the corner past the church driveway, he turned left and accelerated eastward without another glance.

Jud shouted a vile curse in the cab. In that last quarter mile, his resolve had become tempered-steel firm. He had to get rid of Joe Caruso, and it had to be soon. Such an action would require that Jud leave the valley before he had planned to. By the time they found the kid's body, Jud would be a couple states away living a new life. And Joe Caruso would be nothing more than a dead burglar.

●   ●   ●

Joe stayed in the hollow watching the cars and pickups arrive for the meeting. He saw Bradford and Esther drive in, park, and enter the church. Bradford spotted Joe in the hollow from the church steps and waved. Joe waved back, wishing he could walk up to the man and tell him that his long-lost grandson had come home. He kept an eye out for Brenda's car approaching on the road. Was she planning to make contact with her parents tonight? Had she called them to set up a meeting? There were no champagne-colored Honda Accords among the vehicles turning into the church driveway.

Jethro Haig's silver Caddie was one of the last to arrive. Jethro got out and strode toward the church without the slightest glance toward the hollow. His driver, as always, shut off the engine, rolled down the window, and stayed behind the wheel. Rusty never spoke to anyone at the church, and nobody at church spoke to Rusty, as if he was just another inanimate ornament on the car. It would be a challenge to check out the Caddie's tires without arousing Rusty's curiosity, but somehow Joe had to do it.

Velma's car followed the Caddie into the parking lot. Chessy got out and waved to him. He zipped up his tent and jogged toward the parking lot. She started across the cemetery to meet him.

Chessy asked about his day. "It was a really great day," he said, wishing he could tell her what his mother had revealed about Bradford McDermot. Instead he quickly turned the question back to her. She had accomplished some reading she needed to do and felt good about it.

"Do you want to stop by Uncle Thomas' cabin with me?" she said as they crossed the cemetery lawn. "I'm going to sit with him during the meeting, just to make sure he's all right. I was hoping you would sit with us, too."

"I ate supper with Thomas a little over an hour ago," Joe explained. "He sounded real good. He may already be inside the church."

"You ate supper with him?" Chessy said, sounding pleased.

"Yeah, I helped him set up a table for the meeting, and he invited me over for franks and beans. It was very good." Joe thought about his conversation with Thomas. That had been good, too. He would tell Chessy about it eventually. Just before stepping through the doorway, Joe glanced back toward Jethro's Cadillac. Rusty was slouched behind the wheel with his cap pulled down over his eyes, country music wafting from the open window.

A chilly quiet greeted them as they entered the sanctuary at a minute before seven. Bradford and Ezra sat at the table on the platform, huddled in a whispered conversation. Most of the regular church members were present, Joe guessed, and sitting in their usual places. Jethro Haig and Chet Rasby sat statue still, both staring forward. But the usually congenial chatting among members was missing. People just sat and waited for the meeting to begin.

Joe and Chessy slid into a rear pew and scanned the room for Thomas, but he wasn't there. They left enough room on the end of the pew for Thomas to sit when he arrived.

Bradford, in a serious tone, welcomed everyone to the meeting. Joe saw him in new light. Today he noticed a few physical traits his grandfather shared with Brenda: squared shoulders, slightly upturned nose, dark brown eyes. Joe considered the irony. Bradford was a fine man. After a rocky start, Brenda had put her life back together and had become a fine woman. Yet father and daughter had been separated for more than twenty years by old hurts. Joe wanted this family reunion as much for them as for himself.

"Ezra and I decided that we need to begin this meeting with a time of prayer," Bradford began. His gentle command of the congregation gave Joe pause for pride. "God doesn't want us to be divided over this issue. We need to hear what he wants us to do, what will pull us together instead of tear us apart. So for the next few minutes, let's go to the Lord in prayer. Anybody who wants to lead out may do so."

The rows of heads in front of Joe and Chessy bowed in unison, and the room was silent—not a rustle, not a cough. The seconds ticked by. Out of the corner of his eye, he saw that Chessy's head was bowed and her eyes were squeezed shut. Joe kept his eyes open, watching the congregation. They seemed to be frozen in time, no movement, no sound.

Finally, Bradford offered a nice prayer to get things started, asking God for the very things he had instructed the congregation to pray for. In the background, Ezra added an occasional, muffled "Amen" to the board chairman's petition. Joe knew that both men had their biases: Bradford was in favor of selling the property, and Ezra wanted to keep it. But he was convinced that both men wanted unanimity in the congregation more than they wanted to push their respective sides of the issue, and that impressed Joe.

After another minute of silence, another rumbling voice pierced the silence. It took Joe a moment to determine that it was Chet Rasby. His prayer was laced with religious sounding *thees* and *thous, shouldsts* and *couldsts*. But it was soon apparent that Chet was using the opportunity to advance his cause. The man had already determined that God wanted the church to keep the property for future ministry, and his flowery address to God was his way of making sure everyone else understood it. The scattered murmurs of "Amen" and "Yes, Lord" all came from the Rasby side of the sanctuary.

Chet had barely uttered the final amen to his prayer when Jethro Haig raised his coarse voice. He was louder and more fervent than Chet, but his petition centered on the importance of being good stewards of the buildings and grounds God had already entrusted to the Chapel of the Valley. As he prayed, verbal support rose from the McDermot quarter. Joe didn't like Jethro Haig from the beginning. He wondered if he would discover reasons for his dislike to become hatred.

And so it went. Each succeeding prayer seemed to be directed more toward the other side of the sanctuary than up to God. *This is like a spiritual volleyball match,* Joe thought with wry amusement. Two sides trying to outpoint each other by spiritualizing their biases. Joe found it laughable, but the bowed church members were dead serious.

Finally, Bradford cut in to end the "season of prayer" with a booming "Amen." When the two men at the platform table looked up, Joe noticed the minister furtively dabbing tears from his eyes with a handkerchief.

Chessy leaned into him and whispered, "I'm going to look for Uncle Thomas. He must have decided not to come to the meeting."

"I'll go with you," Joe whispered back. So far, Joe was not impressed with the meeting. He would much rather be outside with Chessy. And perhaps he would linger outside while Chessy and Thomas took their places inside. He wanted a look at Jethro's car while the light was still good.

As they slipped out of their pew, the business part of the meeting began. Bradford was introducing the proposal submitted by Jethro Haig that the church sell off thirteen acres of undeveloped property for the purpose of restoring the building fund. As Joe and Chessy tiptoed out the front door, Bradford yielded the floor to Jethro to present his case.

"It doesn't sound good in there," Joe said as the descended the front steps.

"I can't believe these people," Chessy said, shaking her head. "To be honest, I'm embarrassed for them. This is not how Christians are supposed to act, Joe. I hope you don't judge us by what you see in there."

Joe caught the inference, whether intended or not. Chessy and the others were us, the Christians. Joe was still on the outside looking in. He couldn't argue with her. He was learning a lot about Jesus Christ and the people who had committed their lives to him. But Chessy was right, Joe admitted. He was not in that winsome albeit imperfect company.

As they crossed the lawn on a line with the caretaker's cabin, they could hear Jethro's voice rising in volume through the sanctuary's open windows. He was marching point by point through a list of reasons why the church should sell the property, and why he should be the one to buy it. So far the presentation was civil with no interruptions from Chet or the others.

Chessy stopped at the entrance to the cemetery and glanced around. Thomas was nowhere in sight, so they continued across the cemetery lawn to the cabin door. Chessy rapped gently. "Uncle Thomas, are you in there?"

There was no response. She rapped harder. "Uncle Thomas, are you coming to the meeting?"

When the door did not open, Chessy turned to Joe with a troubled expression. "I don't like this," she said.

"He's probably...indisposed, you know, in the bathroom," Joe suggested.

"Would you go look?" Chessy said.

Joe didn't relish the idea of surprising a man in his own home, but at Chessy's request he tried the doorknob. It was unlocked. "I'll tell your uncle we'll wait out here for him," he said.

He stepped inside, leaving the door ajar. The small house smelled of hickory smoke flavoring left over from supper. Thomas was not in the living room or the kitchen, which Joe could clearly see from inside the front door. The supper dishes were still on the table, and a saucepan with leftover franks and beans was still on the range.

"Thomas, it's Joe," he called out, moving slowly through the living room. "Chessy's outside. We don't mean to bother you. We just want to know if you're coming to the meeting."

No answer. No sound of movement. Joe turned toward the back of the house, apprehension growing.

He found the bathroom door open and the room empty. He stepped into the last room of the cabin, Thomas' bedroom. It was also empty. The bed was neatly made and everything in place except for a pair of boots dropped outside the closet door. Joe smiled. He didn't know any bachelor who kept his quarters as neat as Thomas Rasby's cabin.

Joe returned to the front door. "He's not here," he said, stepping outside.

"That's strange," Chessy said. "Where could he be?"

"It's *very* strange because he left his work boots..." An odd thought stopped him. He turned back to the door. "Just a minute. I'm going to check something." He walked back into the little house.

"What is it, Joe?" Chessy said, following him through the living room toward the bedroom.

Joe didn't answer. He entered the bedroom and opened the closet door slowly. The reflected sunlight revealed a pair of soiled white work socks on the floor and a suit and a few shirts hanging above them. Staring at the socks, Joe felt a chill.

He could tell that feet were still in them.

Chessy peered over Joe's shoulder as he slid the hanging garments to one side. "Oh no!" Chessy gasped. Joe bent down for a closer look. It was Thomas, still in his work clothes and socks, crumpled and still on the floor of the tiny, dark closet.

Chessy knelt beside Joe. "Uncle Thomas?" she called out plaintively. Then she attempted to reach into the closet, but Joe blocked her.

"Let me check first," he said. He leaned into the closet on one knee and reached for Thomas' wrist. The skin was cool to the touch, and there was no pulse.

He laid the hand down carefully and leaned out of the closet. "Chessy, I think your uncle is dead," he said.

Thirty-five

JOE SAT ON THE BEDROOM FLOOR next to Chessy, who gazed into the closet and wept softly. Thomas' head was on the floor in the back corner of the closet with his legs folded up under his torso and his arms at his side. In a few minutes, they would have to go tell someone what they had found. But for the moment, Joe knew Chessy just needed time to be sad.

"Remember how he talked about his heart hurting?" Chessy said. "When the men were arguing, he held his heart."

Joe nodded. "Maybe those were warning signs that a heart attack was coming."

Chessy stroked Thomas' foot lightly. "And we thought he was just upset."

"Maybe the problems at the church broke his heart—literally," Joe said.

They sat in silence for several moments.

"Uncle Thomas was praying when he died," Chessy said, wiping tears from her eyes.

"Praying?" Joe said. "How do you know?"

"This was his prayer closet," she said.

Joe had never heard the term before. "I don't understand," he said.

Chessy explained. "In some versions of the New Testament, it says we should go into our closet to pray. It means that we should find a place that is free of distractions. But Uncle Thomas thought very concretely, as you know. To him, if the Bible says closet, it must mean closet. He told me the other night that he takes off his boots and crawls into his closet when it's time to pray."

Joe spoke the words as the thought occurred to him. "Thomas told me he was going to pray for me."

"I think he prays for everybody he knows," Chessy said.

"No, I mean just today," Joe explained, "while we were eating supper. We talked about some things, and he said he would pray for me. Then I left. It looks like he came straight in here. The supper dishes are still on the table."

Chessy said, "He took off his boots and crawled into the closet to pray for you...and just...died. Think about it. One moment, Uncle Thomas was huddled in this closet pouring his heart out to God. The next moment he walked right into God's presence in heaven."

The words hit Joe hard. He didn't know what to say. Finally, he suggested that they go back to the church and tell the minister what they had found. Chessy said she would stay next to Uncle Thomas while Joe broke the news. When he got back, she would have to call her parents and tell them the sad news.

Walking from the cabin to the church, Joe felt like he had been cheated. The mentally shallow but spiritually deep caretaker, this man who seemed to know Jesus intimately, had promised to pray for him. Now Thomas was gone. Perhaps he died before uttering a word to God on Joe's behalf. And there would be no next time. Who would pray for him now?

Approaching the church, Joe heard harsh words pouring through the open windows. The discussion which began almost civilly had escalated to an argument again. Joe climbed the steps, entered the church, and walked straight down the center aisle toward the front. Under the guise of a spirited discussion, church members were lobbing accusations across the aisle like grenades. People on both sides were threatening to leave the church if the vote went against them. Had Thomas been in the room, Joe thought, he likely would have collapsed and died by now.

He walked directly to the table where Bradford and Ezra were sitting. Their faces were shadowed with agony over the fight. Joe hated to make their already bad day even worse.

Stepping up on the platform, he motioned for them to huddle with him. The church members didn't let Joe's presence on the platform stop the argument. Bradford and Ezra leaned in to hear Joe above the din. "Chessy and I went looking for Thomas," he said for their ears only. "We found him in his cabin. We think he had a heart attack. He's dead."

Ezra dropped his head into his hands. "O dear Lord, please, no," he said.

Bradford leaned in even closer. "Dead? Are you sure, Joe?"

"Yes, he's stone cold, no pulse. He's probably been dead for an hour or more."

Ezra looked up, tears forming in his eyes. "Not dear Thomas."

"I need to see for myself," Bradford said. Joe understood perfectly. Had he been in Bradford's shoes, he would need to verify the news, too. "I'll be right back. Will you stay here, Joe?"

Joe nodded, knowing he meant to stay with Ezra.

Bradford left the platform through the anteroom door which led through the dismantled church office to the outside. The room began to quiet as people were distracted by the activity on the platform. Finally, someone called out from the pews, "What's going on, Ezra?" The discussion was suddenly suspended as church members swiveled forward to hear the reply.

"I'll answer that question in just a moment," he said. "Would everyone please be seated?"

Joe could read the concern in their faces. They knew something was wrong, but they did as Ezra asked. Rich and Velma, who had been sitting in the second row, came quickly to the platform in support of the minister, who could not hide his grief.

Thankfully, Bradford did not linger at the cabin. Returning to the platform table, he remained standing. "Folks, I have sad news," he began. "Our caretaker, Thomas Rasby, apparently suffered a heart attack this evening." A collective gasp rose from the congregation. Bradford went on quickly. "I'm sorry to tell you that he passed away in his cabin."

The gasps gave way to sighs and groans and tears. Velma Walls, standing near Joe, clouded up but remained in control. "Where's Chessy?" she whispered to Bradford. He aimed a thumb toward the cabin and nodded, silently communicating that Chessy needed her now. Velma hurried out of the sanctuary.

Turning back to the congregation, Bradford said, "There's no point in going on with the meeting. There won't be any more fighting tonight. You folks are free to leave. I'm sure Velma will notify everyone when the family decides on a time for the funeral."

Some people rose and filed out of the sanctuary immediately. Others remained in their pews, stunned and grief-stricken. The volatile issues of a moment ago were suddenly unimportant. Jethro walked out in silence with the first wave, head bowed, brushing tears from his cheeks. Chet Rasby huddled with his wife, who was weeping. There was no conversation, only an occasional whisper of shock and grief.

Ezra wanted to go to the cabin right away, so Joe joined a small group, including Bradford and Rich, escorting the lame minister across the cemetery lawn to the cabin. Bradford directed Esther to telephone the funeral home in town to send out a van. A handful of parishioners followed behind at a respectful distance. Others silently walked to their cars and drove away.

As the others crowded into the small bedroom to grieve, Joe went into the kitchen to clean up the supper dishes Thomas had decided to leave for later. It seemed right for Joe to pitch in since he had been the supper guest. Jethro and Rusty were long gone, as were the majority of other church people. Joe would have to continue his investigation at another time. He had neither the opportunity nor the heart for it at the moment.

Joe wondered what had motivated Thomas to hurry into his "prayer closet" so soon after Joe left. Was Thomas so moved by Joe's problem that he felt compelled to pray about it right away? It stunned Joe to think that his name may have been one of the last words on Thomas' lips.

When Chessy came out of the bedroom, she borrowed Bradford's cell phone to call her parents. Joe sat beside her in the living room as she tearfully reported the details. Her mother and father would fly up tomorrow.

When the mortician arrived, he asked if any of the men would be willing to help him lift the body out of the closet and prepare it for transport. Joe assessed that Bradford and Ezra were not up to the task emotionally, let alone physically. That left him and Rich. To Joe's relief, Rich quickly volunteered. Everyone else crowded into the living room as the mortician rolled a gurney into the bedroom.

Joe watched Bradford furtively. He was proud of how his grandfather had handled the crisis. He was a wise man and a respected leader. Joe wondered how he would have turned out had he grown up with Bradford as a role model instead of his adoptive father.

The mortician backed out of the bedroom, pulling on the gurney. Rich followed, pushing from the other end. A heavy, black, plastic body bag was strapped securely to the top.

"You think you'll have a service here at the church, Ezra?" the mortician questioned. He pulled white latex gloves off his hands as spoke.

"Yes, Johnny, possibly Wednesday," Ezra said, struggling to get up on his crutches. "We'll confirm day and time after talking with the family."

"And will the interment be here as well?"

Ezra turned to Chessy. "Do you think your mother will want Thomas buried here?"

"Yes, I'm sure this is where he would want to be," she said.

"Call me tomorrow when you know what time," the mortician said, "and we'll have him ready."

"Thanks, Johnny," Ezra said.

Chessy, Joe, and the others stood on the lawn as the mortician's van drove away. A few congregation members had stayed. Most of them expressed their sympathies to Chessy before leaving. She thanked them.

"Is there something I can do for you?" Joe asked her. He knew that his request was at least partially selfish. As long as he was helping Chessy deal with her sadness he wouldn't be left alone with his own.

"I don't know of anything, Joe" she said. "I think I'll go home with Velma. I need to call Mom and Dad again."

"Sure, I understand." Joe gazed at the western mountains as he spoke. The sun had just slipped behind the tallest peak.

"But thank you for being here with me," she added. "Maybe I will see you tomorrow."

"I hope so."

As he watched Chessy and Velma leave, Joe felt a strong arm grip him around the shoulders. It was a manly expression of affection that Joe had appreciated before he even knew that Bradford was his grandfather. Now the big man's touch meant even more. Esther, his secret grandmother, was at Bradford's side.

"We can't thank you enough for everything you have done around here, Joe," Bradford said, his arm still draped around Joe's shoulders.

"You were so kind and helpful to Thomas, and he really liked you," Esther put in. "You're a very special young man, and we're glad God brought you our way."

Joe felt a lump of emotion swell in his throat and tears come to his eyes. He wanted desperately to end the pretense and blurt out what he knew about this wonderful couple. How long would he have to face them and pretend he was nothing more than a traveler in this valley? All he could say in response was, "Thank you."

Bradford asked about Joe's court appearance and how he was feeling about it. Joe explained that it would be sometime later in the week. He did not verbalize his hope that the real burglar would be unmasked by then. Bradford told him that they would stand with him no matter what.

"I thought you might want to know," Bradford continued, releasing his grip on Joe. "that we received a good offer on our farm this morning. We signed the papers this afternoon to get things started."

Joe wanted to be happy for Bradford, but his news brought only sadness. It was the family farm, *Joe's* family. He wasn't sure what the farm meant to him, but he knew what it meant to Bradford and Esther. It was a shame to see it pass into the hands of a stranger.

"That's great," Joe said, only because it's what he thought Bradford wanted to hear.

"It's a concern off our minds," Esther said wistfully. "We can get on with our retirement now."

Joe nodded.

"I hope we can have you out to supper at least once more before you head back east," she said.

"I'd like that very much."

Ezra joined them, having closed up the cabin and locked the door. "I guess old Thomas spoke his mind about the property, and he wasn't even at the meeting."

"Took the wind out of everybody's sails, didn't he?" Bradford replied. "Trouble is, we will have to reconvene the meeting eventually and finish the business."

"When will you meet again?" Joe asked.

Ezra sighed. "I lost a dear friend this evening, Joe. I don't want to disturb his memory by thinking about a meeting that should never have been needed."

Bradford and Esther said their goodbyes and left. Ezra wished Joe a pleasant evening and hobbled back to the parsonage. Since Thomas was no longer around to close up the church, Velma had recruited Rich to do it. Everyone else was gone.

Left to himself, Joe headed out to his camp. It was nearly 8:30, but the landscape was still bathed in golden twilight. Even though he felt somewhat numb from the tragedy of Thomas' sudden death, Joe forced his thoughts back to the puzzle he had to solve—identifying the person who had burglarized the church and framed him. The evening's events had prevented him from inspecting vehicles in the parking lot as he had planned, especially Jethro Haig's vehicle. He still had time today to pick up the trail.

He decided to take one more look at the tire prints preserved in the hardened mud alongside the road. Grabbing a scrap of paper and a pen for making a simple sketch, he hustled up the path to the road. After checking for traffic, he crossed the highway and walked to the spot where he had found the clear prints.

They were gone.

Thirty-six

JOE EXAMINED SEVERAL YARDS OF SOIL on either side of the spot where he was sure he had seen the tire prints, just to be sure. On this stretch of shoulder where the tire prints had been only two hours ago, there was nothing but scuffed dirt, as if someone had purposely busted up the impressions with the heel of a boot.

He's been here! Joe thought with a chill. *He came back to destroy the evidence while we were in the church.* He thought about Jethro Haig—the old man had been in the sanctuary the whole time. But he didn't know that for sure. Joe had been with Chessy in Thomas' cabin. Jethro had twenty or thirty minutes to slip out of the church, cross the road, scuff up the soil, and return to the debate.

Did my visit to Jethro's farm this afternoon provoke the bold move? Joe wondered. *Is he running scared but too polished a thief to show it?* Joe knew he still had to check out the tires on the silver Cadillac. Even without a sketch, he roughly remembered what to look for. But Jethro and Rusty were long gone. If he was going to inspect the Caddie now, he would have to do it in Jethro's driveway or garage.

Joe returned to his camp to smoke a cigarette and think about a plan. Should he tell the local cops what he was doing? He answered himself immediately with a shake of the head. He needed something concrete to show them, something way more convincing than the tire tracks that were now gone. Best case scenario, he needed to find the money in the possession of the thief. The only possible link between Jethro Haig and the money were the tire tracks. He had to go out to the farm tonight and either confirm or dismiss his hunch that Jethro was involved.

He would wait until well after dark, both to assure that Jethro was home and in bed and to utilize the cover of night. *Midnight at the earliest,* Joe decided. He needed a good flashlight and a few other things. Sitting down at the picnic table, he scratched out a quick list. Then he fired up the motorcycle and blazed up the highway toward Yarborough.

•   •   •

Jud sat in the only booth of the tavern on the sleazy east side of Yarborough sipping his third beer. He liked the Eastside Bullpen because it was small, off the main roads, and dark, a place to come when he just wanted to drink alone. It was also a good place to meet someone secretly. Jud had told the guy on the phone to be here by 10:00 P.M. The clock mounted below the neon beer sign on the wall read 10:40. The only people in the place beside Jud were a couple of old drunks at the bar hitting on the barmaid, who was older than they were.

Earlier this evening, it had taken Jud only five minutes to find the tire tracks he had left behind and wipe them out for good while the kid was playing goody-two-shoes in church. But Jud didn't trust a kid who was smart enough to look for tracks. If Joe Caruso didn't disappear and soon, Jud would always be looking over his shoulder. So he decided to pay the kid a surprise, late night visit in the hollow to end his snooping and protect Jud's perfect crime forever. And his new toy, which would also disappear after the deed, would make short work of Joe Caruso.

At 10:55, a man walked into the bar quietly and slid into the booth across the table from Jud. Despite the warm evening, he was wearing a parka and a wool cap pulled down low. Jud expected an older guy. This one was barely twenty.

Waving off the barmaid, the man whispered to Jud with a sneer, "Four hundred dollars cash, right now."

Jud came back just as tough. "Let's see the merchandise."

The kid reached into an inside pocket of his parka and, after a quick glance toward the bar, pulled out the items they had agreed on over the phone. They were wrapped in a plastic grocery sack. He laid his parcel on the table, covering most of it with his hand.

"The money, c'mon," he snapped at a whisper.

Jud pulled a wad of bills out of his jeans pocket and put it on the table. When the kid reached for the money, Jud moved the package to his side of the table. He could feel the butt, cylinder, and stock through the thin plastic. He also fingered a small box of shells.

"Is it clean?" Jud said.

"Numbers are filed off. It's untraceable."

"Then get lost, kid."

The kid stuffed the money into his pocket and left the tavern. Jud slid the package inside his belt and zipped up his windbreaker to cover the bulge. Dropping a ten-dollar bill on the table, he left.

Sitting in the cab of his truck in the dimly lit parking lot, Jud loaded the gun and dropped a half dozen extra shells in the pocket of his jeans. He started the pickup and headed toward Orchard Valley.

Jud parked the truck several feet up a darkend dirt road a quarter mile north of the old church. The shots might be heard by the old preacher, but Jud would be back to the truck and lost in the dust of the side road before anyone at the church knew what happened. Five minutes later, the gun and any unused shells would be at the bottom of the river and Jud would be free.

Tucking the loaded gun into his belt under his jacket, he pulled his cap low and walked out to the highway in the dark. Traffic at this hour was limited to one car every couple of minutes. When lights appeared in the distance, Jud sidled into the brush to hide until the traveler passed.

Jud could see from the road that the church and the parsonage were dark, and so was the hollow. He didn't figure on the kid already being asleep. But if he was, all the better.

Slipping into the trees bordering the hollow, he stealthily crept near the small tent. There was no motorcycle to be seen. The bike was always parked outside the tent entrance, but tonight it was gone and the tent was zipped closed. *The kid must be off joy-riding with that little girlfriend of his,* Jud thought. *But he'll be back, and I've got nowhere else to be.* So he found a dry patch of grass in the trees and settled down to await his target.

● ● ●

Joe walked his bike down the long gravel driveway toward Jethro Haig's farmhouse. He had debated the merits of parking farther away and walking in, but once he saw what he came to see, he didn't care if Jethro heard the bike thunder to life under his bedroom window as he departed. It was just past 1:00 A.M., and Joe kind of liked the idea of waking the old man up with a scare. It might give Jethro another good reason to dislike him.

There were no lights showing in the upstairs windows of the farmhouse, and only a dim light glowing through what Joe thought was the kitchen window. Probably just a nightlight of some kind. The old codger was upstairs sawing logs. The yard around the house, the barn, and the equipment shed was dark. Joe remembered seeing floodlights mounted on the work buildings, so he had to stay outside the range of any motion sensors that could flood the yard with light. The windows above the garage were dark. Joe wondered if Rusty Ewing lived in the house or in this apartment over the garage.

Joe parked the bike behind a large bush at the end of the driveway. Then he followed the darkest shadows around the back of the big shed until he reached the garage. The ATV and the golf cart were parked beside the garage as they were earlier in the day. One of the pickups was there, the other one—the red one—was gone. Could Jethro be out late in the pickup? Joe didn't think so. It was well known that Jethro didn't like to drive the Cadillac; that's why his lazy stepson had a steady job. Maybe Rusty was out with the truck. Joe was glad he hid the bike in case the truck came back while he was still investigating. He had already scoped out his escape route behind the shed if he had to exit the garage in a hurry.

Joe pulled recently purchased work gloves out of his front pockets and pulled them on. Tiptoeing behind the garage, he came to the back corner nearest the house. There was a wooden stairway leading up to the garage apartment, and under the stairway was a side door to the garage. The door was only about thirty feet from what looked to be the service porch to the house. All windows on this side of the house were dark.

Joe didn't know if there was a motion sensor over the side garage door, so he stepped into the open for two seconds and waved his arms, then he jumped back out of sight. He was sure scavenging animals set off the lights throughout the night, so the momentary brightness would cause no alarm in the house if it was noticed. Still, Joe didn't want to be caught standing in the light if someone happened to glance out a window.

No side garage light came on. He tried again, moving farther out into the open, waving his arms, then quickly backing into cover. Nothing. Satisfied, Joe crept to the side door and tried the knob. It turned in his hand, so he slipped in and closed it soundlessly behind him.

With no windows in the garage, it was pitch black. He pulled the small new flashlight from his hip pocket, cupped his hand over the lens, and switched it on. Then he spread his fingers slowly to allow a minimum of light to escape, fearing that the full beam might be more noticeable escaping through cracks in the doors.

It was a two-car garage, but the silver Cadillac was the only vehicle inside. There was a long work bench along the far wall piled high with junk, and the perimeter floor was also littered with tools, picking boxes, car parts, and trash.

Joe moved to the passenger's side front fender of the Caddie, knelt down, and released a little more light on the tire. It didn't come close to matching the prints Joe had seen in the mud. The tires weren't new, but the tread was still good for another 20,000 miles, Joe guessed. And the tires were evenly worn. The back tire looked the same, as did the two on the driver's side. Had the tires been brand new, Joe would have suspected they had been changed out in the last couple of days. But that didn't seem to be the case.

Switching off the flashlight, Joe stood up in the silent darkness. He was wrong about the Caddie, but was he still wrong about Jethro Haig? What about the farm trucks? What if—

Before the question could form in his brain, Joe heard something: a low hum growing louder, gravel ticking on metal. Then he saw a bright sliver of light sweep under the garage bay doors as a vehicle outside slowed and stopped.

The missing truck was back.

Joe's escape route was suddenly blocked. He could not retreat behind the garage and equipment shed without passing in front of the spot where the truck was now parking, or at least not until the driver was back inside the house. Joe had to stay put and hope that whoever had just arrived—Jethro or Rusty or both of them—would not come into the garage.

He moved quickly to make sure the Cadillac was between him and the door he had entered. He wished the police had not confiscated his pistol. He wished he had glanced around the garage when the flashlight was on for something he could use to defend himself if he had to. But he couldn't afford to turn on the light now, so he dropped low behind the Caddie to wait.

The truck engine shut down, and only one door opened and closed. Joe followed the thud of boots on pavement as the driver walked in front of the bay doors. Joe figured the guy was either heading toward the house, the stairs to the garage apartment, or the garage side door. He hoped the man had no reason to rummage through the garage at this time of night. While holding his breath, Joe listened.

When he heard heavy footsteps on wood, he released a silent breath. The driver was ascending the stairs to the apartment. Joe was sure it was Rusty. From the sound of the boots, Joe envisioned the man reaching the landing in front of his door, then he paused, perhaps to find the key on his ring. Then he heard the door swing open and close, then heavy footsteps in the apartment above.

Joe decided not to wait around. Rusty may have reason to come back downstairs. He moved quickly to the side door, opened it without a sound, and followed the dark shadows behind the garage toward the equipment shed. There was the old red Ford pickup parked beside an even older cream-colored GMC. Maybe the red truck was Rusty's. It made sense that he would drive the Cadillac when transporting Jethro, but even a chauffer needs his own wheels when he's off work.

Joe had to check the tires of both trucks. With Rusty inside, the motion-sensitive floodlights at the front of the garage were now off again. Glancing up, he saw a light on in the side window of the apartment. Keeping in mind that Rusty might have a view of his truck from the window, Joe moved slowly in the darkness to where he could squat down and look at the tires of the GMC.

Even the faint glow of the flashlight might attract Rusty's attention. Joe hunkered low, covered the lens of the flashlight with his hand, and aimed the subdued beam at the right front tire. After three or four seconds, he pivoted on his haunches and illuminated the right rear for five more seconds. Then the light went off. The tread didn't match what he remembered from the shoulder near his camp. He moved at a crouch to the Ford and repeated the inspection.

The sight froze him with fear. It was a match, no doubt about it. These had to be the tires that left a mark in the roadside soil near his tent. The tread patterns matched what he remembered. There were even traces of yellow clay. While Joe had been focused on Jethro Haig, it now looked as if Rusty Ewing was the man he was looking for—Rusty, the man who was so far under the radar in Orchard Valley that few people even acknowledged his presence.

Yet Rusty Ewing had been at the meeting last night, slouched in the Caddie as usual, only steps away from the telling tire prints that were scuffed into oblivion. And being Jethro Haig's driver, he probably overheard something about the money, made the snatch, and stacked the evidence against the stranger in the hollow. Nobody even gave Rusty a second thought. Joe wasn't about to underestimate him. If he was capable of burglary and smart enough to frame someone else, what would he do if he was confronted?

Joe had to tell the police in Orchard Valley, but would they believe him? Not likely. He needed concrete proof. He needed to find the money, and now he had an idea where to look. But not tonight. He had to get out of here and come back when he could get into Rusty's apartment. And if he couldn't find the money, Joe didn't know what he'd do.

He glanced up to the apartment window again. He saw no face looking down at him, only cheap, gauzy curtains glowing with faint light. So Joe took off as quickly and quietly as possible toward the Harley. He wasn't about to tip his hand by firing it up in the driveway. He would push it out to the road. He still wanted the element of surprise when he returned to look for the money.

• • •

Jud sat on the edge of the bed looking at the note his boss had taped to his apartment door. It started with his name—at least the name Jethro used for him. It made no sense putting his name on the note since he was the only one who lived in the apartment, the only person to read it. *How stupid!* Jud also hated being called Rusty instead of Judson. When his mother had married Jethro Haig and Jud was a young teen, the old man had started calling him Rusty, trying to be friendly with the kid. Jud didn't like it then, and he didn't like it now. But Jethro was incorrigible. Jud was Rusty to everyone around here, but he had been Judson to his mother and that's what he intended to be called after he left this valley behind.

The only other words on the note were, "11:00 A.M. sharp." It meant the old man probably had a lunch date in the city. Jud cursed at the thought of ferrying the old man into Yarborough, but he had to do it. At least for one more day. Ever since his mother died, Jud had to play the role of the subservient son with Jethro. His mother had taken care of him up to then, and being Jethro's flunky, though it wasn't Jud's idea of a being taken care of, at least it gave him a bed, three square meals a day, a truck to drive, and pocket money—which beat working. Work was something to which Jud had never taken much of a liking. But as soon as he could get rid of Joe Caruso, Jud's lifestyle would change, and Jethro wouldn't be leaving him stupid notes.

The thought of Caruso made Jud wad up the note and fling it into the corner with a curse. He had sat on the ground in the hollow for nearly two hours waiting with gun in hand for the kid to show up, but he never did. It was just a delay of the inevitable as far as Jud was concerned. He didn't get him tonight, but he would get him tomorrow night.

Jud pulled the shoebox full of money from under the bed. He didn't want to count it; just look at it. And the sight instantly energized his resolve to do away with Joe Caruso. Jud was sliding the box back under the mattress when he thought he heard a motorcycle start up in the distance.

It sounded like a Harley.

Thirty-seven

JOE AWOKE BEFORE 6:00 A.M. to the raucous conversation of jays and starlings outside his tent. There would be no going back to sleep. His mind swirled with a slideshow of images flashing through his consciousness. Two recurring images caused him discomfort. The first was the picture of Thomas Rasby lying crumpled, still, and cold in the closet of his cabin. If there was anyone the people in this church and this valley needed, and Joe included himself in that number, it was the kind-hearted, self-effacing Thomas Rasby.

But the sweet old guy was gone.

The second troubling image was that of Rusty Ewing, the nearly invisible "extra" in this cast of characters whom Joe now suspected was the culprit. For all the good Thomas had brought into Joe's life, not the least of which was his niece, Rusty's plot threatened to spoil it all. Joe hoped to turn that around today at Haig's farm, though at this moment he didn't know how he would do it.

Lying in his sleeping bag, Joe considered the events of the last six days in Orchard Valley. It was like a story that had happened to someone else, so different from anything else in his life to this point. Enveloped in a different environment, his thoughts had been stretched in so many new directions. Many of the people he had met had become important to him in such a short time: Chessy, Brenda, Bradford, Rich, Ezra, and poor Thomas. The trip had turned into so much more than he had expected.

And then there was Jesus—the one whom these people claimed as the anchor and purpose of their lives. Joe's thoughts kept returning to Chessy's reference to "us," meaning Christians, and by default implying that Joe was not included in that group. She had not meant for Joe to feel excluded, of that he was sure. But she was right. He was not a Christian. He had not committed his life to Jesus Christ as these others had. He was on the outside looking in. He felt closer to God than he had ever felt before, and he wanted to get even closer. He could not deny that God had heard his feeble prayer in the jail cell and led him to Rusty Ewing. For all the good he had experienced being near Christian people, he felt increasingly isolated and alone for not knowing Christ as they did.

Joe pulled himself out of the bag at 6:30 in the morning and made himself get dressed and washed. Putting away his kit, he heard the screen door slam across the field. He saw Rich passing from the parsonage to the door leading into the church office. He was dressed casually and carrying a couple of books. The man was a perpetual student. He couldn't get enough of the Bible. Couldn't get enough of God. And he had been so willing to share what he knew and what he had with Joe. If anyone could help him deal with this sense of being on the outside looking in, it was Rich.

Joe found himself walking up the gentle slope of the hollow toward the church. He went straight to the side door Rich had entered. Pulling it open, he climbed the stairs, passed through the fire-damaged office, and entered into the sanctuary. Rich was seated on the front pew, bathed in a swath of sunlight pouring in through a side window. A Bible lay open on his lap. "Good morning, Joe," he said, looking up. He gave no indication that Joe's appearance was an interruption. Rather, he seemed glad to see him.

Joe hesitated, questioning his impulsive barging in on the professor. But he might never get this far again, especially if he talked himself out of this opportunity.

"Hi," he said. "Can we talk?"

"Of course," Rich said invitingly.

Joe sat down on the pew. "There's a lot going on inside me right now," he began, "and I guess I need someone to help me process it."

"I'll be glad to help you in any way I can," Rich said.

Joe decided to get straight to the point. "Okay, here's the deal," he began. "Since I got involved with this church, I've felt closer to God than ever before in my life. People have been kind and accepting of me, just as if I was part of their family. You and Chessy have talked to me about God without making me feel condemned to hell. And I can't stop thinking that Thomas was praying for me just before he died. Thomas and Ezra and Bradford and you and the others have made Jesus Christ feel so...real."

"Pretty amazing, isn't it?" Rich put in with a chuckle.

It felt great to be finally telling someone all this, so Joe kept going. "I read the journals my birth mother has kept since I was born, and there was Jesus again, turning her life around, leading her back to the valley so I could find her. I met the most wonderful woman from California who just happens to be here visiting her uncle, and Jesus just seems to be pouring out of her, too. And to top it off, I ride my bike almost three thousand miles away from home and land right in the middle of this, as if God planned it all. It just makes God seem..." Joe paused, unable to find the words he wanted.

"Like you said a minute ago, Jesus seems real to you, like he's a real person instead of a religious icon or a doctrine," Rich said.

"Yeah, Rich, he seems real," Joe affirmed.

"Well, Joe, Jesus *is* real, and he's alive and working in the lives of these people you've met. So maybe that's why he seems so real to you."

Joe was suddenly warmed by the thought that Jesus—the real Jesus Rich was talking about—was beside him right now, speaking through the professor. "Yeah, maybe so," he said at a whisper.

"Do you know why Jesus is real, Joe, and why you sense his realness?"

"Why?"

"Because everything he said about himself and all the Bible says about him is true. He really *is* God's Son, sent to the earth to die for us and restore what our sin destroyed: a loving relationship with God. If what he said wasn't true, then the relationship Christians have with him isn't real. But you have sensed how real he is in the lives of people he has transformed. So that should help convince you everything he said is true."

Joe remembered the penetrating words from Rich's sermon on Sunday: If Jesus' claim to be God in human form isn't true, then any claim of a relationship with him isn't real. Rich's logic seemed irrefutable. Joe couldn't deny the overwhelming evidences Rich shared in his sermon that Jesus was the true Son of God. Neither could he deny the reality of Jesus' love in the lives of his grandfather, his birth mother, Chessy, Rich, and others he had met since coming to Washington. So that left him with only one alternative: Jesus was exactly who he claimed to be.

"So what do you think, Joe?" Rich continued. "Is Jesus real?"

Joe's heart began to race with anticipation. Something good was happening to him, maybe the best thing that *could* happen to him. "Yeah, I believe Jesus is real. I can't deny what I know and what I have seen."

"And do you believe Jesus is who he claimed to be, God's Son come to earth to die for your sin and bring you into a loving relationship with God?"

Joe stopped breathing. His answer to Rich's question—not just the words he spoke but the real answer of his heart—could change everything in his life. It had for Rich, for Bradford, for Brenda, and for Chessy. Joe wanted this change, this nearness to God, more than he had wanted anything in his life. "Yes, Rich, I do," he said with conviction.

Rich opened his Bible and read a few verses out loud to him. It was the same simple, penetrating story that had become familiar to him in the last few days. Rich shared what a simple sinner's prayer sounded like and encouraged Joe to seek God's forgiveness and commit his life totally to Christ.

Joe had never felt closer to God. It was as if the Jesus he had heard about this week had wrapped a manly, loving arm around him just like Bradford McDermot had. So it was easier talking to God out loud than he thought. Joe let the words flow from deep inside, and along with the words came a few tears. It didn't matter to him that Rich was there to hear the words and see his tears. What he told God was right, so he knew what he was experiencing was real.

When Joe was finished praying, Rich said, "One more thing, Joe. I encourage you to tell someone right away about your commitment to Christ. It will help your faith get off to a good start."

Joe thought about Thomas' question last night about having Jesus in his heart. Joe felt sad that he couldn't walk over to the cabin right now and answer the saintly caretaker with a resounding "Yes!"

"I would like to tell Ezra," he said after a moment. "He told me several days ago that he believed God had brought me here for a purpose, and I don't think he was just talking about putting out a fire."

"I think that's an excellent idea," Rich said, beaming. "Come on, I'll go with you."

Ezra was ecstatic to the point of tears when he heard Joe's simple statement of commitment to Christ. He struggled off the sofa just to embrace the young man. Joe felt uncomfortable at the man's affection at first, but sensing the warmth of love and acceptance through his grip, Joe returned the embrace.

Thanking Rich and Ezra for their help, Joe walked back to the hollow. Buoyed with confidence from sharing his commitment with Ezra, Joe looked forward to telling others. He wanted to tell Bradford and Esther, but he was afraid he might let Brenda's secret slip. And he was eager to tell his birth mother that her prayers for his conversion had been answered, but there was another name at the top of his list.

Chessy would be the next person he would tell, but before he could do that, he had some unfinished business with Rusty Ewing. And by the time he reached his tent, a plan had materialized in his brain. It was so contrary to what Joe would have done on his own, it had to be God.

"Thank you," he whispered toward the heavens. "Thank you for everything."

He climbed aboard the Harley at 7:45 and headed off toward Orchard Valley for a brief stop before driving out to Jethro Haig's farm to get Rusty Ewing out of bed.

Thirty-eight

EZRA SIPPED HIS SECOND CUP OF COFFEE and thanked God for bringing Joe Caruso to himself. His leg throbbed painfully, his heart ached for his departed friend Thomas, and the weight of the church squabble and financial difficulties were heavy upon him. But in the midst of it all, God had somehow reached the young man.

"If you can touch a troubled young man, O Lord," he said, "you can certainly untangle our mess here."

He prayed for Thomas' family, those who were grieving the great loss even more than he was, and prayed again for his fractured congregation. Since Saturday's initial outburst between Chet and Jethro, Ezra had been struggling in his prayer for the church. A pall of failure and self-doubt mocked him. He questioned the efficacy of a twenty-two year ministry that had produced, or at the very least allowed, members with such a shallow foundation of Christian charity and compassion. Here they were, fighting like cats and tearing each other apart in the name of Christian ministry. Where had he gone wrong?

After several minutes of prayer, Ezra pushed himself up from the kitchen table, hoisted his crutches into place, and hobbled outside. A wispy layer of ground fog carpeted the cemetery between the parsonage and Thomas' cabin, as though the grounds that he had loved were mourning him.

Ezra found himself pulled in the direction of the cabin. He crossed the cemetery lawn, stopping briefly at Dorrie's headstone to tell her how much he missed her today. Arriving at the cabin door, he found the key on his ring and let himself in. It seemed odd not to knock first or announce himself as he had so many times over the past two decades. Thomas had told him repeatedly that he was welcome in the cabin anytime whether he was inside or not, but Ezra would not think of treating his friend so disrespectfully.

Ezra moved slowly through the living room and kitchen, taking in the details, remembering his friend. Thomas had no need for anything that didn't serve a specific purpose. There were no pictures on the walls, no knick-knacks on the coffee table or shelves. His kitchen utensils were few. Most of them were hand-me-downs from his parents who had helped him set up housekeeping in the cabin many years earlier.

Ezra opened each of the drawers and cupboard doors, some of which were empty. Several familiar items brought pangs of sorrow. Thomas' favorite mug, a birthday gift from Ezra two years ago. A package of Oreo cookies—with four cookies left. How Thomas loved his Oreos. And a cello bag of marshmallows. Ezra would miss Thomas' campfires.

The contents of one drawer brought tears to the minister's eyes. He pulled out a worn checkerboard and box of checkers. Ezra had begun playing checkers at lunchtime shortly after Dorrie passed away. Their daily games allowed the only two residents on the church property to get better acquainted and helped ease Ezra's loneliness for Dorrie.

In the bedroom, Ezra found Thomas' old King James Version of the Bible lying on an orange-crate nightstand beside the twin bed. Thomas could only read at a fourth grade level, but he claimed to have read a chapter every night at bedtime—"except for Psalm 119, because it has 176 verses," Thomas used to tell him sheepishly. "That chapter takes me almost a full week."

Ezra would take the Bible back to the parsonage and leaf through it. You could tell a lot about a person's faith by what you found in his Bible: underlined verses, mementos slipped between the pages, notes scribbled in the flyleaf. Ezra liked to read from the deceased person's Bible during memorial services, and he would do the same at Thomas' funeral, which had been set for Wednesday morning at eleven.

The sliding door to Thomas' "prayer closet" was still wide open. Ezra stood in front of it, fingering Thomas' meager wardrobe on hangers: three work shirts, two pair of work trousers, a threadbare Hawaiian shirt, two white dress shirts, and the gray suit Thomas had worn to church every Sunday morning for probably thirty years. Two neckties were looped over the hanger rod—red with stripes and blue with checks. Both ties had been in and out of style a number of times since Thomas received them as Christmas presents from his late father decades ago.

As the clothes moved on the hangers, Ezra spotted something on the floor at the back of the closet. He pushed the clothes aside on their hangers for a better view. It looked like a thick spiral steno notebook. Curious, he laid the rubber tip of his crutch on it and slid it out of the closet.

Sitting down on the bed, Ezra picked up the notebook and opened it. Ezra knew immediately from the crude handwriting and simple language that the notebook belonged to Thomas, but it took a moment longer to figure out what it was. Ezra could not recollect seeing the notebook before, though that did not surprise him since he had never meddled in Thomas' possessions. So he flipped through the pages with curious interest.

It was a prayer list, he determined. There were names, dates, and comments on each page. Apparently when Thomas heard about the needs and problems of other people, church members and others, he listed them in his notebook. Then he took the notebook into his closet with him and lifted these people and their needs to God in prayer. The notebook was in the closet with Thomas when he died.

As Ezra flipped through the pages, he found his name scrawled on a number of lines. Next to each entry was something he must have mentioned to Thomas during a checkers game or in casual conversation: back pain, an ingrown toenail, the death of a relative, concern for a church member. Ezra didn't realize that Thomas had been so attuned to his needs. Tears rolled down his cheeks as he pictured the humble caretaker on his knees in the closet praying for him.

He turned to the first page of the notebook. The date indicated that he began keeping this notebook a little over three years ago. Was this the only prayer notebook, or was there a library of them stashed somewhere in the cabin which dated back decades? Ezra hoped there were more, and he looked forward to leafing through them, if Thomas' family would allow him the privilege.

Ezra located the place where the used pages ended and the blank pages began. These would have been Thomas' most recent prayer concerns. Perhaps he had been talking to God about them at the very moment of his death.

He glanced over the last three pages. Prominent among the many names written there were those of Jethro Haig and Chet Rasby. Thomas had been terribly distraught over the conflict between these two men and those who sided with them. Everybody had witnessed Thomas' emotional trauma, but perhaps no one had realized that each episode had driven Thomas back to his notebook and his prayer closet. His heart cry for God to heal the rift between the people he loved was documented here in black and white.

Ezra wanted to read these pages in detail, so he decided to take the notebook back to the parsonage. There would likely be some excerpts that would be appropriate for the service.

Just before closing the book, Ezra turned to the last page Thomas had used, the most recent entry. He expected to find an outpouring of angst over the church conflict, but instead, the page was dedicated to only one topic. The heading of the topic was terse and telling: JOE IN TROUBLE.

Ezra knew the entry referred to Joe being accused of stealing Louise Wilkerson's gift from the church office. Had Joe confided in Thomas and requested his prayers? Had Thomas talked to Joe about Jesus, how the answer to all the young man's troubles was the Savior? It's what Thomas had done with so many of the visitors to the hollow over the years. "Joe is in the family now, Thomas," Ezra spoke aloud. "Can you hear the angels rejoicing? Did Jesus tell you, 'Well done, good and faithful servant'?"

Ezra rose from the bed and adjusted the crutches under his arms. He went into the kitchen and found a plastic grocery sack in the cupboard under the sink. Returning to the bedroom, he placed Thomas' Bible and prayer notebook in the sack so he could carry them back to the house. Crossing the cemetery again, he breathed a prayer that the thief would be found.

Thirty-nine

JOE TURNED INTO JETHRO HAIG'S FARM at a few minutes before 9:00 A.M. The night before he had sneaked up to the house in the dark while pushing his bike; today he rumbled loudly down the long driveway and revved the engine a few times for good measure before stopping in front of the bay doors of Haig's garage. The Ford pickup was parked where Rusty had left it, just as Joe expected. Glancing past the building, Joe saw the GMC truck several acres out in the field and Jethro Haig telling his farm hands what to do. It was just as well if the old man was otherwise preoccupied.

Before shutting off the engine, Joe goosed the accelerator a couple of times under the apartment window. *Wake up, Rusty, and take your punishment,* he thought wryly as he turned the key and silenced the engine. Removing his helmet and sunglasses and stepping off the bike, Joe glanced up at the window of the garage apartment. He saw nobody glaring down at him, only the cheesy curtains pulled closed. It was warm enough to stow his denim jacket in the saddlebag, but he purposely kept it on.

Walking to the side door to the garage, he opened it and saw the Cadillac sitting there. He stepped inside the garage long enough to touch the hood. It was cold. The Caddie hadn't moved since yesterday. Joe assumed that Rusty was still here.

At the foot of the outside steps of the apartment, Joe paused. "All right, here we go," he said at a whisper. He ascended the stairs confidently and rapped hard on the door. "Rusty, open up. It's Joe Caruso." There was no response and no sound of movement inside that Joe could hear.

"Wake up, Rusty," he called out, pounding louder. "I know what you did. I can go to the police, or we can talk about a deal."

Again, all was quiet.

Joe lifted his fist to pound again, but the door flew open first. Rusty Ewing stood barefoot in his jeans and T-shirt, thinning reddish hair matted from sleep. But Joe's focus moved immediately to the gun in his hand, which was directed at him.

"Shut up and get in here," Rusty hissed.

Joe hadn't counted on a gun. He had underestimated Rusty Ewing again, thinking burglary and planting false evidence was the limit of the lazy man's capacity for crime.

"Before you use that gun, Rusty," he said, edging into the squalid studio apartment as Rusty kicked the door closed behind him, "you'd better hear me out. Somebody knows I'm here, and I told her what to do if I didn't come back."

Rusty backed further into the room with the gun trained on Joe.

Joe kept talking. "I know what you did, breaking into the church, stealing the money box. You were at the church the day of the storm. You must have heard about the money from Jethro or Thomas, and you started making your plan right then. You decided to get the money and pin the rap on me, the stranger in town."

"You're crazy," Rusty spat, adding curses, "and I have every right to blow you away for breaking into my room." Rusty's gun stayed aimed at Joe's chest, and his gun hand was shaking. There was rage in the man's eyes.

Joe went on. "I also know you used my screwdriver to open the desk. Probably snuck out to my camp that afternoon when no one was looking and grabbed it. The thunderstorm was the perfect cover for you, wasn't it? You couldn't believe your luck. You got in, grabbed the money box, dropped the screwdriver as evidence, and got away without being seen."

"I ought to shoot you right here, right now. And if you brought anybody with you, if somebody comes through that door, I'll do it, I swear. I've got nothing to lose."

Joe's heart began to race. The gun was menacing, and Rusty's threat was just as frightening. His only defense at this moment was to keep talking, so he did.

"Like I said, Rusty, my girlfriend knows where I am. If I don't come back in an hour, she's going to the police. If you pull that trigger, you'll have a hard time explaining all the blood spattered on your walls. Life in prison—maybe the gas chamber. So just stay cool because I have a better solution."

"What solution?"

Joe ignored the question for the moment. He had to get everything off his chest. "When the police found the screwdriver but didn't arrest me, you decided to up the ante. You planted the empty money box near my camp, again when nobody was around. And you probably even called to tip off the cops. But they couldn't keep me in jail, and that gave me time to figure out you were behind the frame up. I've got pictures of the tire tracks from the road before you scuffed them out last night. And if you don't play ball with me today, the cops will find the money, whatever you haven't spent of it, probably somewhere in this room."

"Maybe I swapped out the tires, got new ones, buried the old ones."

"No, Rusty, you didn't. I was here last night, hiding in the garage when you got home. I checked out the Caddie and the pickups before I left. One glance at the Ford's tires and—*whaddayaknow?*—perfect match! If you go changing tires now, the police will find out. I left them a note with my pictures."

Rusty muttered a curse. Joe realized with mounting apprehension that this snake who shamelessly sponged off his own step-father wasn't all there mentally. Joe could see it in his eyes. He had to keep talking until he could get out of the room. "But, like I said, I have a solution for both of us."

"What solution?" Rusty shouted, thrusting the gun closer.

"A fifty-fifty split. You give me ten grand, then I'll turn the pictures over to you and disappear forever—far, far away, east coast, where I came from. Nobody suspects you now, and nobody will ever find me. We'll both be in the clear."

Joe held his breath as Rusty weighed his options. "What's it going to be, Rusty?" Joe pressed. "I have to get back to my girlfriend before she goes to the cops." He hoped his lie sounded more convincing to Rusty than it did to him.

Rusty lowered the gun a little. "Tonight," he said.

"What do you mean?"

"The money ain't here. I'll give you your share tonight. And I swear, if I see you anywhere in this valley after tonight, I'll kill you."

Joe didn't believe Rusty's first promise that he intended to hand over ten thousand dollars, and he doubted that this thief was smart enough to hide the money somewhere else. But he had no doubt that Rusty would follow through on the second part, and he was sure the gunman meant to do it tonight.

"Your place or mine?" Joe said, playing along.

"Midnight at Eastside Bullpen, a bar on Eighteenth Avenue East, corner of Chinook, in Yarborough. You'd better be alone, and you'd better have the pictures."

"And you'd better have the money," Joe replied sternly. He backed toward the door, opened it while staring down Rusty, and slipped out. He wasted no time getting to his bike. Starting up, he saw Jethro Haig glaring at him from the field. Joe saluted toward the old man, then snapped the bike into gear. *Guess you'll be looking for a new flunky after tonight, Jethro,* Joe thought as he raced out the driveway toward the road.

After a lengthy stop in town, Joe headed for Velma Walls' house just outside the small business district of Orchard Valley. He had so much to tell Chessy, but he couldn't tell her everything until after his meeting with Rusty tonight.

"I hope you don't mind me stopping by." Joe was standing at Velma's screen door. Chessy had answered the door, just as Joe had hoped. "If I'm interrupting something, I could come back."

"No," she said, seeming pleased to see him. "I'm just reading for my online class. I could use a break. Velma is at the minister's house making phone calls to arrange the service for tomorrow."

"There's something I want to talk to you about," he said, "if it's all right."

"Sure. I was about to nuke a quesadilla for lunch. Can I fix one for you?"

"Yeah, that would be great."

As Chessy grated cheese over a couple of flour tortillas, Joe said, "How do you feel today, I mean about what happened to your uncle?"

"I didn't sleep very well," she said. "I should be grateful that I was able to spend some time with Uncle Thomas, but I'm going to miss him. How are you doing?"

Joe thought about what he had come to tell her. On that score, he was doing fantastic. But first he had to respond in kind. He answered with conviction, "I'm going to miss him, too."

Chessy explained that her dad and mom would be arriving at the airport in Yarborough at 4:30 this afternoon. Joe felt a mild flash of panic at the prospect of meeting Chessy's parents. He had felt nothing but acceptance from Chessy and the people in the church. But what would Mr. and Mrs. Carpenter think about their daughter hanging out with a "biker" from Pennsylvania?

Chessy exhibited no reservations about introducing him to her parents. Instead, she said that this may be the only positive thing about Uncle Thomas' passing—that Joe would be able to meet her parents.

As Chessy served lunch and sat down, Joe said, "What I have to say has something to do with you and your uncle and other people I have met this week, including my birth mother. This has been the most amazing six days in my life. I never expected my trip to turn out like this."

"Like what, Joe?" Chessy probed.

"Well...sort of...life-changing, I guess," he said. Telling Chessy was more difficult than he had anticipated. He took a deep breath and released it. "What I mean is, thanks to you and Thomas and Rich and others, this morning I came to realize that Christ is real and that he wants a loving relationship with me. And so Rich helped me pray, and Christ has done something inside me."

Chessy's mouth fell open, but she didn't speak. She seemed frozen in shock. The only movement Joe saw on her face was the tears that quickly filled her eyes and spilled down her cheeks.

She reached out her hand and took his hand. "Joe, that's wonderful," she said. Then she could say no more.

"I don't know if your uncle had a chance to pray for me or not before he died," Joe went on. "But my birth mom said she has been praying for me since she trusted Christ a few months ago. And she didn't even know where I was. I think her prayers had something to do with me coming west."

"I've been praying for you, too, Joe," Chessy said, drying tears with a napkin from the table. "Since the day I first saw you in the hollow, I've been praying that you would come to Christ. I just didn't expect it to happen so soon. But I'm so happy for you."

"I want to say something important to you about all this," Joe said, holding Chessy's hand. "You played a big role in my decision, but I want you to know that I didn't do this just, you know, for you. I mean, I didn't do this so we could be together. I did this because I need Christ in my life."

A fresh wave of tears crested in Chessy's eyes and spilled down her cheeks. "Thank you for telling me that," she said, "because that's how I have been praying for you. I asked God to bring you to himself no matter what happens to us."

Having shared his spiritual decision with Chessy, Joe now wanted to tell her everything—about discovering his real grandparents, about Rusty Ewing and the money. But it was too soon. It would be difficult, but he would have to wait.

"Since I'm going to meet your parents," he said, "It's only fair that you meet Brenda Long, my birth mother."

"I would like to meet her very much," Chessy said excitedly.

"What about now?"

"Now?"

"She works in Yarborough in the county building. Would you like to take a ride into the city? I'll have you back by 2:30 at the latest."

"Yes, I'd like that. Lucky for me, Doctor Rich let me hold onto his helmet."

They hastily finished lunch and left for the city.

Forty

JOE AND CHESSY ARRIVED at the county building in Yarborough at 12:45. Leaving Chessy in the hall for a minute, Joe found Brenda and explained that he had some important things to share with her. Brenda welcomed another opportunity to visit. She asked if Joe could wait until 1:00 when she could get away for a late lunch. When Joe agreed, she suggested that he wait for her in the cafeteria of the Yarborough Community Hospital, which was one block away. He said nothing about Chessy being with him. He wanted to keep it as a surprise.

While they waited in the cafeteria, Joe asked Chessy not to mention anything about the burglary charges pending against him, adding, "Everything is going to work out all right. I'll tell you about it tomorrow."

When Brenda arrived at the cafeteria, Joe presented Chessy as a new "friend" who happened to be visiting Orchard Valley as he was. He was pleased at how the two women seemed to hit it off immediately. Joe and Chessy told the sad story of Thomas' untimely death, which led into a brief discussion of the conflict at the church. Brenda expressed her sympathy to Chessy and her concern over the problems at the church.

"Joe has some exciting news to tell you," Chessy said, beaming. Joe thought she was even more thrilled at his conversion than he was.

"I'm eager to hear it," Brenda said.

Joe had been thinking how best to tell his news. "I want you to know," he began, "that your prayers have been answered." Then he waited for a response.

"Which prayers?" Brenda returned with a gleam of anticipation in her eyes.

"I committed my life to Jesus Christ this morning." He summarized his discussions with Rich, which dovetailed so perfectly with the testimony of Brenda's conversion he had read in her journals. "Thank you for putting your story in writing, Brenda," he said, "and for praying that God would bring me to himself and to you."

"You don't know how much it means to me to hear you say those words," Brenda said with tears. "I'm just a new Christian myself, and I wasn't sure if God heard my prayers or not. Finding you this week has strengthened my faith."

She asked question after question of Joe, wanting to know every detail of God's work in bringing him to Christ. Joe gladly answered them, and Chessy added valuable insights into God's working. By the time they concluded, all three of them were wiping tears from their eyes.

Joe and Chessy waited at the table while Brenda went through the cafeteria line. She brought a slice of pie for each of them. When Chessy excused herself to use the restroom, Joe asked Brenda's permission to tell another facet of his story when she returned. Brenda agreed.

When Joe revealed that Bradford and Esther McDermot were Brenda's parents and his grandparents, Chessy dropped her fork. She was even more shocked to learn that the McDermots did not yet know that Joe was their grandson. "Why?" Chessy said, wearing a look of incredulity. Joe knew she would ask. He turned to Brenda to let her answer.

Brenda told Chessy the story of her twenty-five year estrangement from "Dad," just as Joe had learned it in her journals. Then Brenda explained her change of heart toward him as a result of Christ's presence in her life. "He has every right not to have anything to do with me after how I treated him," she concluded.

"But Bradford is a sweet, wonderful man," Chessy argued. "He's also a godly man. He will accept your apology just as you have accepted his. I'm sure he wants to be reunited with you. He's probably been praying for that day ever since you left home."

"I hope you're right," Brenda said with a whimper. "I was so afraid of him for so long. And now I'm so ashamed for running out of his life and for robbing him of his first grandchild. I need courage to talk to him."

"I'll be praying for you, Brenda," Chessy said. "God will give you the strength you need."

In light of Brenda's transparency about her painful past, Joe knew he had to speak. "I need to apologize to both of you," he began. "I mislead you about something, and I feel strongly that I have to clear it up. It has to do with this." He traced the jagged scar down the side of his face with his finger.

"The scar?" Brenda said.

"Yes," Joe said, wishing he could suddenly disappear. "I told you both, as I have told everyone, that it was an accident."

Chessy said, "You didn't fall into a big window like you said?"

Joe shook his head slowly. "No, I didn't fall into any plate glass window. I was thrown into it."

Brenda gasped. "No, please no." Her look of horror communicated that she had not only guessed the truth but that she had been punishing herself for allowing it to happen. He reached a reassuring hand to hers.

"I was at home with my father that night, like I said," Joe began, emotion squeezing his voice almost to a whisper. "We were in the den watching television, one of those big consoles that's a piece of furniture. I was lying on my back on the floor, and I guess I was tapping the television with my shoe. My dad told me to quit kicking the TV. I stopped for a minute. Then I must have started again. He probably barked at me two or three times to stop it. But I was engrossed in the TV show, so I guess I didn't stop."

Joe's hands began to tremble and his mouth turned dry. Something inside begged him to say no more. He was in uncharted territory. He had never told this story to anyone. Years of fear gripped him like chains. He didn't want to go on, but something within urged him to do so: *It's time to tell the truth. The truth will set you free.*

Joe moistened his lips and pressed on. "Suddenly my father jumped up from his chair, grabbed me by my shirt, and pulled me up. He'd had a couple beers. He wasn't drunk; he knew what he was doing. He screamed at me with rage in his eyes, 'When I say stop, I mean stop!' Then he threw me into the window. It broke on impact, and I fell through it to the outside. I guess a shard cut my face on the way down."

Brenda covered her mouth in horror. Chessy's eyes filled with tears. She rested a comforting hand on Joe's shoulder.

"I started bleeding big-time, and it really scared me," Joe said, starting to cry. "Dad had to come outside to get me. He saw the blood and knew he was in trouble. He carried me inside and made me hold a big towel to my face to stem the bleeding."

Joe stopped to get himself under control. If he didn't, he reasoned that he would never finish the story. Brenda and Chessy were also teary. They just remained silent, each of them touching him caringly.

After several moments, he pressed on. "On the way to the emergency room, with me holding a blood-soaked dish towel to my face, Dad threatened to kill me if I told anyone what really happened. I'm serious, he said he would kill me. So I said nothing when he explained to the doctors—and later to Mom—that I had been rough-housing in the den against his wishes and fell into the window. Nobody questioned his explanation. Why should they?

"My father never repeated his threat to me in words, but it was there—in his eyes—every time he looked at me. I knew he could fulfill his promise. He almost killed me that night, so I knew he could do it if he wanted to. Even when Mom divorced him and he moved away, I had this fear that he would know if I told on him, and he would come after me. So I never told anyone the truth. Until right now."

Joe couldn't stop the tears from flowing. He buried his face in his hands to muffle the sound of his sobbing. Chessy and Brenda were crying, too, with their arms draped over him. Joe suspected that there were plenty of turned heads and curious stares around them in the cafeteria, but he didn't care. He felt years of pain and shame pouring out with his tears.

"I'm so sorry, Danny," Brenda wept near his ear. "I wanted you to have a father, but I didn't know he would hurt you. I'm sorry. I'm so sorry."

Hearing her use his birth name made Joe feel especially close to Brenda. "It's all right, Mom," he whispered. "You did the best you knew how. You couldn't know what I was getting into. It's not your fault."

In a few minutes, the tide of emotion receded. "I'm so glad you told me your story," Chessy said. "I feel so honored."

Brenda smiled as she dabbed her eyes. "I feel honored, but I also feel guilty. Thank you for reassuring me, Joe. And I'm sorry I slipped and called you Danny."

He brushed it off with a wave of his hand. "It's a nice name," he said. "I would be proud to be Danny Barnes if I weren't already Joe Caruso."

As they walked back to Brenda's office, Chessy asked Joe about his experience of growing up with such a scar. Joe admitted that it was horrible being ridiculed by his peers and ignored by girls, but the worst thing was telling people that the injury was his own fault.

Outside Brenda's building, Joe embraced his birth mother for the first time, and tears returned for all. Joe and Chessy told Brenda that they would be praying for God to help her approach Bradford.

Just before they said goodbye, Brenda said, "Thank you for calling me Mom, Joe. You don't have to do that if it's uncomfortable to you."

"It felt pretty good the first time," he said, smiling. "I think I can get used to it."

When they got back to Orchard Valley, Chessy invited Joe to go with her to the airport to meet her parents and have supper with them at Velma's. He thanked her but declined, explaining he had to go to the mall to find a jacket and tie for Thomas' funeral. Joe assured her that he would stop by Velma's later in the evening before Chessy delivered them to the motel.

"I'll see you tonight then," Chessy said with a smile that made Joe's knees buckle.

"I'm looking forward to it."

On the way to the mall, Joe sensed his anxiety mounting. The activities of the day had helped him not to think too much about his midnight meeting with Rusty Ewing, and thankfully, he had some things to do before his late night drive into East Yarborough. But his appointment with the gun-toting burglar was coming. He was sure Rusty wasn't going to be there for the "solution" Joe had proposed. Stealing $22,000 in cash seemed to have unleash greater evil in Rusty. He didn't know what Rusty had planned, but neither did Rusty know about the surprise Joe had waiting for him.

BEFORE HE REACHED THE MALL, Joe saw a large thrift store south of Yarborough, so he pulled in. He was thrilled to find a sport jacket, shirt, and tie that matched his best pair of pants. They cost a total of $12.35, but they actually fit well and looked good on him. His outfit wouldn't put him on the cover of a men's fashion magazine, but neither did he have to shell out a hundred bucks for a jacket that would likely hang in his closet until moths devoured it.

Slipping the package into his saddle bags, it occurred to Joe that finding these clothes was not a coincidence. "Thanks, God," he said, feeling genuinely cared for.

Having saved so much money on clothes, Joe wanted to splurge a little on a good supper, but he was due back at Velma's in half an hour to meet Chessy's parents. So he opted for a fast-food grilled chicken salad and milk shake, which he ate at an outdoor table.

Riding back out to the valley, Joe was suddenly overwhelmed by the convergence of circumstances that had brought him to this day. *If it hadn't been for the thunderstorm,* he thought, *I may never have been so deeply and positively influenced by Thomas, Ezra, Chessy, and Bradford.* He could have moved on from the hollow the next day and never been part of what God had in store for Chapel of the Valley. Worst of all, he might have missed the opportunity to talk to Rich and commit his life to Christ.

Joe realized that he may have met Brenda even if he had moved into Yarborough, but had he not become involved with the church repairs, he may have missed the chance to know his grandparents as he did. He may have said hello and goodbye to his birth mother and headed back to Pennsylvania. There were too many coincidences. This whole trip had been orchestrated by God, and yet Joe could have spoiled the music by ignoring the opportunities. Joe was amazed at how he had been led and the fact that he had followed God unwittingly into the light.

Now where would the path wind? What did God have in store for him now? Was Pittsburgh to remain his home? Was he to complete an advanced degree and continue to pursue a career in civil engineering? If so, should he stay in the east? And if his career kept him in Pennsylvania, what would become of his relationships out here? Joe wanted to expand his relationship with his birth mother and his grandparents. And he didn't want to lose touch with Ezra or Rich. How could he do that from nearly three thousand miles away?

And then there was the captivating blonde named Chessy Carpenter. Was she part of God's long-term plan for Joe, more so even than Brenda, Bradford, and Esther? Or was she just another instrument God used to bring him to Jesus Christ? Were their lives like two streets intersecting temporarily or like two roads destined to merge into one? Joe couldn't answer those questions, but he knew he was not at all ready to see this woman walk out of his life.

When Joe arrived at Velma's, supper was over and the dining room table was spread with snapshots of Thomas Rasby taken at various stages of his life. While Velma loaded the dishwasher, Chessy and her parents, Bertram and Lydia Carpenter, were sorting through the pictures, selecting several nice ones to display in the foyer of the church for those attending the memorial service.

The introductions were painless, even enjoyable. The Carpenters were congenial toward Joe with only a passing glance at the scar on his face. Fortunately, their get-acquainted question did not require him to tell his life story. They were more interested in the last six days, obviously having heard some of the story from their daughter. Joe related the key events without delving into all the intricacies of the relationships. The couple was elated at Joe's conversion.

There were a few tears through the evening as Chessy and her parents looked at pictures of Thomas and remembered his life. Joe talked about

Thomas' kindness to him, inviting him in for meals, allowing him to sleep on his sofa after the storm. Joe also related the experience of rescuing Thomas from the roof of the church after the ladder had fallen as the storm rolled in. The stories evoked both smiles at Thomas' big heart and tears at his childlike frailty and fearfulness.

When it was time for Joe to leave, Chessy's parents said their goodbyes in the living room, but Chessy walked him outside. She stopped on the porch steps and sat down. Joe sat next to her. They talked about their awe of the country and how being away from the city allowed such a clear view of the stars on a moonless night.

"So how was your first day?"

Joe knew what she meant: his first day as a Christian. "It's been a great day," he said. "It still is a great day," he corrected himself, reaching over to take her hand. She did not pull away. Joe silently prayed that the day would end as well as it had begun.

"How long will your parents stay?" he asked.

"Not long, maybe until Friday," Chessy said, gazing at the sky. "Dad has to get back to the raisins."

"I like your Mom and Dad," Joe said. "You're blessed to have them."

"Yes, I know," she said. Then after several silent moments, "I'm thinking about flying home with them." She was still looking skyward as she said it.

They were words Joe knew were coming at some point, but he still cringed inside at hearing them. He said, "With your uncle passing away, your visit here is suddenly over, isn't it?"

"Especially with you heading back to Pennsylvania soon," Chessy said, slipping her hand from his gentle grasp.

"I don't know when I will leave," he offered.

Chessy turned to him. "But you have to go back, don't you? You are going to finish your degree, aren't you?"

"I don't know, Chessy," Joe said with a sigh. "A lot has happened in my life this week. I'm not the same person I was when I arrived. I have some things to sort out."

"Do you think you will come back to Washington—I mean, sometime?"

"I would like to come back," Joe said. "I don't want to lose touch with my family here. And I really love this valley."

Chessy slipped her hand back into his. "You know, it's not too far from here to Fresno," she said with a smile in her voice. "Just a good day's motorcycle ride."

Joe squeezed her hand gently. "And I understand a person can get there even quicker on an airplane, and that the planes fly both ways."

Chessy laughed at his gentle jab. She moved closer and leaned lightly against him.

Joe released her hand and slid his arm around her. Her head nestled gently on his shoulder. "The only thing I know for sure right now, Chessy, is that I want you in my life. If it means driving across country on my bike again, I'll do it. This week was not just about me coming to Christ, as important as that is. I think God wanted me to meet you, too."

"I feel the same way, Joe," Chessy said. "I felt this way even before this morning. But after seeing what God has done in your life, I don't want us to be separated by three thousand miles."

They sat in silence for several minutes. Joe relished Chessy's gentle warmth at his side. Finally he said, "I need to go."

"And I need to get back to my parents."

"I have something really important to do yet tonight. I can't tell you about it right now, but will you pray for me?"

"Of course I will. Can we pray right now?" Chessy didn't wait for a response. She just started to pray, thanking God for what he had done for Joe and asking his presence and direction for whatever Joe had to do. It sounded so natural, so genuine. Joe sensed that God was sitting on the porch step with them listening.

"I'd like to hear how it goes tonight," Chessy said after saying the amen, "if you are okay about telling me."

"I want to tell you about it, but I won't know anything until after midnight."

"Will you stop by on your way back to the hollow?"

"You'll be awake that late?"

"I have a pile of reading to do," Chessy explained, "and tomorrow is full with the service and all. So I'm planning to work into the wee hours."

"All right, I'll drive by when I'm finished," Joe said. "If there's a light on in the window, I'll stop."

"There will be a light on."

Joe stood and pulled Chessy up with him. Their embrace and kiss happened so easily that Joe didn't know which one of them initiated it.

After savoring the moment, Joe spoke seriously. "Chessy, if I'm not here by one-thirty, don't wait up for me. My thing tonight may not go exactly as I plan."

Chessy seemed to be searching his eyes deeply for the meaning of his words. "All right, Joe," she said tentatively. "Is this thing you're doing dangerous?"

Joe sighed. "It's nothing illegal, nothing wrong," he said.

It was a very general answer to Chessy's very pointed question, but she nodded in acceptance anyway.

Joe kissed her once more before she could ask another question. "See you later," he said.

Forty-two

THE TEMPERATURE WAS SUPPOSED TO BOTTOM OUT at around forty-two degrees during the night, Joe had heard. So he wore a sweatshirt under his denim jacket. At 11:00 P.M., he cranked up the Harley, idled up the path to the road, and took off toward Yarborough. None of the wonderful people he had met here, including the church people and his new-found family members, knew where Joe was going tonight and what he was doing, but he knew they would all be happy for him when he announced that the burglary charges against him had been dropped and the real thief was in custody. Joe hoped he was healthy enough after it was over to tell the news himself.

Joe knew there were no iron-clad guarantees about his meeting with Rusty Ewing. He hadn't been a Christian very long, but he already accepted that God, for reasons Joe didn't understand, sometimes let bad things happen to good people. Thomas Rasby was a prime example. It was a no-brainer that God was powerful enough to keep Thomas from dying when he did, and Joe could not doubt God's love for Thomas and for the many who grieved his passing. But God let him die anyway.

Not knowing what the real outcome would be tonight, Joe had envisioned a number of possible scenarios, some of which were decidedly less pleasant than others. The security he was counting on could fail. He could get shot or beaten up. With each frightening possibility he gave himself the same advice he would give anyone who questioned Thomas Rasby's untimely death: God is God, and we're not. We do the best we can, and we leave the rest up to him.

Traffic was very light heading into the city. Joe checked his mirror repeatedly until he was convinced that he wasn't being followed by anyone, particularly someone in a red pickup truck or a late-model silver Cadillac. Just to be sure, he took a roundabout route to the county government center downtown, pulled into a deserted parking garage at 11:25 P.M., and drove to the third floor as he had been instructed.

He found the gray trade van parked right where he had been told it would be. The sign on the side of the van read, MIDSTATE HEATING AND AIR CONDITIONING. There was a car parked beside it, obviously an unmarked police cruiser.

Climbing off the bike, he was met by two men who had been waiting in the car. "Mister Caruso, glad you could make it," said one of them in a somber tone. There was no offer of a handshake. A man and woman stepped out of the side door of the van. All four of the people meeting Joe were dressed in casual street clothes—jeans, sweatshirts, Nikes. All of them also wore an olive drab nylon jacket with a yellow star and insignia painted on the front, and each had a holstered gun on his or her hip.

"Hello Chief Jurgen," Joe said.

"This is Lieutenant Rhodes with the Yarborough County Sheriff's Department," the chief said. "He and his team will be heading up the operation tonight. Vic and I go back a few years, so he's letting me ride along even though I'm outside my jurisdiction."

The lieutenant, who was huskier, twenty years older, and a shade taller than Joe with a buzzed haircut, nodded a greeting. "George said you did a good job this morning wearing the wire," he said. "He said the suspect all but admitted his guilt."

"I was scared spitless," Joe said soberly. "I didn't expect him to have a gun."

"That's why I told you not to go into the apartment," Jurgen interjected, remonstrating Joe as he had after his first morning encounter with Rusty Ewing at Jethro's farm. "I told you to call him out, get him into the open where we could see both of you with the glasses. We can't help you if we can't see you. And when you're inside with a crazy gunman, we can't bust down the door to get you or something may go off. Just remember that tonight."

"Can we just get this over with, Chief?" Joe said impatiently. "I'm sorry it didn't go as well as you'd hoped this morning. I'm not a professional at this. I just want to get this guy off my back and clear my name."

Lt. Rhodes went over the plan with everyone as a male deputy slipped a tiny microphone and transmitter under Joe's clothing. Joe's job was to make contact outside the tavern where the team could watch from the undercover van parked nearby.

"We need to see something tonight, Mister Caruso, to make sure this guy's arrest sticks," the lieutenant continued. "We need to see him hand you money which, along with the tape we have from this morning, will prove that he's attempting to buy you off. That's an admission of guilt that will stand up in court even if he doesn't bring the money from the burglary."

"I don't think he will bring any money," Joe said. "I think he just wants me out of the picture."

"That's why you have to stay in the parking lot where we can see you, no closer to him than twenty feet," Jurgen put in. "If he wants you to get in the truck or go into the bar with him or anywhere else, flash the photos and tell him to show you the money or the deal's off."

"But I don't have pictures of the tire tracks," Joe argued. "I told you that was a lie."

"We have some pictures that will look real from several feet away," Rhodes said, handing Joe a plain manila envelope. Joe pulled out two eight-by-ten glossies of tire tracks which must have been taken at another crime scene.

The lieutenant went on. "If he shows you a substantial amount of cash or if he attempts to assault you, we'll be on him like a chicken on a June bug. If he walks, we'll get him eventually."

"But I want to nail him now," Joe said. "He has a gun. He's threatened me. I don't want to be looking over my shoulder while I'm in Washington. That's why I set this deal up with you."

"We want him, too, kid," Rhodes said, "but we don't want you or anyone else to get hurt. Just play it safe and let's hope he gives us what we want."

Two minutes later, the lieutenant and his two deputies left the parking garage to get into position outside the Eastside Bullpen. Chief Jurgen's job was to follow the Harley to the bar from an inconspicuous distance and be on the ready as back up.

"Did you bring my pistol?" Joe asked the chief. "I don't have anything to defend myself with."

Chief Jurgen shook his head. "If he sees a gun, it might set him off. We've got plenty of firepower if he gets nasty. You just get out of the way."

"Yes, sir."

"And if you don't want to do this, tell me now and we will shut down the operation. You asked us to do it, so you can call it off."

"No, I want Rusty out of my life. If we don't do it now, he might come after me, and others could get hurt, too."

The chief nodded. "Then let's roll."

Joe's stomach churned as he drove the six miles east to the tavern. When he was within a quarter mile, he checked his watch. It was a few minutes before midnight. As he had been instructed by Chief Jurgen, Joe turned onto a side street and pulled up to the curb. Joe was supposed to arrive a few minutes after 12:00, not before. The chief's unmarked car kept going on Eighteenth to get into place.

As the Harley idled at the curb in front of a little strip mall that was closed, Joe sensed his anxiety escalating to fear. With a few minutes to kill, Joe's thoughts turned to Chessy. If all went well at the Eastside Bullpen, he would be out to Orchard Valley in an hour explaining everything to her and thanking her for her prayers. He hated to think of someone else driving up to Velma's tonight or in the morning to explain that Joe was in the hospital or in cold storage at a funeral home.

He wished Chessy was with him now to pray for him again. But since he was all alone, he prayed. "I think I'm doing the right thing," he said softly. "Rusty has to pay for what he did. Please help me and the cops get him. And keep us all safe."

Ten minutes later he rolled up to the dumpy tavern and turned into its dimly lit parking lot. The street was dark with no traffic, and there was only an old car and an old pickup in the parking lot. The car, a beater Ford Taurus, was parked away from the building, apparently belonging to the barkeep. The red Ford pickup was backed into a space in the shadows next to the tavern. Joe recognized the silhouette of Rusty Ewing wearing his trademark race car cap behind the wheel.

Out of the corner of his eye, he noticed the van across the dark street in the shadowy parking lot of a small industrial building. He had seen Chief Jurgen's car parked several spaces down the street on the same side as the van.

Joe parked his bike a good thirty feet from Rusty's truck. With the Harley shut down, he could hear twangy music wafting from the window of the pickup. He pulled the envelope of photos out of the saddlebag and planted himself beside his bike in clear view. He stood as still as he could, but his knees were quivering.

Rusty waved him toward the truck. Joe shook his head and stayed put. Rusty stepped out, staying partially behind the door which he left standing open. "If you want to do business with me, you'd better get over here."

Joe slowly opened the envelope, pulled a picture halfway out, and held it up for Rusty to see. He prayed that it looked convincing in the dim light. "I brought what I have," he called out, "now you show me what you have. I want to see the money."

"I can't see the picture from here. Bring it over."

"No chance, not until I see ten thousand in cash." Joe's mouth was desert dry and his voice sounded weak and tinny to him.

Rusty laughed coarsely. "What's the matter, kid, don't you trust me? We made a deal. I've got the money right here on the seat of the truck."

"Then show me."

After reaching into the truck, Rusty produced a shoe box. The lid was on. Joe could tell by the way Rusty handled it that there was some weight to the contents. "Here you go, your half. Ten grand and change."

"Remove the lid, let me see."

"You're crazy, kid. Not out there in the light."

Joe felt his fear boiling into anger at the man who had framed him and was now baiting him into a fight or an assault. "Get this straight, man," he blazed. "I'm riding out of here in thirty seconds, straight to the police, if you don't show me——"

A big car came squealing around the corner and stopped with a screech in front of the driveway. Joe's first thought was that the luxury sedan was blocking the cops' view of him from the van.

With the car's engine still running, an old man bolted from the driver's door and started toward Rusty. "Judson Jerome Ewing, what in blazes have you done?" he yelled angrily. "Where did you get this kind of money? Was it you that robbed the church?" It was Jethro Haig, crimson with rage and waving a fist full of greenbacks at his stepson as he crossed the parking lot.

By the time Joe looked back toward the pickup, Rusty had flipped the lid off the shoe box, pulled out a gun, and leveled it at the charging Jethro Haig. "Stop right there, Jethro. I'm not going to let you spoil this for me. I swear I'll——"

Joe reacted. Dropping the envelope, he took three sprinting strides toward Rusty Ewing and launched himself at the door of the pickup. It flashed through his mind for an instant that this was not what the cops meant by getting out of the way if trouble erupted.

The metallic crunch created by his body slamming hard into the pickup's door was overpowered by a thundering explosion from Rusty's big gun. Stunned by the collision, Joe crumpled to the pavement, his brain suddenly spinning on a dizzying tilt-a-whirl ride. The blur of frantic activity above him was dominated by waves of olive drab. Just before passing out, with the gunshot ringing in his ears, a prayer escaped his fading consciousness: *Don't let Jethro die. Don't let me die.*

Forty-three

"MISTER CARUSO? Hey kid, are you all right?"

Joe opened his eyes slowly and, with some difficulty, focused on the face leaning over him. His head throbbed. "Chief?" he said.

He made a move to sit up, but the Orchard Valley police chief kept him down with a hand on his shoulder. "The paramedics are rolling," he said. "I want them to take a look at you."

Joe closed his eyes until the world stopped doing cartwheels, then opened one of them a crack. "Am I...shot?"

Jurgen smiled thinly. "No, it's a miracle, but nobody got shot. The bullet took out a window in the building across the street. You did clock yourself a good one on the noggin, though. Don't know if he would have shot the old man or not, but you made sure he didn't have the chance."

"What about Jethro?"

"Didn't get a scratch. Of course, he's not the knucklehead who lit into an F100 pickup like a bighorn sheep in mating season." The chief allowed himself a chuckle at the thought.

A siren was audible in the distance and getting closer.

"What happened?" Joe said.

"Seems that Mister Haig got suspicious, having seen you talking with the suspect earlier today. He went into the man's apartment to look around this evening and found a pile of greenbacks stacked in bundles in the middle of his bunk—a little over $20,000. Haig figured out right away it was the stolen money, so he came looking for Rusty. Said he had been to half the beer joints in Yarborough before coming here. Said after he boxed Rusty's ears he was coming after you next. The old guy is fearless."

"Coming after me?" Joe said, opening both eyes to slits.

"Figured you two were in cahoots. You were in the suspect's apartment this morning, and that's where Haig found the money. And then he finds the two of you here. Put yourself in his shoes. What would you think?"

"I see what you mean."

"It took a little explaining," the chief said, "but I think I got the old boy straightened out about you."

Joe felt relieved about that. "What happened to Rusty?" he said.

"The door caught him full force on the right side, knocked the gun loose, and threw him into the side of the building. Sure took all the hot sauce out of his taco. I think his wrist or hand is broken."

Joe thought for a moment. "I guess it wasn't too smart of me to go after the guy. Somebody could have been shot."

"But if you hadn't sent him flying, he might have had a clear shot at somebody. You did a good thing, kid. Stupid, but good."

Working himself up to rest on his elbows, Joe said, "When can I get out of here?"

"Soon as the paramedics check you out. But you'll need to go into the sheriff's office tomorrow morning and tell your side of this story."

The paramedics arrived, examined Joe, and released him with aspirin samples for his headache and a couple of Band-Aids for minor abrasions. "The truck got the worst of it," grinned the young female EMT. "The door is dented on both sides." She left to join her partner who was checking out a banged up Rusty Ewing before he was transported to the county jail by way of the county hospital.

Joe was still sitting cross-legged on the pavement when Jethro Haig walked up. "Sorry my boy did this to you, young man," he said in the gruff tone Joe now understood was characteristic of the old farmer. "Rusty never was quite right in the head. Worried his mama into an early grave with all his shenanigans. Don't know what'll become of him when I'm gone."

Joe stood gingerly. "I'm sorry, too, sir—for Rusty. Maybe the county can get him some help." Joe also felt bad for suspecting Jethro for what Rusty did, but he would leave that apology for another time.

"I suppose you'll be at the funeral tomorrow," Jethro said.

"Of course. I really liked Thomas. In fact, all of you at the church have been very good to me."

"Then I'll see you tomorrow. Right now I need to…" Jethro motioned toward his stepson who was being placed on a gurney by the EMTs under the watchful eye of two uniformed county deputies.

"Of course."

Jethro surprised Joe by thrusting out his hand. "Once again, I'm sorry."

Joe took the hand and shook it firmly. "No problem. See you tomorrow."

After setting up an appointment with Lieutenant Rhodes for 9:00 A.M. at the Sheriff's office, Joe mounted his bike and left for the valley.

•   •   •

Joe pulled up to Velma's house at 1:43 A.M. He was pleased to see a light glowing through the living room window. By the time he reached the top porch step, the front door was open.

"You're late, Caruso," Chessy said in a hushed tone, laughing lightly. When she noticed the discolored knot on his forehead and the scrape on his chin, the smile evaporated. "All right, Joe," she said sternly, "I'm going to fix you some coffee, and you're going to tell me the whole story."

As they sat at Velma's kitchen table draining a pot of decaf, Joe complied fully with Chessy's directive. He told her everything. He included all the details because he didn't want the night to end. With the weight of the accusation finally off his back, he wanted nothing more than to spend time with the person who had so remarkably—and providentially, he was sure—entered his life. He was convinced that Chessy felt the same way about him.

It was Joe who finally brought the meeting to an end. "I need to get out of here," he said as he stood. "The county sheriff's office wants me to come in at 9:00 A.M. to get the details of my story. I'll make better sense if I get a little sleep between now and then."

"Like maybe five hours," Chessy said.

"So I guess I'll see you at the church for the service at 11:00."

Chessy walked him out to the porch where the late-night chill made their embrace all the warmer. "You prayed for me tonight, and I know God helped me," Joe said. "So it's my turn to pray now."

With Chessy's head nestled on his chest, Joe prayed a brief prayer of thanks. Then after a kiss, he left for his home in the hollow.

Forty-four

THE PEWS OF THE SMALL SANCTUARY were full, requiring the ushers to set up folding chairs at the rear to handle the overflow. Joe had been invited to sit with Chessy and her parents in the front row. Being in such a prominent spot, he wished he had spent a little more money on his jacket, shirt, and tie.

Walking down the center aisle with the family, Joe noticed that church members from the McDermot and Rasby families and their respective sympathizers were seated in their usual pews on opposite sides of center. Joe locked eyes with Bradford and Esther as he passed by them. They flashed a warm smile which he returned. Joe knew that the good news of his exoneration had circulated among key members, including his grandparents. He had so much more he yearned to tell them.

A good number of people from the community were scattered among the members where pew space was available. Velma sat at the organ softly playing a selection of musical pieces. The decorations for the funeral were anything but ostentatious—appropriate, Joe thought, for the person being honored. Three floral sprays and two large bouquets adorned the platform on either side of the pulpit. The casket was sturdy and plain, made of honey-colored wood, which also suited Thomas.

Just as Joe and Chessy were seated, two ushers walked forward and opened the casket. From where he was seated, Joe had a good view of Thomas lying peacefully in his only suit and his red-striped tie. The caretaker looked as innocent and vulnerable as he had in life. If the shouting match between Chet and Jethro flared up during the service, Joe expected to see tears seeping out of Thomas' closed eyes.

Unknown to Joe, a woman wearing dark glasses and a smart black suit trimmed in white lace slipped into the sanctuary at the last moment. She took one of the folding chairs, blending in with the sea of faces as Velma concluded the final piece of the prelude.

Ezra had suggested that Dr. Rich be allowed to assist with the service so that he would not be on his feet as long. Chessy and her parents heartily agreed. Rich began the service with an eloquent but heartfelt prayer which was warm with hope. This was not the end for Thomas; this was the beginning of life eternal with his Lord.

Rich then read the obituary, which chronicled Thomas' life and accomplishments and commended his traits of humility, kindness, and helpfulness. The congregation was respectful and silent except for the occasional sniffle. Chessy held Joe's hand firmly on one side and her mother's hand on the other.

Ezra hobbled up the platform steps on his crutches and sat down behind the pulpit on a tall stool Rich had moved into position. He displayed Thomas' well-worn King James Bible and said the Scripture lessons for the service would be a selection of texts underlined by Thomas over the years. For several minutes, the minister just read from the Bible without editorial comment. The words had new meaning for Joe, and he drank them in.

"I usually preach a sermon during a memorial service, but not today," Ezra continued. "My messages usually put Thomas to sleep every Sunday, so I won't spoil his tribute with a dry sermon." The comment was greeted by polite, subdued laughter.

"Instead, I have decided to let Thomas give the sermon today," Ezra went on. "Thomas Rasby was not a public speaker, but his life was an eloquent message of what it means to be a loving, hard-working, need-meeting Christian. Thomas was a big man, not in what he knew, but in how he loved. As the Scriptures say, 'Knowledge puffeth up, but charity edifieth.'"

As Ezra spoke, it seemed to Joe as if he had known Thomas much longer than he had. The minister was right. Thomas had taught Joe something about Jesus every day he knew him. Joe knew those lessons would continue on even though the kind-hearted caretaker was gone.

Ezra continued. "You all know that Thomas Rasby believed in prayer. But none of us knew until yesterday that he practiced it so faithfully." He lifted the dog-eared, spiral bound notebook from the pulpit and held it aloft. "I found this notebook yesterday in the back of his closet. Now, Thomas wasn't much for reading and writing. About the only reading he did was in his Bible. And writing was hard work for him, so he didn't do much of that either. Except for this. The pages are nearly full, and I'll bet there are many more books like it stashed somewhere in his cabin."

Whispers of amazement snaked through the congregation.

Lowering the notebook to the pulpit, Ezra said, "Nothing I say today could be more inspirational than the entries in Thomas' prayer notebook. They are very personal; most of our names are in this book, including mine. They are also very specific because Thomas asked God for exactly what we needed and thanked God for the blessings he provided.

"Like me, you may be quite surprised at what Thomas wrote in his notebook. He greeted you every Sunday morning at the front door and asked how you were. If you told him about a problem or an illness or a worry or a death in the family, Thomas wrote about it in his book. Then he took the book into his prayer closet and talked to God about whatever you told him. Let me share a few examples."

Ezra began to read from the notebook. Each entry was brief: a date, a name—usually first and last, and either an item of prayer or praise.

"April 16. Winnie Ferguson. She has the gout, but you can heal her, blessed Jesus.

"May 4. Reverend Sturdevant. His back pain is giving him no end of trouble. Put your healing hand on our minister.

"September 22. Leonard Rasby. Uncle Leonard is hurting so bad because Aunt Minnie died last week. Give his heart a big hug.

"November 21. Velma Walls. Travel mercies when she drives to Spokane to visit her schoolmate.

"December 19. Jethro Haig. Thank you, Jesus! When Jethro's pickup spun into the ditch on account of the ice, your angels kept him from breaking his neck."

The entries Ezra read were met with gasps of wonder, amused chuckles, or tears of humility from those mentioned by name. Joe sat in awe of what he was hearing. The list of names seemed endless. Some he recognized, most he didn't. And Thomas had taken a personal, prayerful interest in each one, just as he had for Joe.

Ezra paused while he turned a number of notebook pages. "In more recent days," he said, finally finding his place, "Thomas' prayer notebook had a different focus. Here's the entry from May 25, last Saturday: 'Oh Jesus, dear Jesus, I hear you crying. I feel how your heart is broke. Please don't let our church folk fight with one another. It makes my chest hurt.'"

Ezra paused, waiting for a lump of emotion to relax in his throat. There was total silence—no movement, no sniffles, no whispers.

"Then on May 26, Sunday, he wrote: 'They got to yelling after church. You don't care so much about buildings and land that the church should split up over it. But that's what they are fixing to do. They behave like they love the boards and the dirt more than each other. That is not right. And dear Jesus, my chest still hurts.'"

A large tear rolled down Ezra's sorrow-creased face. Joe heard Lydia Carpenter softly weeping. Others in the room had also been moved to tears.

Regaining his composure quickly, Ezra said, "There is one last entry I must read to you. On May 27, the day he died, Thomas wrote: 'What good is a church building if the people inside don't love each other? Blessed Jesus, don't let them move one more board until they can do it together.'"

Ezra pulled out a handkerchief and wiped at his nose. Then he closed the notebook and nodded to a woman listed in the program as Mrs. Winthrop, who stepped to the organ with Velma Walls. She began to sing, "What a Friend We Have In Jesus." Joe glanced at the program. Following the solo, Ezra would pray, then the congregation would be dismissed to the cemetery for a brief graveside service. At the bottom of the page, guests were invited to remain after the interment for a potluck dinner on the church lawn.

Mrs. Winthrop was a little teary, so she only made it through two verses before closing her hymnal and sitting down. Before Ezra could begin his closing prayer, Joe heard a loud shuffle of feet behind him. He turned to see Jethro Haig rising to his feet. Other heads swiveled in the direction of the sudden distraction.

"Reverend Sturdevant." Jethro's booming, gravelly voice instantly dominated the quiet room. "There's something I have to say, and it can't wait."

Forty-five

SEVERAL SECONDS OF AWKWARD SILENCE PASSED. Church members glanced between Ezra and Jethro to see if the minister would allow such an interruption. Finally, Ezra said, "What's on your mind, Jethro?" It was spoken in kindness, but Joe detected a subtle threat in his tone. He guessed that the stoop-shouldered old farmer wouldn't get out five words of argument before Ezra shut him down in front of the entire congregation.

Joe was aware that the story of his exoneration was also the sad story of Rusty Ewing's incarceration, and everybody knew Rusty belonged to Jethro Haig. Joe assumed Jethro was about to apologize to the congregation for Rusty's actions, just as the old farmer had done to him the night before.

Every head swiveled back to Jethro. His eyes dropped from the minister to the casket. Then he turned toward the McDermot side of the church and eyed Chet Rasby narrowly before looking back at Ezra. He cleared his throat noisily. "I just want to tell everybody that I've been wrong." He cleared his throat again. "I...I apologize for being such a hard-nose lately. I've been making a mountain out of a molehill. I lost sight of what is really important."

There was another pause as Jethro gazed again at the body in the casket. "And Thomas, I'm very sorry that I..." Suddenly the dam burst. Jethro Haig's words were overtaken by a prolonged, guttural moan of grief followed by deep, wrenching sobs. His knees buckled slightly, but he gripped the pew in front of him and steadied himself. For several moments, he stood and bawled unashamedly.

Joe's eyes flitted across the congregation. The reaction to the sudden outburst was mixed. Some faces were wet with tears. Other church members sat wide-eyed and open-mouthed, seemingly frightened or confused by the display. One woman sitting behind Jethro, perhaps a relative, reached out a hand to pat him on the arm. Another relative slipped a wad of tissues into his trembling hands.

Stifling his sobs, Jethro stepped out of his row and started unsteadily down the center aisle. Reaching the casket, his grief crested again. Rich moved quickly but without panic to Jethro's side to help him remain upright. Bradford appeared to support him on the other side.

"I'm sorry I caused you such pain," Jethro wailed, gazing down at Thomas' still face. "I'm sorry I hurt your people. I'm sorry...Please forgive me...I'm so sorry."

Joe turned to see several people crying behind him. Others were simply transfixed at what was taking place. Ezra's head was buried in his hands on the pulpit, his shoulders heaving with sobs.

Gaining control again, Jethro turned and started back down the aisle, leaving Rich and Bradford at the altar with the casket. Before he had passed the first row of pews, Chet Rasby sprang from his seat in the fourth row and stepped into the aisle to meet him. His eyes were wet with tears and his face drawn with grief.

"Jethro, I want to apologize to you," he said, voice quivering. "I said some terrible things, and I'm very sorry. I also caused pain to our dear Thomas. I don't want our church divided, and I don't want to lose your friendship. Will you please forgive me?"

Jethro gazed at the man as if measuring his sincerity. Then he said, "Yes, I forgive you. But I have also wronged you, Chester, with a cold heart and hateful words. Will you forgive me?" The men fell into each other's arms and wept.

A man in the fifth row on the McDermot side stood. "I agree with you, Jethro," he said, sniffing. "I've been hard-hearted and stubborn. Chet and the rest of you, I'm sorry for fighting with you over this property issue instead of praying with you about it and discussing it with you. Please forgive me." Then he stepped into the center aisle and approached Chet Rasby. They tearfully embraced and exchanged words of forgiveness.

Next to stand was Edith Winthrop in the front row near the organ. She was too choked up to speak. Clutching a tissue to her face, she met Jethro in the center aisle and confessed her own judgmental attitude toward him.

The scene that unfolded over the next several minutes was unlike anything Joe had ever witnessed. One by one, church members stepped out of their pews and apologized first to Chet or Jethro and then to others across the center aisle. Many, including Chet Rasby, spent tearful moments at the casket apologizing to Thomas for the grief they had caused. Others knelt at the altar beside the casket or in their pews to confess their sin to God. And a few came to Chessy and her parents to apologize for making Thomas' last days so stressful with their selfish arguing. The Carpenters were gracious and forgiving, embracing the strangers and consoling them while they themselves were consoled.

Apparently, the little revival was more than some of the non-members from the community could bear. Many of them slipped out of the sanctuary unnoticed during the distraction. Others stayed and watched, entranced. At one point, Joe caught a glimpse of a woman wearing a black dress and dark glasses seated in the rear of the church. He couldn't see her clearly because of the milling throng, but he wondered if it might be Brenda. The next time he looked around, she was gone.

After about twenty minutes, people drifted back to their pews and sat down. All except for Jethro Haig, who had moved to the other side of the center aisle, closer to Chet Rasby and his wife. "I have one more thing to say," he announced, and the congregation quickly quieted.

Ezra, still perched on his stool behind the pulpit, gave him the okay with a nod. Joe was still in mild shock from what he had already witnessed. He listened eagerly to see what else Jethro had up his sleeve.

"You all know that I have been trying to buy that thirteen-acre parcel out south for a few years now. I was prepared to give the church a good price. That offer was still on the table as of our last church meeting Monday evening, the meeting we never finished."

There was a moment of silence as church members recalled the shocking news that had interrupted the meeting and sent everyone home in tears.

"Thanks to the generosity of our departed sister, Louise Wilkerson, and the courage of our new friend, Joe Caruso, we have some much needed cash in the bank." Jethro glanced at Joe before continuing. "But there is so much more to be done around this church, and Louise's gift just ain't enough to do it.

"But what I want to say now is not about selling the property. I've had a change of heart. I'm taking that offer off the table, and I'm going on record to say we should keep that piece of land, which has been dedicated to the Lord's service."

A ripple of murmurs rolled across the congregation.

"While we were getting things straightened out between us just now, I had another idea, and I think it's what God wants me to do. I'm still going to write that big check to the church, the amount I offered for the land. Only it will be a donation. Part of it will help us complete the repairs on this old building. The rest of it will start a fund for a building out in the hollow."

Gasps of surprise and elation quickly escalated to hearty applause and cheers of appreciation. Then someone called out, "Then I suggest we name the building Haig Hall in Jethro's honor."

The applause started up again, but Jethro quickly waved it off. "No sir, I don't deserve it, and I won't allow it," he said emphatically. "But I will support a motion to dedicate that facility to the memory of our caretaker, Thomas Rasby."

There was a reverent silence. Then someone verbalized the words many were thinking: "Thomas Rasby Memorial Hall. Yes, very appropriate." Unanimity of ascent was manifested in nods and whispers.

Chet Rasby stood again. "I think I speak for all of us, Jethro, when I say thank you for your generosity. I know God will bless you for it. As for Leta and me, we want to be counted, too. We have a little mad money saved up—not much, mind you—but we want to put it toward the building fund. We want this building and the parsonage to stay in tip-top shape."

Bradford was up next. "Thank you, Chet, and thank you, Jethro," he said. "Esther and I have some good news. Well, it's *mostly* good news. We have accepted a good offer on our farm, so in a couple of months, we'll be town folk instead of farmers. We'll miss the farm, but we are ready to slow down a little."

"Congratulations, Bradford," someone called out. Others added their affirming words.

Bradford continued. "We want to be among the first to support the building fund, especially a new ministry facility named after Thomas. So part of the proceeds from our sale will go to that. We hope that others of you will see your way clear to contribute so that Thomas' ministry of caring can carry on."

Another ripple of applause rose, but it was cut short by Ezra's raised hands. His face had brightened considerably during the events of the last several minutes. "Now, now, people," he said, smiling, "this is a memorial service for Thomas, not a fundraising telethon for the church." The congregation's laughter was warm and appropriate.

The minister went on. "I want you to imagine how Thomas would feel today if he were still with us. He would be dancing in the aisle, wouldn't he? In fact, I imagine he's dancing with the angels on the golden streets of heaven at this very moment. Nothing brought him greater joy than to see people serving God and loving one another. And if what I have witnessed today is any indication of what our church is going to look like in the years ahead, Thomas is going to wear out many pairs of dancing shoes up there."

Then he closed his eyes and lifted a simple prayer of adoration to God for all that had transpired and begun as a result of Thomas' life and death.

He had barely spoken the amen when someone began singing melodically another song Joe had never heard. It wasn't on the program, but after only a few words the entire congregation had stood and joined in, singing heartily, "Blessed be the tie that binds our hearts in Christian love." Hands joined spontaneously down each row, even bridging the center aisle. Those nearest the front reached out a hand to touch the casket to include Thomas in the circle of love.

The service adjourned to the cemetery for a brief graveside service. Thomas was laid to rest in the back corner near his cabin. Lydia and Chessy Carpenter tossed flowers on the casket as it descended into the earth.

Forty-six

IT WAS AN AMAZING SIGHT. Folks who had only days ago been at each other's throats were sitting together around the outdoor tables enjoying another sumptuous potluck country dinner. Jethro Haig and Chet Rasby, who had fueled the feud with their personal attacks, were being commended for taking the lead in making things right. The air was festive with laughter and conversation. It seemed a little too festive to Joe on the heels of a funeral, but he overheard someone say, "We don't need to feel badly for Thomas because he's in a much better place. So we may as well enjoy ourselves in his honor. That's what Thomas would want us to do."

Joe walked through the outdoor buffet line and sat with Chessy and her parents. Several people came by to say they had heard about his conversion and were very happy for him. Others came to tell him how happy they were that he had been cleared of the charges against him. These same people visited Jethro to express their sadness over Rusty's trouble.

Joe was clearly not the star of the show today. Most of the people gathering around his table had come to talk to the Carpenters. The farmers wanted to meet Bertram and hear all about growing raisins in central California. The women were attracted to Chessy and her very social and friendly mother, and the conversation never strayed too far from Thomas and how much everybody loved him.

After wolfing down a plate of casserole, fried chicken, and potato salad, Joe excused himself to visit the dessert table. He continued to glance around, hoping to spot Brenda. He was almost positive she was the woman he had glimpsed briefly in the back of the sanctuary during the service, but she wasn't here now. Where had she gone? Why didn't she stay and talk to him? Did the unusual and emotional funeral service scare her away? Did she see her father, get cold feet, and go home?

Feeling the need for space, Joe served himself a slice of coconut cream pie and headed for the church basement where it was quiet. He sat down in a kid-sized wooden chair in a classroom. Ever the optimist, Thomas had kept it clean and ready for the Sunday school children who never came.

"Joe?"

The voice startled him. Bradford McDermot was standing in the classroom doorway.

Bradford stepped inside the room. His wife Esther was right behind him. The big farmer in the ill-fitting brown suit explained, "We were heading over to visit with you when we saw you come in here. Don't mind if we say hello, do you?"

"Not at all," he said, setting his plate aside and standing.

"Ezra told us the wonderful news that you have welcomed the Lord into your life," Esther said, wearing a saintly smile.

Joe nodded. "I don't understand much about being a Christian, but I see God in all you fine people here at the church, including Thomas, and I want God inside me in the same way."

"You'll understand more as you grow in your faith, Joe," Esther said.

Bradford cut in, "We also wanted to hear the story about you and Rusty from last night. We always knew somebody else had taken the money. We're happy the trouble is over with, but we're sad for Rusty and Jethro."

Joe summarized the events leading up to his meeting with Rusty at the Eastside Bullpen. He glossed over his head-on collision with the door of the red pickup and Rusty's subsequent arrest. "I'm glad it's over, too," he concluded. "I just hope Rusty can get some help."

Then he directed the conversation back to the couple. "So you found a buyer for your place?"

Bradford nodded. "We've been praying for God to send the right buyer at the right time, and I guess that time is now. We haven't met the buyer yet—don't even know his name—but we have accepted the offer."

Out of politeness, Joe forced himself to say, "Yes, I'm very happy for you two." But he was not happy about seeing the farm pass out of the family before he had a chance to enjoy any of it.

"We're going to miss the old place," Bradford continued, reaching out to place his hand on Esther's. "But now I can finally start to pay my wife back for her love and support over the years. We're going to travel a little, maybe take a cruise. As they say, this is the first day of the rest of our lives."

Joe's eyes shifted from his grandparents to a woman in a black dress trimmed in white lace who had just stepped through the doorway behind the farmer and his wife.

"Mom? Dad?" she said.

The couple turned toward the voice. It took a few seconds for them to process what they were seeing. Bradford spoke first, gazing at the woman. "Brenda?" he said in disbelief.

Esther clasped her hand to her mouth and burst into silent tears. Bradford stood motionless as if in shock.

Brenda said, "I'm sorry for walking in unannounced like this. It's taken me a long time to get up the courage to talk to you."

Joe felt like he was violating his mother's privacy. He said to no one in particular, "I'll wait outside."

"No, please stay, Joe," Brenda said.

Bradford finally found his words. "Do you know Joe?"

Brenda glanced at Joe. "Yes, Dad, I know Joe. In fact, he's a big reason why I am here today."

"Brenda, this is a miracle to me," Bradford said, tears welling in his eyes, "I'm so happy to see you."

"I don't know how you can say that, Dad, after I have rejected you all these years." Brenda was fighting back her own tears. "Twenty-two years ago you asked me to forgive you, and I tore up those letters. But the same Jesus who made you a new person has now changed my heart. I do forgive you, Daddy. Can you possibly forgive me for hating you all these years?"

"Oh yes, dear one," Bradford said, choked with emotion. "I forgave you a long time ago."

Father and daughter embraced and wept, and Esther soon joined in. Joe stood back, reveling in the tender scene, anxious to be part of it.

Soon the four of them were seated together. Joe could see the question in Bradford and Esther's eyes. *How do you know Joe?*

"Dad and Mom, there is so much I want to talk to you about," Brenda said excitedly, "so much of our lives to recapture. But I must start by telling you about my miracle." She summarized her months of rebellion and hatred after she left home as an eighteen-year-old, culminating in her relationship with Wallace Barnes and pregnancy. Then she rehearsed the painful account of giving her baby, Daniel Lee Barnes, up for adoption, apologizing again to Bradford and Esther for sending their grandchild away.

"When I became a Christian a few months ago," she said, "I began asking God if he would let me see Danny again, just so I could know he was all right. I didn't have much hope, and I told God that I would be all right if he said no to my request. That's when I transferred to the county office in Yarborough, just in case Danny came looking for his birth parents."

Joe stole glances at his grandparents' rapt faces to see if either of them would figure out where Brenda's story was leading. They appeared clueless, which only fueled Joe's mounting excitement.

"God answered my prayer, Dad and Mom," Brenda announced. Joe watched expressions of interest turn to amazement on Bradford and Esther's faces. "My son Danny and I found each other this week. Your grandson is eager to meet you."

"Where is he?" Bradford asked with anticipation. "Does he live in the valley?"

A mischievous grin formed on Brenda's face. "Yes, he's currently in the area."

"This is wonderful, dear," Esther sang with glee. "When can we meet Danny?"

"I think today would be a good time," Brenda said, still grinning. Joe, who was thoroughly enjoying the build-up, couldn't keep from smiling, too.

"You have to understand one thing," Brenda went on. "His name was changed when he was adopted. I have called him Danny all these years, but his legal name is Joseph Caruso." As she said the name, she reached out and took Joe's hand.

The reality broke on Esther first, and she shrieked with surprise and elation. Bradford's face blanched with such a look of shock that Joe hoped his heart would survive it. Then he was engulfed in the loving, tearful embraces of his grandparents.

Forty-seven

IT HAD BEEN A PHYSICALLY TAXING and emotionally draining day for everyone involved in Thomas Rasby's funeral. After the service and potluck dinner, there was much work to be done. Those left at the church had to clean up the dinner mess, tote tables and chairs back into the church basement, and tidy the sanctuary. Thomas was jokingly chastised for so abruptly leaving them in the lurch without a caretaker, but every mention of Thomas ended with words of appreciation for his hard work and loving heart. Several church members volunteered to help with the janitorial and gardening chores around the church until a more permanent solution for these needs could be arranged.

Despite the busyness of the day, when Joe volunteered to build a campfire later in the evening, many agreed that it would be a fitting conclusion to a day in Thomas' honor and promised to come back. So at dusk, when Joe and Chessy had the fire stoked high, Ezra, Rich, and Velma were there. They were joined moments later by Brenda, Bradford, and Esther, who had spent the late afternoon together at the farm reveling in their restored relationship. Brenda had changed from her black dress into jeans and a sweater, which she borrowed from Esther. Chessy's parents were spending the evening with Rasby relatives in the valley.

Ezra had stopped by Thomas' cabin and brought a bag of marshmallows and sticks. Many marshmallows were toasted and enjoyed in the caretaker's honor. The marshmallows brought back fresh memories for Joe and provoked a sharp pang of loss.

Everyone was still buzzing about the miraculous family reunion experienced by Bradford, Esther, Brenda, and Joe. The story was told from every possible angle and everyone agreed that God had done a marvelous thing.

As the fire dwindled, conversation turned from the past to the future. Someone asked Rich about his plans for the summer. He explained that he wouldn't have missed the last seven days in Orchard Valley for anything, but after next Sunday, he would move on to his sister's home in the Seattle area and continue his sabbatical studies.

"I feel very much attached to you people," he concluded, "so I hope you will allow me to come back and visit while I am in Washington."

"You have been a great roommate, Rich, and your room is always available," Ezra said enthusiastically. "Please come whenever you can, and be prepared to preach for us when you do. We love how you share the Word."

Joe had missed Ezra's comment because the wheels in his head were suddenly turning. He noticed something when Rich mentioned wanting to return to Orchard Valley and visit. At the moment he spoke those words, Rich had been gazing across the fire at Brenda, who had smiled in response to his comment. Joe swallowed a gasp of surprise. Rich and Brenda? Had the godly bachelor professor taken notice of his mother?

The two had talked briefly this afternoon when Joe introduced Brenda at the potluck supper after the reunion with her parents in the basement, and Joe had noticed Rich and Brenda chatting as they toasted marshmallows. Had Brenda suddenly become the *primary* reason Rich wanted to come back to Orchard Valley? As soon as he got past the utter slap-in-the-face surprise of the thought, he began to delight in it. Rich needed a wife, and Brenda needed a husband. Why not each other?

Joe leaned into Chessy to whisper what he had just observed. But one look at her eyes revealed that she had also noticed the little sparks flying between the two. Joe and Chessy stifled giggles of delight at what they had witnessed.

"What about you, Chessy?" Esther asked. "What are your plans for the summer?" Everyone turned to hear her answer.

"When I first came up here, I didn't know how long I would stay," she began. "It all depended on my relatives here. Uncle Thomas is now gone, and I have seen my other relatives. So when my parents arrived yesterday, I decided to fly back to Fresno with my them on Friday."

There was a tentativeness in her tone that offered Joe some hope. He was not ready to say goodbye to Chessy quite yet, and he hoped she was thinking the same way.

"But I'm not quite ready to leave just yet," she went on as she glanced at Joe and smiled. "I'm taking some courses on line, but I can work on those anywhere I can plug in my laptop. I just have to finish my exams before the fall term starts in California. But for now, I'm kind of playing it day by day."

"And I'm not ready to give up my roommate," Velma put in. "Chessy and I have had a wonderful time getting acquainted. I think we have bonded, as they say. She can stay with me as long as she wants to."

"Velma has been like a second mom to me," Chessy said. "And there are some other people it will be difficult for me to leave."

Chessy reached for Joe's hand and held it tight with both of hers. He flushed with embarrassment as others around the campfire saw the gesture and chuckled knowingly.

"Joe, you have to go back east for a while, I hear," Ezra said.

Joe nodded. "Tomorrow I'm going into the airport to purchase a ticket to Pittsburgh—a round trip ticket," he announced. "I'll settle a few things, pack some clothes, and fly back as soon as I can. As you all know, I just met my mother and grandparents, and I want to spend some time getting acquainted. And there are other relatives in this area I never knew I had. Also, I thought perhaps I could help Bradford and Esther pack up and get ready to move. They have invited me to move into the farmhouse until they move out, so I may stay out here for the summer."

"You have a graduate degree to finish, I understand," Velma said.

Joe thought about how to respond. His graduate studies were the biggest question mark in his brain since he committed his life to Christ. "When I came out here, I fully intended to return to grad school and complete my engineering degree. That was my big plan—with all the emphasis on *my*. I didn't even consider at the time what God might have in store for me.

"But now he's in charge. It's just that I don't know what he wants me to do. I would appreciate it if you people would pray for God to reveal his will in my life, and I look forward to your counsel and advice. Right now, I don't know what I'll be doing."

"Have you ever thought about being a farmer like your grandfather?" The surprising question came from Brenda, who was eyeing him with a curious expression.

"A farmer? Me, a city boy?" Joe retorted. "No, the thought never crossed my mind—at least not until a few days ago when I spent some time on the McDermot farm. It was fascinating. That's no simple operation. There is a lot to learn. I'm at least eager to know more about farming before I leave the valley."

Brenda nodded. "Well, would you consider staying in Orchard Valley to help me run my farm?"

Bradford cut in before Joe could answer. "What on earth would you want with a farm, Brenda?" he said, almost laughing.

Esther followed up her husband's question. "Yes, dear, what are you talking about? You don't really have a farm to run, do you?"

Brenda turned to her mother. "After my late husband died five months ago, I went through our papers in order to notify our insurance companies of his death. It was important to Dennis to take care of all the bills and finances in our marriage, so I didn't exactly know what we had. I knew he had at least one life insurance policy, and together we had a few investments, but I was not prepared for what I found.

"Unbeknownst to me, Dennis had taken out several policies on himself over the years, and he had maintained other savings and investment accounts he never told me about. He always said I would be well taken care of if he died first, but I never realized that he had been so disciplined with our money. To make a long story short, Dennis left me with a great deal of money. I don't have to work if I don't want to, and I can live very comfortably for the rest of my life and still have money to pass on to my grandchildren."

She flicked an amused glance at Joe, and he felt his face flush warm in the firelight.

"So are you planning to go into farming?" Ezra asked.

"I didn't think it was wise to make any snap decisions after Dennis's death," Brenda continued, "so the money has been earning dividends since he died. After I gave my life to Christ, I began asking God the same question you are asking, Joe: What do you want me to do with my life? I can't explain it, but I began thinking about buying some farm property. It seemed like God was directing me that way. So my realtor started looking around the valley and found a very nice farm for sale. I sensed God nudging me in that direction, but I didn't know why. So I made an offer and it was accepted. Long story short: I have a farm to run now."

"You really bought a farm?" Joe said in disbelief, and Brenda nodded vigorously. Joe leaned forward. "Where is this place?"

"I don't know if you've heard of it, Joe," Brenda said with a serious expression. "It's Bradford McDermot's place."

Joe's mouth dropped open. Brenda maintained eye contact with him and nodded as a grin began overtaking her face.

Suddenly, Bradford leaped off the bench and bellowed, "Brenda was the buyer! Esther, Brenda bought our farm!"

"Yes, Dad," Brenda said, laughing, "I am the mystery buyer."

Whoops of surprise and elation erupted around the circle. Bradford crossed to his daughter and took her in his arms, laughing and crying all at once. He danced her around the campfire, giggling repeatedly, "Brenda bought our farm! Brenda bought our farm!" And everybody celebrated with them.

Joe was on his feet, too, but all he could do was laugh. "I can't believe it. What kind of family is this? You're all nuts!"

Once the hoopla had subsided, Brenda said, "When the realtor mentioned your farm, Dad, I was pretty skeptical. I didn't know if you would sell it to me, but I felt God's direction to make an offer. So that's why I kept my identity a secret."

"All this time I thought it was Jethro Haig," Bradford said, laughing again. "But it was my own dear daughter."

Brenda continued, "Mom and Dad, I want you two to stay at the farm if you like. You don't have to pack up and move. I'm quitting my job when escrow closes, and I would love for you to stay here with me. And Dad, if you will teach me the business, I will hire a crew and run the farm. You two can travel and take cruises to your heart's content, but you will always have the farm to come home to."

Bradford and Esther were overcome with emotion. "God is so good," Bradford said tearfully. "God is so good."

Turning to Joe, Brenda said, "I'm serious about my offer, Joe. I would love to have you join us at the farm and learn the business with me—if you feel so led."

Joe warmed to the thought immediately. "I don't know, Mom," he said. "But it's something I will pray about and discuss with…my friend here." He turned affectionately toward Chessy and gave her a squeeze around the waist.

"I've been wondering," Ezra said with a mischievous grin, "if Joe and Chessy have a more personal, long-term reason for spending the summer in the valley."

Joe felt embarrassment flooding his face with color.

Velma chipped in quickly, "Come to think of it, there hasn't been a McDermot-Rasby wedding in this church for years."

"You're right, Velma," Ezra said, "but something tells me we might have another one here someday."

The laughter around the circle was free of ridicule, but Joe still felt uncomfortable in the spotlight. He stood up and pulled Chessy with him. "You're going to have to excuse us," he said, suppressing his own laughter. "My allergies are starting to act up, so Chessy and I are going to take a motorcycle ride to get some fresh air. Goodnight everybody."

As the couple retreated toward Joe's camp, Velma called out, "What are you allergic to, Joe, weddings?" Everybody laughed.

Joe just gripped Chessy's hand as they ran laughing toward the Harley, and he wondered if the word *wedding* would come up again before his summer with Chessy ended.